DEMON CARD
ENFORCER 3

JOHN STOVALL

Published by
CS BOOKS, LLC

This is a work of fiction. Names, characters, places, and incidents either are the product of author imagination or are used fictitiously, and any resemblance to actual persons, living or dead, business establishments, events, or locales, is entirely fictional.

Demon Card Enforcer 3
Copyright © 2025 Capital Station Books
All rights reserved.

Cover Design: Michael Gladigau

Editors: Amy McNulty, Nia Quinn, Celestian Rince

IF YOU WANT TO BE NOTIFIED WHEN JOHN STOVALL'S NEXT BOOK RELEASES, PLEASE VISIT HIS WEBSITE OR CONTACT HIM DIRECTLY AT

John.W.Stovall@gmail.com

DEDICATIONS

First, as always, to my wife, **Shami Stovall**, *who has made this career, and many other things besides, possible. You are the most amazing person I know. With, and because, of you, my life has elevated multiple times.*

Secondly, to the other members of my writers' group. To **Dana, Ryan, Mary, Emily, James, Kris, and Scott**, *thank you for the efforts you put into this as well. Especially Ryan, whose own card game efforts led to this book directly.*

Third, to my parents, **John and Gail Stovall**. *Your support throughout my life has been over the top, and you are the perfect parents everyone else wished they had. And, in my "master's degree in English" mother's case, one of my editors as well. This dedication, unfortunately, comes too late to reach my father, who passed away. I hope you were isekai'd to some place with a really awesome map, perhaps an alternate magical Earth, to fight for the good one more time.*

*Fourth, to my editors **Celestine Rince** and **Amy McNulty**. Thanks for doing this. I know I don't make it easy.*

*Fifth, I'd like to thank **Chris Zinn,** who supported me on Patreon for multiple years as my single, sole patron, and provided bonus editing, before all this took off.*

*Sixth, I'd like to thank the other people who helped me on my Discord—I got a lot of ideas from them. **Shaodwrise1, Har'Tracyn, Pancakes, True_God_of_Noobs, Seraphion, A Lazy Monster, Deltorian, jjffjhjf, Mikato1, Scion, Tristan, BonzBonzOnlyBonz, DMacks, IHaveManyAliases, KuroYuki, MagmaWave999, OliveBirdy, Section160, SuperWaffle, and Tshandrabal**. Everyone either contributed editing, feedback, card ideas, or help with the website. To all of you: thank you, genuinely. It means a lot to see someone interested, and it helps a lot to get all your ideas for cards and concepts. This book would have been at least fifteen percent worse without you.*

*Seventh, to **Justin**, who is the best voice Wolfe could ever have— and the rest of the team at **Soundbooth** who bring everyone else alive.*

*Lastly, to the Card World peeps: **Kacey Ezell**, who liked this series enough to write Shadow Card Guardian, and to **Rhett, Steve, and Josh** of Aetheon who decided to pay me in advance to write Card Apocalypse. Card World looks to be an absolute minimum of three series and ten books at this point, and perhaps far more.*

CONTENTS

INTERIM CHAPTERS

Malviere's Birthday One: 6:28 A.M.

It was weird, being a card.

Malviere didn't sleep, but she had days and mornings. Her schedule was dictated by the pattern of the rest of her pack. Most days, that pattern was quite predictable—and quite boring.

The pack alpha, Wolfe, woke up early, as did his mate, Shel. Usually with the sunrise. So Malviere began her day at the same time—as did the rest of the house, near enough.

Shel went and woke the female pups of the pack, Shannon and Lucy, while Wolfe went and prepared the food for the pack. He prepared the meat of pigs and the eggs of chickens quite well. Most mornings saw a variant of those two dishes with perhaps one to two extra items.

Shel or one of the others handled every other meal, always, but Wolfe did every breakfast.

Once the food was ready, the new pack Beta, Liam, would come in. He was in charge of escorting the pack pups to school, but he ate with the pups, Wolfe, and Shel as if he were part of the pack. Malviere wasn't sure if he was, but she treated him as if he were. She did the same for 'Grammy,' an elderly human that was also probably a pack member. Grammy contributed little that Malviere could understand.

She wasn't sure why Wolfe let her stay and use the resources of the pack.

Cereboo, a powerful pack Beta, as well as the two tiniest pack members, James and Jason, which were 'Apricot Cavapoos' according to Shel, also joined them to eat. They were fed on the floor, and not at the table with the rest of the pack. Despite that, they made Malviere very happy. She understood them far more than most of the human members of the pack.

Frequently, the two angels that stank of Raphael ate with them as well—but they weren't *real* pack members. Malviere simply refused to believe it.

Even if they fought with the pack sometimes.

After the morning feeding, the pups and Liam would leave to go where the pups could learn.

Shel would then leave to go to hunt those that deserved to be in the Infernal Realms, and Wolfe and Cereboo would go off and do work with the same ultimate goal. Malviere was left alone, and she usually spent half the day playing with Jason and James.

There were others here, cards like her, but their minds were empty, and they couldn't play. And Grammy just read or knit, or worked at a computer on 'business' for Wolfe, till the pups came home.

The pattern was the same five mornings a week, and on the other two days, it started the same but they would all do fun things together, instead. Although only very rarely did Malviere get to choose what they did. Shannon told her that five times was too many times to go to the same zoo.

But it was a weekday, and Malviere sat on her bed, half-thinking, waiting for the day to be the same as every other.

So Malviere was deeply surprised when there was a knock

at the door to her room a few minutes before the pack alpha normally started his day.

She was sitting on the bed they had gotten her, blankets carefully pulled across the top and unused, petting Jason and James. The room had white walls, and a steel chandelier hanging from the ceiling. The chandelier had an old-fashioned, medieval gothic style, but still had modern electric lights in the faux candles—but with a twist.

Malviere stood from her bed and flicked the lights on, casting the previously dark room into a soft red light.

She opened the door and stared out into the richly carpeted hall.

Wolfe and Shel stood there. They were with Cereboo, who was panting heavily from all three heads. Jason and James ran out, jumping at all three, their tails going like they had motors in their butts.

"Happy birthday!" Wolfe and Shel said together before throwing a bunch of confetti at Malviere. Cereboo gave three quiet woofs and licked her.

The alpha and his mate had a cupcake on a tiny plate that both were holding. A single lit candle adorned the top of the cupcake.

Malviere didn't like sweet things, only savory, but she knew a cake with candles was the way you celebrated birthdays. She had seen it for Lucy and Shel both. It was tradition, and she didn't mind tradition.

"My birthday?" Malviere asked, confused, petting Cereboo's head with one hand and taking the proffered cake with the other.

"Yup," Wolfe said, nodding, a half-smile on his face that sat awkwardly on his usually serious mien. He was her deckbearer, and Cerberus' chosen, and she trusted him more than anyone. But even his smiles were sometimes scary.

Shel stepped forward and ruffled Malviere's long brown

hair. "We've been tracking, and today is the day you evolve! So that makes it your birthday! A special day that will mostly be for you, although we have one or two other things we have to do as well. But still, we have a ton of stuff you'll love planned out!"

"Why... I don't change, like humans at least. And as a card, I must obey. Why celebrate my... birthday, as you call it?"

A sudden dark thought entered Malviere's mind. *When I evolve... will I change too much? Will I still be me?*

Shel smiled again, an expression that sat far better on her face than on Wolfe's. "But you remember. So, this is a happy day to remember, I hope."

Joy filled Malviere, briefly dispelling her worries. *I have the best pack. The absolute best pack* ever.

"Thank you," she said, baring her teeth in the pattern of a smile to tell them that she was happy.

Shel smiled even wider, then leaned in and hugged Malviere. "I can't wait! We start with surprise breakfast!"

Malviere followed as the two left, heading for the main kitchen. The dining area had multiple tables in a huge room, capable of seating more than a hundred people. The walls had numerous giant oil paintings of many of the Infernal Lords that couldn't be removed. But the kitchen, while huge, had a space large enough for a single dining table and chairs away from the portion used for cooking. It had been converted into the family's mini dining area.

The Hellmouth Institute created enough food to feed a hundred every night at midnight, but it did so as components—it still needed a cook. But the knives were always sharp, the cutting boards cleaned themselves, and the dishes in the sink did the same and put themselves away as well.

Right now, the sink was full of dirty utensils, so they had to have been used recently.

Wolfe entered the kitchen and turned toward Malviere, motioning her toward the table.

Rather than the customary bacon and eggs, a huge platter awaited her at her usual seat. It was filled to the brim with raw, bloody steak chunks, a pile almost as big as Malviere's head.

"It's all for me?" Malviere asked. She never got hungry, but she loved to eat. Especially meat. The rarer, the better.

"All yours," Wolfe responded. "Wasn't even that hard. It's not like you want the forbidden art of cooking to actually touch your meat. I just told the Institute to give me steak, chopped it into bits, and waved it in the vague direction of the oven for a couple seconds."

Shel laughed, but Malviere barely understood the alpha's humor, most days.

But she understood hunger in her bones, even if she didn't need food.

Malviere set to the food with a will. As she did, all the usual morning companions filtered in—Liam, who looked like a dwarf, the pups Shannon and Lucy, looking newly groomed in nice school clothing, and Grammy, who took a seat and worked on some crossroads while nibbling at food. Cereboo and the cavapoos also joined, and even the unnamed 'Wandering Bulgae Pup' did, in fact, wander in. But it didn't *do* anything, and Malviere ignore it.

It was slightly less creepy than when the Desperate Cultist wandered in and sat, doing nothing, but only marginally so.

A few joyful minutes later, when she could barely move to eat another bite, Malviere sat, satiated, at the table. Wolfe had gone over and prepared bacon and eggs for everyone else, and was now serving it to the entire table, which, unfortunately, now included the angels.

"Making that steak for you wasn't that hard, honestly," Wolfe said as he scooped some onto Lucy's plate. "I could easily include it in future meals."

Malviere didn't respond for a moment. Something else was still nagging at her, strongly enough to put off thoughts of rare steak. "What's it like, evolving?"

"We don't know," Shel said, reaching her hand across the table and taking Malviere's hand.

"You're the first," Lucy said, sitting with her damaged left hand in her lap and daintily forking a small piece of egg with her other. Then she frowned. "I meant the first that is also a companion, sorry. Sorry. I looked on the internet, and a very few orphan cards now have their evolved forms available for viewing on the internet. But not any of the super rare orphan companions."

"You're super-spesh," Shannon said.

Malviere was quiet. "I... I don't know if I'll even like steak, once I evolve. Will I be me?"

"Don't know, kiddo," Wolfe said. "You're a strange one."

Lucy started to raise her hand—the undamaged right one.

"Special and wonderful in a statistically unlikely way," Wolfe said with a roll of his eyes at Lucy, who very briefly stuck her tongue out at him with a roll of her own eyes right back.

Wolfe turned back to Malviere. "But I'll say this much. We have an incredible present for you, something you've wanted for a long time. So, it'll at least be a fun day. I think you'll be fine, though."

"What are we doing first?" Malviere asked, determined to enjoy the day.

Wolfe set the giant platter of food, almost empty, onto the floor, where Cereboo and the cavapoos proceeded to rip at it.

"For the very first present, I actually need to make one more level. You know I don't normally like taking you out of the institute," Wolfe said.

Malviere interrupted. "I know. You told me. If I'm defeated, you'll have to wait another six months to evolve me."

Wolfe ignored her interruption. "But, for today, we'll

make an exception. How would you like to go to the Rat Arena with me?"

Malviere's joy rose. She knew the alpha wouldn't let her fight, but she even loved to just *watch* the pack fight.

Shannon sat up in her seat. "Ah, can we go?"

"No way," Grammy said without glancing up from her crossword puzzle. "You have school. And besides, it's dangerous."

"Yeah, no chance at all," Wolfe said. "Not unless you get your own deck when you're older. I *really* don't want to advertise the connections I have to people they might use to hurt me."

Lucy and Shannon nodded soberly at that.

"When are we going?" Malviere asked eagerly.

A horn that was more dirge than automobile warning system sounded outside.

"I think that's our ride right now," Wolfe said, smiling. "Shall we?"

"You'll make sure Lucy and Shannon go where they're supposed to, Liam?" Shel asked.

"Yup."

"I would *never* cut school without an appropriate excuse," Lucy said stiffly.

Shel laughed. "Well, you might not, but..."

Shannon took her turn to stick her tongue out, and Wolfe and Shel left, laughing. But they pulled Cereboo, Sorenia, and Liurenia back into their deck as they did.

Malviere hadn't gone back into the deck for six months.

"I'll mind the business," Grammy said, and Wolfe gave a backward salute in the air as the three of them walked from the kitchen into the central hall, and from there to the foyer of the Hellmouth Institute. Statues of demons adorned the main hall, as well as a few more paintings, these of various Infernal Realms done in landscape. The carpet was red and thick, feeling happy on Malviere's feet. The foyer lacked the carpet, but had a marble floor, slightly rough, and dark wood paneling that held even more art.

They stepped from the foyer onto the porch through a heavy wooden door, and into the usually empty parking lot. A small garage had been built off to the side, where Liam stored and worked on the pack's vehicles, but that meant that most days the huge lot was nearly empty, as it was all for visitors and customers of the private investigator business, of which there were few.

Today, however, was different. A limousine was pulled up to the front of the Institute—a limousine with a skull engraved on the hood. Standing outside, in a black dress more appropriate to an evening cocktail party than a seven a.m. summer morning, was a very occasional ally of the pack —Miriam.

She leaned over, putting one delicate, beautiful, and pale hand on Malviere's shoulder. "And how's the birthday girl today? Are you ready for some excitement?"

Malviere's Birthday Two: 8:14 A.M.

Malviere half-growled—her voice sickeningly high-pitched in her own ears rather than a proper threat—as the hood was removed from her head.

"Don't you bloody growl at me," the man removing it said with a funny accent. "That's standard procedure for everyone. Even cards with memories."

Malviere glanced around the elevator, which struck her as little more than a cage. It also stank of human fear... and excitement.

"It'll be fine, little wolf," Miriam said, reaching over and musing Malviere's hair. Malviere gently batted the hands away —she was fine, not worried. Just letting the man know what she thought of his shenanigans. And Miriam was a mere ally of the pack, not a packmate, and shouldn't be taking liberties.

"Hah, 'Little Wolfe'," Miriam said, holding up quotes around her nickname. "I crack myself up. It's like she's your daughter."

The comment warmed Malviere some, although she didn't know why. Maybe Miriam wasn't so bad. Malviere bared her teeth in a smile.

"Sometimes she feels like a little wolf," Shel added. "Always growling at people and liking dogs better than humans."

"Hilarious," Wolfe muttered.

The guard with the odd accent laughed. "Yeah, your boy threatened me the first time he came here as well. Like father, like card?"

"That's in character," Miriam said. "For both of them."

The door of the elevator opened, forestalling further commentary, and Malviere stepped out into the room, excited to see the Rat Arena.

She found herself in a huge, flat cave with a modern wooden floor installed, about fifty feet wide, that curved in a circle around the top of a massive arena—an arena that was built into an even larger cave that headed down. Wiring had been run across the natural stone ceiling, held in place by metal prongs hammered into the stalactites and the ceiling itself. A few parts of the cave walls had power lines as well, and they snaked across the smooth wooden floor of the balcony to the tables and the sitting bar that ringed the arena. The air was cool and still.

A huge number of anthropomorphic rats, mostly women in slinky cocktail dresses that seemed like they should have come from an eighty's casino, worked the tables that lined the place, passing out drinks and snacks. Malviere ignored them— somehow, she could sense they were the same magic that made minions, and wouldn't think, talk, or more importantly, threaten the pack.

But there were other people around that might threaten the pack. As Wolfe and Shel stepped out of the elevator, quite a few people gazed at them, many subtly nudging each other or nodding, and many going quiet.

Malviere had been studying the enemies of the pack with Shel and Wolfe—the photographs and files of those they would likely fight someday. She tried to growl again at the huge number of them gathered here. Members of the Weeds, the Singh, and the Renfeldt families were all gathered. A few others were around, independent agents that served the Infernal, Undead, or Elder factions in their hearts, if not knowingly or openly.

Malviere sneezed as cigar smoke washed across her, turning to see the source—a wiry man, young-ish but with thinning hair and bony fingers like he couldn't wait to be eighty. He wore an expensive black and white checkered suit.

"We welcome you to the Rat Arena!" a man said as he walked up.

"Hey, Clive," Wolfe said, nodding to the man with resignation in his voice.

Malviere could sense her alpha's dislike of Clive. But Wolfe didn't seem even slightly violent, so Malviere relaxed, confident this was something she didn't understand yet.

"I'm looking for a man, Zane Richardson. Have you seen him?"

Miriam laughed and held her hand out to Clive, palm down. "Right to the point, Wolfy. Have you no sense of the pageantry of these things? In conversation, as in sex, you need a bit of foreplay."

Malviere's alpha gritted his teeth.

Clive took Miriam's hand, bowed over it, and kissed her skull-ring-encrusted knuckles.

"Can you please just tell me if Zane's here?" Wolfe asked.

"Yeah," Clive said, then raised a single eyebrow. "When you asked us to let him in here, I was pretty concerned, given who he is. But I suppose you have Shel with you, and you guys have never caused me problems. He's at a table at the far end, almost dead opposite where we are right now, on the edge where he can see the fights."

"Thanks," Wolfe said, tipping an imaginary hat to the man

before turning and starting around the huge balcony that surrounded the arena.

"You're no fun at all, Wolfy," Miriam said, shaking her head mock-sadly while smiling. "Is he any fun at all at home, Little Wolf?"

Malviere ignored Miriam—she had another question she wanted answered. "Are we going to kill that man and send him to Cerberus?"

"Just like Wolfe indeed," Miriam muttered sardonically, grabbing a wineglass from one of the anthropomorphic rats they passed and taking a sip.

Wolfe turned to Malviere with wide eyes. "Um... I hadn't intended to. Also, since when do you ask things like that?"

"I was just curious," Malviere said, nervous that she had overstepped her role.

"Yeah, that's fine, ask all the questions you want. I was just surprised you were talking much. Maybe it's because you're about to evolve?"

Malviere thought about his words. Whatever the reason, he had said she could ask more questions, and Wolfe was a blunt man.

So she just asked what she wanted to know. "Why aren't we going to kill him? You obviously don't like him."

Shel snorted and over-dramatically flicked her red hair back. "If we killed everyone Wolfe didn't like, there wouldn't be enough humans left to repopulate the Earth."

Miriam made a drumming motion, sloshing a tiny amount of wine onto the floor. "Ba-dump, tschhh. Rimshot."

"Har har," Wolfe said without any humor in his voice. "I don't like Clive because he's ridiculous—all that 'we' nonsense and his new, ridiculous suit and all the same crazy pageantry as our resident Queen of the Dead."

"You have to admit I do it with more style," Miriam said.

Wolfe rolled his eyes but continued. "Also, even after

nearly two years, the cigar smoke brings back cravings I prefer not to be reminded of."

Malviere didn't understand the last comment. "So, who do we hunt, then, my alpha?"

"Don't call me that again, it's awkward. I'm only after the people that really deserve to spend their afterlife with Cerberus. Murderers, rapists, and the other worst-of-the-worst scum. Also, the people that Cerberus told me need to go to prevent chaos and wanton death in Noimoire—the other three with the cards. I'm not worried about people that run untaxed Arenas like Clive, or people that run a club where drugs can be had like Junior Vampress here. They aren't on the menu."

"Ah, so glad to know you care," Miriam said, batting her eyes at Wolfe.

Malviere nodded to his words. She would keep their targets in mind, for the future.

She was also nearly a hundred percent positive that Wolfe didn't mean she could eat the others when he said they were on the menu. But just to be sure, she might ask about it later.

She bet evildoer tasted great lightly singed and with some steak sauce.

They walked the last little bit in silence. At the far end of the massive balcony, there were almost no people at all—except for one table.

Wolfe stopped. "Stay back a bit, please, Malviere. Behind Shel and Miriam. I don't want this guy to pay attention to you."

Malviere moved to where she wouldn't be easily noticeable or visible.

Wolfe walked up to the table. The man there was small, both short and thin, and looked... precise. He was in a pressed button-down shirt, as well as slacks with a crease in them. His hair was combed just so, and his spectacles were so clean you could barely tell the glass was there. He was eating a salad one vegetable at a time and taking tiny sips of wine while staring into the arena below. Every so often, he would pick up a pencil and make a note on a piece of paper.

As Wolfe approached, the man glanced up, then dabbed his mouth with a napkin and stood, extending his hand.

"Wolfe, I presume?" the man asked.

Wolfe took the man's hand and gave it a single firm shake. "Yeah. You're Zane Richardson?"

The man nodded. "I am. You sure about this? Even after my flight, if you want to back out now, I won't hold it against you. But once I step in the ring, I'm keeping the money."

"I'm sure."

"Alright. I'll head down to the far side entrance, if you don't mind walking back to near side."

"I could use the exercise," Wolfe said.

The man gave Wolfe's two-hundred-and-thirty pound, almost nothing but muscle body the once over and then laughed, shaking his head. "Great."

As they walked back, Miriam asked, "What was that all about? And why did Clive crack that comment about Shel, earlier?"

"The man is an old academy buddy of Rhett's," Wolfe said. "He's now an FBI agent working the trafficking case that your late, lamented brother brought down on everyone."

"Damian was a fuckface to the very end," Miriam said, her voice dark.

Shel laughed. "Such an understatement."

Miriam smiled, but her eyes held no mirth as she continued. "Was Rhett the cop that you guys went all buddy-buddy with?"

"Or something like that," Wolfe said, scratching his arm. "Anyway, the last time I went and served court summons on some witnesses for Rhett and his office, Rhett joked with me about his old buddy that ran a dog deck as well, but was twice my level. So, I got to thinking—I could win a fight like that easily with Malviere here. Although, if she goes down, we'll have to have her next birthday half a year from now. But that would make me two levels in a *very* favorable match-up. So, I asked for his email, then sent him an offer—a hundred thousand to use his yearly arena match-up against me. He agreed."

It seemed... weak, and cheap, to Malviere. But whatever put the deer in the pack's belly, she supposed.

"Wow. You don't think small, do you?" Miriam said.

Shel was the one who answered. "We've been doing stuff like that a lot. Really pushing our card capabilities rather than living large. With all the money we got for selling Damian's cards, I got two match-ups against easy targets for my deck, and made four levels—now we're doing the same for Wolfe. It's a bit of a risk, as Wolfe needs at least one level for the Building card. The guy has to fight him for real, so it won't just be a cakewalk."

"I'll be fine," Wolfe growled. "You worry too much."

"Will the gods reward you with experience if you just pick easy fights?" Miriam asked.

Wolfe took that question. "Shel and I looked up a lot of stuff, and we can agree to 'decks as is' when the offer is made, even if it's a very favorable match-up. Although even that won't work against decks made intentionally easy. But if I'm up against a deck that was built as well as the deckbearer thought they could... well, even if the deckbearer agrees to a bad match-up, I'll get experience."

Shel jumped in again. "The theories the armchair lord predictors came up with is that it mirrors real-life fights—you bring what you have to the table, even if you're not ready, but you don't ever try and lose in a life-or-death situation."

Of course, Malviere thought to herself.

"In-ter-est-ing," Miriam said, dragging the word out. "I'll have to think about that for my own advancement, and that of Derek and Ahmed."

"Where are they, anyway?" Wolfe asked.

"Sleeping it off," Miriam answered.

"Sleeping what—" Wolfe started, then held his hands up. "No, nevermind. Don't answer."

Miriam laughed as they reached the narrow stairs that led down to the arena, but then conversation briefly stopped as everyone walked down, single file, into the arena below.

MALVIERE'S BIRTHDAY THREE: 8:30 AND 10:13 A.M.

They all filed out into a small room at the bottom of the Arena. It was long and thin, with an exit directly onto the arena floor. The room was very simple and appeared to be hewed stone, but a rock plinth nearby said exit and had a modern-day computer screen on it, one not attached to anything else. It was just a glass pane jutting up from the rock with electronic symbols all over it.

Wolfe turned to Malviere. "It's time for your first present —we'll be fighting side by side, with you in the ring. For the Pack."

Malviere felt excitement course through her—excitement to be part of the hunt to bring those that belonged in the Infernal realms their just deserts. Even if this part of the hunt wasn't really... real.

It was training, like when puppies fought each other.

Malviere had a sudden thought. "Don't I have to go back into the deck to help you in this fight?"

She wasn't sure if the idea scared or comforted her. *Who will I be, when I evolve? Will I even remember?*

"No," Wolfe replied. "You don't need to worry about that.

We—me and Zane I mean—agreed to a 'companions out' rule. Clive set it up for us that way before we got here. So, you can participate without resetting."

"Hmm."

"Don't die, though," Wolfe said. "He'll figure out very quickly why you're so important to this fight, and then he'll target you. We have to win fast."

"For the Pack," Malviere said. Even if she wanted to go back into the safety of the deck, she wouldn't. Not when it was against the wishes of the pack alpha.

Wolfe smiled at her. "Yes, exactly. For the Pack."

"Wait," Malviere asked. "Does this mean that I'll get to fight beside brother Cereboo?"

Wolfe smiled even wider, then touched his hand to his chest. "Yup."

He splayed his hands out, cards appeared. Wolfe touched the one off to the side, and Cereboo sprang into existence.

He woofed excitedly, licked Wolfe and Shel, and then came over and licked Malviere.

Malviere loved Cereboo. He was the best, her big brother in spirit if not flesh.

Wolfe put the deck away and walked over to the glass pane. "Get ready."

Shel kissed him and then stepped back, and Miriam said, "Kick his ass, Wolfy."

Wolfe reached out and touched the pane of glass. The Hellmouth Institute card briefly appeared on the screen, and Wolfe froze.

Then, without any further fanfare, Malviere found herself on the rock floor of the arena, with Wolfe in front of her and Cereboo beside her. The instinct to hunt filled her, and she cursed her tiny, weak body. She could only help others hunt. For the moment.

Maybe... maybe she *did* want to evolve.

She glanced ahead and saw their target—Zane—across the field.

"Go get'im, boy," Wolfe said, and Cereboo raced across the arena, woofing happily. He also loved to hunt, perhaps even more than Malviere.

The announcer kicked in a bit late. "We have our second match of the morning! Wolfe, the once enforcer and now reaper of the Grimm family, on one side! Against him stands Zane, the FBI agent investigating the remains of the family and their business."

Very few cheers floated down. Malviere sneered. Of course the worms who were involved wouldn't cheer for either of the people hunting them. They deserved the time they would spend with Cerberus.

Around them, all across the arena floor, rose huge piles of trash. The sounds of skittering and squeaking filled the arena, coming from the refuse about them.

"Wolfe enters with two companion cards already out, giving him a huge advantage!" the announcer continued. "But he got the garbage swarm arena, so every single creature card on the field, even tokens and companions, will be drawing mouse aggro!"

This time the crowd cheered.

Malviere glanced over to see a huge gray rat, not a mouse at all, poking its head from the garbage.

Wolfe brought forth his Demon Portal, summoning two of his Angry Hellhounds—a tier three and tier four—as well as a Lost Hellhound Puppy, from his side deck.

Malviere felt the power of her card siblings. Four of Cerberus' spiritual children, his conduit, and Wolfe himself faced Zane. He was food for the pack, whether he knew it yet or not.

Zane touched a card, trying to delay the inevitable, Malviere supposed.

Mated Pair
Rare Tier-1 Beast Immediate
4 Beast Power available

The deckbearer may immediately play two of the same Beast creature card from their deck. These cards must have the same name and tier both, and must be 1 or 2-power cards.

"Team strats are one of the strongest plays in the wild."

The card flashed and disappeared, and two wolves, normal-looking but for a bluish tint to the fur and lightning across their body. They started running to meet Wolfe.

Thor-Blessed Ravager
Uncommon Tier-1 Beast [Canine]/Lightning Creature
1 Beast Power, 1 Lightning Power
Health: 10
Attack: 3
Magical Attack: 10
Defense: 6
Magical Attack: 6

Special: **Shocking**: Any creature that takes more than 50% of its Health as damage from a single attack is shocked and cannot act the next round

"Thor had a brief period where he wanted his own Fenrir Wolf, and the results can still be found in the most magical parts of the forest."

Malviere was entranced by the wonderful new magical dogs, even if they were empty like most cards. They should be a part of Wolfe's pack, not the pack of their unworthy master. She called to them, "Join us, as Cerberus wills!"

The Thor-Blessed Ravagers switched sides, turning and falling in as Cereboo blasted past them, headed for Zane.

Malviere screamed as pain lanced through her calf.

Her health flashed in front of her face, dropping from thirteen to ten. She turned to see that a rat was hanging from her leg.

Wolfe ran over and stomped on the rat's head, killing it. He fired at a couple more.

Once they had a moment to breathe, he commented, "Alright, ironically, I think we've got Zane in the bag, but we need to stop the arena itself from killing you. You're the mission here, now."

"Sorry, al—" Malviere choked, her words changing. "Sorry, Wolfe."

Wolfe grimaced. "I think *every* creature card will summon a rat—but our creature cards stack bonuses. So, we still need more doggos, even if it means more rats. Wish I had one more power, however. I would have loved to play Litter here."

He touched a card, and another Angry Hellhound appeared. Tier three, and with bonuses from four other canines *and* Malviere. Even the other two, one tier-three and one tier-four, would be insanely strong.

The other deckbearer touched a card, and vines sprang up around everyone except Wolfe and Zane themselves. The doggos and the rats both.

Entangling Undergrowth
Rare Tier-2 Nature Persistent
2 Nature Power

All creatures on all sides lose their base attack and magical attack action.

"The forest's edge is safety for most beasts."

"He's trying to reset and buy himself time," Wolfe said. "I'd bet money he didn't expect you stealing his wolves, but I'll also bet he'll have almost all his power left, given his deck and perks are probably all canine synergy if he's been running this deck long enough to make Level Fifty-Seven.

"Although, shame I don't have Nature. A card like that could give me a real edge in some cases."

"He made a mistake," Malviere whispered, her voice laced with an otherness she couldn't normally call forth as her magic built—an otherness that made her sound like a threat.

She reached out, finding the Tier-four Angry Hellhound with her power.

"Kill."

The Hellhound ripped from the foliage and hit Zane. It was now a full six attack and magical attack higher than its base—which meant it hit for an attack of fifteen and a magical attack of eleven.

Zane was ripped near in half from the first attack, screaming for a mere second.

The magical attack setting his corpse on fire afterward was purely perfunctory.

"They're... wonderful," Malviere said.

"Enjoying the second part of your birthday day?" Shel asked, smiling at Malviere.

Malviere bared her teeth back as she petted the Dread Coyote in front of her with her left hand. Its fur was silky gray-black, and its shoulder came up to Malviere's head. It stared at her with eyes that contained no emotion.

It was empty, like all cards that weren't companions.

Despite that, Malviere had a sense of it. It was a trickster and lone hunter. It wanted to stalk and terrorize its favorite prey—mortals—until they were so tired and scared, they made a mistake. Then, and only then, would the Dread Coyote feed.

It was wonderful.

Malviere ripped at the kabobs in her right hand, tearing a piece of meat from the stick, chewing, and swallowing. It was tough and overcooked, but still quite good.

"Thanks," she muttered once she had swallowed. She bared her teeth at Shel again, and was rewarded with a return smile from the alpha's mate.

Malviere glanced around at the building she was in.

Magical Menagerie
Legendary Tier-2 Building

Null Card: This card may not be played in the Great Game but remains in deck.

This card may hold up to sixty Beast creature cards. Each card must have a different name. Each card added is removed permanently from the great game.

The cards manifest as their creatures inside the building, but will not fight, even to preserve themselves, and will peaceably interact with anyone that enters. If they are slain, they are removed forever.

The Deckbearer gains Beast power equal to the cube root of the different beast cards contained herein.

"Nature draws power from biodiversity, and so can rare deckbearers."

"Do you think the guy who owns this actually got three copies of this card?" Shel asked.

"Maybe," Wolfe said disinterestedly. "I'd think it more likely they got a legendary-rarity generic upgrade card."

Malviere walked over to a Shard Wolf Pup, petting the creature as the humans talked around her. They followed her while mostly ignoring her.

"I know every season had its broken cards, but this thing is crazy. I bet at Tier three it could hold seventy cards, and give four Beast power," Miriam said, then yawned.

She turned her gaze to Malviere. "Good thing I like you and your alpha"—Miriam laughed as Wolfe groaned —"because I don't normally operate in the unholy and forbidden hour of ten in the morning. That's sleeping time for me."

Malviere continued to wander, entranced by all the magical doggos—this menagerie had almost half its cards as canine type, for whatever reason.

"You definitely need one of these Building cards," Miriam said to Wolfe.

Shel snorted. "A *legendary building* card usually goes for ten to fifteen million. Some for far more. It's not happening."

"Not my first building pick, for sure," Wolfe replied. "Although it would be nice. But it costs at least five levels as well."

"Eh. Maybe if you didn't keep giving people their cards back."

Wolfe grimaced. "Always poking me, Miriam. Zane and I made that deal ahead of time—whichever one of us won would give the card they got back. I still got two levels. That's what's important."

"Just saying."

The four of them wandered around for another hour, chatting and jesting. Malviere was silent almost the entire time, except for occasional comments to the creatures she encountered.

But finally, she had interacted with every single creature card here. She could have stayed another ten hours, but she knew the pack would want to move on, even on her birthday.

She glanced up at Wolfe. "Okay, I'm done. What's next for today?"

Shel answered. "Well, next, it's time to expand the den, as you would say."

"Expand the den?"

Shel nodded with a smile.

MALVIERE'S BIRTHDAY FOUR: 2:14 P.M.

Malviere burped.

"It's really weird that you do that," Shel said.

"I like eating," Malviere said, placing the water back down on the table and picking up her burger and taking another bite. It was delicious, barely cooked at all, with only barbecue sauce and bread.

"And if she can eat, why not burp?" Wolfe asked rhetorically.

Some of the sauce spilled down Malviere's front, and she frowned.

Shel grabbed a small towel and dabbed at Malviere, then dipped it in the water and rubbed at her front. "It'll be nice when you're evolved just so that you can jump in the deck in order to clean stains."

Malviere didn't say anything, her mind conflicted. The Wandering Bulgae Pup was at her feet—as were the cavapoos —and she reached down, picking it up and setting it in her lap. She petted it.

"He's going to evolve with you," Shel said. "The Desperate Cult Child as well."

They don't have memories or feelings.

The door to the huge kitchen banged open, and Shannon and Lucy came running in, throwing backpacks onto chairs.

"You didn't do it yet, right?" Shannon asked excitedly, jumping on to a chair near Wolfe.

"If I'd have placed it, there'd be a huge extra building, wouldn't there? Did you *see* a whole extra building?"

"Maybe it was behind the Institute! You don't know."

"We haven't done it yet," Wolfe said.

"See?" Lucy butted in.

"Hey, you were worried too."

"Nuh-uh."

Liam followed the two kids in, gathering their backpacks. "You guys have to do homework tonight, after the placing but before anything else."

"I *always* do my homework first," Lucy replied.

"Shannon, you have to do your homework before anything else except the placing," Liam said.

"Ahh," Shannon whined over-dramatically, and everyone laughed.

"We're expanding the den now?" Malviere asked.

"Yeah. We can wait a little bit, but not too long. You'll be evolving soon."

Malviere felt her excitement and dread both rising. She put the Bulgae Pup on the ground. "I'm ready."

Wolfe walked to the counter and opened a drawer, from which he pulled a long, flat lockbox. He took a key from the drawer and opened the lockbox, then withdrew a manila envelope from it.

"I thought you were going to stop keeping the key right next to the box?" Shel asked.

"Sorry, I'll find a better place for it." Wolfe stuffed the key in his pants and then put the lockbox back. Then he walked over to the group, undid a small string holding the clasp on the manila envelope, and turned it sideways, holding his hand out.

A card dropped into it, and everyone gathered around to stare at it. On the front was a *very* demonic-looking interior room in an old-fashioned library.

Infernal Library
Uncommon Tier-1 Infernal Building
No cost

Building: Null card. May not be directly used in the Great Game.

Special: Creates a library of approximately 10,000 square feet. Any Infernal deckbearer inside may use non-creature cards at 1 less power.

Special: Infernal Cards with the word 'Cultist', 'Tome', 'Book', 'Knowledge,' and 'Forbidden' do not count against the deckbearer's card on field limit. The deckbearer may associate one card with those words in its title to this card, and it will always appear in the deck's first pull.

"Repositories of forbidden knowledge allow Mortals that are so inclined to engage in the dark arts—but they are never without price."

"What's so good about this?" Lucy asked. "I mean... do you even have any cards like that?"

"I have the Desperate Cult Child, who will also evolve tonight. But we are also hoping for excellent synergies with the orphans—I mean, this"—Wolfe raised his hand at the Hellmouth Institute around them—"makes Mortal and Infernal orphans grow up. This"—Wolfe held the card up—

"is an Infernal source of learning. The synergy seems obvious."

"And if it's terrible, we can likely sell it for almost as much as we bought it for and try again," Shel said.

Lucy nodded. "That's smart."

"What will it do to me?" Malviere asked.

"Well, we were hoping it would be 'what will it do *for* you'," Wolfe said. "But we don't know. Let's all go find out."

It was a long walk outside, the paintings of Infernal Lords seeming to stare at her with dark eyes as she walked. Malviere couldn't help but think about the fact that they were about to place a building that was going to change who she was, fundamentally. It was disturbing, bringing forth, even more, her fears about changing. Fears that had been bubbling under the surface since this morning, when they had told her it was the day she would evolve.

The day she would change.

The group, all happy, excited, or both—except Malviere herself—exited onto the front porch, and then Wolfe led them around the side of the building.

Wolfe held the card up, then touched his hand to his chest and brought forth his deck. He concentrated, and the card in his hand disappeared, replaced by the single Lost Hellhound Puppy left in his deck, which transformed back into a Rescue Pup as Malviere watched.

Then Wolf swiped his cards for two minutes. Malviere felt a bit tense—this was her very self they were talking about.

Wolfe finally got the card and cast it onto the ground. A massive building, an old wood-and-stone one, briefly shimmered before disappearing. In its place, a massive new wing of the Hellmouth Institute stood, a mere two stories high but a bit longer on one side. It was seamlessly connected to the Institute itself, but did have its own exterior entrance—a large, flat marble staircase flanked by two statues of the

Nachash the Serpent, Infernal Lord of Forbidden Knowledge.

Shel chuckled. "Remember when you commented about how much it irritated you that Big Man Grimm so openly advertised his connections? And then again when Miriam followed suit, doing the same thing?"

"Yeah."

"Just saying."

Wolfe grimaced. "I didn't pick this look."

But Malviere was just staring at the building, willing the card stats to appear—which they did, quickly. She only paid attention to what had changed.

Library Wing of the Hellmouth Institute
Unique Rare equivalent Tier-1 equivalent Infernal Building

Special: Forbidden Fruit: Any Mortal or Infernal (pre-evolution) orphan that evolves here gains another tier. These benefits stack. If the final card is Tier-6 or higher (or equivalent tier-6) then the location of the nearest undiscovered monster or puzzle box will be revealed to the deckbearer. If any Mortal or Infernal orphan evolves here and reaches Tier-10 or higher, the nearest undiscovered dungeon will be revealed to the deckbearer.

Special: This card will revert to an Infernal Library if it is ever removed from the deck of the deckbearer possessing the Hellmouth Institute.

"The Library Wing of the Hellmouth Institute is where all its brightest pupils go to find incantations or allies to get them ahead—in whatever pursuits they have."

"Wow," Wolfe said, staring at the building as well. Then he

turned to Malviere. "That's pretty damned good for you—two tiers, straight up. I think you'll actually hit the tier-ten mark. That's absurd."

"Absurd in a statistically unlikely, good way," Lucy chimed in.

"Yeah, that."

Malviere was relieved—it would only add tiers. She wouldn't be changed completely. Just be better.

Shannon literally jumped up and down and clapped her hands. "That's so bussin'! Can we enter, take a look at it?"

"You shouldn't use words like that," Lucy said.

"Words you don't understand?" Shannon said.

Wolfe rolled his eyes. "Let's just go inside, girls."

They both half-raced to the huge double-door and yanked it open, running into the library.

"This is crazy weird and scary!" Shannon yelled, but she sounded like she was having fun.

Shel laughed as well, taking Wolfe's hand and yanking on him exuberantly. When he didn't immediately follow, she rolled her eyes, let go, and ran up after her sister and friend. Liam followed.

Malviere frowned. They were treating it like some kind of... demon amusement park. It had real consequences. For the pack... and for Malviere.

"You okay?" Wolfe asked quietly as they walked up the steps.

"I'm not injured, pack al"—she coughed, the words changing—"Wolfe."

"You can call me whatever you wish, I just personally would prefer you use my name," Wolfe said. "Sorry, didn't mean to make that a rule."

Malviere nodded, but didn't say anything else.

Wolfe turned and sat on the great marble step, staring out

at the light traffic on the road at the end of the huge driveway leading to the Institute. He patted the seat next to him.

"Do you want to sit and talk about what's bothering you? You don't have to."

"Why do you think something is bothering me?" Malviere asked.

"Well, I have cooked breakfast for you for almost eighteen months now, and today you're different. More different than today being unusual ought to account for, I mean."

Wolfe stretched. "But I'm not really the 'talk about your feelings type,' in case you couldn't tell, so you've gotta either take this opportunity now or go look at the library with the loons."

Malviere sat beside him. "I'm scared of what will happen. I'm going to be different soon... will I even be me?"

Wolfe laughed. "Anything that starts with any version of 'will I be me' is dumb, kid. Trust me. Less dumb in your case, but... everyone grows up. Everyone changes. Everyone. I'm not the same as I was when I fought my dad, more than twenty years ago. I'm not the same as the man that fought by Big Man Grimm's side. Heck, I'm not even the man I was months ago, before I killed Damian."

"You're not?" Malviere asked. "But... you never evolved."

"Actually, I did evolve—it was just slower. But what you're worried about is merely growing up, I'm pretty sure. Just the Great Game version. Everyone grows up, sooner or later."

Malviere thought about it for a moment.

Wolfe stood and dusted his pants off. "I suppose in your case, you have the actual luxury of growing up only when you want. And it can be nice, being a kid, for a while. But being an adult is better, most of the time."

Wolfe held his hand out, and Malviere took it.

He pulled her to her feet. "Look... You don't have to

evolve. If you want to stay a kid, go for it, as long as you want—enter the deck and start again, until you're ready."

"But it'll make the pack weaker."

Wolfe shrugged. "That's true. But it's up to you regardless. I personally recommend that you grow up—evolve, whatever—but you don't have to. The decision is yours."

"When do I have to decide?"

Wolfe smiled wryly. "I think in the next fifteen minutes or so."

He stretched a second time, his arms pointing up. "Well, I'm going to go see this scary library. You decide as you wish. I promise either will be fine with me."

Malviere nodded, sitting down again on the steps outside the new 'Wing' Building card as Wolfe walked inside.

She had to evolve someday. Malviere knew that much. She had to change, someday.

But she wasn't sure she wanted today to be the day.

MALVIERE'S BIRTHDAY FIVE:
2:45 P.M.

Malviere stared out across Noimoire. She *knew* a great deal of evil lurked there. Not just because of what she had learned, listening to the alpha and his mate, but something instinctual told her. The knowledge and magic that flowed to her from Cerberus, she guessed. She didn't know, really.

She did know that she wanted to fight that evil. Not just assist with her powers, like she was some persistent card. No, she wanted to fight beside the pack for real, sending those that were truly evil to where they belonged.

To do that, she needed to be stronger.

If she waited, she might be better prepared. Wolfe could get more buildings, or more enhancements, and she would be stronger.

But really, in her heart, she just felt scared.

Malviere shook her head. She wanted to cry in frustration, because she didn't know what to do. But she had never cried, not ever.

She knew what it was for, of course, and she had seen Lucy

and Shannon cry more than once, and even Liam once, when he was holding a picture of his brother.

Malviere didn't even know if she could cry.

Being a card was weird.

Cereboo walked out from the library and slumped down next to her, on her left side. He rested his huge right head in her lap, the other two staring out at the town with her.

"You'll have to evolve too, someday, huh?"

Cereboo woofed quietly.

"I think once the alpha has all the cards like you, from that set, he'll choose to evolve you as well. Probably. Are you scared?"

The central head leaned over and licked her face, and Malviere laughed. "Yeah, you're my big brother. Of course you aren't scared."

Malviere stared out at the bright day for a moment. "I'm being silly, aren't I? A real wolf would try to be strong, right?"

Cereboo let out a quiet woof, and somehow, Malviere knew he wasn't offering her advice or taking sides on her dilemma.

Even though she was just a card, everyone was letting her make the choice.

Malviere felt her toes and fingers tingling, filling with magic. She knew the moment to choose was coming rapidly.

She was afraid... but the fear was limiting her.

Before, she hadn't had a choice. When she had been a Possessed Orphan, she had been empty like most cards. Now, she was Malviere, Conduit of Cerberus. She couldn't remember the time before, but she had seen the Desperate Cult Child, and had felt the emptiness of the Wandering Bulgae Pup. She felt little for them, not like she felt for Cereboo.

Now Malviere looked back on *old* Malviere with scorn and

disgust, and a desire never to return. Maybe *new* Malviere would be even more *bussin'*, as Shannon said.

Malviere was still scared.

But now... now she was also excited.

She lay back as the magic rapidly crawled up her limbs, into her torso. "I'm going to do it, Cereboo. You'll still like me once I change, right?"

Cereboo woofed in the affirmative, and Malviere could feel the laugh in his bark, at her silly assertion that he wouldn't always consider her part of the pack.

He stayed with his head on her lap as the magic finally filled her torso and climbed across her head.

Her world disappeared.

Malviere was back in the deck. The nothing place where the magic of the gods was the most accessible. The place she waited, next to her alpha's soul, when she wasn't out of the deck, fighting his battles.

It was a comforting place, and somehow, she was never bored. It was where she had been born, essentially.

And now, it was where Malviere was made anew.

Her limbs lengthened, and she felt places that still had the fat of a human child thinning. The clothes that were somehow a part of her changed, and her hair grew even longer. Subtle physical manifestations of human womanhood manifested.

But those changes were little compared to the changes to her magic, and her mind. The connection to Cerberus strengthened, and Infernal knowledge and power flowed into her. She also gained normal knowledge, and the ability to understand concepts and connections she hadn't, prior.

The magic settled, and Malviere took stock of herself.

She remembered everything. The first time she had awoken, eighteen months ago. The times she had fought beside Wolfe. The time she had been killed by thugs while inside their first home. Her recent fight against the other Dog Deckbearer.

Her feelings for her pack.

Even her previous, silly fear about losing herself.

She was everything she had been before, but now... now she was *more.*

A moment later, the tug came, the tug that meant her pack needed her. Although she suspected strongly that Wolfe just wanted to talk. But she heeded the call.

Malviere appeared next to Wolfe, inside the Library Wing, amid the stacks. The place had the faintest hint of sulfur, which Malviere suspected was too faint for normal human noses to pick up. There were also segments of the book walls that just had the faces of various obscure minions of the Infernal Lords, rather than room for more books. The floor was black tile, and the wood of the shelves was mahogany.

Wolfe and Shel were waiting, glancing at her as she appeared.

"Decided it was time to grow up?" Wolfe asked.

"I did, *great alpha*," Malviere responded, drawing those words out with extra emphasis. She grinned when Wolfe grimaced, and grinned wider when Shel laughed. Malviere hadn't understood, before, that friendly teasing and banter were not disrespect to an alpha—they were things that grew a pack closer.

Now, however, she did. And she reveled in her understanding, the deepness with which it allowed her to appreciate her pack.

Malviere also noted, with pleasure, that her voice had changed. While still feminine, it now had the reverberations of otherworldliness as an undertone. It was intimidating, and lent her a certain gravitas.

"And you're okay, I take it?" Wolfe asked.

"Better than okay," Malviere said, motioning to herself.

She was now nearly five-foot-six and appeared perhaps eighteen. She had long black hair, a long black dress, and slight claws on the end of her fingers. Her shadow was thick and curled up around her, shifting even when she was still. Malviere knew that the spirits of unjustly slain dogs, treated poorly by their pack, dwelled within, waiting for her call—and that the shadow was where hostile magic would weaken considerably before it could touch her pale skin.

She could also feel the power of Wolfe's enhancer card flowing to her, increasing her health and her defenses. *Truly, the best alpha one could want.*

"Can you see your card?" Wolfe asked.

"I can," Malviere said, focusing on it. She could see, from the slight change in their pupils, that Shel and Wolfe were staring at it as well.

Malviere, Conduit of Cerberus

Unique, Legendary equivalent, tier-11 equivalent
Mortal/Infernal companion[Evolved Orphan, Canine]
0 Power [2-power equivalent]
Health: 20[22]
Attack: 2
Defense: 5[6]
Magical Attack: 9[**Death**]
Magical Defense: 15[16]

Special: **Canine Leader[1]**: All other [Canine] creature cards gain +1 to their non-Health stats while she is on the field
Special: **Canine Rush[1]**: Once per round, any one [Canine] card may take an extra attack or magical attack action.
Special: **Canine Lord:** [Canine] creature cards of other deckbearers will switch sides without returning their power.
Special: **Canine Summoner[1]:** All [Canine] creature cards cost 1 less power of any type to summon

Note: Malviere's 'on the field' range is 350 feet.

"Malviere cannot remember any life except that of acting as a conduit for the power of the great guardian of the gates to the Infernal, Cerberus. She aids his chosen hunters on the mortal plane, to bring back those whom Hell has lost."

"Wow," Shel said, her voice hushed. "You got *powerful*, Malviere. You could kill me in a single action if I had no mantle."

Shel shuddered slightly.

"For the pack," Malviere whispered. "*Never* against the pack. I didn't change that much. I will *never* change that much."

Wolfe chuckled. "Good to know."

"So, want to see how the other orphans turned out?" Wolfe asked.

Shel and Malviere nodded in unison. Malviere was curious, and she had a greater understanding of how Wolfe's deck worked. She wanted to know if the new cards, her empty-minded allies, would aid them all.

Wolfe fiddled with the deck, swiping. Cereboo came wandering in as he did, and went over to Malviere, nuzzling her. She petted his head, sensing his continuing fondness for her.

A minute later, Wolfe touched a card, and a human woman sprang forth. She was wearing robes with multiple Infernal Lords' symbols on it, and carrying a tome.

Obsessive Infernal Cultist
Rare, tier-8 Mortal/Infernal Creature [evolved orphan, priest]
1 Power
Health: 9
Attack: 1

Defense: 5
Magical Attack: 4[**Infernal**]
Magical Defense: 5

Special: **Infernal Portal Summoner [2]**: Any Infernal card
with the word 'Portal,' 'Gate,' or 'Summon' costs 2 less power
of any type to play
Special: **Sacrificial [3]:** This card may be sacrificed for three
power of any type to be used for one summoning.

"This cultist has grown up in an Infernal church, and its every
commandment and mystery is dear to her heart."

"Wow," Shel said. "That's... strong. Very, very strong for a
one-power card."

"She will serve the pack well," Malviere said, enjoying the
sound of her own voice as it reverberated with magic.

"Yeah," Wolfe said, giving Malviere the side eye. "Ready to
see the Bulgae Pup?"

"I can't wait," Shel said.

Malviere felt the same way.

Wolfe touched another card, and a fiery dog, about a
hundred pounds, tail held high, appeared.

Bulgae Moon Chaser
Rare Tier-7 Fire [Canine] Creature [Evolved Orphan]
1 Fire and 1 Any Power
Health: 15[17]
Attack: 0
Magical Attack: 9
Defense: 6[7]
Magical Defense: 6[7]

Special: **Canine Tribal**: +1 to all non-Health stats for every other [Canine] on the field.
Special: **Hold on!** This creature survives the first otherwise fatal attack with a single Health.
Special: **Lost in the Dark**: If in the deck, the deckbearer does not trigger deck drawn warnings
Special: **Speedy:** This card may be played as an extra card play within a 30-second period.

"This dark Bulgae has hunted the moon for his master a thousand times. Perhaps the thousand and first he will catch it, or perhaps he will merely learn another ability."

"That's pretty strong," Shel said. "It might be stronger than the Angry Hellhounds you're working on, even the tier-fours."

"You should at least keep one in the deck," Malviere said, shocked at herself for volunteering tactics. "For surprise."

Wolfe raised an eyebrow at her but nodded. "Well, they're rare and tier seven and eight,

so that makes sense. Although the lack of the double attack ability is concerning."

"You should also put the Cultist into the auto slot of the Library," Shel said. "If that was a first draw, in a lot of fights, you would be able to do some truly absurd things—even your demonic portal card would only cost four power and bring forth five power worth of creatures in a round."

Wolfe nodded slowly. "I don't think I have anything else that fits, so that makes sense."

"Maybe you should look for an absurdly high-power dog," Shel said. "Some card with a title like 'Kaiju Mutt.'"

Wolfe laughed. "Sure, sure, we can check. But we'll look at the deck later. For now, we have something else we need to do."

Shel smiled. "Yeah, that's right. We do."

Malviere looked between them. "What's that?"

"Celebrate the rest of your birthday, of course. We have a few more things planned."

"We have reservations at the best Brazilian steakhouse in the city," Shel said. "Also, we—"

Wolfe interrupted. "Hey, don't spoil *all* the surprises."

Malviere smiled. Being a card *was* weird.

But with this pack, it was also good.

PROLOGUE: ONE CHANCE

Fern's Viewpoint

Six days, twenty-two hours, and thirty-one minutes left, you damned baby. You've already wasted almost an hour-and-a-half. Get yourself together! You're not two anymore!

Fern Wachowski tried to breathe in a four-two-six pattern. Four-second inhale, two-second hold, six-second exhale.

It was supposed to lower anxiety, and she desperately needed to be at her best.

But Fern's current level of fear was overwhelming the technique.

"The painting of Gabriel I hate so much, the marble floor, and the computer I work at in front of me," Fern said, naming three things she could see, then moving on to three she could hear. "The sound of the computer humming, my own heartbeat going far too quickly, and the chirping of that idiot bird outside my window."

Finally, three things she could feel. "The chair I'm sitting on, the keyboard beneath my fingers, and *my gods' damned anxiety*!" she said, her voice rising to a high-pitched scream of frustration on the last part.

She was embarrassed at her outburst, even though no one was with her in the tiny room that was her prison.

But her outburst gave her an idea.

She could try to call on an old emotion, to overwhelm the new ones. An old, once-familiar emotion, almost lost beneath her fear.

Anger, Fern. Anger is better than fear. Remember why you started, everything the crime families took from you. Remember what Adam took from you when he caught you. Not what he did, never that—only what he took.

It was hard, but Fern stoked her deeply hidden rage. Her depression, anxiety, and outright terror threatened to overwhelm it and snuff it out. But it was still there, buried deep beneath those worthless emotions that owned her most days.

Finally, she managed to revive her old thoughts of revenge, breaking the cycle of dark, terrible thoughts that had paralyzed her.

Six days, twenty-two hours, and nineteen minutes left. Adam's gone, his children are gone, his deckbearer minions are gone. It's time. The only chance you'll ever have, Fern.

With trembling hands, Fern touched her chest. She felt her power as she had many times before, over the almost two years since Drop Night, when she had been gifted with a deck. It felt of cold metal, but with an edge of deception.

No one is close enough to know when you pull your deck, Fern. It's time. Just do it.

She pushed her hand out, forcing her fingers open and splayed through sheer force of will. She had been suppressing the urge to do this for almost two years, and it was hard to change now.

Four cards popped out of her chest and hovered in front

of her, about a foot away. Three directly forward and one slightly off to the side.

Fern knew almost everything about cards and being a deckbearer. But it was all book knowledge—she had no practical experience. She could pull her status sheet up, and she knew she had a god-gifted deck with a companion.

Which, of all her cards, was the one that most interested Fern. *Please be something that can help save me. Someone that can help save me.*

She touched the companion card to the side, which glowed with purple and metallic gray energy.

A tiny little robot appeared on the floor. Or maybe not a robot... a bizarre cyborg. It appeared to be a human brain, inside a glass case with silvery wires connected to it, all on top of a cutesy white robot body. It was fairly small, perhaps a bit larger than a full-grown male pug.

She stared at it, and a card semi-imposed itself over the creature.

Brain Bot

Unique Rare Equivalent Tier-6 Equivalent Golem/Psychic
Creature [Cyber, Cyborg, Mastermind]
0 Power
Health: 5
Attack: N/A
Defense: 3
Magical Attack: N/A
Magical Defense: 3

Special: **Golem Leader [1]**: this adds +1 to all non-health
stats of every other golem
Special: **Master Deckbearer [Psychic 1]**: Every Psychic card
costs 1 less power while this card is out.

Special: **Psychic Resonator [2]:** This increases the magical attack power of all Psychic immediate cards by 2

Special: **Psychic Brain-Hack**: This card can take control of any one other creature card that does not have resistance or immunity to psychic energy, but may only do so for two total rounds once every hour.

"Brain Bot is loved by no one. But Brain Bot is useful to everyone. Why does no one love Brain Bot?"—Brain Bot.

Fern almost wept when she saw that the attack stats on her companion were 'not-applicable.'

"Damnit," Fern muttered, her anxiety threatening to come back with a vengeance. "I needed a protector, not... this."

The screen on the front of the little robot flashed. A sad emoticon face with a tear, almost eight-bit in appearance, formed, and then the words "Is Brain Bot a disappointment?" appeared.

Fern was startled. She had read, of course, about companions having personalities and memories, but somehow hadn't expected this... thing, to talk to her. For some reason.

But she didn't want to hurt its feelings. "I have to escape, Brain Bot. I wanted a companion that was large and powerful and could fight. You seem really neat... but you're not what I wanted right now, I'm so sorry."

The words changed. "Brain Bot will save you! Brain Bot can do it! Take a chance on him!"

"I don't have a choice anyway, Brain Bot—I have to go now if I ever want to be free again. Now is the time, for multiple reasons."

She turned back to the computer, her hands slightly steadier with a companion nearby, even one that was not optimal for the moment. She took the USB drive out from it—the drive with all the proof of the corruption that wormed through Noimoire. More than half of it was directly traceable to her personal nightmare, Adam Delacruz.

It wouldn't work to try and do things the right way. That was what had gotten her in trouble in the first place, the time she had gone to the authorities when the Renfeldt family had been on to her.

She needed something else. *Someone* else.

She glanced around her ten-foot by ten-foot room. It was beautiful, and had a wonderful twin bed and beautiful wooden desk, but the door was closed, sealed from the outside.

With an electronic lock. To keep a hacker inside.

Adam Delacruz was brilliant, bold, and ruthless as hell. But he had two blind spots. He was *old*, almost two hundred years old, and he didn't really understand modern technology.

Which was how Fern ended up in a room with a computer, held by an electronic lock.

Or, perhaps it was his second flaw, his arrogance. Perhaps he had counted on her fear of him to keep her locked up.

Fern shuddered, her hand going to her back, and the tracery of scars there. She started to hyperventilate again.

But she grabbed hold of herself, thinking about her rage again. Adam had almost been right, about her fear of him. But as her father had once said, 'almost' only counted in horseshoes and her hand grenades.

She stared at her computer again. Land deeds, police incident reports, and intercepted emails from the three major Noimoire crime families were all still open.

As was a profile she had been building for some time, much of it on Adam's assistance.

Ethan Madison Wolfe the 2nd.

It has to be him. He's the only one that has any chance to survive, and is unquestionably not in Adam's pockets. He killed

Adam's son, and ruined his plans with Worldwide Decurion. Adam won't forgive that for anything.

Fern stared out the window, onto the grounds of the giant manse that was Adam's home. A large parking lot with fountains and statues, surrounded by a carefully maintained garden, surrounded in turn by a carefully maintained line of trees to block it from view… and everything was finally encased with a huge stone and wrought-iron fence.

Cameras watched it all.

Fern turned back to her keyboard, fingers shaking. She took the mouse, and moved the cursor to click into a hidden folder. She clicked on two programs, both of which she'd prepared a long time ago.

Her door clicking open was the only sign that anything had changed, but she had disabled all the electronic locks, the cameras, and the alarms.

She felt her pocket again, to make sure the USB drive was still there. Then the other pocket, where the keys to the little used van that she had nicked yesterday were.

Fern walked to the door and opened it. It swung in smooth and silent, and Fern glanced into the hall. Finding it empty, she stepped out into the grand hallway that ran the near exterior of the mansion.

The hallway was ostentatious, with marble floors and crystal chandeliers that she passed underneath as she hurried away from her room. If she headed in the opposite direction, toward Adam's offices, she knew she would find plinths carrying cards inside glass cases—famous cards that Adam couldn't use. A few were even legendary, from the many powerful deckbearers that Adam had defeated over his years, whether Indian chieftains, Nazi generals, or Prohibition mobsters. She was tempted to take some, but there were guards stationed there, and even without alarms, the sound of breaking glass could give her away.

The money wasn't worth it.

Instead, Fern headed in the opposite direction, toward the garage elevator.

As she walked the halls, Brain Bot followed, nearly silent but for the faintest hum as the small cyborg rolled along behind her. He reminded her that she had a deck she hadn't taken stock of yet.

She looked at her remaining cards. A Cyber Sai, an equipment card which added to her attack and could disable electronics. A Mind Blank card, that would do slight Psychic damage—more with Brain Bot out—and cause a deckbearer to lose a card play. And a creature card called a Hack Ninja.

Those cards would have to be enough, although Fern hoped she didn't need anything from her deck.

She reached the elevator and hit the down button. She waited around the side of a nearby hallway, watching the elevator. When it opened, she waited a second to make sure no one came out, then dashed across the hall and slipped into it, holding the door as Brain Bot rolled after her. She hit the garage level button repetitively, feeling trapped until the doors closed.

A moment later, the elevator doors opened, and Fern stared out into the garage. No one was there at the moment.

She hurried over to the old white van with a hanging symbol of Uriel in the window—the one that hadn't been used more than a couple times in the ten years since Adam's most recent children had gotten their driver's licenses. It was a solid vehicle, upgraded to provide protection to his children, although no one had attacked him or his family in ages. Well, not until Caine was killed last year.

Fern opened the van door with shaking hands, dreading every moment that it cost her. Then she helped Brain Bot inside, even though she could barely lift him. Once they were strapped in, she turned the van on, hit the fob to the garage door, and gently pulled the car out into the front driveway.

It had been almost three years since she had driven a car, but apparently it was like riding a bike.

The driveway was a huge circle around marble fountains with statues of angels in them, and Fern pulled out of the circle along the shorter path, entering the main driveway out.

As she drove out, slow and careful, one of Adam's men—Travis—stepped out from the bushes to the side, holding his hand up. Travis was nearly thirty, large and muscled, with a thick black beard and a slight gut. He carried a gun in a side holster, and Fern eyed it nervously.

No one is supposed to be here. Did I miss something, or is this just bad luck?

Travis stepped out in front of the car and motioned for her to stop.

"No, no, no, gods damn it, no," Fern muttered under her breath as she slowed.

Travis walked up, staring into the window. Upon seeing Fern, his eyes widened. "Fern, what are you—"

Then his eyes flickered to the cards still in front of her chest, and then over to Brain Bot, strapped into the front seat.

His eyes widened in surprise. After half a second, Travis stepped back and reached down.

I can't go back! Fern punched the accelerator as hard as she could, and the van lurched forward. The crack of the handgun sounded, and some metallic plinks filled the car, as well as the sound of breaking glass. Fern scrunched up, barely able to move or breathe, but she didn't take her foot off the accelerator or her hands off the wheel.

None of the bullets hit her.

Travis was shouting and waving his hands, and ahead of her, at the end of the path, the gate began to close.

Fern's foot never left the accelerator.

The vehicle picked up speed, going nearly eighty miles an hour when she reached the gate. She slammed into half of it, and the gate was bent out from the heavy van, but it was slung sideways. She left the end of the driveway, crashed through bushes, hit a slight ditch, and finally bounced out onto the road near the house, screaming the whole while.

But somehow, the car didn't flip, and she stopped screaming, but was still hyperventilating.

She happened to glance over at Brain Bot, who had a puke emoji in eight bit on his front screen.

The little bot stopped her emotional train cold, and she almost choked into laughter. She slowed slightly as she sped down the road.

But only slightly. She knew that it wouldn't be but two minutes before Adam's men were after her.

She glanced at the clock. *Six days, twenty-one hours, and fifty-three minutes left.*

I hope you're everything they said you were, Wolfe...

CHAPTER 1

RAMPAGE INTERRUPTUS

"What's on the docket today, Timo?" Wolfe asked.

Mrs. Timo glanced up from the large, dark wood desk with silver skull inlay she was working behind. Her skin was slightly darker than the normal white, either Mediterranean or perhaps Pacific Islander.

She lowered her glasses to stare at Wolfe with brown eyes surrounded by laugh and worry lines both. "It's Mrs. Timo or Grammy, you young whippersnapper."

Wolfe chuckled. "Alright, *Mrs. Timo*, what's on the docket today? More braindead work for the Joliet P.D. and/or D.A.?"

"Yup," Mrs. Timo said, patting a couple thin files on the desk in front of her. "The P.D. this time. They need two people served that live near us in Noimoire, and they want you to take statements from a victim that lives out here as well. The usual rate is being offered."

Wolfe grimaced. *I hate doing that boring-ass work for forty-an-hour, a couple hours a day. I mean, this would be a great job, normally...*

Damian Grimm, the son of his old boss Thaddeus 'Big Man'

Grimm, had possessed a *ton* of expensive cards in his deck before Wolfe killed him. Four rare cards specifically had been quite valuable—the five-power, rare Infernal Champions. Close to as expensive had been the building card that Wolfe had dealt with the night he had killed Damian, and four solid enhancer cards. None had fit his deck—or they'd had prices he wasn't willing to pay, like hideous Infernal features. So Wolfe had sold them all for *millions*.

Most of the money had gone to either purchasing arena matches for himself and Shel that were extremely advantageous, or to buying upgrades for his and Shel's deck. Wolfe had also gotten Liam a knock-off Infernal and Canine deck that synergized with his own. It was far weaker than Wolfe's own deck—but it had still cost almost a million dollars on its own.

Wolfe had a couple hundred thousand left in the bank, which might not sound like a lot for the number of people in his household. Besides Wolfe himself, it was composed of three adults, two children, four self-aware cards and two idiot Cavapoo dogs. But Wolfe also lived inside the Hellmouth Institute, which provided a ton of food beyond the mortgage-and-maintenance-free dwelling it itself was.

So working for what Wolfe admitted would be a solid salary under normal circumstances felt oddly pointless.

But he wanted the contacts with the police, so they would treat his William Madison personae as an ally and not a suspect. Plus, between Wolfe's contract P.I. work and Shel's work as an actual member of the Joliet P.D., he could hopefully explain away any giant windfalls that came from his other activities, once he resumed them.

He sighed and held his hand out. "Alright, pass it over."

Mrs. Timo handed him the three new files, each with a case name and the hiring agency—Joliet PD—written below it in small letters. Each was thin, with each file folder containing only a few pieces of paper. Although the one for the interview had a bit more in it, and Wolfe knew he'd need to review it thoroughly before beginning his own interview.

He thought back to the first witness statement he had ever gotten, from Mrs. Timo herself, and winced. It had been bad. But he knew what he was doing these days, after nearly a full year as a P.I.

Wolfe drummed his fingers on the desk, only vaguely seeing the odd demonic imagery. After a year of living inside his building card, it was just part of the scenery. He decided to try and serve the papers first. It was still fairly early in the morning. Wolfe knew from personal experience that most people involved in criminal activity didn't get up till late, making it easier to surprise them at home.

He took the keys to the newest car—he seemed to lose one every year in some kind of shootout. The new one was a Black Ford-150 truck, with the v8 and all the bells and whistles—as well as a ton of custom mods Liam had put on it. Wolfe was *tired* of losing his cars and wanted one that would survive the next time he was in a fight, even if it was slightly more conspicuous than he liked.

Then he strapped on his STI Edge, more to stop any of the people he had to serve from doing anything dumb than out of any fear he might need to use it.

Then he whistled.

A chorus of antiphonal barks came back, and a moment later, Cereboo busted into the room. The giant, three-headed, black-furred boxer raced past Wolfe and out the front door, barking like a maniac the entire time.

Wolfe glanced at his first card, and oldest companion, as he raced past.

Cereboo

Unique rare equivalent, Tier-7 equivalent Beast/Infernal
[Canine] Companion
0 Power
Health: 12
Attack: 5x3
Defense: 7
Magical Attack: 7[**Fire**]
Magical Defense: 4

Special: **Fungible [Beast, Infernal]:** While in play, Beast and
Infernal power may be spent as if they were the other.
Special: **Infernal Slayer**: +100% Attack and Magic Attack
against other Infernal cards.
Special: **Preferred Typing [Beast, Infernal]:** Gains all the
better type matchups of both Infernal and Beast.
Special: One of the 'Gate to the Underworld' cards. If all 6 are
possessed in the same deck, the bearer will gain 7 Legendary
Infernal or Beast card pulls. Additionally, the deckbearer may
either gain the Mythic 'Gate to the Underworld' Building
Card or evolve Cereboo. Each card was given to a member of
the Noimoire underworld.

"A pup of Cerberus, who was born into a particularly
frisky litter. Cereboo was the runt—not quite as strong,
nor as tough, as his litter mates. But his heart was the
heart of a huntsman, and the blood of Cerberus runs in
his veins. He hunted across the fiery plains of the first
infernal realm, chasing the damned who tried to escape
their fates. Now, he chases many things, but his soul is
still called to chase those who belong in the Infernal
Realms."

A moment later, an eighteen-year-old girl came through
the door. She had red eyes, long black hair, a long, ragged black

dress and fingernails that were almost claws. The shadows swirled around her, a near-physical black energy.

"Morning, Malviere," Wolfe said with a nod.

"Alpha," she responded with a nod back, her voice eerie. "Do we go to serve notice to evildoers that their day of justice approaches?"

"I think in this case we're serving victims notice of when to come tell their story in court, actually. But yeah, it's time to go work."

Malviere nodded her head, and Wolfe caught a glance of her card as she walked out as well.

Malviere, Conduit of Cerberus

Unique, Legendary equivalent, tier-11 equivalent
Mortal/Infernal companion [Evolved Orphan, Canine]
0 Power [2-power equivalent]
Health: 20[22]
Attack: 2
Defense: 5[6]
Magical Attack: 9[**Death**]
Magical Defense: 15[16]

Special: **Canine Leader[1]**: All other [Canine] creature cards gain +1 to their non-Health stats while she is on the field
Special: **Canine Rush[1]**: Once per round, any one [Canine] card may take an extra attack or magical attack action.
Special: **Canine Lord:** [Canine] creature cards of other deckbearers will switch sides without returning their power.
Special: **Canine Summoner[1]:** All [Canine] creature cards cost 1 less power of any type to summon

Note: Malviere's 'on the field' range is 350 feet.

"Malviere cannot remember any life except that of acting as a conduit for the power of the great guardian of the gates to the Infernal, Cerberus. She aids his chosen hunters on the mortal plane, to bring back those whom Hell has lost."

Wolfe followed Cereboo out, Malviere falling in at his side. It occasionally still struck him as odd that, aside from Shel, the two beings he might be closest to were magic cards, not 'real' people. Both were companion-type cards that could think and had memories and even goals.

He walked out of the front office of his business, Madison Private Investigations, and into the foyer of the Hellmouth Institute. The room had marble floors and wood-paneled walls, but the lighting was iron chandeliers with giving off soft red light and there were statues and pictures of Infernal Lords or Champions on the walls.

Wolfe hated the décor, but he couldn't actually remove it from the Hellmouth Institute, so grudgingly accepted it. He pushed his way out of the heavy wooden door—carved with a pentagram, because why not—and out into the front parking lot.

Cereboo was already in the back of his new truck, his front feet on the reinforced roof of the front cab, one head looking back at Wolfe and the other two staring forward.

"Elder brother is excited to hunt," Malviere said, her voice feminine, but with an otherworldly reverberation that made it scary.

She got rather powerful when she evolved, and her new form reflects it.

"I think 'Elder brother'"—Wolfe held up air quotes—"just loves smelling the city. We're not hunting anyone."

Malviere shrugged, then asked a different question. "Why isn't your other companion, the Obsessive Infernal Cultist, coming?"

Wolfe shuddered slightly. He only had two actual

companion cards, but his perk from Level Twenty-Five let him treat one evolved orphan as if it were also a companion card. He kept the Obsessive Infernal Cultist out because she let him play his Demonic Portal cards extremely cheaply. The card normally cost six power and summoned up to five power of Infernal Creature cards from a side deck. But the Obsessive Infernal Cultist reduced it by two. Wolfe had a second one in his deck as well, that would always be in his first hand, so he might be able to summon five power worth of creatures for *two* power, if things went optimally.

But that was only if he needed to fight. The rest of the time, the Obsessive Infernal Cultist was just a thoughtless, silent card that almost appeared to be a human woman, walking around and giving off an entire chasm's worth of uncanny valley.

Wolfe left her home, most days. She didn't just disturb him; she bothered the people he worked with and served papers on as well.

"If we need her, we'll bring her," Wolfe responded.

He went around the driver side door, and Malviere went to the front passenger side door. Before Wolfe could open the door, however, he heard a screech of tires and watched as a van came tearing around the corner from the street into his parking lot, almost tipping over as it did.

Wolfe touched his chest, pulling his deck, and at the same time grabbed his pistol from the holster.

Wolfe aimed his gun at the front of the van as it came flying up. But he shifted his aim when he saw a small, mousey, and terrified-looking lady gripping the wheel, and the three cars that came tearing around the corner after her.

Shit. I should have kept the Companion Infernal Cultist around after all.

CHAPTER 2

IT BEGINS

"Cereboo, ravage whichever fool sticks his head out first!" Wolfe yelled.

Cereboo woofed in acknowledgement and ran in a loping curve toward the enemy's cars,

rapidly pulling ahead of Wolfe.

"Malviere, keep behind me and boost your brother," Wolfe continued.

Malviere took a few steps behind him.

Wolfe glanced down at his deck. As expected, his second Obsessive Infernal Cultist card was available, thanks to his library building card. He saw that he also had one of his Demonic Portal cards.

Normally, his perfect setup would be the Cultist followed by the Portal which would cost four-power for five power worth of creatures.

But Wolfe wasn't sure 'mo' monsters' was the play he should be making. He was pretty sure he was about to be wildly outnumbered by people carrying guns, which would chew through his creatures before they could get unbeatable synergy going.

He had two other cards, one of which was the card he planned to use instead—Cerberus' Home for Wayward Hellhounds.

As the van tore at him, he rushed forward and to the side, praying to his patron that the woman driving wasn't an actor pretending to be scared to ambush him. Two people leaned from the back of the leftmost car and fired at him with pistols. Wolfe's stomach clenched as the near misses stirred his hair.

Well, now I know who my enemies are for sure. Plus, I'll have no trouble with the police when I waste these fools.

From behind Wolfe, Malviere whispered, "Get him, brother." Cereboo sped up wildly, almost as if he were a movie on fast forward while everyone else was just on play.

Wolfe's dog cut in front of the leftmost car, behind the van, and leapt up and snatched one of the gunmen in midair and dragged him to the ground. Both rolled across the parking lot, a pile of screams, snarls, and barks.

Wolfe was glad one was down, but kept his focus. The cars were right on the van's tail, a mere hundred or so feet back—the timing was going to be tricky.

As soon as the van passed him, he touched the card at his chest, trying to put it perfectly into the gap between the van and its pursuers, where it would muck up their attack the most.

Cerberus's Home For Wayward Hellhounds
Unique Rare equivalent Tier-1 equivalent Persistent
1 Infernal, 1 Beast, and 1 Any power

Special: **Puppy Power:** Any Beast with 'Puppy' or 'Rescue' in its title has +50% Attack and Defense.
Special: **Summoner [Lost Hellhound Puppy L/5]**:
Generates a Lost Hellhound Puppy at no power cost every 30 seconds until Level/5 are on the field, rounded up.

Special: **Savior [Beast]:** If any opponent 'sacrifices' a creature card type Beast, that card joins you instead of being destroyed until the fight ends.
Special: **Heart of Gold [Beast]:** You cannot sacrifice Beast cards.

"This card is the only pound in existence that tries to find homes for the few Bad Doggos in the universe. Perhaps with proper attention, they too can be Good Boys."

As the card triggered, rocks rose from the asphalt without damaging it, and rifts of flame and cages formed in the middle of the rocks—the physical manifestation of the card.

The three cars skidded, the two outside ones turning left and right to avoid the obstacle. The last guy that had been hanging out of the car to shoot Wolfe dropped his gun and grabbed the side to keep from flying from his ride.

But the middle car smacked into the rocks, denting the front of the black sports car. An airbag went off, and Wolfe guessed he had a few minutes before those jackasses rejoined the fight.

He stepped forward, putting a rock between himself and the rightmost car and rapid firing his STI Edge into the front windshield. Fortunately, the thugs hadn't gotten bulletproof windows. The windshield collected tiny, spiderweb-crack-ridden holes, and the thugs collected red spots on their chests.

Neither moved, and the car slowed a bit as it rolled past Wolfe, drifting away without a driver. Wolfe stepped back into cover.

Wolfe was tempted to immediately go on the offense for the other cars' worth of thugs, but didn't want to leave an enemy behind him.

He waited for a couple seconds behind the rocks of Cerberus' Home for Wayward Hellhounds. The instant the card summoned the first Lost Hellhound Puppy, Wolfe knew thirty seconds had passed.

He instantly played his second card. The Obsessive Infernal Cultist appeared—a woman appearing roughly eighteen with long black hair who wore gray robes with vague pentagram-esque symbols on them and carried a dark grimoire.

"Stay behind the rocks!" Wolfe called out.

Heavy gunshots sounded out across the parking lot.

Wolfe risked a glance. Liam—who looked like a red haired, red-bearded dwarf, only taller—was running from the garage. Two Angry Hellhounds were running at his side—Wolfe figured he must have heard the fracas and started summoning the same time Wolfe did. He had an automatic rifle in his hands and was firing at the rightmost car. Wolfe grimaced as a bullet from the return fire caught his mechanic and driver in the thigh, and Liam went down with a yell.

Shit!

To buy his ally—and friend—some time, Wolfe switched out the magazine and fired at the other side of the car, plinking the metal and wounding a thug behind the driver seat. Everyone took cover.

The Hellhound Puppy rushed at the rightmost car, barking cutely. Cereboo picked himself off the asphalt, blood from the throat-torn corpse at his feet dripping from his central mouth. He ran at the middle car, leaping at the first thug who opened the door and stumbled, face already bloody and cut, from the backseat.

Wolfe serviced targets as he walked closer, relying on the STI Edge held in two hands to keep people down. He ran out of bullets and rapidly switched his last magazine in. Liam fired from the other side as his two Angry Hellhounds reached the car.

But the driver's side thug had a feel for the flow of combat.

In the seconds that Wolfe left as he switched his magazine, the man leaned out the window and fired rapidly. Wolfe bit back a yell as sudden pain flared through his right bicep, and he dropped his gun just as he was bringing it back up to fire.

Wolfe followed his gun to the warm asphalt and swiped his cards, cussing when his second Demonic Portal wasn't in the pull.

But he did get his mantle, which might have been even more important. He slapped that on.

Master of the Infernal Hunt
Unique Tier-5 equivalent Infernal Persistent [Mantle]
2 Infernal Power
+10 Health, +3 to all remaining stats.

Special: **Cerberus's Champion:** All other [Canine] Cards gain +5 Health and +1 to all other stats, and all [canine] cards gain advantage against Infernal cards.
Special: **Versatile [Infernal]:** This card alters to fit its wearer so long as they have at least 2 Infernal Power
Special: **Grand Pack [Canine]:** [Canine] cards do not count against cards on the field
Special: **Favorable Façade[Canine]:** Count as a Beast[Canine] card for all purposes except type match penalties.
Special: One of the 'Gate to the Underworld' cards. If all 6 are possessed in the same deck, the bearer will gain 7 Legendary Infernal or Beast card pulls. Additionally, the deckbearer may either gain the Mythic 'Gate to the Underworld' Building Card or evolve Cereboo. One card is held by each of the crime families of Noimoire, and the sixth is held within the city by another.

"Sometimes, the demons call a hunt on other demons, and a hunt master is always chosen to lead the chase."

Wolfe felt power as the mantle settled over him, and a faint red glow covered him. His wounds hurt less, the blood staunched, and Wolfe knew he would be far, far harder to hurt.

But it was nothing compared to what came next—he heard Malviere's voice in his mind, wordless but urging him to great feats in Cerberus' name. His movement accelerated and he snatched his gun from the ground. He fired rapidly upward, his hand tracking almost effortlessly at the heads barely visible over the windows. In just a few seconds, Wolfe executed both the back seat thugs with his gun.

It took him a moment to realize what had happened. *I turned myself into a 'canine' card for all purposes... which includes Malviere's ability to double the attack rate of any canine cards, I'm guessing.*

Wolfe assessed the battlefield as he placed his now-empty Edge on the ground and then rose to stand again. He raced toward the car that had slammed into the newly grown rocks. *Five thugs left at the most—two on the other side of the rightmost car unless Liam and his pups have already killed them. Then three left in the car that smashed into Cerberus' Home for Wayward Hellhounds.*

It would normally be suicidal to charge gunmen in a car, even stunned ones in a crashed car, but Wolfe knew his mantle made him far more resilient.

A yip came, and a notification told him that one of his Hellhound Puppies had died.

Another surge of power hit Wolfe. He had a base eight in his attack and defense, modified by four each from the combination of mantle and his perks—and for thirty seconds, he got an additional fifty percent because his Puppy card had died while he was counted as a canine card himself.

He reached the car, and with his double attack rate from Malviere and current eighteen attack with his bare hands, double-punched straight through the back and front passenger side window, killing both thugs by caving their skulls in.

His hands were undamaged.

The battlefield stilled, and Wolfe glanced around.

Cereboo had finished off the driver as well, and Liam and his dogs must have killed the two on the far side of the rightmost car, as there weren't any more shots being fired.

Wolfe headed around the car he had just attacked and then ran toward Liam. As he did, he pulled his phone and put a call into his friend, Lieutenant Rhett Walker of the Joliet PD.

"Hello? Wolfe?" the uptight but masculine voice of Rhett answered on the other side.

"Hey Rhett," Wolfe said. "I've got a bit of a problem here at the Hellmouth Institute, and I'd prefer if you were first on the scene."

"Lovely," Rhett muttered through the phone. "I'll be there in thirty minutes. It's a bit of a drive."

"Thanks," Wolfe said, and hung up.

It was gonna be a day.

CHAPTER 3

ONE WEEK

Wolfe stared around at the carnage. Three cars, twelve bodies, and Liam was shot. Not to mention the lady in the van, which had stopped right near the front door to the Hellmouth Institute. But she wasn't moving, just clutching the steering wheel, so Wolfe headed toward Liam.

Cereboo and Malviere fell in beside him again as he moved. Cereboo was torn up from the fighting, so Wolfe unsummoned and resummoned his pup.

As Wolfe reached his friend, he saw the damage wasn't too bad. Liam had rolled over, and Wolfe could see that the leg wound wasn't spurting. That meant no artery had been hit and Liam would live.

Which was how Wolfe defined "damage that wasn't too bad," after twenty years as a mob enforcer and slightly over two years as a vigilante.

As if on cue, Liam muttered, "I'm okay, and I'll be totally fine once Shel gets off work."

Wolfe chuckled and nodded. *Shel having cards that can heal people probably also has a lot to do with my cavalier attitude toward non-life-threatening wounds. She's brought me back from serious injury on quite a few occasions. And speaking of...*

Wolfe dialed Shel at her private number. She was at work as a new rookie in the Noimoire police department. Her phone rang three times, then went to answering machine.

Wolfe sighed. This didn't seem like the kinda thing you should leave on an answering machine, but... "Hey Shel, it's Wol—William. I just got attacked by three cars' worth of thugs. I'm alive, they're dead. But Liam was shot. It'll hold till you get back. Rhett is on his way, but I think things are about to get interesting again. Love you, see you tonight."

Even after two years, it felt weird to him to tell someone he loved them, but he liked it.

"Can you walk?" Wolfe asked Liam.

Liam held his hand up, and Wolfe pulled him to his feet. Liam took a halting step, grimacing as he did. "Hurts, but I can move."

"Cover me then. I'm almost positive whomever is in the van is not a threat, but just in case..."

Liam nodded, and touched one of the cards floating in front of him. A tier-one Angry Hellhound appeared next to him, and he limped into formation with everyone behind Wolfe.

I've got an entourage, Wolfe thought with a half laugh, glancing at everyone.

"A mighty pack indeed," Malviere said in her otherworldly voice, as if reading his mind.

Wolfe walked up to the van. He saw the woman inside was staring at him as he approached, meeting his eyes in the side mirror.

But her white-knuckled grip never left the steering wheel as Wolfe approached.

When he was nearly there, the lady whispered, "I'm not here to attack you. Please don't kill me, Wolfe."

Wolfe almost laughed at the most ridiculously obvious declaration before his brain ground to halt. *She knows who I really am.*

Ironically, her knowledge made him warier, and Wolfe regretted that he was out of magazines for his Edge. But with his mantle on and Malviere out, he was still ridiculously dangerous. Not that he wasn't always dangerous—but especially so now.

Wolfe reached the window and stared inside. The woman in the driver's seat appeared older at first glance, with dark rings around her eyes and the first sign of wrinkles around their edges. But a second look, at her vibrant brown hair, youthful skin, and lack of any hang in her flesh, placed her in her late twenties. Wolfe was almost positive his first impression was because she had suffered terribly, or been in fear a long time.

The way she gripped the wheel confirmed it, as did the thick black hoodie and sweatpants she wore, that concealed most of her from gazing eyes.

She was breathing oddly, long deep breaths, a slow hold, then letting it go.

On her opposite side, a brain in a glass case, carried by a small, white wheeled frame, was buckled into the passenger seat. A card appeared over it. *She's a deckbearer.*

"Um, hello?" Wolfe said.

"I need your help," the woman whispered after a moment, still only staring at the side mirror rather than directly at Wolfe. "I can make it worth your while."

"You're sounding crazier than a soup sandwich," Wolfe said. "Or at least way ahead of where this conversation ought to be. Start at the beginning. Who are you?"

"I'm Fern. Fern Wachowski. But that's not important.

What's important is that Adam is gone for"—she glanced at the dashboard—"six days, twenty-one hours, and thirty-two minutes more. That's how long before he comes back and kills us both."

Wolfe frowned. "Not helping the whole soup sandwich thing."

Fern took a deep breath, then whispered, "The seat beneath me, the wheel I'm gripping, the air conditioning."

Wolfe was getting impatient, but gave her a moment. While Fern breathed and talked to herself, he glanced back at the scene of carnage. *I hope no one had heard the commotion and called the Noimoire police. I think there's a decent chance, since the lot has a lot of distance from everyone else. But gunshots are loud, and we fired off a ton of bullets in that fight.*

Fern finished whatever breathing exercise she was doing and finally looked at Wolfe directly.

"I'm involuntarily working for Adam Delacruz," she said. "You don't know him, but he's Caine Delacruz's father."

Wolfe remembered Caine, the man that had worked for Worldwide Decurion—the organization that had been trafficking criminals for organs and other nefarious purposes. Caine had been killed by Damian, technically, but only because Wolfe had been trying to kill them regardless.

"I keep tabs on the remaining three crime families for him. Adam works with them. He plans to assassinate you a few weeks after he gets back because you killed his son, with the help of said families."

Fern slowly and deliberately released the wheel with one hand. She reached inside her hoodie pocket and pulled a USB drive out, handing it over to Wolfe. "Everything I know about all their operations, which is a lot, is on that drive. It's yours."

Wolfe fingered the drive. "Why?"

"You can't be working for Adam, since you killed his son. But I know you've been quietly looking into the crime families, who I want dead as well—because they support Adam, and for personal reasons as well."

That all sounds like personal reasons, but I don't need to know. "So... you want me to take this information and kill a ton of people?"

Fern returned her hand to the wheel and stared ahead again, then recited in a monotonous voice, "I investigated you after you killed Caine. I know you're keeping a growing list of everything you can about the crime families on your computer —including lists of who has certain cards. I know most of your information is through Rachel Lyons, your girlfriend, who's working for the Noimoire police department, since it matches the files in the police databases, mostly. I know about the Gate to the Underworld set. I think you aim to finish the other crime families off. I want that as well. This will help."

Wolfe raised his eyebrows at the recitation. *Alright, I guess I'm going back to storing information the old way—on paper. I had no idea someone was, or could, look at my personal computer. I wonder which idiot in my household downloaded what that let Fern look into things.*

"What do you want in return?" Wolfe asked.

She turned her head back again, staring at Wolfe with haunted eyes. "It's yours. But I would want you to protect me from Adam, if you will. He's coming for you, one way or another. But I'll still be safer with your protection than without, when he sends people after me in turn."

"He's going to send people after you?"

Fern nodded.

Wolfe motioned to the Hellmouth Institute. "And you want to live in a gigantic demonic building?"

"If I never see another symbol of Gabriel, I'll be happier."

Wolfe glanced at the symbol on the side of the van. He was almost positive it was a Divine symbol, but he didn't know which archangel it referenced. *Not Gabriel, I guess. Huh.*

Wolfe turned his attention back to Fern. "Alright, well, you can stay here for now. I don't know that's it's perfectly safe, but it's something."

Fern turned the van off, slowly removed her seat belt, and stepped from the van. Wolfe took a few steps back to give her room as she exited. Something told him she wouldn't appreciate large people near her.

Fern glanced up at him once she had exited. She took a deep breath and whispered, "You can do this, Fern. Anger is better than fear."

Wolfe raised an eyebrow, then glanced over at Liam, who rolled his eyes then shrugged. Wolfe silently chuckled to himself. *Yeah, that's how I feel about this chick as well.*

Fern took another deep breath and then looked up at Wolfe. "I can do something else for you, as well. I'm going to pull my deck, okay? I'm not attacking you."

"Sure," Wolfe responded.

Fern went through the motions of touching her chest over her heart and then pushing her hand out, fingers splayed.

Two cards with purple light, and another glimmering with gray light, appeared.

Golem and Psychic. That's an odd combination.

"Wrong cards," Fern said.

"You should see my alpha trying to pull his mantle," Malviere murmured.

Fern didn't respond or acknowledge Malviere at all, just staring at the cards in front of her for a full minute, the time before you could switch into a new hand. Then she swiped the cards sideways. The three cards seemed to move sideways into nothing, and three more came from nothing to rest floating in front of her. Two were gray, and one purple.

She reached out and touched the purple card, and light flashed around her.

Fern's appearance changed. She now had long red hair, a

freckled face, and green eyes, all on a roughly twenty-one-year-old body.

Wolfe blinked as he stared at a near-perfect copy of Shel, the love of his life.

"I can change your appearance with my cards. It only works on any given deckbearer once per day, like healing cards, and my length of play for my cards is only five minutes... but, for a tiny bit at least, we can disguise you."

Her appearance briefly shimmered, and Wolfe was looking at Fern again. Liam whistled. "That's useful. The gods put very few cards in that can affect the world outside the Great Game, you know."

"A lot more this season," Fern replied, her voice stronger than it had been. "But... when it's time to hunt, you can catch them unawares. For a bit, at least."

She reached back inside her hoodie pocket and glanced at her phone. "You've got six days, twenty-one hours, and twenty-seven minutes before Adam gets back. You have to clear the Noimoire underworld before then."

It was Wolfe's turn to whistle. "You don't think small, do you?"

"It has to be this way," Fern said.

Wolfe frowned. "I'm not sure I should launch a war of murder against the gangs... I've been giving thought to trying to get them all arrested, instead. Doing it the"—he held up air quotes—"right way."

Fern started to tremble. "You can't, Wolfe. Even if you had time, Adam's connections will keep them on the street. And you don't have time. You won't live if they all go on the offensive at once, and neither will Rachel. They're going to do it soon, right after Adam gets back, like I just said. You have to finish them, *now*."

"You're sure?" Wolfe asked. "I thought I covered my tracks fairly well..."

Fern's breathing and speech were both speeding up. "Look at the evidence I gave you! It's all there. If you wait for them to hit you, it'll be too late. Then, once they've killed you, Adam will have me back. I'll never escape again. My choices will be death or servitude forever, if he doesn't just torture me to death for my betrayal."

She paused her talk, almost choking as she hyperventilated. "You have to, hit them, first. Now. For, both our, sakes. *Please.*"

CHAPTER 4

THE DECISION TO GARDEN

The Joliet PD vehicle pulled to a stop in front of Wolfe, away from the huge mess. A huge mess that was starting to *really* smell in the unusually hot Joliet weather. The normal copper-and-shit smell of violent death was already being reinforced by the smell of rot and decay, and Wolfe's nose wrinkled.

"Hey Rhett," Wolfe muttered.

The door to the car opened and Rhett stepped out. "Holy crap, William. Even for you, this is… impressive."

"Just use my nickname Wolfe," Wolfe said.

Rhett grimaced. He appeared, as always, like the poster child for military recruitment. Rhett was of a height with Wolfe, six-foot-two, but even more muscular. He also had military cut hair, intense blue eyes, and chiseled features.

Even his police uniform looked ironed.

Rhett was probably one of Wolfe's closest friends, and his most reliable after Shel, but he was also a bit much sometimes. *Who irons their police uniform?*

Rhett glanced around, his head taking in the scene while

his body remained almost at attention. His nose also wrinkled at the smell.

"What happened here?"

"I was attacked by twelve guys in three cars," Wolfe responded. "They drove in, shooting wildly and inaccurately, and I used Cerberus's Home for Wayward Hellhounds to cause an accident. Then Liam and I killed them all—Liam had an assault rifle, and I have a very strong deck."

Rhett nodded. "That's it? Nothing else?"

Wolfe consciously didn't let his gaze head to the garage, where Fern and her van were currently hiding. "Nope. They just drove in and attacked me. I ended them. Play stupid games, win stupid prizes."

Rhett frowned at Wolfe's flippancy. "With anyone else I'd assume you were hiding something, but you do have a lot of people that would want to off you for one imagined slight or another."

"And a few real ones," Wolfe quipped again.

This time Rhett nodded as if that were sage commentary. "Yeah, I could see you actually slighting a few people enough for them to murder you. I damn near wanted to when we first met."

"Heh," Wolfe muttered. Rhett had a point. But suffering fools had never really been Wolfe's strong point...

Before they could say anything else, the sounds of sirens interrupted their conversation.

"Great, the fine boys in blue from the Noimoire PD are here," Wolfe muttered.

Rhett frowned again. Wolfe swore Rhett was gonna have wrinkles before he was forty, and he already had resting 'stern' face.

"C'mon, you can't blame me for being irritated with the Noimoire PD," Wolfe said. "We've got history, them and I."

"Most of the men that betrayed their oaths are dead or

appealing life sentences," Rhett said. "I think you should give the new ones a bit more credit—your own girlfriend among them, I might add."

Wolfe rolled his eyes but held his tongue. On the one hand, Rhett was probably right. On the other, Wolfe had a long and contentious relationship with the police, and not even close to all of it had been Wolfe's fault. Two of the biggest defining moments of his life had been thanks to utterly corrupt cops.

Wolfe and Rhett waited in companionable silence as the Noimoire police cars—*eight* of them—pulled into his large parking lot.

"Down, down, hands on your head!" one shouted as he came out with his gun pointed at Wolfe.

"I've got this, officer!" Rhett called out. "You're late. We're fine."

More and more police officers boiled out of the cars and headed for Wolfe. He sighed, and decided to comply with them, despite what Rhett had said. Wolfe went to his knees and lay on his stomach, hands behind his back, as the officers rushed him.

His mind was on Fern's words, however. Between this and what she had said, he already knew this was going to be a whole *thing*.

"Six days, fourteen hours, and nineteen minutes," Fern muttered where she sat at the center of the dining table, surrounded by Wolfe's allies, a newly purchased laptop in front of her.

"Would you stop doing that?" Wolfe muttered back.

Shel laughed. Wolfe paused for a moment and appreciated

his wonderful, beautiful girlfriend. She was gorgeous, with brilliant red hair, equally intense green eyes, and youthful, tanned skin. But Wolfe had been with beautiful women before.

What really made Shel special was that she was truly kind and supportive of Wolfe, a fundamentally good person. Raphael, a Divine Lord, known as the Archangel of Kindness, had picked her as a chosen deckbearer, and that choice made sense to anyone that spent time with Shel.

Liam and Malviere kept quiet.

Wolfe probably shouldn't be so irritated at Fern. She had obviously had some seriously bad things happen to her. But, it had been a long day, and Fern had brought that day to him.

Rather than going to serve papers, as he first planned, Wolfe had instead spent hours talking to police officers. With Rhett there, things had gone better than expected, but twelve bodies were still twelve bodies.

Wolfe hadn't told anyone about Fern the whole time. He'd just repeated his story that gangbangers ambushed him outside his residence, and that he, Liam, and their decks had fought them off. Since Fern had been hiding in her car past the fight the whole time, the crime scene bore out his story.

After being handcuffed, Wolfe had been arrested, over Rhett's objection. The Noimoire police officers had been relatively solicitous, but they'd still stuck him in the back of a car and interrogated him. The investigation had taken hours—coroners, detectives, blood-spatter guys.

Only when it was discovered that two of the men had been men arrested at the warehouse where Wolfe had put an end to the human trafficking operation had things gotten better. After that discovery, the police had pretty quickly convinced themselves everything had just been a retaliatory hit against Wolfe.

But finally, the scene had been cleaned—mostly, Wolfe was

gonna have to hire someone to power wash his parking lot—
and everyone had gone home. Including Wolfe.

"So, you've all heard it," Wolfe said. "The question is—do
I start murdering people?"

"Continue murdering people, my alpha," Malviere said in
her otherworldly voice.

From under the table, Cereboo whuffed a couple of times
from multiple heads. Wolfe swore his dog was laughing at him.
Wolfe was never sure how much Cereboo really understood,
and most of the time his pooch acted like a normal pooch. But
Cereboo could clearly follow complicated commands shouted
in English. So he probably understood a lot, actually.

He also gave Malviere the stink-eye. Ever since his card had
evolved, she—it?—had gained a sense of humor. A dark sense
of humor, and she occasionally poked Wolfe, as well. Not least
of which by calling him 'alpha,' which always sounded to
Wolfe like the title an edgy thirteen-year-old would revel in.

"I think you have to," Liam said. "The evidence that Fern
showed us was pretty convincing. They've already paid people
to be available to take you out. I mean... It's not really even
hitting them first at this point. They've literally paid multiple
assassins to take you out in a few weeks."

Shel, her eyes sad, nodded. "And, well, there's Cerberus's
message."

"Cerberus's message?" Malviere asked, intrigued. Liam
also perked up in interest.

Wolfe sighed. "I was told, when I received this deck, that if
I didn't get all six cards, whomever did would pretty much
destroy the city, or maybe just make it evil. It was a bit
cryptic."

"You talked to the gods?" Liam asked, wide-eyed.

"More like the gods talked at me," Wolfe replied.
"Although I was hardly handed a list of Cerberus's
commandments."

No one said anything.

"That's it, then?" Wolfe asked. "Shel, you don't have an opinion that we should do things Rhett's way?"

Shel shook her head, her face tragic. "No. I want to do it the right way. I really, really do. I desperately don't want to risk or lives, freedom, and careers again. But Adam is the third-most important politician in Illinois, a multiple-time war hero—"

"For the Confederacy, at least the first time," Liam muttered.

Shel nodded as she continued, "—and he's a billionaire. There's no way we're taking him down fully in a legal manner. And all the crime families have obviously, openly decided to kill you—as has Adam himself."

Wolfe was legitimately surprised at how easily Shel was going along with this. That had been his single biggest concern with going on the offensive—that Shel would be upset.

But with her on the side of murdering everyone... well, the card had been played.

"Alright, then, how do we do this?" Wolfe asked.

Fern turned the computer around. It had lists of the living locations of prominent members of all three gangs, places they conducted their illicit activities or kept the profits of same, and had vague schedules and protections for most of the prominent members.

The Singh and Renfeldt families, Wolfe could immediately see, were going to be problems.

But the Weeds, a loose collection of criminals much like the Cobras had been, were going to be less of a problem. It looked like their leader, the aging Chester Ambroise, travelled with few guards.

Wolfe knew the Weeds gang. "Looks like the petty thievery and fencing guys didn't feel like they would be attacked."

Fern nodded. "They've picked up a lot of the drug trade

that the Grimm family lost, and they have multiple deckbearers. I have learned that it's not Chester that has the card you're looking for, it's his younger brother, Pierre. Who specifically handles the drug transactions now."

"Is he a harder target than his older brother?" Wolfe asked.

Fern shook her head. "No. At least, not usually. Tonight, after midnight, they'll both be on the Noimoire docks, moving product."

"Tonight, you say?" Wolfe asked.

"Yes."

"Do they have the usual agreements to keep the police away in place?"

Fern nodded, and Wolfe stroked his chin before putting his hand down.

One last question. "Do you know how strong they are?"

Fern glanced down. "Only kinda. Chester's had his deck for almost forty years, like your boss once did. It's a Nature and Beast deck. His brother just got his Infernal deck in this last drop, gifted of Belphegor, Infernal Lord of Sloth."

"Are they good fighters?" Wolfe asked.

Fern waggled her hand back and forth with ambiguity, still not meeting Wolfe's eyes. "They're both older, so I doubt they're personally tough. I also don't know how many levels they've made. I would bet almost anything that Pierre is a lot lower than you. But Chester could be very high quite easily, higher than you certainly. He's had twenty times as long to level. Plus, they both made *a lot* of money over the last two years, both from picking up where the Grimm family failed and from working for Adam. They could have some very strong cards. They have a couple other deckbearers with them as well, although they don't just keep them around as guards."

Wolfe glanced at Shel, who shrugged. "I'm sure the three of us—you, me, and Liam—can handle them."

Wolfe shook his head. "I need to do this alone."

Shel frowned and started to open her mouth.

Wolfe cut her off. "You'll be nearby, with Fern, in case something goes wrong. But I need her illusions. This has to be an extremely fast hit, and it has to be unknown who did it."

"They might figure out I was behind it," Fern said. "I mean, they know I hacked them once."

Wolfe smiled a shark's smile. "That sounds like a story. But will Adam's people admit to the gangs and mob families that you're gone? Without some extra reason?"

Fern smiled, the first time Wolfe had seen her do so. "No. No they will most definitely not. Adam hates to admit weakness."

"So, we're in the clear," Wolfe said, still baring his teeth. "I mean, you keep saying I've got six days. So that's two days per family, with illusions and your pre-existing access to keep them confused, right?"

"The hunt will be good," Malviere said. "But what about your other packmates? Like Rhett?"

Wolfe's smile slipped. "Rhett will *absolutely* not be down with this, and we shouldn't let him know anything. Ever. Under any circumstances."

"What about the vampire?" Malviere asked.

It took Wolfe a moment to get what she was talking about. "Miriam?"

Malviere nodded, and Shel perked up as well.

"You know, she might be helpful somehow... I'll give her a call."

Wolfe glanced at everyone, his heart racing with excitement and fear both. "And then we hunt."

CHAPTER 5

HERE WE GO AGAIN

"Wolfy, is that you?" came the sultry voice from the other end of the phone, although Wolfe could hear the semi-hidden sardonic edge to her voice. Miriam always sounded like she was having a subtle laugh at the world.

Wolfe rolled his eyes. "Yeah, it's me. I want to meet to talk, and I'm on extremely tight timeline. It's important."

"Well, since it's *important,* I'll have one of my boys drive me over in the limo with the tinted windows," Miriam said. "You know how much I hate to have the sun touch my fair skin."

"Let's meet somewhere else. It might not be the best for your health if we're seen together, before... things."

"Ooh, you know how to excite a girl," Miriam said, her voice faux breathy. "Perhaps we can meet at the local Deckburger?"

Wolfe ground his teeth. Recently, Miriam had learned the story of Wolfe and Shel's early stops at a Deckburger, and had been bringing it up constantly.

"How about we just meet in front of my old house?" Wolfe responded. "We both know where that is."

"Oh, Wolfe, you tease," Miriam said and laughed. "Gonna make me eggs for breakfast again?"

"Hanging up now," Wolfe replied, and did.

Shel smiled. "Always a character, huh?"

Wolfe nodded. "Alright, let's go let her know what's happening. Fern, you should come with us."

Fern started. "Are you sure?"

Wolfe nodded. "Miriam is an ally. You'll be safe. You told me you had access to the business dealings of the gangs through Adam, I know—but Miriam launders all their money and might know more, or have access you don't."

Fern nodded, clutching her laptop to her chest.

"Six days, seven hours, and fourteen minutes," Fern muttered quietly as she stared out the window of the van they were all in.

It was nearly midnight, and the city streets outside the van were dark, both from the fog rolling in off the lake and from the lack of streetlights. All of Noimoire was dangerous, but some parts hid it beneath glitz and glamour. The part they were in now, the poorest parts near the old docks, didn't have the energy left to hide what it was.

Most of the lights weren't functioning, most likely because they'd been looted for their copper by the local meth heads. Despite that and the fog, Wolfe could make out a few people on the streets outside. The first were a pair of men sitting fairly far apart that were almost certainly drug dealers. Down the street from them was a woman with a young body that Wolfe would bet had an old face, dressed in a miniskirt that would have left only a tiny bit to the imagination in the daylight. Last, but not least, a thin, nerdy guy in a damned white polo was walking the street, probably looking for drugs for some party.

But no police. Miriam was arranging a few 'incidents' near them, but away from the docks, to distract the police even further away.

"Wish that idiot with the polo would leave," Wolfe muttered.

No one responded to that any more than they had responded to Fern muttering how much time they had before Adam got back. The tension in the van was palpable. They were all staring at the small collection of cars at the far end of the dock, and the boat in the water just past the end of the dock. Multiple people were loading and unloading stuff from the ship.

Wolfe's phone buzzed, and he picked it up.

"It's as go as I can make it," Miriam said without her usual flirty banter, the tension in her voice notable as well.

Wolfe hung up.

"Malviere and..." Wolfe paused, "creepy Obsessive Cultist, with me. Cereboo, stay back a bit—I'll call you if needed, but you're more recognizable."

Wolfe opened the door to the van and stepped out, and Shel slid into the driver's seat. "Good luck, my love," Shel said, her voice faux casual.

Wolfe patted the new knife at his belt. "I'll make my own luck."

Malviere opened the back door and the Obsessive Cultist and Cereboo both slipped out. The Obsessive Cultist walked close to Wolfe. He frowned as he glanced at her. She appeared to be an eighteen-year-old woman with black hair and pale skin carrying an eldritch tome. But she was creepy in the extreme—her eyes never flickered around, she never said anything, and her face rested placidly.

Malviere, in contrast, looked excited.

"My first true hunt since I became the real me," she said, her voice reverberating with a darkness, the hint of the howls of damned souls in it.

"Yes. But be quiet," Wolfe said. *She's almost as creepy as the dead-eyed cultist, in her own way. Scarier, really.*

Fern leaned out the window and touched her hand to her chest, pulling her deck. Wolfe dismissed the notification, hoping no one was close enough to see it. It wouldn't be a problem for him—his deck contained an evolved Bulgae Moon Chaser, which hid his deck pull from notifying anyone.

Fern must have gotten her card in the first pull, because she touched a purple card in front of her, and magic settled around Wolfe. He watched as his hair lengthened, became blond, and his skin shifted to a pasty white. His nails lengthened, one cracked, and it appeared as if dirt appeared under them. His clothing appeared older and baggier, dark gray with wine stains on them.

"You made me into a hobo."

"It'll be good, trust me. The gray will be harder to spot, and maybe people will think this was a drug hit by a crazy person," Fern responded. "Now go, please. The five minutes are counting down."

No one is going to think I'm a hobo when I'm using cards, Wolfe thought. But it didn't matter—all that mattered was they wouldn't recognize him. So he just nodded to Fern and took off into a jog, Malviere and the Obsessive Cultist running behind him.

He crossed the street and headed toward the huge parking lot surrounding the docks, shaking his head as he went. *I remember being ambushed at this dock by the Cobras—and guarding product shipments on multiple other occasions.*

But now it was his turn to ambush people at the dock. *Turnabout's fair play.*

Wolfe kept low, hoping the night fog would hide him. He made it to the edge of the parking lot, half-hiding behind one of the defunct streetlights. A quick look revealed little—just vague shapes loading and unloading on the ship.

Wolfe was tempted to sneak up slowly, but he knew his illusion had a time limit. He pulled his deck, reveling in the fact he wouldn't inform anyone. He immediately summoned his second Obsessive Cultist—the one guaranteed to be in his first hand because of his new building card, the Infernal Library Wing of the Hellmouth Institute.

Obsessive Infernal Cultist

Rare, tier-8 Mortal/Infernal Creature [evolved orphan, priest]
1 Infernal Power
Health: 9
Attack: 1
Defense: 5
Magical Attack: 4*[**Infernal**]
Magical Defense: 5

Special: **Infernal Portal Summoner [2]**: Any Infernal card with the word 'Portal,' 'Gate,' or 'Summon' costs 2 less power of any type to play
Special: **Sacrificial [3]:** This card may be sacrificed for three power of any type to be used for one summoning.

"This cultist has grown up in an Infernal church, and its every commandment and mystery is dear to her heart."

With two of the Obsessive Infernal Cultists out, Wolfe could now use his Demonic Portal card for two power—and that card summoned five power of Infernal Creatures from a side deck he had established.

Wolfe took a chance, waiting the thirty seconds to get the next summon. Each Demonic Portal card allowed Wolfe to create a side deck of five creature cards, and they all stacked together. Even though Wolfe had only a fifteen-card deck, two of them were Demonic Portal cards now, which let him maintain a ten-creature-card side deck. Wolfe had a lot of interesting options, now, in the creature department.

He had a few extra Demonic Portal cards at home, and when he had five really good cards, and enough leveling pips to up his hand size and deck size at the same time, he was going to expand the deck again.

Wolfe used the Demonic Portal card, and brought forth two creatures from the side deck that having demonic portals allowed him to create.

The first was a Hellhound Puppy, which he left in the greater pack to guard the Obsessive Cultists. Then he summoned a new creature from his side deck, one he was almost positive no one had seen before—and the costliest card he had in his deck.

Black smoke boiled from the point he had summoned it, spreading over fifty feet in every direction—the insubstantial body of the demon, which quickly engulfed Wolfe and his team of cards, the smoke not quite touching them at any point. Wolfe glanced at the card.

Smoke Demon
Rare Tier-1 Infernal Creature
2 Infernal, 2 Any power
Health: 13
Attack: N/A
Defense: N/A
Magical Attack: N/A

Magical Defense: 11

Special: **Incorporeal**: Physical attacks cannot hit
Special: **Choking 50':** All enemies that need to breathe suffer
-2 to all stats within 50' of the Smoke Demon, and take 1 true
damage every 30 seconds.
Special: **Sacrifice Obscured [3]**: This creature may be
sacrificed at any time. If it is, for the minute and a half after,
no creature may attack any deckbearer or creature if within
250' of the spot of death, and vision is reduced to 5'.

"I suppose, where there's smoke, there's fire. Or in these
bugger's case, where there's hellfire, there's smoke."

Wolfe had added quite a few cards to his side deck,
including ones he'd gained from Damian, or had bought with
all the things he had sold from Damian's deck. The Smoke
Demon was just one of them, but it had been quite expensive.
It had a few situations where it would be extremely useful.

Wolfe ran, inside his own Smoke Demon, as it rolled
forward. He hoped that in the dark it would seem only a
darker patch of fog. His entire group followed, obscured,
Cereboo at the very back of the Smoke Demon.

Wolfe saw the first member of the Weeds gang ahead, a
lookout leaning against a car, staring bored out into the
darkness. As the smoke roiled forward, the thug straightened a
little, fingering his gun.

But he was slow to realize the threat and the smoke rolled
across him. Immediately, the thug began to choke and cough,
briefly trying to cover his face with his hand.

Wolfe eschewed his usual STI Edge in favor of grabbing his
new knife—a huge hunting blade. He rushed from the smoke,
and the thug opened his mouth to cry out.

Too slow. Wolfe slammed his knife up under the chin of

the thug, not quite killing him in a single hit, but utterly incapacitating him. The thug fell down, choking on magical smoke and his own blood both.

Malviere ran up, and grabbed the darkness that swirled around her. She moved her hand toward the thug violently, and the darkness parted. A spectral dog lunged out and bit the thug where he lay, near dead, on the ground.

The spectral dog didn't inflict a physical wound, but the man stilled, his flesh graying, and rot wafted from him.

Wolfe got a no-experience kill notification for the thug.

"My first personal kill during a hunt," Malviere said.

Wolfe glanced at the quickly rotting body. "Congrats. Do you eat what you kill?"

"Gross," Malviere said, half-gagging. The most human reaction Wolfe had nearly ever seen from her, outside of her appreciation of rare steak.

"Julio?" came a call from outside the smoke, deeper into the fog, toward the ramp onto the boat.

"Ah, shit," Wolfe said. He hated it when the low-level thugs were smart about stuff. "Let's go!"

Wolfe rushed across the parking lot toward the man that had called out.

The man yelled again, louder. "Julio? Answer me, man!"

Wolfe briefly saw the man at the bottom of the ramp, gun out, staring in confusion and growing horror as the smoke rushed him. Just before it hit, the man raised his gun and fired rapidly and blindly into the smoke.

He missed Wolfe, but a yip and notification of death told him that at least one bullet had found his Lost Hellhound Puppy.

The yells around the boat told him that his surprise had been lost.

CHAPTER 6

PULLING WEEDS

Wolfe pulled his Edge. The thug that had shot the pup barely had time to widen his eyes as Wolfe stepped forward out of the smoke and blasted the thug in the chest with three clustered shots.

The thug somehow managed to stay upright long enough to take two steps backward. That despite massive blood pouring from the holes in his chest and what had to have been outrageous static shock. He collapsed off the end of the pier in the tiny space between the boat and the docks with a splash.

Furious hacking and coughing came from the edge of the boat as multiple thugs lined up and shot into the semi-darkness around Wolfe. One grazed his arm, doing two damage, and he cussed, firing wildly at his assailants to keep their heads down as he ran up the ramp.

One thug died as a spectral mastiff flew up from the pier and bit the thug, and he got a notification that Malviere had killed him. Wolfe kept shooting as he ran full tilt up the boat and managed to catch one thug in the face, blowing his head off.

However, Wolfe's lunatic charge, despite the fog and the

Smoke Demon, put him in the open for crucial seconds. A red-hot pain ripped through him as a bullet tore through the flesh of his side, and Wolfe nearly fell off the ramp, slamming into the railing at the side of boat entrance and falling back down the ramp.

Wolfe let go of his gun and grabbed the ramp to keep from going into the lake, which would have brought his rampage to an end—and probably ended him as well. He managed to stabilize and not get shot again long enough to flip his deck and touch a second Demon Portal card. He almost summoned his 'usual' but went for two more of his odd cards again, still hoping to get through this without any stragglers reporting who had really attacked the Weeds.

He summoned a Chain Demon and an Annoying Imp, each of which was in the deck because of an unusual feature it provided.

Chain Demon
Uncommon Tier-1 Infernal Creature
3 Infernal Power
Health: 25
Attack: 6 x3
Magical Attack: 0
Defense: 8
Magical Defense: 5

Special: **Forced Confession:** If total damage dealt to any target exceeds half that target's Health, the target is rendered immobile. If held immobile, the target must truthfully answer all questions put to him.

"The inquisitors of the Infernal Realms have far more tools at their disposal than their mortal counterparts."

The brief puff of red energy that heralded the Chain Demon cleared to reveal a creature that was nearly ten feet tall, wreathed in chains, with a few moving away from the mass of the body like tentacles. It stood over Wolfe protectively as Wolfe clutched the damp and dirty ramp up into the boat while his side bled.

The Annoying Imp was a mere two feet tall, red with slight horns and wings that appeared too small to support its weight in the air. It appeared at the top of the ramp, and its card revealed its two tricks, tricks that Wolfe hoped would save him—Taunting and Dodge [3]. The creature forced every other creature to attack it, and it had a seventy-five percent chance to avoid any physical attack.

But instead of a creature appearing, the air around Wolfe grew cold. A snowflake fell onto his arm, and as he stared at the field around him more fell, obscuring things even further.

Wolfe's opponent, who he hadn't even seen yet, had played an unexpected card—Demeter's Finale.

Demeter's Finale
Legendary Tier-3 Nature Persistent
2 Nature Power

This card gives advantage to all cards with the words 'Unseelie,' 'Winter,' 'Ice,' 'Snow,' 'Blizzard,' or 'Cold' in its title or keywords, and everything else is treated as if it had disadvantage against all targets. All other advantages, disadvantages, and resistances are ignored by all cards. (Immunity is unaffected.)

Any card that inflicts damage with the Cold type gains 3 Magical Attack.

The creatures are almost certainly going to be coming, Wolfe thought. But the real problem was that with type disadvantage, every one of Wolfe's creatures would inflict half damage against everything they attacked, making it harder to clear the thugs and get to his real targets—Chester and Pierre Ambroise.

The dulling but still agonizing pain in his side reminded Wolfe that he was already down to eleven of his thirty-two health—a normal mortal would have died already from the damage sustained.

He hit a second card in his deck, pulling Brimstone, one of his paired set of magical guns, and fired along the boat, keeping the thugs' heads down as he lurched back to his feet and onto the ship deck proper, off the ramp.

The Annoying Imp was shot in the first couple seconds as Wolfe made it to the top, but the Chain Demon followed him, and most of the thugs foolishly fired at the Chain Demon.

But two shot at him, and he hit the deck and rolled around the edge of a metal shipping crate to avoid being hit.

On the deck, at the edge of the swirling fog near the front of the boat, two creatures appeared. One was titled Winter Witch and the other was titled Carnage Demon—and its card showed a four-power cost.

I need to change this dynamic fast, I'm already losing.

Mentally, Wolfe summoned Cereboo and Malviere both—his plays weren't working well enough.

Then he 'detonated' his Smoke Demon, triggering the 'five-foot visibility' and 'creatures can't attack' functions.

Immediately, the smoke everywhere thickened. Wolfe managed to stop from coughing. *This smoke may not be damaging, per se, but it can't be good for me. Ninety seconds to change things up.*

He dismissed the remaining creature card—the Chain Demon—to recover the mana as he kept behind the crate. The rate of fire dropped off, and people calling names, like this was a demented game of Marco Polo, started.

I guess it's almost a game of Marco, Polo. Where the losers die.

Wolfe swiped his deck, almost cheering when he saw the card he wanted—his Mantle. *If anyone sees this they'll likely put one and two together. I need to end this fast.*

Wolfe touched his Master of the Hunt mantle card, which settled over him, giving him renewed vitality and increased ability both. As well as speed from Malviere, if her ability would work without line of sight.

Wolfe, energized, ran around the opposite side of the crate. *Twenty-one health again—less than my starting amount, but more than a normal chump, anyway. And my stats are far higher.*

He almost immediately ran into a thug who stared at him wide-eyed. The thug had long, dirty-blonde hair and a pock-marked face. Wolfe punched the druggie-looking obstacle in the sternum before the thug could pull bring his gun up. Wolfe felt bones snap beneath his empowered strike, and the man collapsed, eyes bugging, to briefly claw at his chest, mouth open, before dying.

Wolfe ignored the corpse and kept going. He knew the thug hadn't signed off on killing him, but he worked for the Weeds—a criminal organization that had signed off on killing him. The thug had voluntarily joined this life, and had reaped what he'd sown.

Fuck around and find out.

He did hit his next card—Hellfire. A second infernal gun appeared in his other hand, and his attack went to eighteen, which was an absurd level, doing something like five times the damage a normal chump with a gun would do.

Wolfe rounded the corner of the crate. He couldn't see anything, being effectively blinded from the thick smoke, fog, and snowflakes. He raised Brimstone and Hellfire and dual-fired off a couple rounds into the smoke back in the direction of the docks. He didn't wait, running past and behind the next crate in the line. Wolfe's random aggression was rewarded with both a yell and a death notification.

Wolfe continued to run past, headed for the end of the ship. Since he hadn't seen either Chester or Pierre at the loading area, his next best guess was that they were near where the creatures had appeared—the front of the boat.

He dashed through the thick smoke, heading past all the crates and along the side as the boat narrowed.

Wolfe slammed into someone running the other way, no time to slow or change direction as his enemy appeared. The middle-aged man with a salt-and-pepper rock star hairstyle was bowled to the ground as Wolfe hit him, slamming backward hard into the deck on his back, gun out.

Wolfe only needed a third of a second to assess the situation—just a fraction less than the man he hit, who was obviously Pierre Ambroise.

He fired downward with both his Infernal pistols before Pierre managed to fire upward, and blew his target's chest open in a massive splash of blood and bone.

A deck of cards appeared in the cavity of his opponent's torso, but before Wolfe could react at all, another man came lunging from the smoke, shirt pulled up across his mouth.

The older man with the gray ponytail reached out and touched Wolfe with one hand while another touched a card.

A blast of ice exploded across Wolfe from the point that Chester Ambroise's hand lay on his arm.

CHAPTER 7

FOUR OF DEMONS

Wolfe grit his teeth, nearly screaming as cold so intense it burned ripped through him. His magical defense was a nine, currently, and the attack did eleven actual damage, dropping him to fourteen health.

He also dropped Brimstone and stumbled two steps back, and he gained penalties to his stats.

But he didn't drop Hellfire.

As Chester walked forward, a smug smile on his face, pulling his own gun up. Wolfe didn't give him the chance. He swung the butt of his Infernal pistol at his opponent and connected just as Chester's eyes were widening in surprise.

Wolfe had expected it to kill him in a hit with his increased stats, but he forgot about the disadvantage that he carried from Demeter's Finale. Rather than doing fifty percent more damage against mortals, he did half damage.

Ice shattered around Chester Ambroise's face and the hit sent Chester sprawling sideways into the boat railing to collapse on his side.

Apparently, he also has a mantle.

Neither Wolfe nor Chester hesitated. Chester ignored his gun in favor of touching a card and reaching for Wolfe's ankle, scrambling on all fours to reach Wolfe. Wolfe was faster. Propelled by the supernatural speed that Malviere provided, he leapt back and rapid fired into Chester's head, shoulders, and back.

Chester grunted at the first two and then screamed out, "Let me live, I'll—" before the third shot sent him to the ground, whimpering. Wolfe's fourth shot stilled him, and Wolfe made nearly a level-and-a-half.

Wow... he was higher level than I thought. Shame he didn't die better. That felt slimy.

Wolfe knew damn well Chester was a horrible human being whose legacy was hundreds if not thousands of shattered lives, but shooting a man to death over a long enough period to let him start begging felt ugly.

Wolfe shook it off. He'd seen people suffer far more for far longer. And the sporadic gunfire around the smoke and fog-filled night told him the thugs were still hunting him, or perhaps trying to fight Malviere. Either way, he needed to move.

He reached down and grabbed the pile of cards from Chester—it was larger than any pile he'd grabbed before. Then he took the pile from the chest cavity of Pierre's corpse.

Forty cards stared at Wolfe, a mix of Infernal red, Beast brown, and aquamarine Nature cards.

Wolfe wasn't sure if the two decks together were a better haul than the one he'd gotten from Damian, but he bet it'd be close either way—and he already had a fourth card from the 'Gates to the Underworld' set.

At least he assumed he did.

Before Wolfe could check to be sure, a notification popped up, telling him that the obscuring effect from the smoke was gone. The fog would limit visibility, but once the physical smoke cleared, it wouldn't limit it enough to stop the thugs from emptying their magazines in Wolfe's direction.

And he had seconds left on the disguise as well.

Wolfe carefully tucked every card into his jacket and zipped the interior pocket, took a deep breath, and ran at the front of the boat. He leapt up onto the railing and then hurled himself of the end of the boat, counting on his massively increased stats and Malviere's boost to carry him through.

He hit the water like a missile, diving deep, and then swam as hard as he could, powered by his magics, toward the next pier over.

Wolfe, soaking and freezing, followed by a newly resummoned Malviere and an unharmed Cereboo, tapped on the back window of the van.

Fern nearly shrieked and started hyperventilating. Shel leaned way over from the driver's seat and opened the back door. She gave Wolfe a fearful-eyed once over before seeing that he was, if not unharmed, at least going to live. She touched her own chest and willed her deck into existence even as she straightened up and then patted Fern on her shoulder. "It's alright, it's just Wolfe. You're fine. You're fine."

Fern's breathing slowed, and she started her routine of naming things.

Wolfe ignored that and stepped into the van leaving wet footprints in the carpet and then sat in the driver's seat.

"How'd it go? Are you okay?" Shel asked, giving Wolfe a glance in the rearview mirror as he transferred what was practically half of Lake Wisconsin from his clothing to the back seat of the van.

"I'm alive, they're dead, and I've got their cards," Wolfe

said, patting his jacket with a squelching sound. "Plus, I'd bet no one identified me. So, wounds aside, I'd say it was a damned successful run."

Cereboo leapt into the van and immediately headed to the far back, and Malviere took a seat in the row behind Wolfe.

He had unsummoned the Obsessive Cultist a while ago.

Shel touched a card, and a Veteran EMT card appeared next to Wolfe on the seat. The veteran healed him for eight health. Then two rookie EMTs, both tier-two now, appeared and healed Wolfe for eight each as well—doubling the four a tier-two could heal because a Veteran was on the field.

The twenty-four health was enough to heal every wound Wolfe had, and he sighed in pleasure despite still being half-frozen from the lake. His arm healed, his side healed; even the graze to his shoulder and various bruises disappeared.

"Better than sex," Wolfe muttered.

Shel laughed and arched an eyebrow at him in the mirror. "It's not an exclusive service, you know. You can have both."

Wolfe laughed throatily. He admitted to himself that he felt a desperate need for Shel after surviving his fight and having his wounds removed.

He glanced at Fern, who was huddled on the front passenger seat, arms around her legs, muttering to herself. *Although that's a bit awkward to talk about at this exact moment.*

But it was moot, as Wolfe felt another need more pressingly than any mere carnal desire.

He unzipped the inside of his jacket and pulled out the decks he had taken.

Shel turned to stare at them excitedly, and even Fern was pulled from her anxiety enough to turn and stare. Malviere moved to hover over Wolfe's shoulder, staring.

He quickly cycled through them, seeing multiple cards

that would be fascinating to deal with, both Beast and Infernal.

But finally, he came to the card he wanted.

Conduit of the Infernal Six
Unique Legendary-equivalent, Tier-three equivalent Infernal Enhancer
0 Power

This card will alter its stats to fit the most prevalently mentioned lord of the six that sent these cards to whichever lord is mentioned most by other cards in the deck. If none are present, this card gives +5 Health.

Special: **Gate to the Infernal:** If all 6 are possessed in the same deck, the bearer will gain 7 Legendary Infernal or Beast card pulls. Additionally, the deckbearer may either gain the Mythic 'Gate to the Infernal' Building Card or evolve Cereboo. Each card was given to a member of the Noimoire underworld.

Wolfe brought his deck out, looking for which card to replace. He was cognizant that he would almost certainly need to increase his deck size soon—too many of his cards were becoming null cards or were in for very specific things they did to the deck rather than putting a creature on the field.

There simply wasn't room to add anything to his deck.

He had his two companions and his three set cards, which by themselves occupied five of his fifteen card slots. He had the second Obsessive Cultist which was always picked first to drive the cost of his Demonic Portal cards down, of which he had two—his only way to put non-orphan creature cards on the field. He had his Bulgae Moon Chaser evolved orphan which prevented his deck from being detected when he pulled it and was a strong card on its own.

Of the remaining six, three were his mantle and the paired Infernal Guns cards. Then he had the Infernal Library card, which was the other half of his Obsessive Cultist trick, his enhancer card, Caretaker of the Lost, and Cerberus' Home for Wayward Hellhounds, his Infernal-Rift-enhanced No Kill Pound, which, in addition to summoning lots of Canine cards gave him some ability to shape the battlefield.

Wolfe had three leveling pips, and was damn close to a fourth. But just to up his deck size, hand size, and add a single enhancer slot he would need six leveling pips.

Wolfe sighed and spent two of his pips to add an enhancer slot, and then, temporarily, removed the second Obsessive Infernal Cultist by switching it for the new set card.

Then he swiped cards till it came back up.

Conduit of the Infernal Six
Unique Legendary-equivalent, Tier-three equivalent Infernal
Enhancer
0 Power

This card grants advantage against Infernal to the deckbearer and all creature and companion cards in the deckbearer's deck. Additionally, any cards in the deck with the word 'Hellhound' in their title gain +1 to all stats. Any one card the deckbearer possesses may be treated as if it were Infernal as well.

Special: **Gate to the Infernal:** If all 6 are possessed in the same deck, the bearer will gain 7 Legendary Infernal or Beast card pulls. Additionally, the deckbearer may either gain the Mythic 'Gate to the Infernal' Building Card or evolve Cereboo. Each card was given to a member of the Noimoire underworld.

Wolfe quickly described it for Shel, and she started the van up.

As they drove, she briefly glanced back in the mirror. "Are you going to add it to your deck?"

Wolfe nodded. "I mean, yeah, I'd be a fool not to. But I need to get more cards in the deck soon—every card I have is critical to my build, and at a minimum I'm going to want three more spots for the set cards and two more Demonic Portals. I need more levels."

Shel nodded. "Well, we can always go to that dungeon we learned about when Malviere became an evolved orphan at Tier-ten."

"I thought we still hadn't found the actual entrance," Wolfe replied.

Shel shook her head and passed her phone back. "Miriam's team finally found it, sorry. She called this morning. It's a Volcano Dungeon she said, so I assume elemental. Hopefully a team of us could handle it."

"You have to kill the others before Adam returns," Fern said quietly.

Wolfe stared at the phone, then looked at Fern. "One is down. We still have six days—making three levels so I can up my deck will be fine."

He passed the phone back. "Let Miriam know we'll meet her at the dungeon. But tomorrow. Tonight we need to rest and recuperate."

"Well, you do," Shel said, smiling. "The rest of us are fine."

CHAPTER 8

"VOLCANO" DUNGEON PREP

Everyone watched as Wolfe spread the rest of the cards out on the table. He'd gotten a ton of both Infernal and Beast cards from the Ambroise brothers.

The light from the ceiling chandelier was low and slightly reddish tinged, and the table had a complicated etching of a decorated pentagram across it. Wolfe and team had gotten pretty used to the décor. Liam, Shel, and Malviere simply watched as Wolfe spread the forty cards he'd gotten across the table, no one really commenting. Cereboo lay down, one head against Shel's leg, the other against Wolfe's.

"Alright, I'm going to put everything that's not great into a sell pile. While we're figuring out the good stuff, can you check out the prices on everything else online, Liam?"

Liam nodded, his red beard so long it vaguely swayed as he did.

After a few minutes of sorting, Wolfe had made two piles. In one pile was the stuff on one on the team could use—whether it was because it was Nature, or because it wouldn't fit in Wolfe's deck well.

Liam was already moving cards from that large pile to a

third pile, and making notes on a piece of paper, keeping track of prices.

The second pile had the 'maybe' cards.

Most of the stuff in Chester's deck hadn't fit well, as he had been running a clear 'Winter' theme. But five cards stood out as potentially useful—a Tier-3 Sheltered Den and four Tier-2 Dire Wolves.

Sheltered Den

Uncommon Tier-3 Beast Persistent
1 Beast Power Persistent

Any controlled Beast creature that doesn't attack for 30 seconds gains twice the Defense and Magical Defense until it does attack, and may not be the target of area of effect or environmental effects. Any Beast creature with the Leader, Pack, or Tribal keywords gains +2 defense.

"Cover from the elements is the basis of any real good beast den."

Dire Wolf

Uncommon Tier-2 Beast Creature [Ice-Age, Extinct, Canine]
2 Beast Power
Health: 12
Attack: 7
Defense: 5
Magical Attack: 0
Magical Defense: 5

Special: **Canine Tribal [1]**: +1 to all attacks for every other canine on the field.

Special: **Ice Age**: This creature gains resistance to Ice energy attacks and Immunity to Ice energy environmental effects

"The famed Dire Wolf of the Ice Age, a pack predator to be feared, back at the will of the gods for your entertainment."

"Those two are interesting," Shel said, glancing at them. "More of a true side-deck situation, but in certain situations, that Sheltered Den, especially, could be interesting."

Wolfe nodded, but his gaze was already going to the other cards.

Pierre's deck, in addition to the conduit card, had contained multiple other cards that were interesting. Wolfe was pretty sure he wouldn't want to use a few, but he had the strong and interesting ones out anyway.

First were two cards that named Belphegor, the Infernal Lord of Sloth, a companion and a persistent.

Malviere *growled* as she stared at the cards. Her voice was a mix of girl and beast, with an otherworldly reverberation behind it.

"Not a fan?" Wolfe asked.

Shel laughed.

Malviere bared her teeth before speaking. "The cards of the other Infernal Lords should be destroyed. They represent everything wrong with this world."

"Calm down, Cutenstein. I'm just looking," Wolfe said. *For now.*

The first card, the companion, showed a fat child sitting inside an opulent hotel.

Tuvagi
Unique Rare-equivalent, Tier-6 equivalent Mortal/Infernal [Demigod] Companion
0 Power

Health: 22
Attack: 10
Defense: 4
Magical Attack: 0
Magical Defense: 4

Special: **Apathetic:** This card may only take an action every other 30-second period.
Special: **Aura of Apathy:** -2 to all non-health stats of all cards on the field opposed to Tuvagi
Special: **Pain of Effort:** Any card that that takes an action, and any non-allied deckbearer that uses a card, take one true damage.

"This child of Belphegor by a mortal priestess embodies the Sloth he represents. His true strength is its appeal to others."

Belphegor's Rest
Rare Tier-1 Immediate
3 Infernal Power (available)

All creature cards, minions, and companions on the field are returned to the deck of their deckbearer, and may not be brought forth again for 5 minutes. This does not work on any card with 'Loyal,' 'Determined,' 'Passionate,' or 'Obsessive' in the title or keywords.

Against Monsters, this causes them to be unable to take actions for 90 seconds.

"Whatever the reason, whatever the name, whatever the excuse... 'giving up' is the greatest failing of every species on Earth, and only a tiny few escape it."—Kelricktra, Baron of the Wasting Wastes.

In addition to those cards, Wolfe found two more Infernal cards that were decently interesting.

Both were persistent cards, and seemed to feed into the deck that won while doing nothing that the Belphegor cards Pierre possessed had apparently represented.

Good Intentions
Rare Tier-1 Infernal Persistent
3 Infernal Power

Every non-infernal card used by any non-allied deckbearer on the field costs one extra 'Any' power, and inflicts one damage to the deckbearer using it. The Deckbearer that used Good Intentions gains 1 Infernal power for each card so used.

"Sometimes, the Road to Hell is paved with good intentions"
—too many demons to count

Unending Decadence
Uncommon Tier-1 Infernal Persistent
1 Infernal, 1 Any Power

Every creature card used by any deckbearer on the field gains a 1 any power (available) upkeep. Failure to pay causes the card to be sacrificed and does 1 true damage to the card's controller.

"It is almost impossible to come back from the descent of a civilization into decadence, without a cleansing that is extraordinarily painful."

"I kinda wish we could have seen the Conduit of the Six card before it switched over," Wolfe said. "This deck is borderline hilarious in its methodology. I definitely won't use them, so they're not out, but even the creature cards were basically fat sacks of defense that did light chip damage constantly or punished people for using cards. This whole thing is a troll deck."

Shel and Liam both chuckled perfunctorily.

Shel twisted her finger in her hair. "The question is, can you use it?"

Wolfe reached out and touched the Sheltered Den card. "Maybe. I think that this one will be useful when we go into the volcano dungeon. My gut tells me that'll have a lot of environmental damage."

Shel nodded to his words and continued with her thoughts. "What about the Unending Decadence card? Synergized with Cerberus' Home for Wayward Hellhounds, you could screw with everyone at no additional cost to yourself. Combined with Good Intentions, you'd mess with everyone."

Wolfe frowned and pursed his lip to the side. "The question is—would it be worth losing *five* power to do so? *Eight* with Cerberus' home? I mean, that's considerably more than half my deck. And anything I remove will hurt my current strategy considerably."

There was another pause.

"Well, perhaps you could switch something in for just the Sheltered Den, and we can go make levels in the dungeon?" Shel said.

Wolfe pulled his deck out again.

It was insanely tight already, but his gut was telling him he'd benefit from having the card.

But only if he had enough creatures on the field.

"I'm gonna try something a bit different on this one," Wolfe said. "I'm skeptical at how effective shooting things in a Volcano Dungeon will be. But since I have an immense increase to my creatures at the moment with the new Conduit card, I'm going to remove Hellfire and Brimstone and just carry my trusty Edge. The difference in attack is limited for the power cost."

"But they give you a power being in the deck, almost like enhancers," Shel responded, her brow furrowed.

"I know," Wolfe replied. "But the Obsessive Cultist removes two from the Portal Card, or can be sacrificed. It's the better play for the moment."

"You just removed that."

Wolfe scratched the back of his head. "I know. But given this and the dungeon, I'm thinking I need to go a different route."

Shel nodded to his words. "That's it then? None of the other amazing cards?"

Wolfe shook his head. "Without a serious deck makeover, or just more cards in deck, I can't really benefit. Although that means we have a decently solid deck I haven't removed anything from at all, except the set card. We could put some of the weaker creatures back in and give it to someone to use."

Shel laughed. "You sure? It seems like this deck would screw you over."

Wolfe glanced back at the cards. *Yeah, every one of those is designed to hit nearly everyone including allies and even the deckbearer, except Good Intentions.*

"Alright, I'll just keep them with me, along with Hellfire and Brimstone, in case I need to substitute some stuff."

"You don't want me to add them to the sell list?" Liam asked. "And do you want me to leave the Infernal cards off?"

"Just sell everything from that first big pile. How much was it?"

The piece of paper slid across the table, propelled by a gentle push from Liam. Wolfe glanced down. *Eleven million. We won't get that much selling them to Gavin's, but we'll probably get seven to eight million, or closer to ten if we do straight trade for cards. Damn.*

"Most of Chester's cards were either higher tier or higher rarity," Liam said.

"Maybe we can look at getting you some better cards as well, Shel?" Wolfe asked.

"I'd like that a lot. But let's look at my perk options when I hit Level Twenty-Five myself, and we'll see what fits best then, okay?"

"Sure, hun, whatever works." Wolfe yawned.

"Can I maybe get a new card as well?" Liam asked.

"Sure," Wolfe said, yawning a second time.

Shel smiled at him, then yawned herself. She stood and stretched. "Well, shall we get to bed? It's going to be a long day tomorrow."

"Lead the way."

CHAPTER 9

INTERLUDE WITH A CRAZY PERSON

The Ekron Eternal was vastly less impressive in the daytime. The neon lights weren't lit. The half-naked vampire statues, rather than tantalizing with their flaws hidden by dark light, just appeared as garish, cheap decorations. And there wasn't a line of people waiting to get in, just a slightly stained ramp leading up to the door.

Even Wolfe's cards felt that way.

"I remember this place being far more impressive," Malviere said in her otherworldly voice.

Fern, Liam, Malviere, Shel, and Wolfe were all staring up at the building from the parking lot across the street—the one beneath the Eternal was closed.

Wolfe couldn't remember the last time he had been to the Ekron Eternal during the day. "Yeah, it's pretty obvious that Big Man Grimm wanted to have this thing shine when the moon was up, and gave fuck-all fucks about how it looked during the day."

Shel giggled musically. "Fuck-all fucks? It's been a while since you've thrown out a cringe one-liner. I've missed them."

"Har har," Wolfe grumbled as they walked across the street.

Shel leaned over and pecked him on the cheek. "Love you."

Wolfe's heart warmed, but he couldn't bring himself to utter the words in front of Fern and Liam. It felt private, even if he enjoyed saying it to Shel.

She rolled her eyes at him but smiled at him affectionately. Wolfe couldn't help but notice how healthy Shel appeared. She smiled easily, her skin was tan, and she had lean muscle across her entire body. Wolfe knew she'd picked up the second stage of fighting perks as well from her constant training.

There were times Wolfe doubted his choices, despite Cerberus himself letting Wolfe knew he needed to follow his path. But seeing the powerful, happy, confident woman Shel was now, instead of the weak, pale girl that had almost died but for him, reassured him.

As they approached the door, it opened, held by a tall, muscled, black man dressed in a slick grey suit and carrying a pitchfork. Derek, an ally of Wolfe's from his first clashes with the cobras after he'd gotten his deck.

Wolfe jutted his chin up at the pitchfork. "She's still got you doing that, huh?"

Derek rolled his eyes. "Miriam, right?"

Wolfe chuckled. For most people, that wouldn't be an answer, but for Miriam, it made total sense.

They crossed the dance floor of the Ekron Eternal. The red lights were off, and white ones were on. The lack of fog and thumping music was also different. Much like the outside, seeing it all in the light made it far less impressive, perhaps even a bit cringe.

But the back booth was as impressive as ever. Big Man Grimm had made a huge leather booth that surrounded a massive dark oak table. The table had been replaced, but was nearly the same as Wolfe remembered.

But the people were different. Big Man Grimm was dead, and his eldest son had left the business, occasionally fighting over inheritance with Miriam. Theodore, the accountant, was dead. And every single lesser lieutenant was dead except for Piper, who was in jail.

Only Wolfe and Miriam, of the original group that had once sat this table even semi-regularly, remained. Everyone else was new.

Derek took his seat on the 'side' that Miriam occupied, sliding in next to Ahmed. Ahmed always made Wolfe laugh—his deck was based almost entirely on cards they had gotten in the Frozen Cairn dungeon, and the cards were vaguely themed like the images the gods had placed in old Egyptian packs, before that realm had interacted extensively with the outside world and joined the general pool of cards.

So Miriam had Ahmed dress up in a pharaoh's outfit, including having the open shirt and ridiculous beard, and he carried a staff with an ankh on it.

At her other side was Victor, the one-time information broker. Victor was short for a guy at five-foot-seven, almost painfully thin, and pale white with faint acne scars and brilliant green eyes under greasy, black hair. He was dressed in a suit much like Derek, although a black one. But otherwise, he had no theme yet.

Miriam herself took the cake, however. She was dressed in a diaphanous, black-lace dress that showed off equally black underclothes beneath. She had in her usual red contact lenses, with her usual black makeup around the eyes, to complement her long black hair.

Wolfe did a double take. *Wait... those aren't contact lenses.*

"What happened to your eyes?" Wolfe asked. "Surgery?"

Miriam, who had been lounging back on the giant leather booth—probably to show off her figure—shuddered dramatically. "Gods no. I know they can do that, but I'm not risking my eyesight on that. No, I got a new enhancer card, and this was the manifestation."

Wolfe slowly nodded. "Alrighty then. Did you get it for the powers, or because it gave you red eyes?"

"A little of column A, a little of column B," Miriam said. She reached over and gracefully picked up a glass of wine, sipping at it with black-lipstick-tainted lips, then licked the rim of the glass while staring into Wolfe's eyes.

Shel snorted and giggled.

I wish she wouldn't constantly flirt with me.

"So, Shel told me that you finally found a way to get to the dungeon that we located when Malviere evolved. Is that true?"

Miriam laughed throatily and leaned back again, wineglass held languidly in one hand. "No, I called you over here on that false pretense because I couldn't think of any better way to proposition you again."

Ahmed grimaced and Derek rolled his eyes.

Wolfe snorted. "Okay, fine then, tell me how you located it."

Miriam shrugged gloriously and swirled her wine. "We had to drill."

"From inside the sewers?" Wolfe asked.

"Yeah, and let me assure you, it was hell to cover up and pay for," Miriam said, a hint of seriousness entering her voice. "I only trusted four guys, and they've all been compensated extremely well for working for over half a year in the sewers, unable to talk to anyone, mostly when we'd arranged other projects nearby."

Wolfe nodded. "So what is it? Shel said it was a Volcano dungeon."

Miriam gave another exaggerated shrug. "Something like

that, yeah, although I haven't gone and checked it out, and no one's gone in. It's a door, surrounded by falling lava that comes from nowhere and goes nowhere. It gives off heat, but you can pass close to it without burning up. I didn't send anyone in, so I don't know its name or if it's really a volcano dungeon."

Maybe I should change my deck back, Wolfe thought. He had made changes on a false assumption. He wasn't sure, but he had the cards in his pocket, so he could do it if he needed.

Screw it. "Shall we go then?" Wolfe said, starting to scoot out.

"In a moment," Miriam said, holding her empty hand up slowly. "We still need to talk."

"What about?" Wolfe asked. "We just need to get to the dungeon and run it. I really need a couple levels."

"Sure, sure," Miriam said, nodding. "But... you just killed Chester and Pierre Ambroise, right? Carved the heart out of the Weeds?"

Wolfe nodded. "Yeah. You helped me do it, remember?"

"Like it was yesterday," Miriam said airily. "Because it was."

"Smartass."

Miriam chuckled musically. "So... is this it, then? Are you planning on slaughtering the remainder of the gangs?"

Wolfe glanced at Derek, Ahmed, and Victor.

"My men," Miriam said, running one hand over Ahmed's chest provocatively, "are loyal."

"It's way less cool when you do that, and way more cringe, when we're in normal light and the sound of 'oonce oonce' isn't battering my ear," Wolfe said, nodding at Ahmed. "But fine. I'm aiming to take out both the crime families over the next couple days."

"The next five days, twenty-one hours, and twenty-two minutes," Fern muttered.

Miriam glanced over and raised an eyebrow.

"You get used to it," Wolfe replied to the unspoken question.

Miriam leaned forward, most of her flirtatious demeanor gone as she stared at Wolfe intensely. "All three of the crime families have a ton of their money in my club at the moment, being laundered. I can stop paying it out, but it'll cause problems *really* quickly. In a day or two for the Renfeldt and Singh families... and it'll be a problem whenever the Weeds end the infighting to see who will inherit. It'll hurt the remaining families a bit, although not immensely. But I'll also start moving on other territories. I have plans, Wolfe... But your war is my trigger. So are you committed to the others?"

Wolfe glanced again at Shel, who subtly nodded.

He turned back to Miriam. "Yeah. It's go. I aim to end all the remaining crime families in Noimoire in a blaze of destruction."

Miriam nodded, leaning back again and smiling, her eyes alight. "I can't wait to see the destruction you carve across the landscape, Wolfe."

Then she glanced at Fern, Shel, and Liam in turn. "How many are you bringing to the dungeon?"

"Shel for now—she needs to make Level Twenty-Five and get her perk."

Miriam nodded. "Of course. May I bring one of my boy toys as well?"

Derek laughed, and Victor smiled, but Ahmed frowned. *Interesting dynamic they have there.*

Wolfe was torn. It had been his dungeon, and Miriam already owed him in the dungeon department... but she had helped to physically open a path to the dungeon after Wolfe had found it when he had evolved Malviere nearly a year ago.

He made a decision. "Very well. But only for the first floor if there's more than one, then we reconsider, fair?"

She held her glass out to him in a mock toast. "Fair and more than fair, Wolfy."

"So, *now* can we go?" Wolfe asked. "I have places to be and people to kill."

Shel laughed again. "Ooh, two in a day."

Miriam laughed.

CHAPTER 10

THREE SPIRITS, PART I

The four of them—Wolfe, Shel, Miriam, and Derek—walked through the tunnel underneath the earth. They were trailed by *six* companion cards—Wolfe's three; Sorenia and Liurenia; and Malik, Eater of the Dead, the card Wolfe had gained for Miriam last year when he had killed Tracy, the deckbearer for hire that had been working for the traffickers.

"I can't believe you're coming to a dungeon in a cocktail dress," Wolfe said to Miriam.

The only concession the mafia princess had made to the fact that the dungeon might be dangerous had been switching her stilettos for black tennis shoes and grabbing her golf club. Other than that, she was dressed as she had been in the club two hours before.

"I can't believe someone sold you an assault rifle," Miriam replied.

Wolfe hefted the new AR-15 he was carrying. "It's not an assault rifle."

Miriam laughed musically and rolled her eyes. "And yet, I bet you assault someone with it."

Wolfe widened his eyes and obviously rolled them right back.

Miriam shifted the subject. "I doubt the dungeon will let you in with an assault rifle."

Wolfe shrugged. "We'll see."

He knew she was most likely right. Most dungeons were odd about what could go in, and the older the dungeon, the less it tended to allow modern weapons, especially larger ones. Most dungeons let pistols in, and a few let some pretty heavy ones in—there was a documented case of one allowing someone in with a tripod-mounted, belt-fed machine gun— but there were more that wouldn't even allow pistols than those that let people in with semi-automatic rifles.

The dungeons had always been picky. There was a hilarious story he'd heard way back in high school from one of his cool history teachers. Mr. Hammonds, Wolfe thought. It had been about one of the English kings that had tried to take a ballista into a dungeon and been rejected.

Still, after his close call on the boat against the Weeds gang, Wolfe knew he needed to up his game. He was wearing a bullet-proof jacket and carrying both his STI Edge in its holster, and an AR-15 in his hands.

Then Shel busted up laughing. "No one sold him an AR-15. It's mine."

Wolfe frowned as the other two chuckled and Miriam said, "That makes sense."

Wolfe saw a glow up ahead. "Oh look, we're here. Shame we can't talk about this anymore."

The group of four walked up to the gate. It was as Miriam had described it—a solid door in the side of the rock, metal, with no handle. Around the door was lava coming from nowhere, pouring down past the door on either side, and returning to nowhere. Wolfe immediately started to sweat, but even when he got close, he was never close to getting burned.

Wolfe touched the door of metal.

A notification popped up. *No firearms are allowed inside the dungeon.*

Wolfe grimaced and turned to the others, placing his AR-15 on the side of the gate. "No firearms at all, not even pistols."

Derek and Shel groaned and pulled their pistol holsters off, setting them next to Wolfe's semi-automatic rifle.

"My club is looking *pretty* smart right about now," Miriam crowed.

Wolfe patted his new hunting knife even as he set his own STI Edge down. "I'm doing okay in the 'up close and personal' department."

Derek half-heartily hefted his own pitchfork. "I'm doing... not miserably."

Miriam laughed musically and placed her hand on his shoulder. "You'll be fine, my little imp."

Wolfe eyed Miriam. *I know she told me she hams it up as camouflage, to convince people she's not dangerous, but I think she just loves the games as well.*

Miriam pulled her deck, touching her hand to her chest and then splaying it outward. Bone-white and purple cards, four of them, appeared, as well as a fifth bone-white card off to the side.

"Ooh, got it in one," she said, touching a purple card.

The vague outline of an eye appeared, staring at the dungeon entrance. "So, this is a level one to a level thirty-five dungeon, group, with Fire, Elemental, Life, and Mortal types. It's called Loowitlatkla's Fall, and has three levels."

"Hmm," Wolfe muttered.

Shel pulled her phone out.

"You're getting reception down here?" Wolfe asked, bemused.

She laughed. "No. I did a bunch of research on dungeons

last night, after you fell asleep. I kept the stuff on my phone so we could reference it inside the dungeon, but this also works."

She paused, scrolling something on her phone, then spoke again. "Most dungeons have a floor per ten levels, and a boss at the end of each floor, with a single sub-boss on each floor as well." She scrolled again. "Plus a final boss. But that's just the usual, almost fifty percent of dungeons deviate from that. And group means it's designed to challenge three-to-four deckbearers at a time, so we're pretty much on spec for this."

"Although way over level for most of it," Wolfe said as he reached over and touched the metal door again.

Without any warning, he found himself sweating in the near-burning heat of a huge cavern. He was standing on a ten-foot-wide ledge around a lake of lava. But at the edge of the lake of lava, impossibly, were small, bright green plants. And the rest of the dungeon was a riot of colors as well. Cereboo, Malviere, and the Obsessive Infernal Cultist had appeared next to him the second he entered.

Wolfe got about twenty seconds to stare before a bat, made of fire, flew at Cereboo.

Least Firebat
Dungeon Monster Fire [Bat] Creature
Health: 3
Attack: N/A
Defense: 1
Magical Attack: 4
Magical Defense: 1

Special: **Incorporeal:** This creature is not affected by physical attacks

Special: **Thorns [Fire 3]**: Whenever this creature is attacked in melee or brawl, the attacker takes three true damage as Fire.

"I hate elementals."—Hoyaneh, Iroquois Deckbearer

Wolfe stepped back against the gate, and Malviere called out, "Fall" in her otherworldly voice. Black energy shaped like a dog hit the bat even as it hit Cereboo. Cereboo yipped from two of his heads, but the bat disintegrated.

Wolfe removed the '0 xp' notification—the bat had been equivalent level of two, far too low for him to gain experience.

A moment later, Derek appeared, and after that Miriam and Shel stepped in.

Miriam fanned herself with her free hand, beads of sweat forming on her instantly. "Maybe I should have been naked."

"Please don't," Wolfe responded, and Miriam chuckled.

A few more bats were flying across the lake, but nothing else seemed out of the ordinary. Wolfe did see a single tunnel exit on the far side, however.

"Shall we?" he asked, pointing.

Light beams from Sorenia and Liurenia cleaved the Fire Bear Cub in twain.

Derek called out, "Ding!"

Shel clapped her hands silently. "Congratulations, Derek! That's two levels, right?"

Derek nodded. "Yeah. The Frozen Cairn was nice, but aside from two losing arena battles, I haven't had any other chances to level, so this has been wonderful. Especially since with you and Wolfe and your insane decks around, this is basically just me being power leveled."

Derek clasped Wolfe on the shoulder. "You've always had my back, man."

Wolfe shrugged out of it. "Miriam has your back, not me. I

just appreciate a guy that can be relied upon to not be utterly incompetent."

Derek nodded with a half-smile.

"How much further to the first boss, do you think?" Miriam asked. "I mean, I'm getting some nice experience. But I'm also pretty tired of watching Malviere, Sorenia, and Liurenia just burn everything down while the rest of us do jack. Plus, getting *no* cards is pretty irritating."

"Well, that bear cub was level nine, so I'd bet we're about to find the first boss," Shel replied, her eyes staring at nothing while she checked notifications, Wolfe assumed.

Shel continued. "And if we're getting no cards now we can expect to get an extra-large reward from the floor boss. Dungeons are usually pretty consistent in output."

The group walked from the tunnel into the next cavern. It was about fifty feet on a side, with a few tiny rivulets of lava throughout it. There was an exit on the far right side, but a gate of stone was across it.

In the center stood a giant—a man, twelve feet tall, covered in stone, and carrying a massive stone club.

"I don't think my own nine-iron is going to do much," Miriam said with a cute frown. "In fact, I'm beginning to regret having brought it."

Wolfe stared at the boss card.

Stonecoat Scout Leader
Dungeon Monster Boss, Elemental [Earth, Humanoid]
creature
Health: 100
Attack: 10
Defense: 10
Magical Attack: N/A
Magical Defense: 7

Special: **Stone skin:** This creature has resistance to all physical attacks

"If he survives, he'll bring the others."—Sachem, Iroquois Chief

"Watch the lava, I think that's what makes this fight even slightly dangerous to us," Wolfe said. He'd had a hand of cards out for some time, waiting for the moment to actually fight, as opposed to letting the companion cards handle everything.

He touched his second Obsessive Infernal Cultist, summoning it onto the battlefield.

At the same time, Cereboo raced toward the Stonecoat Scout Leader. Malviere whispered words of power, and the already pumped-up Cereboo flew into action. He hit the Dungeon Boss six times, each for a net of two damage, knocking off an eighth of the creature's health. But that was mere seconds before he was slammed with the club. He was picked up and carried through the air, taking just over his health in damage and dissolving into red light.

A tiny Imp poked the Stonecoat, chipping it a tiny bit.

Wolfe glanced over at Derek with a raised eyebrow.

"My deck isn't that great," Derek said sheepishly.

"You will pay for hurting Big Brother," Malviere intoned, slamming her spirit dog into the creature. At the same time, light beams from the two lantern angels hit it. The damage was more than Cereboo's teeth chewing on it. Malviere's Death attack did nothing, the dog dissipating against the creature.

Elemental Type was immune to Death, Wolfe remembered.

By contrast, each Light beam carved significant damage into the creature, inflicting a net of seventeen more damage.

Wolfe tossed his Demonic Portal, going for the maximum creature build. He dropped a Gehennan Kennel Master and the Tier-four Angry Hellhound. The Hellhound was instantly effected by the Kennel Master's Motivation ability, and made an attack that doubled up—a net hundred and twenty-one damage physical attack and a net forty-nine-point magical attack for another eleven damage.

Liurenia and Sorenia fired again, and Malviere used her own ability to give the Angry Hellhound another attack. The stone on the enemy cracked, and the blood began to leak through the edges.

Miriam screamed, a noise half sound, half mental pressure, but the Elemental ignored her psychic attack as well.

Wolfe was a bit annoyed when the Stonecoat Scout Leader clubbed his hellhound out of existence, but he swiped his cards, got another Demonic Portal, and brought out two Tier-Three Angry Hellhounds and a Lost Hellhound Puppy.

Two vampires began whaling on the boss, as well as a couple more imps.

The boss went down to a horde of creatures and companions the next round, dropping a pack of cards and a separate single card.

"That wasn't that hard," Derek noted.

Wolfe wasn't so sanguine. "Maybe. But that was a level ten boss, and we've got someone over thirty and someone almost twenty-five. Our decks aren't the best against the Elemental type. Also, I'm gonna switch my deck back and put Brimstone and Hellfire back in; this wasn't what I had thought when I originally did all this."

What will I do with what is almost an entire shut-down deck I have now?

"Should we stop?" Shel asked as she walked over and picked up the pack and card that had dropped from the boss.

Wolfe snorted as he made adjustments to his deck. "Definitely not—that was easy, even if it was only because of our level advantage. Let's get you to Level Twenty-Five and get some more cards. I'm sure we'll be fine till at least the next boss."

He put his deck away, and walked over to where Shel was. "Speaking of more cards, what did we get this time?"

Shel held the card out to him.

CHAPTER 11

THE THREE SPIRITS

T he card showed an old lady in slightly furry hide clothing, tending a hearth fire, with injured people in beds behind her.

Loowitlatkla The Fire Tender

Unique Rare Equivalent, Tier-1 equivalent Mortal/Fire
[Civic] Creature
1 Mortal or 1 Fire Power, 1 Any power
Health: 11
Attack: N/A
Defense: 3
Magical Attack: N/A
Magical Defense: 3

Special: **Tender to the Arch of Fire**: While this card is on the field, no enemy deckbearer cards may cancel, control, or auto-kill any Fire type card.

Special: **Healer [5]**: When this creature enters the field it may fully heal one other creature card or restore 5 Health to a deckbearer

Special: Dungeon Exchange: This card *may* be exchanged at
the end of Loowitlatkla's Fall

"Loowit was once an old woman of such heart and kindness
that the gods granted her eternal life."

"That's a pretty solid card, hun," Shel said. "I think this
dungeon must be crazy old, since that's an old Amerind spirit
according to some other card information I've seen. A pretty
minor one in the grand scheme of the releases."

"Old it may be, but it's also batshit insane," Wolfe said.
"We're not even remotely in the right place geographically if
it's referencing Mt. St. Helena. Let's move forward though—
prizes are prizes, even when handed out by a schizophrenic old
dungeon."

Miriam giggled. "Deck sets, dungeons, and monsters are
released in sets around all people that have a connection. So
you get stuff that isn't near where it references. I mean, that
one chosen lady that Shel fought in the Rat Arena last year
had monsters that were only seen in overland monster form in
Iraq, but have been released as cards here in the U.S."

"Thanks for the impromptu history lesson," Wolfe
muttered.

"What about the card pack?" Shel asked.

"We'll open it after the next boss," Wolfe said. *Might as
well make deck decisions with more than a single pack.*

Wolfe moved to the passage forward, which was blocked
by a stone gate. As he approached the stone gate, it shattered.

Wolfe raised an eyebrow. "Subtle."

Miriam giggled. "What gave you the impression anything
would be subtle? The lava bats flying at your face, or the
twelve-foot-tall stone giant?"

"Heh," Wolfe offered, his only commentary as he moved
forward.

Shel and Derek chuckled as they followed, and Miriam giggled. Wolfe swore she did it as an affectation.

The passage was short, with smooth rock walls. At the end it turned into a beautiful cavern, with glowing mushrooms and rivulets of water going nowhere. It sloped gently upward, and Wolfe followed it, his muscles clenched as his head tracked, waiting for an attack. But none came.

At the top of the beautiful cavern, a door looked out. Wolfe first saw a beautiful, star-filled night sky and crescent moon. He stepped out into a forested mountainside with a single owl hooting. Beneath him on the mountain, he saw a cluster of huts in a large clearing, near a pond. A single fire kept the night at bay.

Wolfe shivered. *The night and the cold air. I'm sure I'll adjust in a moment, but I still have sweat from the volcano on me.*

Shel came out from the cave and glanced around as well. "I don't see anything besides the village. Should we search around or just head for it?"

"Let's just head for it," Wolfe replied. "I think, based on the little I know about dungeons, that unless something immediately presents, we should just head for the obvious lead."

Miriam emerged from the cave. "Yeah, everything I've read on dungeons supports the idea that they rarely hide the ball. They may have hugely challenging and complicated puzzles, but they rarely have anything that is particularly hard to find. Checking a drawer for a prize is about the limit."

"I keep forgetting that under all the crazy you're actually a learned individual. In law school, even," Wolfe said.

Shel laughed.

"*First* in my class in law school," Miriam replied, and touched her finger to her lips, way too coyly for what she had said.

Wolfe gave up the conversation with an eyeroll. The only winning moves in conversation with Miriam were not to play.

Instead, he turned down the mountain side and headed to the obvious next location in the dungeon. As he got close, he could see that the village was composed of five longhouses, he assumed of Cedar, matching the trees around. Each was close to the others, making five narrowing paths into the fire in the center, where the single woman worked the fire.

As they approached, the woman glanced up from her fire. She was wearing the exact same outfit that Wolfe's card, Loowitlatkla, had worn.

In fact, she looks exactly the same, Wolfe thought.

The old woman spoke in a language that Wolfe didn't know, but the meaning of her words somehow penetrated.

"Who comes to the village of the Cowlitz?" she asked. "I, Loowitlatkla the Hearth Keeper, ask as is my right."

Wolfe stared at her, and a 'card' popped up.

Loowitlatkla The Hearth Keeper
Dungeon NPC
Mortal/Fire [Civic] Creature
Health: 11
Attack: N/A
Defense: 3
Magical Attack: N/A
Magical Defense: 3

Special: **Healer [5]**: Every thirty seconds, this card will heal one other creature card or restore 5 Health to a deckbearer. It will choose whomever is nearest.

"Loowit was once an old woman of such heart and kindness that the gods granted her eternal life."

She really is the same person as the card we just got.

"Is this one of those situations where they only have a few responses?" Miriam whispered while staring at the old lady. "Like that sheriff in the werewolf dungeon?"

"Don't know," Wolfe said, then waited.

Loowit did nothing.

Wolfe stepped forward. "I, Ethan Wolfe, come before you."

"A good name," Loowit said. "A strong name. You could continue on to the meeting, the safe path."

She paused dramatically. "But we have need of you here, Ethan, if you're brave enough."

Wolfe grimaced—his name reminded him of his father, whom he hated.

"Will you defend us, Ethan?" the woman asked, picking up some sticks and tossing them into the fire.

"From?" Wolfe asked, crossing his arms.

"Will you defend us, Ethan?" the woman repeated, again picking up sticks and tossing them into the fire.

"From?" Miriam asked, laughing. The woman repeated her entire spiel.

"Stop that!" Wolfe replied. "Obviously, she's gonna loop till we say 'yes' or—"

A notification appeared. *You have begun a special level twenty-four group encounter. Defeating this encounter will grant the reward for the second floor, as well as an extra award.*

"Son of a..." Wolfe trailed off as Miriam giggled maniacally.

Loowit turned and smiled at him. "I'm glad you'll defend us, Ethan, because the Stonecoats are almost upon us. If you can hold, Chief Tyee Sahale comes here to gift me. He can defeat them. We just have to hold here."

"Well, that—" Wolfe began.

But Loowit wasn't finished. "The braves at this village will help defend us, but we must survive. If you are strong and powerful enough to keep us all alive, I'll have a great reward for you as well as what you'll get from the chief."

"Tower Defense," Shel said, and Miriam nodded.

Wolfe had looked up enough dungeons to know what they were talking about. Before he could say anything, two men, dressed thickly in hide and carrying a stone hatchet, came out of each of the five huts and took up a position in the spaces.

Five ways in, and two braves in each.

Wolfe stared at them.

Tyee Sahale Brave
Dungeon NPC
Mortal [Civic] Creature
Health: 20
Attack: 6(9)
Defense: 6(9)
Magical Attack: N/A
Magical Defense: 5(8)

Special: **Ally of All**: This card, so long as it's within 250' of another card, counts as on the field, allied, and in the deck for purposes of gaining any beneficial effect from a deckbearer or their cards.

"A brave that served the legendary first chief of the Cowlitz."

Snapping sounded, and Wolfe glanced up from his examination. Multiple Stonecoats were coming through the woods. Each appeared the same as the Stonecoat scout, although their Health was lower. But there were a lot of them.

"The braves are getting the bonuses from Sorenia and Liurenia," Shel reported. "They've got nines in most of their stats now."

"Good, because we get a bonus prize if we keep them alive," Wolfe replied. "I'd really like to do that, since I doubt we'll get another chance at this. And it'll still only take two hits for the Stonecoats to kill one. That's way better than the one it would have taken before, but..."

Wolfe examined the field again. "Let's try and fight forward against what we can. Shel, do you still have the Guiding Light card?"

She nodded.

"Try and get that out, to give the braves a third buff, and then keep healing them if you can."

Three Stone Coats moved up, crashing their way out of the forest. Each was a twelve-foot-tall stone man.

Wolfe moved out into the space between the buildings where they were headed. He brought forth Cerberus' Home for Wayward Hellhounds along the forest edge, to give him a constant supply of monsters to block and empower.

Cereboo went on the attack, barking madly from all three heads and charging past Wolfe on the right. He sped up dramatically as Malviere boosted him, biting madly but only slightly effectually at the Stone Coat. The angels fired light beams. Shel played Guiding Light—it had apparently come up for her in the first draw. Miriam dropped a vampire Wolfe hadn't seen before, and Derek put his mantle over himself—the same Imp Lord mantle that Wolfe had gotten him two years ago—the one that empowered imps.

Wolfe pulled Brimstone and started plugging away as the fight went on. His pistol ignoring type advantage gave him a significant advantage as he fired away.

The fight lasted for a good two minutes—two exhausting minutes. The Braves, now at an eleven attack, joined the fight as well. They occasionally got hit, but Shel just healed them up. Cereboo was slain, but Wolfe got his second Obsessive Infernal Cultist out and brought forth two Angry Hellhounds and a spare Lost Hellhound Pup. Imps and vampires appeared, did chip damage, and were slain.

But they kept both braves alive without taking any damage to the actual deckbearers on their team.

Wolfe was glancing around as the last Stone Coat went down.

A notification popped up. *Combined level of encounter is twenty, more than ten below current level. No experience gained.*

Wolfe frowned, but before he could get really angry, he was interrupted by Shel's whoop of joy.

"I made Level Twenty-Five off the three kills," Shel reported.

"Nice!" Wolfe said, glancing around. He felt brief elation, an emotion that didn't come to him all that often, that they had emerged victorious. *That wasn't that hard for a team of four. Although we are quite over level since I think this is the start of the second floor. Well, me and Shel at least.*

"What options did you get?" Wolfe asked.

Shel was staring off into space. "I only got five. I got—"

Three more Stonecoats came crashing through the undergrowth in front of them, interrupting Shel. At the same time, Wolfe heard another set of crashes 'land' between the cedar longhouses over to the side.

"Shit," Wolfe said, just staring for a second. "That's what I get for thinking something might be easy."

CHAPTER 12

THE THREE SPIRITS, PART III

Wolfe dodged to the side and the club smashed into the ground. He fired Brimstone into the side of the Stonecoat, doing significant damage, but the giant kicked out before Wolfe could move. Wolfe was sent rolling into the side of one of the cedar longhouses, hitting hard and slumping onto his side. The hit had inflicted ten damage, and would have knocked a normal human to the very edge of death.

He righted himself and fired another round of shots into the Stonecoat from the sitting position. The stone giant, chewed, beamed, and shot, finally slumped to the ground. *Six down of the nine from this third round*, Wolfe thought. Cereboo was gone, and even Malviere had been slain. Only the continuous pump of creatures from both the Police Academy and Cerberus' Home for Wayward Hellhounds had allowed Wolfe and Shel to fight that many.

But it wasn't over yet.

Wolfe leapt to his feet with a wince. His group was down, but he wasn't sure how Miriam and Derek were doing—he didn't want to lose the special reward, whatever it was.

Shel yelled, "Liurenia, Sorenia, jump the building and keep the stonecoats off the braves!"

The two angels obeyed, leaping into the air and flying across the cedar longhouse.

Wolfe didn't wait to see how it turned out. He ran into the center of the tiny village, headed for Loowit for a quick heal before he went to fight the last couple.

He saw that Miriam was there, her teeth elongated and her eyes red—she had her vampire mantle on. But at the same time, blood covered half her body and her arm was mangled.

Wolfe stared for a second.

She tried to grin at him, but her face was a rictus of pain. "Don't worry about me. I zigged when I should have zagged, but I'll live. Derek needs help!"

"The fight?" Wolfe asked as he ran past the healer, letting Miriam take the benefit despite his own wounds.

"We're losing it, but no braves are down yet—but I don't think Derek is going to last long."

Loowit dropped some herbs into the fire, which turned blue and wafted smoke across Miriam. Her arm straightened a bit, and she reached out with her other to touch a card—one of her weak Sexy Vampires, the shirtless male one that looked like he was trying for a combination of cocaine chic and a six-pack.

Wolfe rushed around the side. Derek was on the ground, trying to crawl away from the fight. Fortunately, the angels were taking the beatings from the two remaining stonecoats, and neither was attacking Derek any further.

A Rookie Riot Police and a Lost Hellhound Puppy came running around the corner as well. Neither did much damage, but Shel leapt around the corner after. A flash of light left her hand and hit one of the stonecoats in the head, dropping it.

She was wearing her Martyr mantle, with blood dripping

from all of her eyes, including her new third eye. But her wounds were healing.

At the same time, she reached out, touched a card, and a Rookie EMT appeared. It healed Wolfe almost entirely, thanks to the synergy bonus with Police Academy.

Damn that girl's become amazing, Wolfe thought, remembering briefly back to when she'd needed saving in nearly every fight.

But he didn't let his fond thoughts distract him. He put his own magical gun to work shooting the other. Liurenia was broken by another club strike, but after that, the last stonecoat went down to the collection of angels, dogs, imps, and one implausibly hot vampire boy all whaling on it.

Derek was healed by Shel at the same time. He rolled to his side, glancing up at the sky.

"Get up," Wolfe said.

Derek didn't move. He just continued to stare at the star-filled faux sky the dungeon was projecting. "I'm sorry, Wolfe, but I'm gonna lay here for another minute, thanks."

A notification appeared, telling Wolfe that this had been an equivalent of a level twenty-eight fight. He got a solid amount of experience, jumping to scrape into Level Thirty-Three from the Level Thirty-Two he had just made from wave two. Then another notification popped up.

For clearing the second floor via challenge, you gain an additional 100% of your current level.

Wolfe dinged to low thirty-four.

"Wow," Shel said. "That's level Twenty-Eight for me."

Yeah, she's a hell of a badass now, Wolfe thought, smiling at Shel. He never wanted to lose her, and he never wanted to be apart from her.

"Yeah, this was incredibly lucrative, even if rather painful," Miriam said. "No pain, no gain, right? Point is, I'm into my low twenties."

Then she followed Wolfe's gaze, and laughed. "And you're just here mooning over Shel, huh? Not even thinking about your levels?"

Wolfe flushed. "I just happened to be looking in that direction."

Miriam giggled again. "Why don't you marry her?"

Wolfe stopped, floored. Somehow, that hadn't really ever entered his thoughts, but... *Why don't I marry her? I mean, most other women barely even interest me anymore, and she's perfect. She's kind and supportive, but also smart and at least kinda badass.*

Shel was flushed as she looked back at Wolfe.

I'm nearly one-hundred-percent positive she'd say yes. Nearly.

Just then a rustle shook the trees again, and Wolfe glanced over. More stonecoats were walking out from the forest— twelve this time.

"Are you shitting me?" Wolfe asked. He, and his team, might be a touch higher level, but no one had picked leveling benefits or changed cards—or even looked at the pack they had gotten. Nine Stonecoats had been enough to nearly kill Miriam and Derek.

I don't think we can handle that many. Wolfe hated to give up, but he hated the idea of watching Big Man Grimm's daughter die even more.

Wolfe was prepared to voice the decision to leave, but Derek pipped up with, "How is this fair? I thought we just got a completed message and bonus experience!"

Wolfe stared for a moment. *Wait, it did say we won!*

Before Wolfe could respond, an arrow slammed into the eye of one of the stonecoats. Men of obvious Amerind heritage, wearing goatskin clothes, came flying out of the woods. Some shot bows, and others used axes. But all moved with supernatural speed.

One of the new men hit a stonecoat with a swing of a stone-headed axe, and the stonecoat *disintegrated,* exploding into a spray of blood and particulate matter across the trees.

Alright, supernatural strength as well.

More of the men poured from the woods. Wolfe could see that they all appeared powerful and healthy—tall, without blemish, and with lean runners' muscles throughout their body.

But even among these men, three stood out. One was older, perhaps in his late thirties. Two were younger, one a bit taller, the other a bit more sturdy, but both bore a resemblance to the older one.

The older one threw an axe, and it hit one in the chest, exploded through it, and slew another on the far side.

Wolfe grimaced. "Okay, dungeon, I get it, these are important and powerful dudes."

Miriam giggled again. "Ah, does Wolfy not feel like the wee little alpha anymore?"

Shel came up and put her hand on Wolfe's shoulder as the last of the stonecoats were vanquished with ease, and Wolfe let go of the retort he had planned. The corner of Shel's mouth was twitching, and Wolfe reminded himself, again, that the only way to win the game of repertoire with Miriam was not to play.

The battle ended after a mere thirty seconds with the complete and utter victory of the Braves. The three most impressive of them, obviously the chief and his two sons, came walking toward Wolfe. At the same time, Loowit stepped out from her fire, moving toward them. The three uber-men and the old lady all met where Wolfe was at the same time.

The older man spoke. "I came to reward you, Loowitlatkla, for your true kindness and selflessness to the tribe, but I see that enemies sought to lay you low. Have my braves defended you, then?"

"Ooh, stilted conversation time," Miriam sang out. "I can't wait!"

"Yes, Chief Tyee Sahale," Loowit replied. "But they were led, and protected, by these great heroes that you see before you, braves even stronger than the ones you left here."

Wolfe stared at Chief Tyee, trying to see his card.

Chief Tyee Sahale, Level 194 equivalent
???

Wolfe grimaced. *Oh, fuck off, gods.*

"Well, I, and my sons Pahto"—Chief Tyee clapped the taller one on the shoulder—"and Wy'east"—the stouter one—"thank you for your service, heroes."

Then the chieftain turned back to Loowit. "Well, I came here to reward you for your good deeds, kindness, and selfless service. You have tended the Stone Arch Fire for almost a hundred years, and I would that you were able to do so for another thousand. So, as my reward to you, I will give you eternal life."

"Ah, gotta love the exposition," Miriam said.

Chief Tyee held his hand out and touched Loowit's head. Wolfe could feel a pulse of magic flow through the pair, but nothing visibly changed.

Chief Tyee stepped back, smiling indulgently.

But Loowit awkwardly bowed her head, her hand on her back. "My chief, I am truly thankful for your gift. But, I would ask to not be an old woman for eternity. Please, return to me my youth."

Chief Tyee nodded again, and he went over and placed his head on the old woman a second time. The same energy passed between them, but this time, Loowit changed. Her back straightened, her hair became lustrous, her skin smoothed, and her figure became fuller. In mere seconds, she appeared to be a young woman of about Shel's age.

An utterly gorgeous young woman, and Wolfe had to tear his eyes away from her. When he did, he could see that Derek, Miriam, and the chief's two sons were also all staring.

But Shel was looking at Wolfe, smiling. Wolfe grinned sheepishly, and Shel smiled back.

But, apparently, Loowit wasn't done. She turned to face Wolfe and his team. "My chief, I would ask a second boon. These people kept every single one of your braves alive when we were attacked by the evil stonecoats. Perhaps, chief, we could entrust the care of the Stone Arch Fire to them, and I could live a life, marry, and have children?"

"Yes, you should marry a chieftain's son," Pahto said.

At the same time, his brother said, "Our children would be beautiful."

The chief ignored his sons and turned to face Wolfe, his eyes piercing and shrewd. "I suppose, given the bravery and success they showed, that we can indeed do so."

He stepped forward, and held his hand out. In it was a card.

When no one stepped forward, Wolfe stepped forward and took the card.

"Thank you, wandering braves," Chief Tyee said. "We'll be going, but I'll instruct my own companions to leave a feast for you, as you have triumphed greatly over adversity, and that should be rewarded. Take care of the arch—it was the heart of our civic life, and it represented life for hundreds of tribes. It is a great honor you have earned, but it is burden as well. But for now, I bid thee farewell."

The chieftain stepped back, waved, and turned. Everyone started to walk off, and the entire scene faded, every person disappearing as they walked away, and the buildings fading as well. What was left was a fire, and next to that, a huge stone slab filled with berries, cooked meats, and clay pots of water.

And *another* card where Loowit had disappeared.

Beside the stone slab lay four hide blankets.

Before anyone could say anything else, three packs of cards dropped.

Wolfe stepped over and picked them up, pulling his previous card pack and then pointing to the stone slab. "Shall we eat, see what we got, and level?"

"Hell yeah," Derek said, and they all moved toward the smell of barbeque.

The trees rustled again, and Wolfe braced himself. But what came out was not another stonecoat—instead, a man of obvious Amerind complexion, shorter but with broad shoulders, traipsed out from between the trees. He was carrying a huge sack made of hide over his shoulder.

He glanced around. "Is this the camp of the heroes? I was waiting where it was safe, but word of your bravery and victory spread, and so I've come to trade if you so desire."

CHAPTER 13

THE THREE SPIRITS, PART IV

"I'm going to set up shop over here, heroes," the trader said, and moved to the side of the clearing. A tent magically appeared, and the trader began setting up a stone table near it.

Wolfe resummoned Cereboo and Malviere, then sat cross-legged at the stone tablet, reaching over and tentatively grabbing a hunk of cooked meat. He gave it a sniff, then bit into it. It tasted a bit gamey to him, but not that different than beef.

But as he ate it, he got a notification that he had received healing.

Shel had kneeled down on Wolfe's right and glanced at the card before grabbing some of the meat herself. She munched on it with one hand while she looked at the card.

Then she glanced over at Wolfe, her eyes shining. "Glad you pulled us through that—this card is insane."

Miriam lowered herself to the ground in an almost perfect match for Shel, but on his left side.

"This could be some kind of male erotica novel," she said,

smiling at Wolfe and licking her lips. "Two beautiful girls, each kneeling to one side of you..."

Wolfe snorted but ignored her—usually the best way to deal with Miriam.

Derek rolled his eyes and tore at the meat he had grabbed.

Malviere, Cereboo, Sorenia, and Liurenia all took seats along the opposite side of the slab, and Cereboo started wolfing down the meat with all three heads. Wolfe noted that somehow, the level of meat never really went down.

He held his hand out. "Mind if I take a gander at the card?"

"Gander?" Miriam asked, giggling.

Wolfe flushed. "My dad used to say it."

"I think it's a great word," Shel said, smiling at Wolfe and staring in his eyes before passing the card over.

The card showed a large fire with leaf-green energy around the outside, near a confluence of rivers and pathways. It was tended to by numerous youthful Amerind women, led by an older woman that resembled Loowit, although it was hard to see the detail on the small picture to be sure.

Stone Arch Fire
Unique Mythic equivalent Tier-1 equivalent Life [Civic] Building
0 power
This creates the Stone Arch Fire. It adds +1 Fire power to the deckbearer, and doubles the effect of any other Civic Building in the deckbearer's deck.

This building card is not a null card. In addition to being placed as a building, it may be played as a persistent for 1 Life, 1 Fire, and 1 any power

Special: **All Healer [5]**: All allied deckbearers and cards heal 5 every single round

Special: **Civic Leader [1]:** All of the deckbearer's [Civic]
subtype creature cards gain +1 to all non-health stats
Special: **Death Ward**: The deckbearer's creatures may not be
killed by automatic removal effects while this card is in play
Special: **Fungible [Life, Fire]**: Life and Fire power may be
spent as if they were the other

"Heat is life, cold is death. Never let anyone tell you fire is only
for burning."

Miriam let out a long, low whistle. "Wow... aren't you a
fire deckbearer as well, Wolfe?"

"What?" Wolfe asked, briefly confused. "Yeah, I am...
technically. But I've not really worked that angle of my
deckbearer abilities at all. This card is basically just one bonus
power."

Miriam smiled at him. "Well, you don't have to ignore
your Fire energy anymore. You could take one Life power and
then put the Stone Arch Fire in your deck. You could heal
yourself every round, and protect your creatures from death
effects."

"That's silly," Wolfe said. "I mean, Shel is the one focused
on police and other civic things."

"But the Hellmouth Institute benefits from other
building cards," Shel said. "If you had this, it would probably
give a huge bonus to any future orphans you get."

Warmth spread through Wolfe at Shel's words, a sort of
spiritual match to the fire they were sitting next to. *She always
tries to support me. This card could obviously benefit her deck,
but her first move was to try and make me stronger. I really
don't deserve a girl like her.*

A tiny piece of Wolfe was tempted to take the Stone Arch
Fire, because it would benefit him. It would benefit him far
less than it would benefit Shel, but it was still their first Mythic

card. His old loner instincts wrestled his new instincts, but were thrown to the ground.

That's old me talking. The guy who only trusted himself and Big Man Grimm. If I really do want to marry Shel, then her strength is my strength, and it benefits me more in her deck.

Wolfe shook his head. "This is wrong for me, or at least a lot better for you, Shel. I can't easily move into a deck that benefits from or focuses on Civic cards, and this plays heavily into that paradigm."

"It'll make you stronger," Shel said.

"It would make you far stronger than me. Sure, I could use it, and it might make me a bit better. But I need to either give up the Occult Library building or spend ten leveling pips, then get enough Fire type cards to benefit. Like I said earlier— I gave that path up when I picked my level twenty-five perk. This should go to you, Shel, assuming no one else objects."

Miriam patted Wolfe on his forearm. "I'm not taking cards from this dungeon, Wolfe. I mean, unless you give them to me, obviously. But I owe you, remember? Even without taking cards you're just power leveling me and Derek here anyway. Also, even outside the moral considerations, it's unlikely that these cards would benefit us much, given our typings."

"I don't know..." Shel said.

Wolfe was surprised it was this hard to get her to just take the card, but she had always played second to him. Which in some cases made sense, but not in this case.

He thought about his intentions to Shel for a moment, then continued. "Look... we look like we might be together a long time, right? If you're stronger, I'm stronger."

"For the Pack," Malviere said, her occult voice echoing with mystic portent.

"Love, honor, and community are the strengths that Raphael bequeathed to mortals, I think you meant to say," Liurenia replied tartly, fluttering her dove wings.

The dark energy around Malviere pulsed. Wolfe's companion narrowed her eyes and glared at Liurenia, then opened her mouth to retort.

But Wolfe beat her to it. "Let's just see what we have for other cards, we'll come back to this."

Miriam clapped her hands once. "Yeah, I want to see the other ones. What was the card that Loo lady dropped?"

Wolfe held it out and the four humans gathered around. It showed a beautiful lady, young, with Amerind features—the person they had just seen.

Loowitlatkla, Whose Face Launched A Thousand Braves
Unique Rare Equivalent, Tier-1 equivalent Mortal/Fire
[Civic] Creature
2 Mortal or 2 Fire Power, 2 Any power
Health: 23
Attack: 3
Defense: 6
Magical Attack: N/A
Magical Defense: 6

Special: **Maddening Beauty**: When this card enters the field, half (randomly chosen) of one enemy deckbearer's creatures on field will switch sides, except for Golem, Elemental, and Undead ones. They remain on the side of the deckbearer till this card leaves the field. The power of the cards that switched sides is returned to their deckbearer.

Special: **Healer [5]**: When this creature enters the field it may fully heal one other creature card or restore 5 Health to a deckbearer

Special: Dungeon Exchange: This card *may* be exchanged at the end of Loowitlatkla's Fall

"Loowit was once an old woman of such heart and kindness

that the gods granted her eternal life. But she requested beauty to go along with it, and that was a different story."

"I aspire to be this spirit," Miriam said, then stood. She struck a pose in the middle of the clearing they were in, her arms akimbo, black-dress-hugged body on display. "Think I could make two of you fight over me?"

Wolfe rolled his eyes, and Derek snorted. Shel just ignored her.

"Anyway, it's pretty interesting," Miriam said with a drawl as she sat back down and grabbed some of the berries from the stone slab filled with food. "The card is potentially very powerful, but it costs a lot of power and it can be undone moderately easily. Not as good as the Arch, certainly."

"*Well*, that's because it's a rare and you're comparing it to a *mythic*," Wolfe said.

Miriam shrugged and aped his voice for her first word. "*Well*, I'm still a tad underwhelmed. But who cares. let's just skip to the fun part and see what drops from the packs."

Wolfe pulled out the card packs they had gotten.

Each of the card packs had stylized picture of a fish and a bird of prey, each composed of black-and-white lines and shapes rather than being a composite whole. It was vaguely Aztec, but Wolfe wouldn't have bet anything he cared to lose on the image's cultural origins.

Written across each pack in English were the words "Cycle of the Fifth Sun, Twilight." Two were labeled common, one uncommon, and one rare.

"Wow," Shel said, pulling her phone out and typing at it.

"Pretty sure this is a zero-bars location," Wolfe said. "The gods don't provide Wi-Fi passwords."

"I downloaded a lot of information into my phone, including set releases and known cards," Shel said absently as she scrolled, through a document and not the internet, apparently.

"Here it is—The Cycle of the Fifth Sun, Twilight. Released in 1510. The second to last time a new world set was released exclusively in Central and North America. It was known as a set with a much higher rate of enhancers as specialty cards, and had a large number of unique creatures granted in dungeons and from roaming monsters."

"Well, let's see what we get," Wolfe said. He passed the card packs over to Shel.

"Why me?" Shel asked, taking them.

"Your perk for opening better packs," Wolfe replied.

"It only works for Mortal and Divine packs, basically," Shel said, then held them back. "You open them. You have the Caretaker of the Lost card, remember? You might get an orphan out of it."

"Does that mean the gods would make new cards?" Miriam asked suddenly, leaning forward. "I mean... there weren't even orphan cards that far back."

"Maybe they'll just give us one from the current set?" Wolfe asked.

"I hope this means new cards," Miriam said. "That would be so cool. Even if it's just a common, it's also kinda a unique."

"Yeah," Shel responded.

Wolfe took the card packs and opened them. The common packs produced eleven commons and an uncommon, the uncommon two uncommon cards and four commons, and the rare pack gave two commons, two uncommon cards, and *two* rare cards.

But no orphans. He snorted after going through them all, and Miriam giggled, probably guessing what he was snorting at.

He then sorted them into piles—Mortal, Beast, Undead,

Infernal, Divine, Light, and then one big pile for everything else, to match their types.

"No Psychic cards at all, huh?" Miriam asked.

Wolfe shook his head no. "No Meta either, although no one here uses those."

Then he held out the Mortal cards. There were a couple common Mortal creatures, one of which was a 'tribal pathfinder' that was incredibly weak but allowed pulling *any* other Civic card from the deck and immediately playing it for its normal cost.

Shel briefly gave thought to it but passed.

Then there was an uncommon mortal and Nature enhancer that showed a man on an altar, his chest open, blood pouring down into plants around the altar. It gave Nature cards a boost but required a Mortal card to be turned into a null card.

"So, no Mortal cards that are useful to me at all, really," Shel said.

"Sorry," Wolfe said.

He glanced at the Beast cards as well, of which there were four. Two were 'Cautious Deer' which were very weak but ignored the first attack against them and could be sacrificed for health. The third was a 'Fish-filled River' persistent that cost only one Beast power and made all Mortal cards cost one less power if their cost started between two and four. Wolfe didn't care about any of those. But the last one was quite interesting to him.

It showed a hairless dog that vaguely reminded Wolfe of a whippet, staring with glowing eyes.

Xolo Spirit-Warder
Uncommon Tier-1 Beast [Canine] Creature
2 Beast Power
Health: 7

Attack: 2
Defense: 3
Magical Attack: N/A
Magical Defense: 3

Special: **Delicacy**: Sacrifice this card to heal a deckbearer for ten health. This power may only be triggered once per day.
Special: **Protection from Undead:** All other allied creatures gain +100% Defense and Magical Defense against undead.
Special: **Death, Undead Immunity**: This creature is immune to all undead and death damage.

"The Xolo Spirit-Warder is a dog that protects mortals from the many undead terrors. It's also a delicacy served at funerals."

"That's pretty weak, and a lot of the time you won't be able to sacrifice it, because of Cerberus' Home for Wayward Hellhounds," Shel said.

Wolfe nodded. "For sure. But as a side-deck creature card, there are situations where it could be *really* useful, and a solid portion of my deck empowers it. I mean, it's a specific deck counter *dog*. I couldn't ask for a better uncommon."

"Your pack grows," Malviere muttered, giving Liurenia the side-eye.

"Well, I, for one, think this dog's anti-undead bias is reprehensible," Miriam said with a pompous air and swirl of an imaginary wineglass. Then she giggled.

Wolfe rolled his own eyes, but he was smiling. He was happy to see Miriam happy, and excited that a card was finally for him.

But he was more excited to see what else there was on offer.

There were two undead cards—a common card called a

'Camazotz Bat' that was a one-power Undead and Beast creature that was a vampire as well.

The second was the rare card. It was called Last Messenger of Camazotz, and was a medium-weak four-power vampire creature card that, when it entered, allowed an immediate play, at zero power, of a second vampire card of three power or less.

Wolfe sighed, and handed it over to Miriam, who clapped her hands and took it. "Can I also get the cute bat please?"

Wolfe handed that over as well, wondering if the books between him and Miriam would ever balance. Although helping the last living child of the man who had saved him, and whom Wolfe had failed to save, was a worthwhile goal in itself. He let it go.

There was only *one* Infernal card, although it was also an uncommon and a Beast card. For a brief moment, Wolfe was excited.

Tezcatlipocan Smoke Jaguar
Uncommon Tier-1 Infernal/Beast [Feline] Creature
1 Infernal, 1 Beast, 3 Any Power
Health: 25
Attack: 6 x3
Defense: 5
Magical Attack: 4[**Death**]
Magical Defense: 4

Special: **Incorporeal:** This creature does not take damage from non-energy sources.
Special: **Dual Attack**: When this creature makes a physical attack, it also makes a Magical Attack on the same target.
Special: **Tribal [Feline]:** +1 Attack for every [Feline] card on the battlefield

"Offspring of a normal Jaguar and the mighty beasts that

Tezcatlipoca sent to slay the beings that once lived under the first sun."

"That's like one of your Angry Hellhounds on steroids," Shel said. "I mean, for five power, its stats are grossly weak, but it makes *six* attacks on a single target every time it attacks. A few buffs and that thing would be insane."

"Yeah, but unless I'm gonna switch over to a cat deck"— Cereboo whined—"which I'm not, it's barely better than one of the Angry Hellhounds and takes *five* power. Not really helpful to me."

Shel nodded. "True."

There was a single Divine card—which was also a Light card.

Couatl of the Second Sun

Uncommon Tier-1 Divine / Light [Couatl, Civic, Sun, Ascendant] Creature
1 Divine, 1 Light, 2 Any Power
Health: 20
Attack: 3
Defense: 8
Magical Attack: 10[**Light**]
Magical Defense: 10

Special: **Guardian of Propriety:** Control of any other Mortal or Divine card may not be taken from the deckbearer while they control this card on the field
Special: **Ascendant Metropolis [1]:** For every [Civic], Divine, or Light Building

keyword in the deck, and every [Civic], Divine, or Light persistent card keyword on the field, this card gains +1 to its Defense and Magical Defense.

"The Second Sun was an age of prosperity, guided by Quetzalcoatl, until mortals drifted from religious propriety."

"Wow," Shel said. "That synergizes *really* well with my deck. Like really well. I didn't even know this card was a thing, from my prior research."

"Well, it was a card from a geographically exclusive set from over five hundred years ago," Wolfe said as he handed it over to her.

They moved on to the next cards.

Light had done well in general—it had two more commons and the other rare as well.

Hint of the Sixth Sun
Rare Tier-1 Light [Sun, Ruin] Persistent
2 Light Power

Sixty seconds after this card enters, every non-undead creature on the field that belongs to a deckbearer is reduced to zero health.
Thereafter, the deckbearer controlling this card can play creatures at 1 less of any type of power cost. If a card would go to zero power, it instead costs 1 (available) any power.
"What will come in the age of the Sixth Sun is anyone's guess."

"Wow, if there was anyone with a powerful mixed Light and Undead deck, this card would be insanely amazing," Miriam muttered. "I'm almost tempted."

"You play *vampires*," Shel said with a laugh. "Really doubt you'll find more than five cards in all of existence that have a useful synergy with both types."

Miriam rolled her eyes.

"It was just a thought."

There was only one other Divine card—a Baby Couatl, which was a one-power creature that could be sacrificed to bring out any other card, up to four power, with Couatl in the keywords.

Shel hemmed and hawed, but decided that she didn't have enough Couatls to justify it.

There were three Fire cards. One was a common low-damage immediate that Wolfe ignored, but the last two were also interesting.

Burned Sacrifice
Uncommon Tier-1 Fire Immediate
1 Fire Power

Sacrifice any Mortal or Beast card. Immediately play from deck or sidedecks any one Infernal or Divine creature or persistent of four power or less.

"Many gods answer to the fire that burns in the chest cavity."
—anonymous Aztec Deckbearer

"Wow," Wolfe said. "That card is... dark. But it could be hugely useful for me."

"If I do put the Stone Arch Fire in my deck, it could also be extremely useful for me," Shel said.

"As would this one," Wolfe said, holding it out.

Friendly Campfire
Common Tier-1 Fire/Life [Civic] Persistent
1 Fire or 1 Life power

While this card is in play, Fire type immediate or Persistent cards that do damage may be used to heal [as true healing] any target instead. This cannot affect any deckbearer more than once per twenty-four hours. All **Food** or **Delicacy** special effects are doubled.

They all stared at the cards. Wolfe had his Xolo Spirit-Warder in front of him, Miriam had her Camazotz Bat and Last Messenger of Camazotz cards, and Shel had the Mythic Stone Arch Fire, the Couatl of the Second Sun, the Burned Sacrifice, and the Friendly Campfire.

"What do we get if we trade in the Loowit cards?" Miriam asked.

"Didn't it say we had to wait to the end of the dungeon?" Derek asked.

Shel nodded to the trader, who had finished setting up. "Pretty sure that this guy can trade now, because we won the special contest."

"Then I can pick my perks?" Shel asked.

Wolfe nodded. "Yeah, we'll get you sorted out for sure, sorry. This is like when I picked mine—let's see our cards, then check your perks, then get your final form, so to speak, worked out."

Shel stood from the stone slab, wiping meat grease on her pants. "Alright, let's go see what he has to offer."

CHAPTER 14

THE THREE SPIRITS, PART V

W olfe wiped his hands on the grass and then stood as well. He was fully healed from the meal, and felt rested and pleasantly full. The evening air was cool and pleasant around him.

He walked over to the trader, followed by most of his team. The trader was patiently sitting cross-legged with a nice wooden board in front of him. On the board were multiple cards, but when Wolfe tried to look at them, the images swam in his vision.

Wolfe frowned. *Cute trick, gods.*

"So, what can we trade you?" Wolfe asked.

The trader smiled amiably. "If you have any Loowitlatkla, Pahto, or Wy'east cards, I can exchange them here."

"Just four cards?" Wolfe asked, assuming that the chieftain's sons would only have a card each, unlike Loowitlatkla.

"If you have any Loowitlatkla, Pahto, or Wy'east cards, I can exchange them here," the trader said, his smile unchanging.

"Joy," Wolfe muttered, then tried something else. "What cards do we get for trading?"

Barely more than an animatronic doll, the trader repeated, "If you have any Loowitlatkla, Pahto, or Wy'east cards, I can exchange them here."

"Now who's making the NPCs repeat themselves?" Miriam asked with a laugh.

Wolfe growled out, "I thought that might get an actual answer, but apparently we need to trade and just see."

"Trade the 'Face who launched' version," Shel said suddenly. "I don't think it synergizes that well."

Wolfe held the card out, and the trader reached out. The second he touched the card, it shifted, and he pulled his hand back again with nothing in it.

"Thank you, hero!" the trader said in a cheery voice.

Shel, Miriam, and Derek all crowded around the new card.

Spirit of Mount St. Helens
Unique Legendary equivalent Tier-1 equivalent Fire/Life Enhancer
0 Power

This card adds 1 Fire power to the deckbearer. This person will have their weight doubled for purposes of resisting being moved. +20% lifespan.

If the Spirit of Mount Hood and the Spirit of Mount Adams are also both in the deck, it adds an additional +5 Health, +2 Defense, and an additional +40% lifespan.

"After the destruction, Chief Tyee changed all three participants into mountains. Loowitlatkla became Mount St. Helens, her life-giving fire with her always."

"That's solid," Miriam said. "Very solid. A Fire power, which would make it way easier to use the Arch or other cards. And I need to get some lifespan cards myself for sure. Shit, that'll probably be worth an extra seventy years, given how old you are, Shel."

Shel twirled her finger in her hair. "It's only truly amazing if I also get a point of Life power, really. Or rely on the Friendly Campfire. I mean, I need ten leveling pips to be able to put Artenia in my deck, so that makes it a bit of a challenge to get all the things we're looking at in place."

"Imagine if you did, though," Miriam said excitedly, putting her arms over Shel's shoulders and then lightly stroking Shel's red hair. "You'd have *five* power types, which all synergize at least a bit—Mortal, Divine, Light, Life, and Fire. You could get some crazy cards with those combinations, rare shit that would be way less expensive since it required such specific things." Miriam leaned in closer, her mouth inches from Shel's ear. "You'd become one of the greatest deckbearers ever."

Shel shrugged her off, slightly red in the face.

Miriam giggled again. "Do you think the other two spirits are the brothers? And that we can get them at the end of the dungeon? I bet they are."

"Probably," Wolfe said. "I don't think we would have seen them if this was a multi-dungeon quest."

"I really want to get those cards. The spirit mountains, I mean," Shel said. "Also to see what other cards we could get. This dungeon has been insanely valuable to us. Like insanely."

"It's been pretty good to me," Miriam said. "But not insanely good."

Wolfe nodded. "Yeah, it's been good to us all. Although a lot of that came from being over-level and beating the special. We aren't going to be able to just waltz through the next floor like we did this one."

Shel laughed. "I saw you get kicked into a wall."—

Derek interrupted with a shudder. "And I nearly died."

Shel continued. "It was hardly a waltz."

"Do you want me to trade the last one in?" Wolfe asked, moving on from the argument he was pretty sure he would lose.

Shel focused inward for a moment, biting her lip in thought. Then she nodded. "Yeah, I don't think the abilities will be enough to justify keeping it, especially since I won't use many fire cards that need to worry about losing control of regardless."

Wolfe handed it over and went through the ritual again.

He got back a new card—a mantle.

Stone Circle Fire Tender
Rare Tier-1 Fire/Life [Civic] Mantle
1 Fire or 1 Life power

All other Civic Cards gain +2 to all non-health stats.

If the Stone Arch Fire is in the deck, all healing powers are doubled and may target any entity.

"Those that tended the Stone Arch Fire were the heart of the numerous Cowlitz tribes."

"Is that better than the Resilient Martyr?" Wolfe asked, staring at it.

"Maybe?" Shel said. "I mean... it's very different. No stats, and no self-healing. But it adds stats to my various civic cards, like the Rookie SWAT, and then that will double some day from all the angels and stuff. I could go for it, especially if I do decide on the Stone Arch Fire build."

Wolfe nodded, then put all the cards down. "Well, we

know what cards we have, for the moment... and have some idea of what we'll get going forward in the dungeon. I think you should pick your perks now."

Shel nodded.

"But first, can we see your deckbearer stats?"

Shel nodded and pulled up her stats on her phone, showing them to Wolfe and Miriam.

Rachel Lyons Status:
Level 28 Deckbearer (14 Levels pending)

Deckbearer Perks:
Lost and Lonely God-gifted Start: +1 Companion card

Deckbearer Perk 1: Divine Favor: When pulling from a Mortal or Divine pack, one random card will be a rarity higher. If pulling from a mixed deck, at least one card will be either Mortal or Divine.

Deckbearer Perk 2: Guiding Light of the Divine: Gain 1 Light Power. May have one extra card in play so long as it's a Mortal (Any EMT, Police, or card with the 'Civic' subtype).

Deckbearer Flaw: Pacifist: May not gain attack from mantles

Deckbearer Stats:
Cards in Deck: 15 (1 pip)
Cards in Hand: 4 (1 pip)
Cards in Play: 3 (1 pip)
Length of Play: 5 minutes

Specialty Cards:
Companion: 2 (5 pips)
Minion: 1 (1 pip)
Enhancer: 1 (1 pip)
Type 1 and Power: 1 Divine
Type 2 and Power: 3 Mortal (3 pips)
Energy 1 and Power: 1 Light

Personal Perks:
Inborn Perk 1: Small: -1 Attack

Acquired Perk 1: Police Training: +1 Attack and
Defense. Does not stack with other training.

Acquired Perk 2: Expert Shooter: +3 Attack and
Defense only when using firearms. Does not stack
with other training.

Personal Stats:
Health: 20
Attack: 5(7)
Magical Attack [None]: 0
Defense: 6(8)
Magical Defense [None]: 5

Wolfe stared for a moment. "So, no matter what, you
could either add a companion slot for Artenia, or you could
add a Life power if you need."

Shel smiled up at him. "And I already have the enhancer
slot for the mountain, but it'll take five more leveling pips to
add slots for the next two if we—I—go down that route. And
a building slot would cost five more pips. It's a challenge to do
everything, regardless of what specific path I choose first."

Her eyes fuzzed out for a moment, and then she started

reading out loud. Wolfe did his best to focus, and for once, everyone else did as well—even Miriam wasn't quipping.

Civic Pride: The deckbearer counts as a [Civic] sub-type and [Police] and [City-Guard] keywords herself and gains the legendary 'Agent Geared' card, which will create a side deck for civic equipment cards that can be summoned and distributed below power cost. Gain 1 Legendary Mortal equipment card pack.

Precious Martyr: The deckbearer gains +10 Health. Every time this person is wounded, all allied cards gain +50% to all non-health stats for the round.

Divine Entourage: Gain one companion slot, and Divine companions don't count against cards on field.

Master of the Lost and the Lonely: Orphans gain +1 Tier when they switch over, and any card packs or non-orphan cards gained from orphan advancement are gained twice. Any one [evolved orphan] card of no more than 2 power may be treated as if it were a free-slot companion card with a 0-power cost.

Nurse of the Chosen: Gain 1 Life Power, and the first time per week any entity is healed by this deckbearer, they lose 1 injury level as well. Gain 2 Legendary Life packs from any set that is represented in the deckbearer's deck.

"Those are some impressive perks," Wolfe said.

Shel blinked her eyes and then looked at him. "Yeah, some of those are amazing. I can't believe I got offered the Master of the Lost and the Lonely as well."

"Probably shouldn't take it," Wolfe said. "I mean, I can already work on making sure that the orphans are being raised up when we get them."

Shel slowly nodded. "I can see builds around all of this... I mean, I was hoping I'd get the companion option. That will save me a good fifteen leveling pips, which is huge."

"Yeah," Wolfe said, then reached over and grabbed another cut of cooked goat from the slab. Derek had finished eating, and sat back with a sigh.

Shel was still talking. "But... being able to heal injuries is also huge. And since we just got a lot of cards that could benefit from me having Life power, including a mythic, well, that power is also kinda a big deal. And two Legendary packs is huge... I'd instantly be a powerful Life deckbearer as well."

Wolfe nodded, his own mind mulling over all the possibilities.

"No, you want power," Miriam said with certainty, and without her usual banter. "The Civic one gives you that. Plus two, modified by your other stats, and then nearly doubled, is insane."

"*You* want that," Shel said. "I've got Wolfe, so nothing bad will happen to me. I can afford to be a healer, or have my angels."

"Wolfe might not be around to protect you some day," Miriam said. "And those are some permanent upgrades, even if minor, you can't normally get. Combined with the new mantle, your Civic cards could do insane damage."

Shel was biting her lip. "Maybe..."

Then she turned to Wolfe. "What do you think I should take?"

CHAPTER 15

BECOME THE RINGBEARER

"I think you shouldn't worry about me or Miriam," Wolfe said. "Do what your soul calls you to do."

"In my soul, I want to be the light to your dark," Shel said. "You once told me that it was my job to save people. I guess I like our roles. You slay those that would break people, keep me safe... and I heal the broken ones. Maybe it's not the strongest path, or the smartest. It probably isn't. But it's the one that calls to me the most."

"Then why did you become a police officer?" Miriam asked, sounding more curious than judgmental.

"I could do so right away, or near enough," Shel said. "Being a nurse, or more so, a doctor, takes a long time. Plus, officers still save people, and can respond to emergencies as well. Plus, I don't want to be hopelessly weak, I just don't want to make my entire focus around fighting people."

"So, are you going to alter your deck, then?" Wolfe asked.

"Let me think about it a bit," Shel said. "I mean, I want to, but I want to think about the leveling specifics a bit more. I think we should see how the rest of this dungeon turns out before I pick leveling perks and finalize my cards for a while."

"I'm gonna add the Xolo Spirit-Warder into my subdeck, in place of the Chain Demon," Wolfe said.

"For me, I'm just gonna add the Camazotz to my deck now. I think it already fits, and requires no leveling pips," Miriam said.

"Alright, well, with those less-than massive changes, I think we should take a break," Wolfe said.

"Boo!" Miriam called out excitedly. "We're kicking ass. We just handled a Level Twenty-Eight encounter! We could go all the way!"

"That's what she said?" Shel asked with a chuckle.

Miriam paused. "By the gods, I can't believe I didn't do that intentionally. I'm losing game."

Wolfe cut in. "Look, I want to switch in Liam for Derek—apologies, man, but I need him to get some levels too."

"Yeah, no, don't even worry about it," Derek said, smiling at Wolfe with perfect white teeth. "You told me one floor and gave me two and I made over ten levels. I'm crazy excited, thank you. Heck, I'll probably be picking my own level twenty-five perks soon at this rate."

"Boo!" Miriam called again, but she was half-laughing. "We can do it!"

"Hey, fair's fair," Wolfe said, as casually as he could. "You got some great cards. Speaking of which, I have some chores I want to do. Can you take Shel home with you?"

"Home with Miriam?" Shel asked, baffled. "What chores do you have?"

"Just some stuff I need to take care of," Wolfe said nonchalantly, rubbing his hand through his short hair.

"Why didn't you tell me before we left?" Shel asked.

"Look, I don't do this often, can I just take the truck and have Miriam take you home?" Wolfe asked.

"I mean, yeah, that's totally fine," Shel said. "Sorry, I wasn't trying to nag, just confused."

"Thanks," Wolfe said. "I appreciate it. Also, please, keep Fern with you. I owe you one."

"Nah, I think some girl time together could be great," Shel said, smiling at Miriam.

"Ah yeah," Miriam said. "We'll hit all the clubs."

"Or we could talk in your club," Shel said.

"Fine, fine, ya killjoy. We'll just hang at my club."

"Well, you two work it out. I'm sure between you, you can have fun without breaking something serious. But let's get out of here, I have something I need to do."

Something I have no idea how to do.

"Mrs. Timo!" Wolfe shouted as he banged the giant front door of the Hellmouth Institute open. "Mrs. Timo!"

"I'm in here, Wolfe. No need to shout," Mrs. Timo said from the room she used to receive the ten or so non-government clients they'd had since they opened their P.I. business.

Wolfe walked in. She was behind the computer again, leaned back, moving the mouse slowly and occasionally clicking something. A glass of water was beading on the infernal-themed desk the computer was on. It looked like she had barely sipped at it.

Wolfe frowned. *She's playing solitaire again. On the other hand, I haven't given her any work, and the girls aren't home from school yet, so...*

He shook his head. It didn't matter, and he had other things to ask.

"You were married once, right?" Wolfe asked.

Mrs. Timo looked up from the computer. Normally, her sun-dried skin looked like it was set in permanent laugh lines, and she smiled easily. But at the moment, one eyebrow was up.

She lowered her glasses and stared over the rim at him. "So, what brought this up."

"Never mind that," Wolfe said, waving off the question. "Just, were you married?"

"Yes, of course," she said. "We didn't do the whole out-of-wedlock thing in my time."

Wolfe laughed mirthlessly. "I'm pretty sure your time was still after the sixties, and they certainly did that then. But again, never mind. Just tell me this: how did your husband propose to you?"

"Ol' Jack?" she smiled in reminiscence, settling back in her chair again but still staring at Wolfe over the rim of her glasses. "Well, it was very romantic. He took me out on his boat, you know. I thought he was going to spend some time fishing with me, but instead, when he opened up his tackle box, there was a ring. He got down on his knees right there and held it out to me."

"It was romantic when the ring was in the bait with his fish?" Wolfe asked.

"Well, we were both in the fish business, way back in the day. That's how we met, in fact, you jumped-up hooligan," Mrs. Timo said.

Wolfe frowned. "You don't use the word 'hooligan,' normally. You're just playing around. I really need to know."

Mrs. Timo rolled her eyes again. "I was telling the truth. I was trying to say that it was romantic to me, or at least special in that it referenced how we'd first met. I guess that's what's important—it needs to be romantic or special to Shel."

"I didn't say anything about Shel," Wolfe replied.

"Sure, hon, whatever you say. I won't tell Shel, don't worry."

Wolfe glanced around in panic. "Shh! Stop saying it out loud, you old bat."

Mrs. Timo laughed. "Good thing you pay me to play solitaire with a mouth like that. Most people would take offense."

Wolfe felt his frustration rising—he hated being in situations where 'being able to punch someone' didn't establish who was polite to who.

But he tried—Mrs. Timo was a nice old bat. Even if she was one. "Sorry. I'll keep it together better. But if we're talking about this, um, theoretical situation, then I'd like to ask, theoretically, what you think Shel would like."

Mrs. Timo picked up her glass of water, frowned at it, and then gave it a wipe with a handkerchief she pulled from a pocket. *Who still uses handkerchiefs?*

"Well, where did you meet? Maybe you could propose to her there," Mrs. Timo said, taking a sip of her water.

Wolfe's mind briefly jumped to the Snakebite Club where he had killed the Cobra lieutenant Frankie.

"I, um, kinda burned it to the ground," Wolfe replied.

Mrs. Timo laughed, sucked water into some part it didn't belong, coughed, and sprayed water across the computer screen in a fine mist. She kept coughing and laughing, half-choking, while trying to dab the water away from the screen with her already damp handkerchief. Wolfe ran over and pounded her back, not knowing what else to do.

"Stop," Mrs. Timo coughed again and waved her arms at Wolfe. "Stop hitting me. Hurts worse than the water in my lungs. I'm a frail old bat, dammit, remember?"

Wolfe took a step back. "Yeah, sorry, I was trying to help."

Mrs. Timo ignored him. "Also, I can't help but say—of course you burned it to the ground."

"Haha," Wolfe said deadpan. "But seriously, what other advice do you have?"

"The same advice. Just find something special to both of you, and build your proposal around that. I mean, you're over six feet, you have way more than six figures, and I'm sure you're—"

She pointed vaguely at his groin.

"I'm not talking about that with someone's grandma," Wolfe ground out.

"Whatever. You aren't the worst-looking, either. I'm sure if you just manage not to completely muck it up Shel will be happy to marry you. Just go get a great ring and do it halfway right."

"I don't want to do it *halfway* right. Maybe you're onto something, but Shel deserves more than my usual stupid-ass way of doing these things. I need a better proposal than anything I've thought of so far."

"Okay, *how* did you meet?"

"We haven't told you that story in the whole year you've been here?" Wolfe asked, scratching his head. "Well, um, I saved her from getting a different kind of six—six feet under."

"Always with the cringy one-liner," Mrs. Time said. Then it was her turn to scratch her head. "Well, I doubt 'saving her life' is a reasonably duplicable situation, so I guess it'll need to be something else."

Wolfe frowned. "Well, what about the ring?"

"I know how much you have in the bank," Mrs. Timo said. "More importantly, Shel knows how much you have. Big ol' rock."

"Right, right. Where can I get a good ring?"

Mrs. Timo rolled her eyes at him. "For that, you have the internets."

"Some secretary you are."

CHAPTER 16

BECOMING THE RINGBEARER, PART II

Wolfe was back in his old stomping ground—well, really, he was back in Big Man Grimm's old stomping ground. His old stomping ground had been a lot poorer, but he had spent a day or two every week in the ritzy, high-priced district where the Ekron Eternal was located.

Which was apparently where all the other high-end pastimes and shopping were located as well.

He eyed the Gavin's Card sign above him again—it was the same billboard, and the same company, that had been advertising by the back entrance to the Ekron Eternal two years ago when Wolfe had first gotten his deck on Drop Night. The actual sign had changed, and now showed an evolved orphan Mortal/Angel fighting an Imp Lord, the deckbearer in the background. Not quite as understated as most ads for the card auction company, but still well done.

But Wolfe wasn't here for cards *or* for the Ekron Eternal, although he thought it ironic that he was a mere couple blocks from Shel. He had been tempted to park in the Ekron Eternal garage, but didn't want to chance alerting her to what he was about.

So, he found himself in the parking lot of *Michelle's*, the most famous high-end jewelry store in Noimoire, if the internet had any idea what it was talking about. It occupied a fairly small storefront, maybe seventy or so feet—which would be big for some places, but felt small for a 'most famous in—' type of place.

A low, mournful warble came from the bed of his truck behind him, and Wolfe turned to Cereboo. "I'll be back, buddy. Just give me a few minutes to get this ring—hang out with Malviere, okay?"

Cereboo warbled again, but settled into the bed as Wolfe walked toward the jewelry store.

There was a man in a suit waiting out front, however, and Wolfe's eyes automatically tracked to the slight bulge that was likely a gun in a chest holster under the suit. The man's eyes tracked over Wolfe for a second as Wolfe walked up, but then slid away with disinterest.

Wolfe snorted. Given a choice, he dressed casual, ate casual, and pretty much tried to do everything in a fairly pedestrian manner. He associated upscale things with either his father, whom he still had dark memories of, or Big Man Grimm, whom he had once deeply respected but who represented a lifestyle he was trying to leave.

But Wolfe knew what he needed to look like to blend in with the crowd. He had put a suit on, shaved down to the slightest hint of stubble, combed his hair, and put a nice watch on, even though everyone used their phones and the watch was a blatant affectation.

But it was expected, and a nice suit was camouflage. No one suspected the guy in the suit was a criminal, ever, and men like the fancy security guard at the door might as well be blind for all they could see past a man's clothes.

Wolfe's sardonic musings were cut short as the man in the suit reached over, grabbed the door, and opened it. "Welcome to Michelle's, sir. I hope you find what your heart desires."

Wolfe laughed, running the jingle he had just heard on their website through his head. *Michelle's... where you find her heart's desire.*

Spoken in a husky female voice, of course.

As Wolfe walked into the store, he was confronted by a veritable piece of art, or perhaps the display room of the treasury of a particularly vain deckbearer champion from the medieval era.

The store had almost fifteen-foot-tall ceilings from which hung numerous complex crystal chandeliers. The windows on two of the walls were clear glass, almost floor-to-ceiling but not quite. They had a rounded top and were sub-divided into smaller windows, looking like the stained-glass story windows of a church of Uriel he had once been to, except they were made of clear glass.

But the ceiling and walls paled in comparison to the contents of the floor. Multiple display cases, each layered with ever smaller circles, like a wedding cake, decorated the floor in a honeycomb pattern. And on each of the ostentatious display tables were hundreds of pieces of jewelry, whose price tags, on the bottom most rung of each display case, started somewhere around 'this month's mortgage,' cruised through 'or you could have a car,' and ended on the very top somewhere around 'would you prefer a legendary card?'

Most of it was diamond jewelry, but by no means all of it.

Along the walls were a group of huge, brooding guards, and wandering the floor were a group of young, beautiful women and a few distinguished-looking men. A couple of them were guiding a few old couples, and one douche-bag-looking man in his thirties, around the display cases, but most were just waiting.

As Wolfe stared at the insane display of decadence around him, one of the waiting women, who was even more alluring than the jewelry, walked up to him. She had long blonde hair, a lithe, youthful body, and a black dress that was nearly spraypainted on, revealing nothing but hinting strongly at everything all the same.

"May I help you find something, sir?" she asked, her voice more upbeat and perky than Cereboo after the time he had drunk an entire can of Red Bull.

Wolfe was a hundred percent into Shel, and had also seen a ton of pretty girls in his life, clothed or otherwise. It still legit took him half a second to tear his gaze from the woman and stare into her face—it took an insane amount of money to look that sexy and not cheap, but she had pulled it off.

But Michelle's could afford the best. It was well known, whether in Wolfe's old line of work or the absolute upper ends of the jet set, that a beautiful woman moved product fast.

"I, um, I'm looking for an engagement ring," Wolfe said.

"Excellent, sir!" the woman said, giving him a hundred-watt smile. "What is your price range?"

"Just show me some good rings," Wolfe growled, irritated with the question.

"Of course, sir, right this way," the woman said without missing a beat or allowing her smile to falter.

She put her hand on his arm, which Wolfe pulled away from her, and then, again without missing a beat, led him over to the first display table.

This lady is as good at her job as I am at mine, Wolfe thought, tempted to leave for a more accessible store with someone a bit less over-matched against him in selling skills.

But he didn't leave. He wanted the best for Shel, and this was apparently where that was found.

He stared briefly at a two-million-dollar necklace. *The*

reasonable best. Pretty sure she'd be mad if I spent that much on a ring anyway.

"Here are our most popular diamond engagement rings," the girl said, motioning vaguely to the table. "Cheaper ones are on the bottom, and the more expensive ones near the top."

"Uh-huh," Wolfe said non-committedly.

She just kept going, now pointing to specific pieces. "You'll find collections from the Summer Flower set, work from Alvond, and even some from Michelle's very own artists here, on these shelves. Over here we have..."

Wolfe tuned her out, letting her perky voice become little more than elevator music.

He didn't want a ring because it was brand name or had a famous designer, and didn't think that would matter to Shel either. Instead, he looked at the rings, trying to feel for one that would be special.

How do you capture the essence of a wonderful, amazing woman whose life you saved, but who in turn gave you a reason to live and grow? Wolfe couldn't help but wonder. *What the hell kind of diamond symbolizes all that?*

Each of them had been a pivotal point in the other's growth, and each had moved on to a near completely new life after finding the other. Not just a new life together, but new ways of doing things, new goals for themselves. Everything had been different.

For both of them, that difference had been pivotal to a better life.

The diamonds, meanwhile, all looked the same to Wolfe. Not literally the sane—some were shaped like hearts, some had a huge central stone, some were clusters of smaller ones, and many were surrounded by other stones. The bands were different metals, and different thicknesses.

But it still seemed utterly banal to Wolfe. There was still a sameness. They looked like every stone some enforcer's girl had shoved under Wolfe's nose, the same as every commercial Wolfe had ever seen for an engagement ring.

They didn't match Shel, either in personality or, for that matter, against her coloration—her fiery red hair, her brilliant green eyes.

The lady touched his arm, and Wolfe started, realizing he hadn't heard her talking for a few seconds. As he tried to run her prattle back through his head, he realized she had asked him a question, from the tone of her last words.

"What?" he asked, wincing.

"I'm sorry, I was asking if these stones are not to your satisfaction," she asked. "You've been frowning at the display the whole time. Perhaps you could give me a bit of guidance into what you're looking for?"

"Something... different," Wolfe said, aware of how inadequate that sounded. He tried to clarify. "Different from normal, I mean. Not just different than these stones here."

She smiled again. "Well, although diamonds are the most preferred main stones for an engagement ring, they are certainly not the only option. A few people prefer other gems. We have small selection of emerald engagement rings, if you'd like to peruse that."

Wolfe thought back to his earlier musings. *At least they'll match Shel's eyes.*

"Yeah, let's see those."

The lady hesitated. "I must warn you, sir, that the emerald engagement rings tend to be a bit pricier, and we have none of the cheapest tier."

"Did I ask, girl?" Wolfe growled out, immediately irritated at the subtle assertion he might not belong here. "Just take me to the emeralds."

Again without the tiniest crack in her smile, or the tiniest hesitation, the woman walked smoothly across the floor. "Of course, sir, right this way."

Wolfe was led past a couple where the wife was oohing and aahing over various pieces of jewelry, and whose husband was typing away on a cellphone, to one of the massive display tables on the outer edge of the floor. It seemed to be an 'odds and ends' table, with multiple smaller collections of jewelry.

"Here is our collection of emerald engagement rings, sir. I hope you find one to your liking."

Wolfe stared at them. They did feel more 'right' to him, but at first, none truly called to him. But as he looked around, he saw one that had the least complex of Raphael's symbols on it—a heart with dove wings, in this case, all made from tiny emeralds, with a large one set in the center.

"May I see that one, please?" Wolfe asked, pointing.

"An excellent suggestion, sir," the lady said. "Since Raphael is one of the archangels that is considered a patron of marriage, in its capacity to bring people together and create joy, along with—"

"The ring, please," Wolfe said, motioning to her.

She took a key from her dress—Wolfe had no idea it could store anything at all, and wasn't a hundred percent sure where it had come from—and unlocked the case. Then she gently lifted the ring out, like it might get hurt, and handed it to Wolfe.

The band was gold, and the emeralds a brilliant green, not that different from Shel's eyes.

He looked at the price sticker. Ten thousand dollars, which was half a damned car, but still pretty low for a place like this. He was pretty sure that Shel wouldn't want to him to actually spend ridiculous amounts of money on a ring anyway.

Although in his soul, he considered even this to be ridiculous for jewelry. But he wanted to do right by Shel.

"Emeralds symbolize hope, loyalty, new beginnings, and transformation, like transforming a single life—"

"They symbolize transformation and new beginnings, specifically?" Wolfe asked. "Seriously?"

She nodded.

"Who decides this stuff?" Wolfe asked.

"I... I don't know," the lady said, finally caught a touch flat-footed. Then she rallied. "But it's been the same associations all three years I've worked here, and Michelle's doesn't make errors in these matters, sir."

Good enough.

"I'll take it," Wolfe said, fishing in his pants and pulling his wallet out, then taking his debit card from its sleeve and handing it to the bemused lady.

She didn't take it, just motioning to a counter in the back. "Right this way, sir, and I know you'll be satisfied with your purchase."

Wolfe gave her one skeptical eyebrow raise. *How could you know that?* But he followed her through a veritable dragon's hoard of jewelry to the back.

She stepped to the counter and pointed to a slightly older but still gorgeous woman with hair almost the same red as Shel's that was working the back counter. "Taylor will take care of you for this last part. Thank you for allowing me to help you in your search for the perfect ring for your fiancée-to-be."

"Uh-huh," Wolfe said as Taylor wrote something down. After a few more seconds, the first lady left.

Wolfe didn't talk for a bit, hoping this was good enough for Shel. It felt right, but this whole experience had been *way* outside Wolfe's wheelhouse.

"Would you like to donate to the Chosen orphan's home?" the lady asked.

"What?" Wolfe replied. "Donate? Like to charity?"

"Yes," the lady replied. "An orphan's home."

"People are donating to orphans?" Wolfe asked.

Taylor nodded. "It's been the latest thing in charity, what with the new cards and all from the Drop Night. A lot of the well-to-do are making that their charity of choice."

Wolfe had never been much for charity. If he wanted to help someone, he would damn well help someone. He wouldn't give the money to some bureaucrat who would take most of it on the way to someone else.

Hells, he was paying to raise two near-orphans himself, right now, Shel's sister Lucy and Mrs. Timo's granddaughter Shannon. Neither were actually orphans, but since Wolfe housed them, fed them, paid for their schooling, and paid Liam to drive them around, he thought it was good enough for government work.

But... He thought it would be an extra nice gesture for Shel.

"If I pay enough, like another ten thousand, can I get a certificate or something, proof of the money going to help orphans, and put it in my future fiancée's name?"

Taylor looked taken aback by the request, but she also rallied almost immediately. Decadent or not, Wolfe had to admit this place hired and trained well.

"I'm sure we can make something that will work, sir. And be beautiful to boot."

About twenty minutes later, with the ring in his coat pocket and a certificate in a beautiful filigreed case in his *other* coat pocket, against his chest, Wolfe walked out of the store, heading for his car.

His phone buzzed, and Wolfe pulled it out.

Shel was calling.

He answered, and his blood went immediately cold. He heard screams and gunshots.

"Shel!? What's happening?" Wolfe yelled into the phone.

"They're trying to kill us!" Shel yelled back. "At the Ekron Eternal, they're trying to kill us all!"

Wolfe burst into speed, running for his car. *It's only three blocks to the Ekron Eternal!*

"*Who's* trying to kill you?" Wolfe asked as he ran.

"Everyone!" Shel answered.

CHAPTER 17

REBURN

Wolfe squealed out of the parking lot of the Michelle's jeweler, the box with the certificate a lump on his chest and his heart a hammering lump *in* his chest. Even though it was only three long blocks to the Ekron Eternal, Wolfe floored his F-150. Given his modifications, making his truck considerably heavier than the model normally was, it took over six seconds to hit sixty miles per hour. Every moment Wolfe spent pressed back in his chair as he waited ate at his sanity, his fear for Shel nearly overwhelming him.

If she's dead, I'll leave a trail of corpses through this city like it's never seen before.

Cereboo was in the bed of the truck, one foot on the hood, barking madly from all three heads. Wolfe could, at this point, hear the differences in his barks. Even when fighting, Cereboo's calls usually sounded like he was having fun. But now, his voice aligned with his deckbearer's dark thoughts, and Cereboo called a different emotion to the world.

Rage.

Malviere sat beside him in the truck, her eyes intent as she leaned forward, her own tiny fists clenched. Wolfe's first Obsessive Cultist, the one that functioned like a companion, sat in the cab behind him, completely passive as usual. Both stared out at the glitzy lights of the city as the F-150 flew down the street like a bat out of the Infernal.

Wolfe blew past cars that were going around forty-five, swerving into the other lane for a slight stretch, blowing his horn like a madman. Fortunately, it wasn't yet late enough that the upscale club and shopping district was very busy, and he wasn't as hampered by the traffic that wouldn't fully manifest for a few more hours.

Wolfe let out a dark bark of a laugh. *Plus, if I get police following me, it'll probably help. Still weird to think that, even after two years.*

But no police were anywhere in sight, and Wolfe heard no sirens.

Wolfe opened his glove compartment and took his trusty STI Edge from its container as he drove, and touched his hand to his chest, pulling his cards.

Wolfe frowned. He hadn't gotten his mantle first—of course—but his Obsessive Cultist was once again there. Wolfe summoned it into the back seat, next to the first one.

I've got my perfect portal set-up, at least, and this time I had the sense to keep the Cultist with me.

A few seconds later, the Ekron Eternal was in front of him. Wolfe slammed on the breaks and turned incredibly sharply into the parking lot, the wheels on one side of the truck briefly losing traction. Malviere grabbed the 'oh shit' bar next to the window and hung on, and the two Obsessive Cultists slammed into the inside wall of the truck behind Wolfe.

A brief, shocked bark sounded and Cereboo was launched from the back of the truck, rolling down the sidewalk in front of the Ekron Eternal and landing in some manicured bushes in front of the entrance. *Fuck, didn't think that through.*

"Sorry!" Wolfe screamed out of his window.

Wolfe got a notification that his pooch had lost half his life, and he unsummoned him. Wolfe would need him later, he was almost positive. Later... and intact.

His mind was wrenched from any further consideration by what he saw. Three men were in front of him, all dressed in leathers with the Weeds gang symbol on the back, each one slightly hunched as they watched the front entrance. But they whirled around as Wolfe came screeching into the parking lot, bringing up gods-damned *submachine guns* and pointing them at Wolfe.

And they didn't hesitate for a second. Wolfe's windshield was suddenly a mass of spiderweb cracks.

But Wolfe neither so much as flinched nor hesitated himself. Despite having almost no visibility, he gunned it, and followed the vague shapes he could see through his busted front window. One of the thugs, dumber than your average turtle, actually tried standing in place and just shooting. He met the bumper of the modified F-150 and disappeared without a fuss.

Of the remaining two, one of the Weeds ran toward to Wolfe's left, for the decorative vampire statues and bushes, and the other thug leapt over the metal railing onto the ramp that normally kept the lines of people waiting to get into the Ekron Eternal.

Wolfe didn't want to bet his truck against the metal railing, so he turned and slammed into the other, who joined his idiot companion as 'bumper jelly.' Wolfe dismissed the 'no experience' notification as he came screeching to a halt.

He stepped out of his truck of the driver side, his truck between him and the last thug. Wolfe kept his head down as the thug on the ramp emptied his magazine into the side of Wolfe's vehicle. In that moment, when the thug ran out of bullets, Wolfe leaned over the hood and shot the miscreant with his STI Edge in a tight cluster of hits to the chest.

Wolfe rushed around the front of the truck, noting the splatter of blood but utter lack of dent on the hood. He called out, "Malviere, Cultists, with me!"

The he rushed to the bar on the ramp into the club, placed his hand on it, and jumped over. He heard the doors to his truck opening, but barely paid attention. He needed to hurry, and while he hoped the support kept up, he wasn't betting Shel's life against their speed.

Wolfe looked down at the thug he shot, and hesitated for half a second before grabbing the submachine gun and a spare magazine. He didn't know the weapon as well as his own pistol—or pistols in general, for that matter—but figured some heavier firepower might come in useful at some point.

Although the weapon raised a ton of questions. *Where are street-level thugs like the Weeds getting heavier weapons? It's like the Cobras, before, with the damned rocket launcher they almost blinded me with in this very building? Can I get weapons like this?*

He decided not to bring forth a card or creature from his deck in the second 'draw' period. He wanted to wait for the Demonic Portal cards or his mantle to show up. Hopefully in the next draw.

Instead, he hit put the submachine gun over his shoulder so he could carry it with the strap, grasped his STI Edge firmly, and went around the corner into the interior of the club, slamming the glass door open with his shoulder, his pistol held forward.

It was still day time, so there was no smoke or innocents to confuse him like the last time he had been in a fire fight in the Ekron Eternal. Merely a few statues. The whole place was tacky without the smoke, lights, and thumping club music. But it had one major advantage—everything was easily visible.

Wolfe saw four men covering nearly the entire open area, but they were faced away from Wolfe, covering exits from stairs and the elevator.

With a completely clear dance floor, it was easy. Wolfe shot one in the back twice, shifting targets right after. But his enemies all moved fast again, whirling to face him. Wolfe dived behind a statue of two near-naked vampires making out as he discovered the drawback to the open floor—it was great for him, but it also made it easy for *them*, as well.

A brief, intense stream of gunfire erupted from the three remaining thugs, all vaguely in Wolfe's direction.

As the statue slowly disintegrated from machine gun fire, and the far wall filled with holes, Wolfe swiped the cards in front of him.

Two Demonic Portal cards, but still no mantle.

Of course.

A brief silence filled the club, more pronounced for the racket of a second earlier, and Wolfe knew his enemies had made a huge tactical error.

They had all hit empty at the same time.

Wolfe touched one of his Demonic Portal cards, hurling his most common play—Two Angry Hellhounds and a Lost Hellhound Puppy—into the field for a mere two power.

A chorus of barks and screams came, and Wolfe figured he had his moment. He went around the side, his own STI Edge up. One of the men went down as Malviere stepped into the club through the front door, her face covered by black hair. Her visage and aura of black energy made her the scariest thing in the room. Three quick, easy, measured steps forward were all she needed, and she reached her hand into the aura and flung it forward. The spirit of a massive Doberman peeled from her and sailed into one of the thugs, biting the screaming man, who died as his heart stopped and his flesh went pale.

The other two thugs fared no better. One was hit by two

Angry Hellhounds and went down in a welter of blood and screams. The last seemed fine for a moment as the adorable Lost Hellhound Puppy bit the last thug on the leg, growling and worrying at it. The thug screamed and tried to beat the card to death with his sub-machine gun, but he seemed mostly okay.

Until Wolfe put a stop to all that with another well-placed cluster of shots from his Edge to the distracted thug's chest.

A quick glance around showed Wolfe no other threats.

Keeping his gun out, Wolfe ran over to the booth that he normally met Miriam in. There was some blood, and a few bullet holes, but the only corpse Wolfe found, fortunately or unfortunately, was Victor. He had a bullet hole to his temple, just off dead center.

Wolfe was normally a pretty simple man, with his emotions ranging between 'content' and 'enraged,' but he felt another as he glared at Victor's corpse, as if his rage could bring back his old compatriot: Sadness.

Fuck.

Wolfe went way back with the information broker. He had saved Victor's daughter, Janelle, from a bad situation once, and they'd been a lot closer—although not close, per se—since the event. But even before that, Wolfe had known Victor almost as long as they'd been in the business. And Victor had helped Wolfe out more than once, and had been one of the few remaining people from the old life that Wolfe had liked.

But Wolfe had seen guys he liked die before. He shook it off.

Where in the Infernal realms is Shel? Wolfe glanced around.

He had a sudden thought, and ripped his phone from his pocket. He had a missed call from Shel a minute ago, and a text that said, "We retreated to the suites above, third floor."

With a last regretful glance at Victor's corpse, Wolfe rushed out of the booth for the elevators.

He reached them, slammed the up button, and waited. He slapped his pistol against his thigh in a rapid-fire pattern, anxious and edgy from even this tiny delay.

After a moment, the elevator chimed and the door slid open. Wolfe walked in, with Malviere and the two Obsessive Cultists following him. Wolfe hit the third-floor button, and waited.

The elevator quickly reached the third floor, and Wolfe walked forward even as it was chiming. At the same time, he flipped his deck, and four new cards appeared, as well as Cereboo.

As the door slid open, Wolfe was faced with a black-haired man, one eye missing, the other so empty of giving-a-shit it might as well have been a rock. The man was holding a massive Desert Eagle 44 Magnum, aimed right at Wolfe's chest. A massive Chinese-style dragon with a skull instead of a head was curled in the hall behind him.

"Goodbye," the man said, pulling the trigger.

The bang was the loudest thing Wolfe had ever heard.

CHAPTER 18

REBURN, PART II

The bullet slammed into Wolfe's chest with a metallic bang even as Wolfe was taking a step forward. He was pitched backward, slamming into the elevator floor on his back. He hurt—quite a bit—but he was still moving somehow.

Surprised to be alive, but not about to look a gift horse in the mouth, Wolfe shot his hand out and touched his mantle before the enemy deckbearer could finish him off.

The man also didn't hesitate and shot Wolfe three more times in quick succession, once in the head and twice in the chest. Wolfe's noggin rang, and he got a notice of being stunned. But with the mantle, Wolfe was still tough enough to survive the experience of being repeatedly shot. Although even with his mantle he lost eighteen health.

Half-blind and stunned, Wolfe still ripped his own Edge from the holster, but the man leapt on Wolfe and pinned the gun away at the same time. He tried to bring his own gun around but Wolfe caught that.

As Wolfe fought the man, wrestling for control of each

other's gun, Malviere hurled a spirit dog out the door at the dragon, accomplishing nothing.

The dragon, however, slammed its way inside, its bulk occupying the front of the elevator. Skeletal claws raked out, killing each of the Obsessive Cultists with a single blow.

"The deckbearer, Malviere! Kill the deckbearer," Wolfe shouted. "It all ends if you accomplish that!"

"I cannot, my alpha," Malviere said, her spooky voice filled with regret.

Right, even if she's basically a person now, she has to obey the rules of the Great Game and attack cards first. I have to solve this.

Wolfe's head cleared and the stunned notification went away.

Wolfe jerked both hands to the side, causing his opponent's face to fall toward him. At the same time, he slammed his own head up into his opponent, and the man reeled back, his nose absolutely pulverized, his face split, and his eyes crossed. With Malviere still out—however briefly—and his own mantle and modifiers, Wolfe was deadly at any range. As the man fell back, Wolfe ripped his hand from his enemy's and tried to bring his gun around.

He managed to get most of the way, but the man got lucky in his scrabbling and managed to push it away just a bit before Wolfe pulled the trigger. Wolfe's enemy still screamed as the bullet ripped through his side. He dropped his own gun to poke a card now revealed by them briefly separating, and a black mantle settled over the man, turning his flesh pale and giving him red eyes.

Wolfe slapped his own card, betting everything that the man had become Undead type, before the man fell back to being chest to chest with Wolfe.

He summoned the Xolo Spirit-Ward.

When the man attacked next, his blows slowed right

before they hit Wolfe. Malviere was cut from the attacks by the dragon, but they didn't finish her—and she triggered her power, speeding Wolfe up.

The total difference in the capabilities between Wolfe and his opponent was now ridiculous. Wolfe yanked and twisted, *snapping* the man's wrist with his total freakish power. Wolfe's enemy screamed, but still tried to get the purchase to punch Wolfe back. Wolfe brought his knee up into the side of the man, a blow that would, under normal circumstances, be weak from lack of leverage and distance. But with his current attack score, magic stacked upon magic, it audibly cracked the man's ribs.

His opponent never stopped, and his one eye never even became fearful, not so much as a widening of the pupil as they fought on the once-pristine floor of the elevator, both of them spilling blood across it. Wolfe slammed the heel of his palm into the man's face, once, twice, three times before the skull finally collapsed under the magically empowered strikes.

Then he fired repetitively into the dragon before it could finish Malviere off—it dissipated into nothing.

Wolfe pushed the twitching near-corpse from him and dragged himself back against the wall of the elevator.

"Are you okay, my alpha?" Malviere asked.

Wolfe cocked one eye up at her. Blood was running into the other eye from the shot to his head, which had scored along his bone, if his quick check with his fingers was anything like accurate.

"Do I *look* fine?" Wolfe asked.

Malviere's lips twitched. "No, my alpha, you most emphatically do not. You look like you ought to be dead."

At that moment, the man next to him gave one final spasm and completed his transformation to corpse. A shit stink filled the tiny elevator, and Wolfe gagged.

"Dammit, this guy was holding a whole damn loaf in for

some reason. What a lovely addition to the day. I think this might be the most squalid thing that has ever happened in the Ekron Eternal, and we had some really bad ones in my time."

Malviere nodded to his words.

Wolfe dragged himself standing, grabbed the cards that had appeared on the corpse of no-face, and glanced into the elevator mirror. He was busted up, with wounds all over the place, mostly the massive shot to his head. He looked like an extra in a zombie movie.

But he had very limited chest damage.

He opened his coat and pulled out the filigreed metal box with the certificate for Shel. The lid was shot through, but the bottom was merely heavily indented, and Wolfe had only a bruise where it had been.

"For only ten thousand dollars a day, *you* could save the life of an ex-enforcer," Wolfe said, his voice whimsically sappy.

Malviere giggled, a sound more like creepy horror-movie child than happy, but Wolfe knew it was legitimately a noise of enjoyment for his card.

Wolfe put the shattered case back in his pocket—now it was charity for Shel and a great story, he figured—and exited into the hall, carefully.

Now that he wasn't fighting in an enclosed elevator, he heard banging, yelling, gunshots, growling, and other indistinguishable noises from way down the hall. A hall he remembered well, with not-yet-changed-out symbols of Beelzebub, plush red carpets, and painting of the Infernal Realms on the walls.

Wolfe knew he had to go have a whole additional fight, but was in agony—he would have been worried about how much he could help Shel under normal circumstances, even though he would have tried, of course.

Finally, however, he had a partial solution to being wounded that didn't require Shel already be by his side. He sacrificed his Xolo, and felt the familiar warmth of healing flow through him, restoring him to 'okay,' with twelve total damage of his thirty health, and no injury penalties.

He rushed quietly down the hall, resummoning Cereboo and then swiping his cards as he did.

He reached the end of the hallway. Three men were there, all with decks floating around them. One was hauling a body back from a door that led into a stairway going up, a body that Wolfe didn't recognize, fortunately.

The scene put Wolfe out of sorts for multiple reasons. He had no idea there *was* a fourth floor to the Ekron Eternal, for one, and for the other, one of the three men was *Ahmed*, one of Miriam's men—and fuckboys.

Somehow, no one seemed to have heard Wolfe run up, probably because a hail of gunfire was coming down the stairs.

"Send more cards!" Ahmed snarled.

"We need another way onto the roof," one of the other two men said. "It'll take too long for the three of us to overwhelm them with sheer card numbers. Your incompetence infuriates me."

The man was tall and muscled, and held himself with the deadly grace of a killer. But he also had red scales across his arms and claws on his hands, and his back had wings sprouting from them.

"You told me the police aren't coming, Nathan," Ahmed snarled.

"That's Mr. Leopold, fool. The police can't pretend they were far away forever, especially since this is a fire-fight that's now on a roof," the man said, then held one hand up. "Never mind. I'll just go out the window and fly up, and handle this myself. If you'd done your damn job instead of thinking with your dick, none of it would have come to this."

Wolfe had heard enough. He knew that Ahmed wasn't very dangerous, since he had been there when they got the cards that made up most of Ahmed's deck in the Frozen Cairn dungeon.

He also sensed that this Nathan Leopold character was incredibly dangerous.

But his mantle was on.

All of it flashed through Wolfe's mind in a fraction of a second as he shot the third man in the head, blowing his entire skull apart with his still-enhanced stats. Ahmed whirled, running into a door and bouncing off to try and escape, but the dragon-winged man leapt hard into the *wall* next to him and blew through it.

Ahmed touched one of his cards, and a massive crocodile with ice rime across its body appeared.

Wolfe casually blew Ahmed's chest apart with three easy shots at less than twenty feet.

The wall next to Wolfe exploded outward. Wolfe was blown through the wall on the other side and into the next room, a nice suite with chairs, bed, and a desk that was also blown apart, leaving shattered chunks of wood across the ground. He took twelve more damage.

Malviere and Cereboo both disappeared in a brief flash of blood before becoming particles that flowed back to Wolfe.

Wolfe picked himself up off the floor even as Nathan flew through the door. He grabbed Wolfe by the wrist and yanked him toward him. Wolfe swung a punch with his other hand, and Nathan blocked, wincing as his arm cracked.

"You have a powerful mantle, criminal. It won't be enough."

"Go fuck yourself."

Nathan dodged the next blow without letting go of Wolfe's arm and then claw-punched Wolfe in the side, doing another two damage. As Wolfe stepped back, he kicked Wolfe low, tripping him back onto the ground.

Somehow, Wolfe knew where the next blow would come,

and blocked the stomp-kick to his head with his own arm, hissing in pain. At the same time, he scrabbled through the shards on the ground, grabbed one, and stuck it in Nathan's leg. The man grunted in agony and stepped back.

Wolfe tried to stand, but in an insane display of ignoring pain, Nathan caught him on the way up with a kick from his own wounded leg, and Wolfe was flung back a couple feet, hitting the ground on his back again.

"It doesn't have to be this way," Nathan said, his dragon wings fluttering to give him balance as he yanked the piece of wood from his leg with a hiss.

He tossed it onto the ground. "Just give me Fern, and you and whomever that's left here can live out their pathetic lives, at least until we come for all the criminal scum like you."

What a day to try and get engaged.

"Answer's the same, numbnuts. Go fuck yourself," Wolfe ground out, leaping up and back ward, slamming his back into the outside wall of the suite, next to a grand viewing window covered in curtains.

Nathan snarled, "So be it," and rushed forward.

Wolfe reached up, yanked the curtains down onto Nathan as he came in. Nathan still hit him shoulder first, and something within Wolfe cracked. Wolfe punched Nathan twice, trying to use his opponent's temporary blindness as an advantage. But at this close range, it was way less of an advantage than Wolfe had hoped for.

Nathan grabbed him and lifted him a few inches from the floor, which deprived Wolfe of any leverage.

Then Nathan spun in a half-circle, building a tiny bit of momentum, and threw Wolfe through the third-story window, into the late afternoon sun, in an explosion of glass.

CHAPTER 19

A HERO'S REWARD

Wolfe sailed out into the open air, a trail of glass following him. His arc terminated, and he came back down to Earth, a fall of around forty feet, trying his best not to tense and make the inevitable collision with the ground worse. He prayed his mantle would somehow let him survive.

He slammed into the roof of a parked Lamborghini, smashing it half apart, the glass from the third-story window tinkling around him even as the glass from the car's windows blasted away from him.

With a cinematic sweep of his dragon wings, Nathan came leaping out of the window after Wolfe. He fell down, arresting his speed and guiding himself somewhat with his wings, his foot aimed for Wolfe's chest.

Wolfe was *badly* injured, and was pretty sure another blow would send him onward to the gods. He wasn't about to go down without a fight, however... and Nathan hadn't pulled a creature, for some reason. A potentially fatal mistake.

Wolfe reached out and touched his Infernal Rift card, banishing Nathan for ninety seconds to a faux Infernal realm.

Ninety seconds... I hope it's enough.

Wolfe was nearly dead. He rolled off the car, onto the sidewalk. An older lady, plump but not fat and in a nice skirt-and-blouse combo that matched her wide eyes, asked, "Are you okay?" as Wolfe landed on the sidewalk with a groan.

"Never been fucking better," Wolfe answered as he tried to hobble back toward the entrance to the Ekron Eternal.

It wasn't busy, per se, but four cars were stopped, and their drivers—and one twelve-year-old or so boy in a passenger seat —were looking at him. A couple pedestrians across the street were as well. It was bright and sunny out, even in the late evening, completely at odds with how Wolfe felt a day like the hell he was now going through ought to look. *It should at least be night.*

A clump of people was at the end of the street, where Wolfe had entered the Ekron Eternal, guns and car bumper blazing.

I've still got to save Shel.

Maybe she figured out what's happening and got away? She'd have let me know, right?

Wolfe pulled his phone out, but it was broken in half. *Fuck.*

He swiped the deck and then summoned the Obsessive Infernal Cultist that had reappeared, the one that acted as a companion card.

Now I just need a portal, but I've got only a hot minute left before Nathan comes back.

Wolfe was very genuinely concerned about that. He had bought himself a tiny chance to recover and win the fight. But Nathan fought like Wolfe, instinctually... like he was born to it. Problem was, Nathan seemed even more trained and deadly, something Wolfe had never actually encountered before.

And Wolfe was hanging onto his life by a few measly health points.

I need more of an advantage, Wolfe thought as he stumbled down the street, moving as fast as he could to get back into the Ekron Eternal, and hopefully find some tactical advantage, before Nathan came back.

It quickly became apparent he wasn't going to make it. *I need surprise and power, somehow, without getting hit myself.*

Wolfe summoned his Bulgae Moon Chaser, with its speedy trait that let him use it without an action. Then, in the same summon, brought forth Cerberus' Home for Wayward Hellhounds, blocking half the street with it. He quickly positioned himself behind the kennel stones, as he had done quite a few times before.

Then he swiped his cards again. *Thirty seconds left.*

Nathan appeared, dropping to the car roof with a resounding crash, right where Wolfe's chest would have been.

A few people screamed as a half-dragon appeared, and began moving away from the scene, although a couple were filming with phones.

At the same time, Wolfe brought forth Malviere. He prayed that it would all be enough, as he wasn't sure he'd be able to get a Demonic Portal out without a second Obsessive Cultist.

Nathan stood, shuddering briefly, and touched one of the cards in front of his chest. A massive Red Dragon appeared next to him.

Wolfe leaned out from and cut loose with the submachine gun, unloading it at Nathan in a sustained burst. Even with his strength, it was a bit hard to control, and only a few bullets hit. At the same time, his entire pack of cards, including now two of the Lost Hellhound Puppies, charged the dragon.

Nathan dropped back behind the car and crouched till Wolfe hit empty, then stepped out. He looked at Wolfe, then up at the roof of the Ekron Eternal.

"I don't have to beat you," he said. "Just her." He crouched and prepared to jump, his wings snapping out.

Oh fuck!

For some reason, Wolfe hadn't seen the move coming. He lurched forward, just as Nathan leapt.

His mantle disappeared, and Nathan executed an impressive five-foot vertical jump, but nothing else.

Wolfe almost swooned with relief—and blood loss, probably. Then, he bared his teeth in a savage, feral grin.

Nathan looked irritated, but little more. He touched his deck again and another dragon appeared.

Wolfe brought forth the second Obsessive Cultist. *The next hand will have two Demonic Portals, almost certainly.*

Nathan looked around the street, then shrugged. He ran across to one of the stalled cars on the road, an old Volvo. He punched through the window, and grabbed the old man driving.

"No!" Wolfe yelled, trying to sprint forward, but his own mantle faded, and the pain came crashing in. Wolfe collapsed to the ground.

"Another time," Nathan said with a tight smile, then pitched the old man he was holding out of the car and to the hard asphalt of the street as his dragons fended off Wolfe's dogs.

Wolfe growled in frustration as Nathan expertly backed the car around and drove off, easily dodging one brave driver that tried to crash his car into him. The dragons simply disappeared after that, not having actually been killed.

With a sigh of pain and frustration, Wolfe rolled over and sat back against one of the 'Cerberus' Home' cages. He glanced over at Malviere. "Today started out so well. A dungeon run, a trip to the jewelry store where I actually found something I liked. What happened?"

"I'd ask if you're okay again," Malviere said, ignoring

Wolfe's mostly rhetorical question. "But the answer is obvious. What can I do to help?"

Wolfe held his hand up, and Malviere reached down and took it. He pulled himself to his feet with her help, conscious of all the eyes watching him.

"We need to get to Shel," Wolfe said. "This could easily be a trick. He can probably get his mantle back in a few minutes and then fly back to attack her."

Wolfe dismissed Cerberus' Home, but kept the Bulgae Chaser out. Then he summoned Cereboo.

He had his entire core team with him—Cereboo, Malviere, and the two Obsessive Cultists.

"Let's go." Wolfe hobbled down the street, still ignoring the stares of the crowd. He was worried someone might try and arrest him, so he dug out his investigator's badge and flashed it around, hoping no one would pay too close attention, or be too concerned with his obvious Infernal deck.

No one bothered him as Wolfe made his way down the street toward the front of the Ekron Eternal, still pushing himself despite his agony, blood weeping from his injuries. He had to get to Shel.

At that very moment, as if by providence, Shel came around the corner, through the small crowed of people gathered there. She was followed by Miriam, Fern, and Derek. She flashed her police badge in unknowing mimicry of Wolfe as she did.

Wolf felt his heart ease as Shel appeared. She was a vision, one he had been desperately afraid he would never see again. Her brilliant red hair, intense green eyes, and muscled but still willowy frame were the sight he longed for the most.

She halted abruptly, her breath catching as her gaze fell upon him. Her eyes widened, flickering up and down the length of his battered frame, each glance betraying her shock at the sight before her.

Shel, Fern, Miriam, and Derek stood nearby, their clothes torn and smeared with blood, but strangely, not even one of them bore the marks of pain or injury. They were ragged and disheveled, yet untouched by whatever violence had left its mark on him alone.

"You should see the other guy," Wolfe quipped.

"We did," Miriam replied, her usually boisterous voice quiet. "All three of them. Two without heads and one without a face."

Shel stepped forward. "You saved me again. I don't think we would have made it against Nathan, not him and his team and his gunman."

"Who *is* Nathan?" Wolfe asked as he forced himself to stand a little straighter. "He was asking for Fern."

Fern simply hugged herself, staring at her feet. "Nathan Leopold is Adam's right hand. An ex-Navy Seal, and a true fanatic of Adam's beliefs. He is almost level fifty, and he has been awarded nearly every medal the military offers. He wasn't supposed to be back."

"Lovely," Wolfe muttered.

Shel touched her chest, pulled her deck, and summoned a Rookie EMT. Wolfe felt a huge portion of his health restored, and breathed a deep sigh of relief.

"Thanks, Shel, truly. I cannot tell you how bad that guy threw me a beating."

"You saved me again, Wolfe," Shel repeated, her eyes staring at him as if no else around mattered. "You killed the three deckbearers trying to murder me, took an explosion for me, did enough to save our lives."

"Yeah, I still got my ass kicked," Wolfe said. It was a bitter pill to swallow.

"But you saved me, which is what you set out to do," Shel repeated again. "You always save me. Always."

"I guess I did accomplish my goal, and senior officer

jackass didn't," Wolfe responded. *That is what matters, in the end. Although I need to be stronger for the next time we meet.* "Now let's—"

Shel reached out and took Wolfe's hands, startling him briefly into silence. She was still staring into his eyes. "Wolfe, I love you."

He held his breath, my chest tight. He couldn't look away from her, but for some reason, words were difficult.

"I want to spend the rest of my life with you," Shel whispered.

"I'm probably going to die before you," was all Wolfe managed to say—too much a realistic to avoid pointing out the truth, too sarcastic to avoid the quip.

"If you go before me, I'll wait patiently until we're reunited again at the gates of the afterlife. Wolfe—I love you. More than anyone. More than anything."

Shel's lip quavered, and a happy tear rolled down her cheek as she continued speaking. "I admire you more than I could have imagined admiring any man three years ago. I want that forever, Wolfe. I feel more cared for, safer, and even more inspired with you than with anyone I have ever been around."

Wolfe glanced around at the people around him, who were all looking at them. One or two had phones out.

He felt his heart warm, but also his cheeks. "I love you, too, Shel, but maybe we should head inside or—"

"No," Shel replied intensely. She wiped the tear away and steadied herself. "I'm tired of waiting. I should have done this a year ago."

Shel dropped to one knee, shocking Wolfe into silence. Then she reached into her damaged police-issued workout sweats, and pulled forth a small case, holding it out to Wolfe. She opened it up, and Wolfe saw that there was a wide golden band inside with writing carved into the interior.

Wolfe's throat tightened. His gaze was locked on hers, his thoughts solely on this one moment.

"Ethan William Wolfe, would you do me the honor of marrying me?"

Cereboo barked happily and Miriam golf-clapped.

Even random people in the gathered crowds *dawwed* and cheered, despite not knowing anyone involved.

The irony of the situation wasn't lost on Wolfe, but his chest was filled with knots, and his face hot. It was still difficult to find the right words. Obviously, the correct word was '*yes*,' but... It wasn't enough. 'Yes' didn't fully capture his feelings.

How could a simple three-letter word embody the essence of love so eternal that Shel wanted to be together even in the afterlife?

After a ragged breath, Wolfe reached into his own pocket and withdrew a similar-looking case. Shel's eyes went wide, her eyebrows knitted in confusion, and then in realization.

"You got me a ring?" Shel blinked, her eyes glazing with even more tears.

Wolfe opened the case. "I wanted everything to be perfect..." Then he sardonically glanced around at the dreary street, the random crowds, and the blood splatters that marred almost everything. This wasn't how he imagined his proposal going, but he had to admit—the setting was more representative of their time together.

With a trembling hand, Shel plucked the emerald ring from the case and slipped it onto her elegant finger.

"Sorry this took so long," Wolfe whispered. "You're right. We should've done this sooner. I should've—"

Shel interrupted him again, leaping up and flinging her arms around him, hugging him as tightly as she could. "I love you, Wolfe. I love you so, so much."

As if it was a signal, everyone on the street started clapping and cheering, even Malviere. Cereboo let out a happy series of barks, and Wolfe clung to Shel.

Maybe it hadn't been such a bad day after all, Wolfe thought, holding back a laugh. He couldn't remember the last time he felt so...

Right.

Maybe that wasn't the right word, but that was how he felt.

"I got you something else, too, but it kinda got shot up in the fight..." Wolfe started, but Shel just clung to him, tears of happiness streaming from her eyes, and Wolfe decided to leave everything else for later.

This was a moment for joy.

CHAPTER 20

RETURN OF THE RIGHTEOUS

Fortunately—since Wolfe's car had to be towed away—Miriam wanted to continue to hang with Wolfe, and she was prepared to lend them her skull-motif limousine to do it.

In fact, she seemed downright determined to continue to be around him. She said she felt safer with him. While Miriam wasn't nearly to Fern's level, the situation clearly seemed to have taken a toll on her as well. She was sitting with her arms wrapped around herself in the back of the limousine, with Derek next to her, across from Wolfe and Shel, who were arm in arm, with Shel laying her head across his chest.

Fern sat in the far back, breathing oddly and talking to herself while typing away rapidly at a keyboard. Malviere was against the window dividing the occupants from the driver. Cereboo lay on the floor.

The whole place smelled faintly of blood and fear-sweat, no doubt from the clothing even though Shel had utterly healed everyone with her impressive new Nurse of the Chosen powers.

"So..." Wolfe said, breaking the awkward silence of the last few minutes as the limousine headed toward the Hellmouth Institute.

No one answered.

"Look, I get that the situation was scary, but I need answers," Wolfe tried again. "What happened? Why were you attacked, and how did they know to come after Fern in the first place, or even where she was?"

"They were after Fern?" Miriam said, looking up at Wolfe, her eyes strangely happy. "Why do you think they were after Fern?"

"Because some dude that threw me from a third-story window asked for her?" Wolfe said, half a statement, half a question.

"Nathan?" Fern asked, glancing up from her laptop. "Nathan said he wanted me?"

"Yeah, that douche-canoe. The 'right-hand man,' or whatever. I mean, why would he have even been there if they weren't after you, Fern?"

Miriam leaned back, slowly recovering her aplomb. "Well, Ahmed said that Dustin was offering a reward for my death since I stole a bunch of money from the Weeds."

"Who in the Infernal realms is Dustin?"

"Newly promoted head of the Weeds, once third in command," Miriam said, smiling at Wolfe. "He was the one whose head you removed from behind instead of the front."

Wolfe grunted at that.

She glanced over at the man nest to her. "Derek, would you be a dear and fix me a martini, please. Beaten, not stirred."

"You get over shit fast," Wolfe said.

Derek just rolled his eyes and reached for a glass in the corner of the limousine.

"Given my family, I credit a genetic predisposition to being able to deal with darkness," Miriam said. "But also, I thought this was my fault. I thought my decisions led to

Victor's—and a couple more of my people's, for that matter—death. But without Nathan being there, me, Derek, and Shel could have beaten everyone, and now that you're saying that, I can see the whole thing."

"The whole thing?" Wolfe asked.

"Of course," Miriam said. "I mean, think about it. How *would* Nathan get a strike team together, and hide his involvement? He could only do it because the Weeds had an excuse to go after me! He was just using that to get Fern."

"So, then, wouldn't it kinda still be your fault?" Wolfe asked.

Miriam stopped, frowning.

Shel pretend-slapped the back of Wolfe's head, then snuggled back against him even harder.

Wolfe frowned, and gently rubbed the top of Shel's head for a moment as he digested everything.

Then he looked back at Miriam again. "Why was Ahmed working for the bad guys?"

"The bad guys, huh?" Miriam asked. "What are we?"

"The less bad, bad guys. Just answer the question."

"After we got back from the dungeon, Ahmed proposed to me," Miriam said. "The bastard claimed he wanted to be exclusive with me. When I said no, he became angry and stormed off. I assume that was when he decided to sell me out, although he claimed it was to the Weeds."

Fern turned her computer around, showing an almost incomprehensible series of bank transfers, her head down, her breathing still odd. "It wasn't for that—it was for me. This here is a record of a two-million-dollar transfer from one of Adam's bank accounts to Ahmed's account."

Wolfe stared at it. "That looks way more complex than a bank transfer."

Fern nodded once. "It is. But it's three dummy accounts and a walking transfer."

"Walking transfer?" Wolfe asked. He had thought he was part of the underworld, but this was new to him.

"Someone clearly took it out at one bank, and put it into an account at another. To break the trace," Fern replied matter-of-factly.

"Then how do you know?" Wolfe asked, fascinated despite himself.

"We have both ends. Anyone tracking the account would just see a withdrawal. But we see the exact same amount of money enter a person-of-interest's account thirty minutes later."

Wolfe decided to drop it—Fern was really good at what she did, he guessed, and he'd trust her.

"So they're still after you, in other words?"

Fern nodded, and her breathing went ragged. "The computer in my lap, the seat I'm on, Cereboo licking my foot."

Wolfe looked down—Cereboo's left head was indeed licking Fern's sandaled foot. "Knock that off."

"I don't mind," Fern said. "It tickles. It helps keep me grounded."

"Continue," Wolfe said, and his dog let out a series of huffs that sounded suspiciously like laughter to Wolfe.

"So, Ahmed shot Victor, then?" Wolfe asked.

"Yeah," Derek replied, then rubbed his chest. "He shot me first, but apparently, I wasn't dead before your wonderful fiancée managed to bring me back with her incredible healing. I'm still busted up inside, despite her healing removing some injury levels. I feel like I snuggled up to death before getting brought back."

Miriam leaned over and kissed him on the cheek. "Well, you're alive now."

"But Victor got shot?"

"Yeah, while I was pulling my deck, Ahmed got another

shot off and hit Victor in the head," Miriam said, angrily wiping at one of her eyes as she talked. "After that, he managed to retreat, and we couldn't go after him since the thugs were attacking us."

Miriam shuddered, then accepted the glass Derek gave her and took a long sip. "I nearly died of gunshots multiple times, but Shel saved me."

"Well, you and Derek kept the thugs off me while I did," Shel said.

As the limousine turned into the parking lot of the Hellmouth Institute, Wolfe slashed his hand through the air. "Wait, none of that matters. Are we sure that they were after Fern, ultimately?"

"They were," Fern said. "Although they're after you now, as well."

"Right," Wolfe said. "Okay, here's what we're going to do. We're going to find a safe place for Fern to stay. Genuinely safe, with someone I can trust no matter what."

"Who's that?" Shel asked again.

Wolfe sighed. "My favorite person in the whole world."

Wolfe rapped on the white door in front of him. It was older, slightly cracked around the edges, as was the concrete walkway leading from the driveway to the front door. But the yard was recently mowed and trimmed, and the flowers all looked healthy.

It was even swept.

The door opened, and Rhett Walker stared out at Wolfe. "What the hell are you doing at my house at nine at night, William?"

Rhett was dressed in workout shorts and a white t-shirt,

and Miriam whistled. Wolfe grimaced—Rhett was the same height as Wolfe, but a touch younger and even broader of shoulder and more pronounced of pec. Wolfe was never sure why, but Rhett's looks had always irritated him.

Probably because Wolfe knew that Rhett had once had a thing for Shel, even if he'd helped Wolfe rather than getting him out of the picture.

"Just use my nickname, Wolfe," Wolfe responded to Rhett's use of his fake name 'William.'"

Rhett scowled. "Who are these people with you?"

Wolfe motioned to Miriam. "This is Miriam Grimm"—Rhett's eyes widened as Wolfe motioned over to Fern—"and this is Fern, um..."

"Wachowski," Fern said.

"Right," Wolfe said, then faced the lieutenant again. "I actually need to ask you a huge favor, Rhett. I can pay."

"What's the favor?" Rhett asked, his face suspicious.

"The mob is after Fern," Wolfe said, keeping it simple if slightly inaccurate. "They tried to kill her at the Ekron Eternal today—"

"Oh my gods," Rhett said, pinching the bridge of his nose. "Was that you? Of course that was you."

"He saved my life," Fern whispered.

"And mine," Miriam said.

"They found fifteen bodies," Rhett replied.

Wolfe did a count in his head. "I think I was only responsible for a bit more than half that."

"You crack me up," Rhett said, but his voice was legitimately angry. "I thought you were going straight. It sounds like, in the last forty-eight hours, you've been responsible for more than twenty deaths."

Wolfe grimaced. "Every one of those came looking to die."

He carefully didn't mention the fight with the Weeds on the boat.

"Should I arrest you?" Rhett asked.

Wolfe tensed. Rhett was a good guy, but his position always made things a tiny bit dicey between them.

Wolfe motioned to Fern. "Look, she'll explain everything to you. If you want to arrest me after that, I won't resist. But please at least look at what she has, and you'll understand what I'm up against, and what she is up against as well. Just listen to her, okay?"

Rhett stared at the mousey girl in front of him, breathing carefully and clutching her laptop close. His face softened as he watched, some combination of pity and tenderness.

Wolfe would have bet anything that Rhett recognized the signs of abuse.

He turned back to Wolfe. "Alright. Tell me everything you talked about was hypothetical."

Wolfe almost laughed—it was a throwback to another conversation. "It was all hypothetical."

Miriam stared between them and then burst into laughter. Wolfe was reminded that she was now a law student, nearly graduated, and still first in her class. She obviously got what Rhett was doing.

"So, where are you guys off to now?" Rhett asked. "Or do I want to know?"

"Actually, nothing nefarious. We're gonna run a dungeon I found, outside your jurisdiction," Wolfe said.

Rhett glanced up. "Wait, really?"

Wolfe nodded.

"Actually, can I ask that you repay the favor by taking me on the run? I could use some levels, badly."

Fern glanced up and tentatively raised her hand. "Actually... could I get in on that as well?"

CHAPTER 21

RETURN TO LOOWITLATKLA'S
FALL

"**S**on of an Infernal," Wolfe cussed as he stared at the notification.

The Dungeon of Loowitlatkla's Fall allows a maximum of four people inside at a time.

Wolfe waited for a moment, and everyone stepped back out of the dungeon entrance, into the tunnel that had been dug.

Wolfe, Shel, Miriam, Rhett, and Fern was 'everyone.' Derek was here, but he was already sitting on the ground against the tunnel wall. Given his injury, he had begged off being a part of the dungeon.

"We have one too many," Wolfe stated.

"Obviously," Miriam said. Then she went over and sat down against the wall next to Derek, and leaned her head on his shoulder. Her dress was completely ragged—it was the same one she had met them in nearly twelve hours ago, and it had tears from the adventure, and a few bullet holes. Wolfe was honestly surprised she hadn't become an involuntary nudist at this point.

Although in Miriam's case, would it really be involuntary?

I mean, she has been running the dungeon in a diaphanous cocktail dress...

"You guys go," Miriam said, waving at them. "Wolfe has already done *insanely* right by me and Derek, and I'll be honest—after a dungeon run and then getting shot near to death more than once and only saved by Shel, I'm a bit... Shell shocked."

Miriam chuckled tiredly at her own joke, the frowned when no one else joined in. "Okay, so that wasn't my best joke. A bit weak, even. The point is, I'm exhausted by the events of this day. I'm tired in my *bones*. The Level Twenty-Five perk would have been nice, but I'll sit this one out."

Wolfe nodded. He was deeply tired as well.

But tired was for chumps.

He couldn't stop. Nathan had taught Wolfe that he wasn't strong enough, and someday, Wolfe would have to face him again. He had to work to make himself ready for that day.

Plus, from other things Fern had said, Wolfe knew that Nathan had nothing on Adam himself. So even Nathan wasn't the goal. He was just a stop along the way.

"You're sure you want to do this, Fern?" Wolfe asked. "I mean, you are Level One, right? You know this'll probably start around Twenty-Three and go to around Thirty-Five."

She nodded firmly without answering, her breathing still ragged.

Wolfe was half convinced he was going to regret it, but he wasn't one who would stop someone from pulling themselves up by their bootstraps, no matter how likely they were to kill themselves.

Wolfe had been helpless more than once, when he was much younger. Even being a mob enforcer, risking arrest or getting shot, had been far preferable to that feeling of utter weakness. He wouldn't wish that helplessness on anyone, not even his worst enemy.

If someone deserved to live at the mercy of someone else, Wolfe would as soon shoot them and be done with it.

"My love?" Shel asked, putting her hand on his shoulder.

Wolfe shook the brief black mood from himself. "Sorry, stray thought. Let's just do this." *Maybe I really am a bit tired.*

Wolfe stepped forward, into the gate for the third time. The heat was the same, and he reemerged in the same cavern from before—near a pool of lava, and also sweltering.

At least this time no fire bat attacked him.

"They're gonna make us walk all the way back, huh?" Wolfe asked as Shel appeared next to him. "The dungeons don't have some kind of transport system?"

"None that I've ever read about, my love. Sorry."

Shel stepped forward from the gate and first Rhett, then Fern appeared through it after a moment.

"So... where are the monsters?" Rhett asked as he glanced around at the cavern, which was lit by the glow of the lava. "I've never been in a dungeon, but this seems empty."

"We have a bit of a walk," Wolfe responded. "Through a long, hot tunnel and then down a long slope."

"Do you try and make everything sound sexual around me on purpose?" Rhett asked, rolling his eyes.

"Eh, just comes natural, I guess."

Rhett motioned with his hands. "Well, lead the way, then."

Wolfe pulled his deck. "Just in case, before we go, let's everyone play all of our companions."

Wolfe played Malviere and Cereboo and his mindless Obsessive Cultist. Shel brought out Sorenia and Liurenia.

Fern played Brain Bot to the rocky ground. He rolled in a half-circle, then, on his front in eight-bit drew a little heart and printed out "Brain Bot is in august company."

Rhett touched a card, and a near seven-foot-tall human in

battle armor with vague police accents appeared, a badge on his chest. He looked like a body-builder that had cybernetics strapped to him, along with a police stache.

Butch Cyber
Uncommon Equivalent, Tier-5 equivalent Mortal/Golem
[Civic, Cyber, Veteran] Companion
0 Power
Health: 25
Attack: 5
Defense: 10
Magical Attack: 0
Magical Defense: 5

Special: Civic Leader [1]: Grants +1 to all non-Health stats of all other allied Civic cards on the field
Special: Bulwark: This card must be attacked before any other cards of the deckbearer, or the deckbearer, may be attacked.

"I'm a test program for the efficacy of enhanced protectors of the citizen body"

"You got a new companion card?" Wolfe asked, raising an eyebrow.

"Yeah, a much weaker one—"

"I'm not weak," Butch said, his voice a deep, pseudo-electronic baritone.

Rhett rolled his eyes. "Sorry. I meant to say a lower-rarity, lower-tier one. It took selling almost every card we got in our little scuffle in the warehouse, but he's worth it. My deck tends to set up slow and he buys time."

Wolfe laughed. "Fair."

Wolfe took in everyone. "We all ready?"

A chorus of yeses, three woofs, one blank stare, and an eight-bit "Brain Bot is ready!" answered him.

Wolfe nodded to everyone assembled, then turned and set out at a brisk pace, following the path back. He was feeling good about their chances. This dungeon had been made five hundred years ago if Shel's earlier information had been accurate—and Wolfe expected it was. Wolfe knew that there had been a bit of power creep since then, most of it with the introduction this set of Companion cards and the free companion slot. Wolfe was fairly sure that they were all stronger for their level than the dungeon would have been prepared for.

Although the dungeon was going to reach Level Thirty-Five, which would be... interesting... with a Level One in the party.

It wasn't that long before he reached the campfire and the stone slab. From there it was easy to find the route—whenever one of them wandered off the path, the tress and undergrowth became rapidly impassable, but everything was an easy forest path in the correct direction.

As they were walking the forest path, a series of arrows suddenly shot from the forest, high into the sky, and then rained down. Wolfe briefly saw a notification that it was a 4-strength AoE attack.

"Everyone down!" Wolfe yelled, hitting the ground.

Everyone else tried to dodge, but arrows managed—magically, Wolfe suspected—to hit everyone except Rhett. Yells, shouts, and growls met the attack.

"We need to move forward!" Wolfe cried out, yanking an arrow from the meat of his upper arm.

Fern was huddled on the ground, an arrow sticking out of her shoulder. Wolfe grabbed her, yanking her along.

Shel started to reach for one of her cards and Wolfe yelled "Get Fern" as they ran.

The Rookie EMT that appeared healed Fern, the arrow popping from her shoulder as it healed.

Wolfe ran into the forest, looking for enemies. He quickly found them when he broke through the treeline into a burning village. This was a full village, not the tiny thing they had defended before. Hundreds of huts, and raging through them were almost a hundred enemies—but they were also fighting each other, two groups of fifty or so, with civilians running around, screaming and occasionally dying.

Wolfe glanced at the figures. There were cards named "Pahto something" and "Wy'east something" that were functionally the same, plus civilian cards.

Pahto Elite Brave
Dungeon NPC
Mortal [Soldier] Creature
Health: 30
Attack: 9
Defense: 9
Magical Attack: N/A
Magical Defense: 9

Special: **Feeder:** Whenever this creature kills a Beast, Plant, or Nature creature it heals fully.

"A brave that served as the personal guard of the first son of the legendary first chief of the Cowlitz."

Pahto Elite Hunter
Dungeon NPC
Mortal [Soldier, Archer] Creature
Health: 20
Attack: 9
Defense: 6

Magical Attack: N/A
Magical Defense: 6

Special: **Incoming Ambush [4]:** So long as at least one card matching this creature is on the field, every incoming enemy, including deckbearers, takes a 4-strength physical attack. Does not replicate additional similar abilities if one has already triggered in the 30 seconds.

"One of the greatest hunters in the legendary first tribe of the Cowlitz, now allied with the chief's eldest son."

Cowlitz Tribesman
Dungeon NPC
Mortal [Civilian, Civic] Creature
Health: 20
Attack: 3
Defense: 5
Magical Attack: N/A
Magical Defense: 5

"A citizen of the Cowlitz Nation."

In the center, near a fire, Wolfe could see the young, beautiful version of Loowitlatkla, sitting on the ground and weeping.

A civilian woman ran up even as Wolfe was taking in the fighting. She was a young Amerind with paler skin and black hair, covered almost head to toe in goatskin clothing.

"Help us! Each of the sons of Chief Tyee has a camp on the outskirts of the city! If you can defeat them, you'll save us! The more of us you save, and the more of our buildings you prevent from burning to the ground, the greater your prize will be!"

Wolfe hadn't even considered the buildings, and glanced at one.

Burning Cowlitz Long House
Dungeon Structure

This building will burn to the ground in seven minutes. Any Elemental [Water] card played in the village will add two minutes to the timer. Any Ice or Elemental [Water] attack against the building will add 5 minutes to the timer. A Civic creature solely dedicated to keeping the building from collapsing will delay the rate of time loss by 50%.

"War, what is it good for?"

Wolfe counted ten burning buildings. Son *of a...*

"Shel, Rhett, Fern—handle everything here! Set up near Loowit in case she's still healing. Keep the civilians alive with healing and cut down the soldier cards as fast as possible. Your decks synergize"—*well, two of them*—"and I think you can save most of this. Watch for the buildings when you have the chance!"

Neither one nay-said Wolfe as they started moving, but Shel called out, "What are you going to do?"

"Hunt," Wolfe said, and Cereboo let out a braying yell. Wolfe brought forth his second Obsessive Cultist.

I have a few moments to set up, I bet.

Part of Wolfe was tempted to try and empower himself significantly, but he had his mantle in this pull, and no Demonic Portals. That meant that he could add the mantle, which would empower his cards, and then likely put *six* creatures on the field with his remaining power and cards on field, so long as he sacrificed an Obsessive Cultist on the last play.

Puppy Pack time, Wolfe thought sardonically, using the name that Malviere had given his deck.

He raced down an obvious path on the left-hand side of the village. He immediately played his mantle. He had already spent one of his eight power, and this further reduced him by two more. But it let him put any number of cards on the field so long as they were canine, and empowered them.

Master of the Infernal Hunt
Unique Tier-5 equivalent Infernal Persistent [Mantle]
2 Infernal Power
+10 Health, +3 to all remaining stats.

Special: **Cerberus's Champion:** All other [Canine] Cards gain +5 Health and +1 to all other stats, and all [canine] cards gain advantage against Infernal cards.
Special: **Versatile [Infernal]:** This card alters to fit its wearer so long as they have at least 2 Infernal Power
Special: **Grand Pack [Canine]:** [Canine] cards do not count against cards on the field
Special: **Favorable Façade [Canine]:** Count as a Beast [Canine] card for all purposes except type match penalties.
Special: One of the 'Gate to the Underworld' cards. If all 6 are possessed in the same deck, the bearer will gain 7 Legendary Infernal or Beast card pulls. Additionally, the deckbearer may either gain the Mythic 'Gate to the Underworld' Building Card or evolve Cereboo. One card is held by each of the crime families of Noimoire, and the sixth is held within the city by another.

"Sometimes, the demons call a hunt on other demons, and a hunt master is always chosen to lead the chase."

Wolfe ran along the path, but it took more than thirty

seconds to reach his destination. He tossed down a Demonic Portal card, drawing forth five power worth of creatures—he picked his Gehennan Kennel Master and an Angry Hellhound, tier-4. The portal cost two power, reducing his power to three and his cards on field to zero.

Wolfe reached a small clearing. Inside, he saw Chief Pahto, an elite brave, and a named shaman. The Chief had two hundred life and strong stats in the mid teens, and the Shaman had fifty health, stats in the low teens, and a powerful healing ability.

Wolfe played his second Demonic Portal while sacrificing his Obsessive Cultist. It raised the cost to four, but the cultist gave three power, and so Wolfe was left with two power. He used the power to summon two Angry Hellhounds and a Lost Hellhound Puppy.

He glanced at his Angry Hellhounds, now that they had what was nearly the maximum possible buffs Wolfe could give.

Angry Hellhound
Common Tier-4 Beast/Infernal (Canine) Creature
Two Beast or Infernal Power
Health: 14(19)
Attack: 9(20)
Defense: 5(7)
Magical Attack: 5 [**Fire or Infernal**](16)
Magical Defense: 5(7)

Special: **Dual Attacker:** When this creature makes a physical attack, it also makes a magical attack on the same target.
Special: **Empty Mind:** Immune to all mind-affecting debuffs.
Special: **Canine Tribal [1]:** +1 to all attacks for every other canine on the field.
Special: **Hunter [Escaped Damned 1]:** Gains +1 Attack for every Escaped Damned on the field.

Special: **Reformed Doggo**: This card gains type advantage, and loses type disadvantage, against any Infernal, Undead, or Elder card, and any card with the word 'criminal' or 'villain' in its title or type.

"It could be argued that most things in the Infernal realms are angry, but these hellhounds take it to an entirely new level— and this one has torn many a spirit to the point it needs to reform on many an occasion."

Malviere trigged one Hellhound with her fast-attacking ability, and it hit the Shaman, slaying it in a single grab of the neck and violent shake that ripped the Shaman's throat out entirely. It did four hundred damage, netting zero for combined type, and then second attacked as an Infernal Magic attack for three-hundred and eight-four base magical damage. The shaman was obliterated by the single strike, taking almost eighty damage net.

Wolfe ran over and slew the brave, just to get his pack and their insane stats focused on the bad guy.

Each of the three Angry Hellhounds hit the Chief. They ripped into his legs and arm, each doing the same base damage. Chief Pahto took less damage thanks to his higher stats, and cach did only did about fifty net each.

But Cerberus hit as well, biting into the chief's stomach and back, and he did another twenty-five damage. Malviere managed another twenty or so with her Death attack.

Wolfe couldn't help but feeling smug. At full synergy, with a couple perfect rounds of set-up, his deck was *insane*.

The Chief slammed his warclub down on an Angry Hellhound, killing it, but Wolfe summoned the Bulgae Moon Chaser with his last power, keeping the other ones at full power.

The next round, the Chief died to the first attack power of

Malviere. Wolfe received a notification that it had been a Level Thirty-Five encounter, and he gained another level.

A card dropped from the dead boss, and Wolfe grabbed it. It was a decently strong rendition of Chief Pahto, a Mortal subtyped for a couple things that didn't subtype to anything their team used.

Based on his summoning and such, Wolfe was pretty sure only two and a half minutes had passed.

He turned and sprinted toward the other chief's base, back along the path. He started dismissing his demonic Portal summons and trying to reset. It would take a minute to return to the village, so if he could somehow resummon everything in the same order, and presumably win in the same time, he might be able to end this before any buildings burned down.

CHAPTER 22

LEVELING ONE MORE TIME

Wolfe returned to the center of the mock Cowlitz village, which had ascended to a new and improved state: not being on fire. He had finished the second fight under the seven-minute mark, but it had been close, as the cards hadn't quite cooperated the second time for his uber-dog strat. Despite that, he saw that two of the cedar longhouses appeared to have burnt down, and a couple civilians were dead in the streets—not dissipated into energy like most monsters or cards did when defeated.

He could hear mothers weeping, and the air smelled of burnt wood, with an undertone of burnt flesh and a coppery blood smell mixed in for maximum pathos. *Way to rub it in, gods.*

Loowit was still at the base of the fire, weeping as well.

"What happened?" Wolfe asked, motioning to the two houses.

"Arsonists," Rhett said. "Some of the archers apparently had extra fire arrows, and ticked down the timers. We hit them specifically and hard after that, but they still got two. Sorry."

"It's fine," Wolfe said. *Nothing can be done by bitching now.*

Wolfe was distracted by three people walking into town. One was Chief Tyee. The other two were his sons, still covered in dog bites but newly restored to...functionality, Wolfe supposed.

They both appeared downcast.

Tyee marched up to Loowit, his sons slouching after him. He took her chin in his hand and faced her up at him.

"I am disappointed in you, Loowitlatkla," he said, then turned and glowered at his sons before returning his gaze to her. "Not as disappointed as I am in my own sons, but I am still displeased. Why would you not choose one? If you had merely chosen, this feud could have ended."

She spoke, fresh tears running from her eyes. "I am sorry, my chief, but they were both so strong, and so wonderful, that I could not choose."

"And now their selfishness and pride, and your indecision, has burned many of the villages of the Cowlitz. But for these heroes here"—he motioned his other arm to vaguely take in Wolfe, Rhett, Fern, and Shel in turn—"the very heart of our people would have burned. I cannot allow this to stand."

"What will you do with us?" Loowit asked.

"I love you all, and honor the good even though I punish the bad. I shall make each of you a spirit of one of the mountains that look at the heart of our people, and yours shall burn forever with the fire you once tended, that brought us all life."

Loowit bowed her head, still weeping, and Chief Tyee waved his hand. His two sons and Loowit all disappeared, and in the distance, three mountains rose, one smoking.

Chief Tyee turned to Rhett, who was nearest him. "Thank you, heroes, for your timely aid—you saved most, but not all, of my people's heart. I will give you these in turn."

He handed two packs and a card to Rhett, then turned, walking off. As he went, he faded from view. At the same time, the fire in town cleared, and a portal appeared in the place the fire had stood.

A moment later, the trader came back, walking into the devastated town like nothing was amiss. He began setting up his stand near the city center, across from the portal.

Wolfe already knew he was going to trade the two cards they had gotten. He headed over to the trader, offering the chief's sons creature cards in order to get the two enhancer mountain cards—the spirits of Mt. Hood and Mt. Adams.

He walked back to the group, where they were staring at the card that Chief Tyee had handed to them.

The picture on the card showed Chief Tyee banishing the three to become mountains.

Displeasure of the Divine
Legendary Divine Persistent
2 Divine, 6 Any power

This card banishes for 30 minutes any three cards that are in play. While banished, these cards do not return their power to their deckbearer, nor do they return to the deck. If this card leaves play, the other three cards return to the field as if just summoned.

"The First Chiefs were so powerful that they can turn those that displease them into geographical features."

"That's quite impressive, especially for someone that has companions on the field that can fight for them," Rhett said.

"I don't have eight power, even with all the enhancers and such," Shel said. "And it doesn't really fit my style. I think, if it were up to me, I just sell it and try and get something else."

Wolfe held the two cards he had gotten out. "Well, if you want, you can take enough enhancer slots, and the building slot, to be able to add the three spirits of the mountain and the Stone Arch Fire building into your deck."

Shel nodded. "I still can't believe that two years ago I was just some stupid jumped-up kid, and now I'm a card officer with a deck that has legendary and mythic cards in it."

She turned to Wolfe. "In case my proposal earlier didn't clue you in, I love you so, so much. For everything."

Wolfe looked away. "Sure. I love you too. But let's open the packs and see what we get, this has been the longest day ever, and I want to get some sleep. We have a lot to do."

Shel tool the two packs from Rhett's hand and then handed them, along with her two legendary Life packs, to Wolfe. "I want you to open them. Four more chances to get an orphan that doesn't even exist yet, based on your perk."

Wolfe still wasn't sure if taking the ancient packs had been the best idea, as merges would be terribly hard to come by. But he had to admit, the cards they had gotten had synergized with Shel a lot. Maybe they would again.

He opened the first Life pack, which was listed as a 'Cycle of the Fifth Sun, Twilight, Legendary Life' and had a picture of a river filled with fish coursing across the packaging, still in the ubiquitous pseudo-Aztec line drawing style.

Four uncommon cards, a rare, and a legendary card, all Life cards, fell into his hand. Wolfe passed them to Shel immediately.

No orphans, but there were immediate heals, and two persistent cards for the rare and the legendary—both of which felt like they had almost been made for Shel.

The first showed a Couatl with hands holding a glowing sun over an Aztec-style village.

Quetzalcoatl's Blessing of Promise

Legendary tier-1 Divine/Life [Vitality, Civic] Persistent
2 Life or Divine Power, 2 Mortal Power

Target [Civic] Card you control with power cost 3 or less.
This card becomes a token copy of it. While this card is on the
field, [Civic] cards you own cost 1 less of any power to play
and you may have 2 extra cards on field so long as they are
[Civic]. Cards reduced below 1 power become cost 1 Any
Power (available) and gain Speedy.

"Times are changing and a new age is arriving. I cannot
promise that it will be better and already there are omens that
it will be a dark age for your people, but I promise you, I will
care for you and watch over you, so that you may find comfort
and rest after your last days."—Quetzalcoatl

The second card showed a rainbow sun glowing over an
even more complete Aztec metropolis.

Shard of the Second Sun
Rare tier-1 Fire/Light/Life/Divine [Sun, Civic, Ascendant,
Vitality] Persistent
2 Power of either Light, Life, Fire, or Divine

Special: Gift of Quetzalcoatl: While this card is in play each
allied creature gains +1 to each non-Health stat for each power
type and each subtype it shares with this card.
Special: Ire of Quetzalcoatl: While this card is in play all
creatures that don't share a power type or a subtype with this
card suffers -1 to all non-Health stats.

"A fragment of Quetzalcoatl's grand Sun Stone, it carries
within it the light and fire that nurtures life and protects
civilizations."

"Well, no orphans, but those are some *good* cards for your deck," Wolfe said.

Shel's eyes were wide as she stared at the Blessing of Promise. "With this card and Stone Arch Fire on the field, I'd heal *everything* for twenty a round, and remove a step of injury penalty the first time it occurs. More than that with the Fire Tender Mantle."

"Well, at a certain point it's overkill," Wolfe replied.

Shel nodded, but she had a faraway look in her eyes.

Wolfe opened the second pack. A few more cards spilled out. The Legendary card was actually not very useful at all—it was a Life spirit that healed and increased healing dramatically, but given Shel's capabilities, it really was pure overkill. Wolfe and Shel quickly decided they would sell it.

But three of the uncommon ones caught Wolfe's eyes. The first was a Couatl that cost one Life power, but two rounds after it entered, could be sacrificed to bring forth any other couatl at no power cost. It was called a Growing Couatl.

The second was an uncommon building called Civic Irrigation. It showed canals and a few wells around an Aztec-style town.

Civic Irrigation
Uncommon Tier-1 equivalent Life [Civic] Building
1 Life Power

This card expands to grow one hundred feet around every building that was placed next to it. It adds 25% to the effect of all buildings owned by other deckbearers that it touches. All effects round to the nearest whole number of the effect. This building may not modify another Civic Irrigation building regardless of who owns it.

"Rivers are fine, but they must be directed to grow life. An expert guiding the irrigation can bring teeming life where before there was nearly nothing, and cities will follow."

"Wow..." Shel said, grabbing Wolfe's arm again. "That would be *amazing*. I mean, can you imagine? If I had that, the Stone Arch Fire would double its effect!"

"So?" Wolfe asked, trying to think through why she was so excited.

"It would make the bonus fifty percent! And then every single plus one would become a plus two on any buildings that anyone had! Can you imagine? You'd add more to growth of orphans, you would add even more to their tier, you would pick two cards to start your hand with..."

Wolfe eyed her. "You seem to be sacrificing a lot for other people. Don't you want to increase your own deck?"

She laughed. "No. I want to heal the world, to save those that deserve saving, like you told me more than a year ago. And now, maybe Liam, or Miriam, or even Rhett here could place buildings and get a greater effect as well."

Wolfe nodded slowly. It made sense, he supposed. She was the light to his darkness, no doubt about it. But...

"Either way, you need fifteen leveling pips to put two buildings in your deck, and you need twenty-five leveling pips to put the remaining Lantern angels in. You're going to have some hard decisions."

Shel's excitement faded. "That's true."

Then they glanced at the last card together. It showed a baby Couatl, more of an iridescent green than the rainbow of most of the couatl cards they had seen, crawling from the remains of a shell.

It was an orphan card, which meant that even if it was officially not a unique card, there would only be one in the world most likely.

Couatl Hatchling of the Sixth Sun
Uncommon Tier-1 Life Minion [Orphan]
0 Power
Health: 7
Attack: N/A
Defense: 3
Magical Attack: N/A
Magical Defense: 8

Special: Will fetch normal objects and such with a decent degree of precision and help carry up to five pounds.

Special: **Orphan Evolution [Unique]:** If kept 'alive' for five straight years, will turn into a Rare equivalent, Tier-4 equivalent creature card, gaining notable power. The deckbearer will also gain a common Life pack from the same set as the orphan. If ever 'killed,' the timer resets.

"Well, that is nearly everything," Wolfe said. "Are you going to do your final build now?"

Shel nodded. "I'm going to take the entire collection of Mountain Spirit cards, which will need five more pips of enhancers."

Wolfe held them out, and Shel took them.

Spirit of Mount St. Hoods
Unique Rare equivalent Tier-1 equivalent Elemental / Life
[Earth] Enhancer
0 Power

This card adds +1 Defense, +1 Magical Defense, and +3 Health. This person will have their weight doubled for purposes of resisting being moved. +20% lifespan. They restore an injury level per day.

"After the destruction, Chief Tyee changed all three participants into mountains. Pahto became Mount St. Hood, who watched over the Cowlitz."

Spirit of Mount St. Adams

Unique Rare equivalent Tier-1 equivalent Elemental / Life [Earth] Enhancer
0 Power

This card adds +2 Defense and +5 Health. This person will have their weight doubled for purposes of resisting being moved. +20% lifespan.

"After the destruction, Chief Tyee changed all three participants into mountains. Wy'east became Mount St. Adams, who sheltered the Cowlitz."

Shel continued. "Then I'm going to take a building slot for the Stone Arch Fire card. That will leave me with seven pips, and I can decide what I want to do after I make three more levels."

"And your cards?" Wolfe asked.

Shel was typing out on her phone, and she passed it over. Wolfe scrolled down, seeing where she was at.

Rachel Lyons Status:
Level 31 Deckbearer (7 Levels pending)

Deckbearer Perks:
Lost and Lonely God-gifted Start: +1 Companion card
Deckbearer Perk 1: Divine Favor: When pulling from a Mortal or Divine pack, one random card will be a

rarity higher. If pulling from a mixed deck, at least one card will be either Mortal or Divine.

Deckbearer Perk 2: Guiding Light of the Divine: Gain 1 Light Power. May have one extra card in play so long as it's a Mortal (Any EMT, Police, or card with the 'Civic' subtype).

Level 25 Perk: Nurse of the Chosen: Gain 1 Life Power, and the first time per week any entity is healed by this deckbearer, they lose 1 injury level as well. Gain 2 Legendary Life packs from any set that is represented in the deckbearer's deck.

Deckbearer Flaw: Pacifist: May not gain attack from mantles

Deckbearer Stats:
Cards in Deck: 15 (1 pip)
Cards in Hand: 4 (1 pip)
Cards in Play: 3 (1 pip)
Length of Play: 5 minutes

Specialty Cards:
Building: 1 (5 pips)
Companion: 2 (5 pips)
Minion: 1 (1 pip)
Enhancer: 3 (6 pips)

Type 1 and Power: 1 Divine
Type 2 and Power: 3 Mortal (3 pips)
Energy 1 and Power: 1 Light
Energy 2 and Power: 2 Life (From Perk, Stone Arch Fire)

Energy 3 and Power: 1 Fire (From Spirit of Mt. St. Helens)

Personal Perks:
Inborn Perk 1: Small: -1 Attack(nullified with all three Spirit of the Mountain enhancer cards)

Acquired Perk 1: Police Training: +1 Attack and Defense. Does not stack with other training.

Acquired Perk 2: Expert Shooter: +3 Attack and Defense only when using firearms. Does not stack with other training.

Personal Stats:
Health: 35
Attack: 6(8)
Magical Attack [None]: 0
Defense: 11(13)
Magical Defense [None]: 6

Card List:
Companion
Sorenia
Liurenia

Building
Stone Arch Fire

Enhancer
Spirit of Mt. St. Helens
Spirit of Mt. Hood
Spirit of Mt. Adams

Mantle
Fire Tender

Persistent
Quetzalcoatl's Blessing of Promise
Police Academy
Guiding Light

Immediate
Barter the Soul
Burned Sacrifice

Creature
Couatl of the Second Sun
Rookie EMT x2

"I'll keep some cards, and I will probably need to move to twenty cards soon. But there are some seriously strong plays in that deck at the moment. But I would benefit from a few powerful Mortal cards with the subtype Civic if we can find them."

Wolfe nodded. "Still, your deck is coming along very nicely."

"As are you, Shel," Rhett cut in. "I'm impressed. And your salary will be huge now that you're past level thirty."

Shel nodded to his words.

"However, what would you say to us opening the next packs?" Rhett asked. "The ones we can all use."

CHAPTER 23

THE LAST PRIZES OF THE DUNGEON

Wolfe took one of the general rare packs, then tore it open and dumped it into his hand.

Most of the cards weren't that interesting. Wolfe did get a second Xolo Spirit-Warder, and the rare was a 'Shattered Mayan Calendar' that was a 1 Golem or 1 Meta power persistent that stopped all creatures and persistent from advancing any timed effect so long as it was in play. It felt highly situational to Wolfe, but Rhett took it for his deck with everyone's consent.

Wolfe opened the final pack of cards, also a rare one. He had been underwhelmed with the number of cards he had gotten for his deck from this entire run. Although Shel was building toward an *insane* mixed civic and healing deck, which Wolfe was extremely pleased with.

Two common cards, two uncommon ones, and *two* that were rare—for a second time in this dungeon, an uncommon had upgraded to a rare card.

One of the uncommon cards was finally psychic—a card called 'vision quest' that took 2 psychic power and stopped the deckbearer from playing cards the next 30 seconds, but afterwards restored all power to the deckbearer even if cards were already on the field. Effectively, all the cards of the deckbearer that were on field already had their power cost reduced to zero. It seemed risky to Wolfe, but Fern wanted it, and he passed it over after a nod from Shel.

But both the rare cards were, somehow, canine subtype although neither fit perfectly with Wolfe's deck as both lacked Infernal. Excitement bubbled in his chest regardless.

The first showed a ruined, dead city jutting out of the ground, filled with spirit dogs.

Fragment of Itzcuintlan
Rare Tier-1 Undead/Beast [Spirit, Ruin, Canine] Building
0 Power

The Fragment of Itzcuintlan creates a 250,000 sq. feet ruined park, with fragments of buildings and a permanent fog within it. Within 10 miles of this location, all dogs have 30% increased lifespan and do not get sick. Within the location, and in all adjacent contiguous buildings, all undead cards except **Itzcuintlan Spirit Dogs** have their Attack and Magical Attack set to N/A.

So long as this card is in the deck, whenever a [Canine] of the deckbearer is reduced to zero health, there is a 50% chance that an **Itzcuintlan Spirit Dog** token card will be called into play.

In the event that the deckbearer has more than one fragment of Itzcuintlan, each additional one past the first adds +1 to all non-health stats of all [Spirit] and/or [Canine] cards rather than increasing summoning chance.

"The first realm of the underworld is sometimes known as Itzcuintlan, the land of dogs, because the spirits of dogs guide their kind owners onward in their journey to their final resting place."

Itzcuintlan Spirit Dog
Undead / Beast [Spirit, Canine] Creature
Token, 1 power equivalent

Health: 6
Attack: N/A
Defense: 10
Magical Attack: 4[**Death**]
Magical Defense: 2

"The ethereal nature of the Spirit Dog makes it extremely hard to seriously injure with normal weapons."

"Okay, so, I'm extra glad I didn't take the Stone Arch Fire and left it to you," Wolfe said, staring at the card. "I mean, I barely have any leveling pips, but this has a great deal of potential for my deck. A huge amount of potential, really."

Shel nodded. "Yeah. Except that by not being an Infernal card it limits the benefit of Hellmouth."

Wolfe winced. "Oh, yeah. My bad."

Then he paused. "Although, technically, the Conduit of the Infernal can make a card act as if it's Infernal."

Shel nodded, but held a hand up. "Don't forget, even with that, it still requires ten leveling pips, so…"

Wolfe frowned. "Well, let's keep it as a possible. It would be pretty amazing in my deck if I can afford it."

Shel didn't say anything else, she just leaned up on tiptoes and planted a kiss on his cheek.

Wolfe glanced at the second card—another orphan from

the modifier provided by his 'Caretaker of the Lost and Lonely" enhancer. This one showed a skeleton. But the creature wasn't just normal remains. The bones of the body were clearly human, but the skull was canine. The creature card showed Aztec markings all over the bones.

Get of Xolotl
Rare Undead / Beast [Skeleton, Canine, Demi-God, Orphan]
Minion
0 Power

Health: 20
Attack: N/A
Defense: 3
Magical Attack: N/A
Magical Defense: 3

Special: **Orphan Evolution [Unique]:** If kept 'alive' for ten straight years, will turn into a unique Legendary equivalent, Tier-1 equivalent, five-power creature card. The deckbearer will also gain a common Undead or Fire (choose one) Building card from the same set as the orphan. If ever 'killed,' the timer resets.

"The non-unique card turns into a unique one?" Shel asked.

"Guess so," Wolfe replied. "I just hope it stays canine. This might be the best pack I've ever drawn from, even if I never really saw myself going with any Undead cards."

"So, what are you doing for level?" Miriam asked.

"Well... I already added in the enhancer, and upped my cards on field and in hand. I think, given my build, that my next best bet is to simply save pips for a building card slot. That Fragment of Itzcuintlan is *insanely* good for my deck."

"Especially if I can work up to the Civic Irrigation card," Shel said. "Three in four times a dog card died, it would spawn a replacement that could stop other cards from attacking you while you set something up."

"Yeah."

"So, what are you looking like at the moment?"

Wolfe pulled his status chart, and recited it. Rhett and Fern paid attention. Wolfe was a touched worried, but not much—Rhett was a damned boy scout, and Fern already had enough to bury him if she wanted.

"So... any changes to your deck?" Shel asked.

Wolfe nodded. "Yeah. After everything, I'm adding our spare two Demonic Portal cards, the orphan, and putting every single creature except the Bulgae Moon Chaser and the Obsessive Cultists into the portal side-deck."

Ethan Madison Wolfe Status:
Level 36 Mortal [3 pips remaining]

Deckbearer Perks:
Lost and Lonely God-gifted Start: +1 Companion card

Deckbearer Perk 1: In the Thick of it: +50% to all numerical benefits gained from mantles

Deckbearer Perk 2: Man's Best Friend's Best Friend: Gain 1 Beast Power. May have one extra card in play so long as it's a Beast (Canine or Hybrid Canine).

Level 25 perk: Master of the Lost and the Lonely: Orphans gain +1 Tier when they evolve, and any card packs or non-orphan cards gained from orphan advancement are gained twice. Any one [evolved orphan] card of no more than 2 power may be treated as if it were a free-slot companion card with a 0-power cost.

Deckbearer Flaw: Fallen: May not gain Divine Power, nor use Divine cards unless they are also Infernal or Corrupted.

Deckbearer Stats:
Cards in Deck: 20 (3 pips)
Cards in Hand: 5 (3 pips)
Cards in Play: 4 (1 pips)
Length of Play: 5 minutes

Specialty Cards:
Companion: 3 (three free from perks and cards, 1 must be an evolved orphan acting as a companion)
Building: 2 (5 pips, one free from cards)
Minion: 3 (3 pips, 1 free from cards)
Enhancer: 2 (3 pips)

Total Power: (upgraded 5 times): 8 -1 (Infernal Rift) +1 (Infernal Gun set) = 8. (Total pips 15)
Type 1 and Power: 5 Infernal (5 -1(Infernal Rift) +1 (Infernal Guns))
Type 2 and Power: 2 Beast
Energy 1 and Power: 1 Fire

Personal Perks:
Inborn Perk 1: Vicious Killer: +25% to all Attack and Defense, check twice for Attack modifier and take the best

Inborn Perk 2: Tough as Nails: +10 Health

Acquired Perk 1: Crafty Street Fighter: +3 Attack and Defense

Personal Stats:
Health: 30/30
Attack: 10
Magical Attack [None]: 0
Defense: 10
Magical Defense [None]: 5

Deck: (20 cards, 3 companions, 2 Buildings, 3 Minions, 2 Enhancers)

Specialty:
Companion:
1x Cereboo (Gate to the Infernal set card 1)
1x Malviere
*1x Obsessive Infernal Cultist

Building:
1x Hellmouth Institute
1x Infernal Library (Library Wing of the Hellmouth Institute) (locks Obsessive Infernal Cultist to the first pull)

Minion:
1x Get of Xolotl

Enhancer:
1x Caretaker of the Lost
1x Conduit of the Infernal Six (Enhancer, Gate to the Infernal set card 4)

Standard:

Mantle:
1x Master of the Infernal Hunt (Mantle, Gate to the Infernal set card 3)

Persistent:
4x Demonic Portal (each adds a side deck of 5 Infernal creatures, 20 creature total side deck)
1x Cerberus' Home for Wayward Hellhounds

Immediate:
1x Infernal Rift (Gate to the Infernal set card 2, adds 1 minion and 1 building card)

Creature
1x Obsessive Infernal Cultist
1x Bulgae Moon Chaser

Equipment
1x Hellfire (Infernal Gun set card 1)
1x Brimstone (Infernal Gun set card 2)

Side Deck: (20 Infernal Creatures)
1x Gehenna Kennel Master
2x Tier-4 Angry Hellhound
2x Tier-3 Angry Hellhound
2x Tier-2 Lost Hellhound Puppy
1x Fireborn Hellhound
1x Smoke Demon
1x Chain Demon
2x Xolo Spirit-Warder (modified to Infernal by Conduit of the Dark Six)

Wolfe finished his recitation with, "And I've got room for one more card in deck, and up to eight more creatures in the side deck for the combined Demonic Portals."

Rhett nodded. "It's a very strong deck, Wolfe. But we should head back now."

At Rhett's words, Wolfe felt his exhaustion seeping up from his very bones. The amount he had done today was impossible to overstate. Two levels of a dungeon, followed by ring shopping, followed by a fight to save Shel that had nearly killed him, followed in turn by a third dungeon level.

Wolfe nodded, his agreement more heartfelt than usual. "Yeah. I'm done as well. Let's go."

Wolfe leaned against the door frame with his forehead as he banged on the door to Mrs. Timo's bedroom. Every single bedroom in the entire Hellmouth Institute was the exact same size, and came with the same furniture. You could move furniture around the Institute, but if you moved it back, it would regenerate inside the place again.

But the bas relief demon faces that made up the doors had a central nose you could hang things from, and each of them hung with an art project from one of the girls—a stylized name. This one had been done by Shannon, and showed a poorly drawn series of waterslides and fish around a pond with the words "Mrs. Timo's room" drawn on it.

The sign was garish and childish and clashed horribly with the décor, but it did mute it—it was far less sinister.

Of course, the place also smelled just the tiniest bit. Not of brimstone or smoke, as you might suspect, but rather the faintest hint of disinfectant in a slightly-too-chilly-but-not-cold building... just enough to be creepy.

But the sign helped a little.

Wolfe raised his fist, about to bang again, when the door opened. Mrs. Timo stared out at him, her gray hair frizzy and her eyes blurry behind her glasses. She was dressed in a thick woolen nightgown and a pair of ratty once-pink bunny slippers.

She stared at him owlishly for a moment. "Wolfe? What in the Infernal do you want at this hour? I swear you acted like a mutt before you got your deck."

Wolfe dropped his fist, pulled his head back from the door frame, and reached into his pocket. He took out ten cards and a scrap of paper.

He held it out to her. "Here, you old bat."

She took the cards and stared down at them, her eyes wide. "What's this?"

"Well, if things go badly, it might be severance pay," Wolfe quipped.

"What?" Mrs. Timo asked, still not raising her eyes. "I've only worked for you for a bit over a year."

"Look, the situation is too long to explain, and I'm *way* too tired to re-live the shitshow that today has been," Wolfe replied. "But the long and the short of it is, I need you to take Liam, as well as Lucy and Shannon and our useless Cavapoos, and get out. I got you some tickets to Tahiti."

"And the deck?" Mrs. Timo asked. "Why the deck?"

Wolfe sighed. "In case stuff goes bad. That deck is designed to win by doing nothing, and it's got some rather nasty cards for it. I mean, I know a stiff breeze will kill you, but hopefully it won't come down to you actually fighting. Work it out with Liam, I'm not sure. But I'd rather not have to worry about my people under attack."

"What made you think of this?"

"I told you," Wolfe began, then hesitated and scratched his head. "No, never mind. I guess I didn't. They found Fern and attacked her, and on the way home tonight, I had the sudden thought it could happen to my people next, since a badass deckbearer named Nathan saw me. So I need you to get out before he does anything insane."

Mrs. Timo nodded. "When do I leave?"

"Four hours from Noimore International," Wolfe said.

Mrs. Timo nodded a second time, a single sharp nod. "I'll get changed and get moving then."

Wolfe nodded and turned away even as Mrs. Timo began to shut the door.

But after a few steps, Mrs. Timo called out, "Wolfe?"

He turned, to see one of her eyes staring out from the mostly closed door. "Yeah?"

"Did she say yes?"

Although beyond tired, Wolfe's face lit up. "Asked me, technically. I'll tell you all about it when this is all over."

Mrs. Timo gave another half nod and finished closing the door.

CHAPTER 24

LAST IDYLLIC MORNING

Wolfe rolled over to see Shel, still asleep underneath the blankets except for her head. Her face was at peace, with wispy strands of her red hair across her face. She breathed easily, just noticeable enough to show she was alive. Wolfe marveled at her beauty in the soft, slightly red-tinted light of the late morning sun coming in through the windows of the Hellmouth Institute.

Shel twitched suddenly, her face creasing with worry even though her eyes were closed. Wolfe reached across the blanket and gently stroked her hair.

She gave another violent twitch and then snorted, sitting up in bed, staring around groggily. One of Wolfe's t-shirts was draped around her frame. Wolfe himself slept in the buff, but Shel had lived in a tiny trailer with multiple siblings, and she was rarely comfortable naked, unless the two of them were specifically engaged in sexy activities.

Speaking of engaged... "Good morning, my badass fiancée."

Shel blinked her eyes, and she held her hand up, staring at the emerald ring she hadn't taken off even to sleep. Wolfe appreciated that she liked it, but leaving it on overnight struck him as crazy.

"So, it really means new beginnings?" Shel asked as she stared at the ring. "The emerald, I mean."

"That's what the lady said at Michelle's, and she seemed pretty sure. She said her fancy store didn't make mistakes about that stuff."

Shel's eyes lit up and she threw her arms around him, hugging him hard and kissing his neck. "I love the sound of that. I love the ring, and I love you too, most of all. Thank you. For... everything. That sounds about right."

Wolfe couldn't stop the smile that split his face; his heart warmed to hear it all. But he gently disengaged, pulling back from her. "When we're done with this whole thing, we need to get married, and then go on an amazing honeymoon."

She smiled again. "Where would you go?"

Wolfe hadn't given it much thought—he had been focused more on thoughts of safe, worry-free nights with Shel then where they spent the days.

But he did his best to give it some honest thought as he stared into her eyes. "Maybe Rome? We could maybe compete in the Colosseum Arena, then visit the Temple of Mercy, perhaps. Maybe some of the Chosen of Raphael will have advice for you."

She smiled. "It's a date."

Wolfe nodded, but his own face went serious. "Right now, though, we have work to do. We need to get ready, and then we're going shopping—one way or another."

Shel tilted her head at him, mimicking Cereboo's questioning head tilt. "Why did 'shopping' need a dark threat appended to it?"

"I'll talk about it later, for now, let's get ready."

"How do we do that?" Shel asked.

Wolfe stood, casting aside the blankets and rooting around

for a pair of workout shorts. "The same way we do every morning—eat some fluffy scrambled eggs, and follow that up with a quick workout."

"And then shopping?"

Wolfe nodded.

Shel got out of bed, walked silently over to her dresser, and took a pair of workout shorts and a smaller t-shirt out before heading out into the hall, presumably for the bathroom.

One of the few things that Wolfe didn't like about his new living situation—besides the omnipresent demonic décor—was the fact there was no 'master bedroom.' So he had to go outside to get to a shower.

On the other hand, this floor alone had ten bathrooms, each with its own shower. Which wasn't the worst. So Wolfe grabbed a towel and headed for his own date with a hygiene ritual.

"So, are we hunting today, my alpha?" Malviere asked from the back seat of the truck.

Wolfe stared out the crack-free windshield of his *spare* modified black Ford F-150 as he drove down Ninth Street, through the heart of one of Noimoire's main commercial districts. After the last couple years, Wolfe had learned that for him, been prepared meant assuming he would have a car filled with lead at some point. He wasn't going to let that slow him down this time.

"No, Malviere, we aren't going to hunt, at least not right now. We're going to shop—"

"Booo," Malviere interjected.

"—for hunting tools," Wolfe finished.

"What?" Malviere asked, excitement returning to her

voice. She leaned forward over the seat, her head appearing between Wolfe and Shel.

Shel chuckled from the front passenger seat where she sat staring out the window, next to Wolfe. She was now dressed in tight faded jeans and a pink blouse that exposed her belly button, under a large jacket left hanging open. Wolfe knew she kept her own police Glock-17 in a holster hidden by the jacket.

Wolfe answered Malviere. "I need to get better gear. I nearly got myself killed when I went after the Weeds, because I did things like I always do—I relied on my natural talent and my Edge, and now, my cards. But I almost got killed doing it. I don't want to do that again, and I really don't want to subject Shel to that. So, instead, I'm going to get what we need."

"What do we need?" Malviere asked, the normal-to-the-point-of-banality conversation made more interesting by her voice.

"You'll see," Wolfe replied smugly.

"You do know that I can't use anything that will alter my stats unless it's a part of the Great Game, right?" Malviere asked.

"I've always wondered about that... what happens if I put a bullet-proof jacket on you, for example?"

"It won't work," Malviere said with certainty in her creepy, echoing voice.

"Well, I wanna try," Wolfe said, suddenly feeling mischievous and like he was thirteen years old again for no reason he could discern. "For science."

"To see what happens and laugh your ass off?" Shel asked with laughter in her voice.

Wolfe solemnly nodded.

Shel changed the topic. "I don't know exactly what you're trying to get, but I doubt if you can actually get better weapons—or any weapons, quickly. This is Illinois twenty-twenty-six. Getting guns is very hard, even for an investigator working with the police. Getting serious hardware will be nearly impossible."

Wolfe smiled a shark's smile. "Well, if it comes to that, I have some ideas about how we might get some upgraded weapons as well."

"It makes me happy when you smile like that," Malviere said as she hung over the back of the seat and stared at him. "It means that some bad guy, somewhere, is definitely going to go see Cerberus soon."

"Or at least have a very bad day," Shel said, smiling at the comment.

Wolfe saw his target and turned into the parking lot. It was a massive Jack's Sporting Goods store. A bit of online research had showed him that with the ever-increasing crime rates in Noimoire, Jack's had started carrying most of the things that Wolfe would need.

He parked his spare truck a ways back from the front, deep into the parking lot where his vehicle wasn't near anyone else. Once he turned the truck off, he exited onto the pavement. There was a slight chill in the early afternoon air, despite the sun shining down on them.

Shel and Malviere followed him out, and Cereboo jumped down from the cab. Each fell in around him, almost automatically from all their time together. With Wolfe just a hint in the lead, the four of them walked toward Jack's. A few people followed him with their eyes—Cereboo and Malviere cut a distinct picture, and while deckbearers were relatively common, seeing someone with cards out *wasn't*. Most deckbearers, Wolfe included, preferred to keep a slightly lower profile, but since Adam and his cronies clearly had a bead on Wolfe, he preferred his companions out and ready. In fact...

"Shel, just in case things go south, can you bring Sorenia and Liurenia out?"

Shel touched her chest in the ubiquitous fingers-splayed

pattern and pulled her cards. She had six in front of her—four in the main set and two off to the side.

She touched the first one, and Sorenia appeared.

She briefly sent Malviere an irritated glance before giving a slight bow to Shel. "Thank you for bringing me forth, deckbearer."

Cereboo woofed happily and ran up to Sorenia, jumping up and licking her. As always, the three-tongues-to-one-defending-hand contest went in Cereboo's favor.

A moment later, Liurenia appeared as well.

The whispers and stares intensified, and a few children were pointing at them.

But Wolfe wasn't worried about it. He had already been discovered by his enemies, at some level. Although the Weeds honestly might not know he had been involved in the assault on them. Regardless, it was best to be protected physically if anonymity couldn't shield him any longer, and four companion cards would make it hard for anything but a sniper shot or massive bomb to finish him off.

Wolfe walked to the front of the store. People moved away from his entourage, giving them a free path into the store, and Wolfe took it. He pushed through the large glass doors into the interior, where he found himself surrounded by a bevy of mannequins covered in team jerseys, boxes of tennis shoes, hats with logos, and the like. He could easily see more practical gear surrounding the central part—fishing poles on one wall, baseball clothing and accessories in another. But he wanted something a bit more specific.

A young lady, not nearly as polished as the one from Michelle's, but still looking at him with respect, stepped to his side. "May I help you, sir?"

Wolfe had been in many stores in his lifetime, and stores of this caliber didn't normally have sales staff approach customers. *I could get used to the deckbearer treatment.*

He nodded to her. "I'm looking for the clothing section—specifically, the line of armored clothing that the internet says you carry here."

The internet? Shel mouthed, silently laughing.

But the lady just nodded like it was the most reasonable thing she'd ever heard. "Of course, sir. Right this way."

CHAPTER 25

GEARING UP

Wolfe shrugged the jacket on. It was far heavier than most jackets, but not a huge strain on him. Although it had a similar feel to running with light weights on.

Wolfe pulled his stat sheet up, but his defense stat remained the same.

"How much does this protect someone?" Wolfe asked the lady helping him.

Shel was the one who answered. "Most of the tests that have been run—and yes, some of them were as horrible as that sounds—indicate that a decent set of armored clothing is worth a plus one to defense, for people that can easily handle the extra weight."

"Then why doesn't it show up in the stats?" Wolfe asked.

"Items and gear not in the Great Game do show up, but only on the actual combat notifications, not in base stats. Like, just because you're carrying your Edge, it doesn't say you have three higher attack, right?"

"What's an Edge?" the lady helping them asked.

"My pistol," Wolfe replied absently.

The lady gasped, her hand going to her throat. "Sir, if you have a gun, you have to leave or we're calling the police."

Wolfe stared at her, irritated. "It's in my glove compartment in a locking case right now. You can untwist your panties. Also, I'm a private investigator that works with the Joliet and Noimoire police forces."

The woman nodded quickly. "Okay, well—"

But Wolfe wasn't done. "Also, I have here"—Wolfe pointed at Malviere—"a card that can throw Death energy from her shadow, hitting harder than a normal gun would most times. Why would me having a pistol make me any scarier?"

"Boo!" Malviere said while making a comical face at the saleswoman, who flinched slightly.

The lady stuttered, but Shel came to her rescue. "It's fine, it's a rhetorical question. Wolfe doesn't have his gun with him, so we can all move on."

Then she put her hand on Wolfe's arm, leaned up, and kissed him on the cheek. She also whispered, "Play nice."

He rolled his eyes but made no further comment about the pistol. Instead, he held the jacket up. "How much for two sets of this in my size and two in Shel's?"

"Uhh…" The lady's eyes phased out and Wolfe could see her mouth moving. "That would be nine hundred and sixty plus tax."

"Let's do it," Wolfe replied. Then he turned to Malviere.

She spoke before he could say anything. "It won't work."

With her echoing voice, the statement sounded like a pronouncement of doom.

But Wolfe was feeling ornery. "I mean, you can hide behind a car," Wolfe said. "Why can't we put a jacket on you?"

Malviere just stared at him.

Wolfe shrugged out of his jacket.

"Um, deckbearer, sir, are you sure you should be

naysaying the gods? It doesn't feel like a good—" the saleslady began, nervously, holding a finger up.

Wolfe threw the jacket around Malviere's shoulders. Shel stepped back and the saleslady cringed.

Malviere just shimmered, and the jacket fell through her, landing anticlimactically on the floor.

The saleslady heaved a huge sigh of relief. "Thank Michael."

"What a crock of..." Wolfe muttered.

The saleslady lady stepped up. "Well, um, deckbearer, it looks your companion was right. Is there, um, anything else I can help you with?"

Her voice was patently insincere on the last question, and Wolfe could easily tell he didn't fit this lady's taste. but he still had some things he needed.

"Take me to your drones, worker drone," Wolfe said.

"Our drones?" the lady asked at the same time Shel half swatted Wolfe's arm.

He sighed. "Sorry, I wanted to see your aerial drones—the ones you can drive around, that have a camera on them. They usually have four fans on them to help them fly?"

"Oh, right, this way," the lady said, hurrying off down the aisle.

"You didn't seem to like the saleslady, alpha. How come?"

Wolfe gripped the wheel as he headed toward his next destination, in a slightly poorer part of town. Not seedy—or not seedier than most of Noimoire—but older and in need of a paintjob and some pothole filling.

He sighed. "Eh, pearl-clutching types have always irritated me. I mean, if I was gonna cause trouble, I would've fucked someone up long before she heard I owned a gun. It feels like overdramatic shit for no reason, or just a programmed response."

"Where are we going?" Shel asked.

"I read about this store—it sells guns and ammo. I mean, normally we had other ways, back in the day, of getting a piece. But I'm assuming we should at least start legal."

"Start?" Shel asked.

Wolfe shrugged but didn't say anything.

"You know, if we need bigger guns, we can always use the AR-15's that—"

Wolfe laughed. "Yeah, I'll just take your AR-15, the one you bought now that you're a police officer, all official and whatnot. As in, it's in the records. I bet it doesn't take them any time at all to arrest you."

"Well, if you buy stuff like that here, they'll arrest *you*," Shel said.

Wolfe shrugged again. "I don't think they're going to sell me what I want here. But maybe. I'm just exploring options. And I might want ammo."

Shel turned. "Wolfe, what's this all about? Really, I mean?"

Wolfe gripped the wheel, swallowing his first, angry response. *That's old Wolfe. Shel loves you.*

He took a deep breath and tried to explain, his voice tired from the last couple days, his mischievousness spent. "I've messed up, Shel. A lot."

"You saved me, and we cleared the dungeon."

Wolfe stared ahead, seeing almost nothing as he talked. "In the last forty-eight hours I've nearly died three times to jumped-up thugs and almost let you get killed once, all because I didn't plan and didn't prepare. I've got a lot to live for, now. A wonderful fiancée. Friends and family I want to take care of."

"You are taking care of us, wonderfully," Shel inserted as Wolfe turned down another street.

Wolfe just kept talking. "I'm used to being the baddest guy in the room. That was good enough against the Cobras, and against Damian's dumb ass. And, I guess, it was good enough against the Weeds, with help from Fern. But even then, it was barely good enough. And Nathan... he threw me from a third-story window. Luck of the gods I didn't die, and I *have* to be out of luck at this point. I need to be better."

Shel laid her hand gently on his shoulder. "Nathan is an ex-Navy Seal, Wolfe."

"Yeah, well, I was stupid even before that. I took the elevator up, and just chilled before I opened the door. Some deckbearer thug shot me in the chest. Not sure if I would have died without the surprise body armor, but it's very possible. And then they would have killed you."

"You were tired."

Wolfe frowned. "Stop making excuses for me, Shel. I need to be better."

Shel sat back, silent for a moment as Wolfe turned his car into a tiny parking lot fronting a row of small, dirty-looking businesses. One of them had a "James' Guns and Ammo" sign.

Wolfe turned the car off, but before he could get out, Shel put her hand on his arm again.

"Wolfe, wait, please," Shel said, her hand lying lightly, not restraining him.

Wolfe sat back.

"Okay, yeah, not at least moving to the side of the elevator was dumb. But you *were* tired. The problem is, you're not a paramilitary guy, or even a cop. Your training is 'thug,' and even if you were the best thug ever, it's not exactly an uncommon or high-tier course, you know?"

"Get to the point, love."

"You need *training*, Wolfe. I wasn't lying about you being tired. You made the mistake because you were exhausted, and freaking out about me—which I love. But you weren't *thinking*."

"Tell me how you really feel," Wolfe growled out sardonically.

Shel just kept going. "Training takes care of that, because your unconscious mind, or maybe muscle memory, knows what to do. How many times have you trained going after people from inside an elevator?"

"Never," Wolfe admitted.

"Exactly. What you're about to do, going into a gun store and buying a bunch of heavier guns... it's not going to work. Or if it does, you'll just end up on cameras and in ledgers and files. We need another plan."

Wolfe hesitated, but he knew Shel was right.

Still... "I'm not sure I can beat Nathan right now. I have to have an edge on him. I've never gone up against someone that can fight like me, or, probably, even better. Even Charleston was just relying on power and cards and sheer viciousness. Nathan fights different."

"So, get the training yourself," Shel replied.

Wolfe stared at the ceiling of the car. "We're supposed to be fighting two more gangs and part of Adam's crew over the next four and a half days, Shel. I don't have time for training."

Shel acknowledged that with a single nod. "Then what's your other plan? I mean, you keep hinting you have some other plan on how to get enough gear to make up the difference, right?"

Before Wolfe could answer, Shel laughed. She nodded to the back, where Malviere sat. Piles of boxes were in nearly every space Malviere didn't occupy. "I mean, you already have a giant collection of armored clothing and drones. I assume that counts for something in the gear department. But what was the plan for the rest of it?"

Wolfe stared at the store in front of him for a moment, but then nodded. "Well, it would require an entire other mission, probably dangerous itself. But I did have another plan. It occurs to me that once upon a time, the Cobras had heavy weapons, including a damn rocket launcher. I never got an explanation of how that happened. Now, I saw that the remnants of the Weeds have heavy weapons—or, at least, heavier weapons."

Wolfe paused, and Shel motioned at him to keep going.

"So, it stands to reason that if this Adam character has been behind a lot of this, he might be the reason they're able to get the weapons like that. He might have a source... but he also might have a stash. If I use *his* weapons in these attacks, it'll most likely lead back to him. And maybe with all the right gear, I can even the playing field against the Singh and Renfeldt families... and against Nathan."

"How would you know or find out, or do anything about it?" Shel asked.

"Fern. She knows all about Adam's operations, and from what she told me about her ex-boss, the one thing he might not be prepared for at all is for me to go on the offensive against him."

CHAPTER 26

A NEW METHOD, AN OLD METHOD

Wolfe was a having a bit of Déjà vu as he stared out the window at the warehouse on the river front in Noimoire. Between the people he had dropped to feed the river crabs, and the time he and Rhett had almost died themselves here, Wolfe would have been happier to never return.

But that wasn't the main reason he was having Déjà vu. The main reason was Fern sitting in the back of his truck, helping him to prepare for another "hit" type of mission.

Wolfe had called her to ask where Adam kept the good stuff. An hour later, she had called back with a location. But she hadn't stopped there. Instead, she had asked him to get an entirely different drone than the ones Wolfe had gotten earlier. It was a mini-drone that still had a camera but couldn't be heard over ambient city noises when it was over a hundred feet away, apparently.

She had made a few modifications to it, then asked Wolfe to get multiple silencers, which he had stopped by Miriam for, and various head-sets and Bluetooth communicators and some odds and ends. Wolfe had gotten them as well, and Fern had modified those next. Something to do with frequencies that Wolfe hadn't 100% understood, although he got the basic idea she was trying to keep anyone from listening in.

Wolfe stared back at Fern. She was hunched over, breathing in the weird way she did to lower anxiety. But Wolfe couldn't help but think how dangerous she really was, despite the least threatening exterior he had ever seen. Barely twelve hours after he had called her, she was sitting in the back of his truck with two laptops and a drone controller around her. One laptop was running some kind of hacking program, and the other was monitoring a newly mounted, highly complex camera on the mini-drone. And she was flying the thing despite her odd breathing.

Wolfe adjusted a Bluetooth communicator in his ear, that matched the headset that Fern wore. He felt more like a deadly soldier, and less like a warrior or thug, than he had ever felt.

I have a guy in the chair, Wolfe thought, bemused. *A badass guy in the chair even if she looks like she'd lose to a stiff breeze or stray bad thought.*

"There are three guards," Fern said, her voice monotonous from where she was hunched in the back, surrounded by her computers. Almost like she was a computer herself. "They're operating independently, so you can murder one without another nearby to hear or see. Two are walking the exterior of the complex, and if you hit one the other will find it about ten minutes later. But one is on the railing walkway around the top, and might see anything."

"What kind of warehouse has a walkway around the top?" Wolfe asked exasperatedly.

"Apparently the kind where high-level villains store illegal weaponry," Shel said, smiling at him slightly.

Fern ignored the byplay. "If you walk up the river side, there is a bush you could hide behind until the perfect moment. I already gave you the preferred pattern for the attack—Wolfe up close, Shel with the AR-15 from the bushes."

Shel nodded, but she was biting her lower lip.

"And you have the laptop?" Fern asked.

Wolfe patted the device lying against his side.

"You should go," Fern whispered. "I'll be with you so long as you're outside, and will warn you on anyone incoming once you're inside."

"You think this'll work?" Shel asked Fern.

"Probably," Fern responded. "And if it does, it'll give you at least improvement in our chances against Nathan, and ultimately Adam. But things can always go wrong."

Her voice dropped even lower, and Wolfe could barely hear it. "We all know that things can go wrong. We know it intimately. But that can happen whether we try or not."

Wolfe nodded and stepped from his truck into the cool night air of Noimoire, carrying the laptop. Shel followed him out, carrying the AR-15, now with a tripod stand and a silencer.

The two of them left the road they were on, heading over the lawn of the warehouse they were at and to the river's edge.

Wolfe's earpiece crackled to life. "No one should have a visual on you, move now."

Wolfe motioned to Shel and started running down the tiny riverfront, a few feet above the river itself. Soon, he saw the bush they had identified. He ran up to it and crouched down behind it, and Shel landed next to him a couple seconds later.

"Okay, just sit tight for a moment. You can probably pull Malviere out as well, but do it fast and put the deck away again —the glowing cards might give you away through the bush once they show up."

Wolfe nodded, touched his chest with splayed hand, and then pushed it forward. He immediately hit Malviere, who swirled into existence lying down next to him. Wolfe dismissed his deck.

"We're hunting, alpha?" Malviere asked.

Wolfe nodded and pointed up ahead, toward the corner of the building, where a bored-looking man, a bit overweight, was walking around in an obvious perimeter. He had a gun holstered at his side, but nothing else.

Wolfe knew the guy working the top had a semi-automatic rifle, however.

"Alright, set up," Wolfe said. He got ready to run himself.

Shel started to set up the tripod, but her hands were shaking slightly. Wolfe watched as she managed to get it set up and took aim at the railing where the upper guard would come around the side.

Her eyes were watering, and a single tear slid down her face.

"Shel?" Wolfe asked, thrown back on his metaphorical heels as he squatted on his physical ones, staring at his fiancée.

She wiped her face. "I'm okay, Wolfe. It needs to happen. Just do what you have to do."

Wolfe stared at her for a moment. "You don't want to kill him?"

Shel shrugged. "I hate hurting people. In defense of you, or others, I've done it, sure. But I've never just shot someone like this before, okay? It's a new experience."

"He's a bad man," Wolfe replied in a whisper. "I mean, this isn't a random security guard. This is one of Adam's people—I mean, he's carrying an illegal weapon, he has to know he's not on the side of right at some level."

Shel shrugged, then replied at the same volume, her voice monotone. "I said I'll handle it."

Wolfe was torn as he watched. He tried thinking back to their time together. Shel had never been the one to pull the trigger in any situation close to this. She had lured the head of the Cobras back, and she had fought with them in a warehouse, but she had never just killed someone without them being a direct threat at some level.

Wolfe sighed. He felt like he was being an idiot, but he also knew he didn't want his fiancée to experience this. It was his job to shield her from whatever tiny darkness was left—or, even if it wasn't his job, it was what he wanted to do.

He reached down and picked up the rifle, then whispered, "I'll handle this."

Shel started to sit up, but Wolfe put his hand out and shook his head no. "Shh. Wait till people are gone."

Shel subsided, and the guards completed their track, giving them a brief moment.

"I can handle it," Shel repeated.

Wolfe shook his head. "I'm sure you can, but you've never assassinated anyone. This feels like a huge step we probably shouldn't have you take, for multiple reasons, now that I think about it. No matter the plan Fern had. Let me handle this part —you be here to keep me alive."

Hope I don't regret this, but I do think this part is well within my usual capability, even if there is a certain irony to abandoning the plan and relying on raw skill.

Before she could argue, Wolfe hurled himself around the bush, running for the wall of the warehouse they were aiming for. As he did, he pulled his deck, praying to Cerberus for luck for once.

And he got it. His mantle was available in his first draw, and he slapped it, a feral glee filling him.

The red light settled around him and he picked up speed, feeling the power of the card coursing through him. He ran to the wall and leaned back against it.

"That was idiotic," Fern's voice came through the com. "But your white knighting aside, the guard will be there in ten seconds, give or take a second or two."

He took breaths as quietly as he could for the remaining few seconds, and as soon as the guard stepped around the corner, Wolfe punched him in the head so hard that the thug's head caved in. Wolfe grabbed him before he fell, his movements supernaturally quick. He laid him against the inner wall.

Fern's voice crackled to life. "You've got five minutes before the second ground guard reaches the spot. Around the corner, about twenty feet along the wall, is a ladder you can reach to get to the top. Upper guard is going to pass it in about twenty seconds, along the railing directly above you. If he looks down, he'll spot you. If he doesn't, you can probably go around the corner and climb the ladder a mere twenty seconds after that without him hearing. If you're careful."

Wolfe nodded, even though Fern couldn't see him—or not enough to see him nod, she could probably see him through her eye in the sky. Then he counted the time to himself, staring up at the railing surrounding the upper level of the warehouse. The soft metallic clink of the guard walking across it came around the corner, and Wolfe silently pointed his STI Edge up, holding his breath as the guard walked.

Every nerve was on fire—this had been what the AR-15 had been for, to silence this guard before he could see what Wolfe had done. Wolfe didn't breathe as the footsteps went past him, the guards gait slow and steady.

After a moment, when the guard was barely past him, Wolfe stepped around the corner, then exhaled.

Thirty seconds later, he ran at the wall, leapt up, and grabbed the ladder. A boost of power from Malviere gave him extra impetus, and he pulled himself up, his new phenomenal combat power translating somewhat to raw strength, over the railing in a move that would normally have required one of the upper percentage points of human physiques, but that he could manage with his mantle.

Then he willed Malviere gone. After a moment, her red and brown lights swirled into his deck. Wolfe re-pulled the deck and re-summoned her.

"Alright, just lean around the corner and finish that man for me. As quiet as you can. I don't want to chase him over the metal railing."

Malviere nodded and leaned around the side.

Wolfe held his gun, ready to go around the side if things didn't work.

Malviere threw her shadow at the target. A ghost dog formed and raced where Wolfe couldn't see it.

But a notification popped up, telling him that the target was dead.

Wolfe breathed easily.

Then he leaned over the side of the railing and waited. A moment later, he pulled his trigger once, the silenced shot turning the last guard's head into mist thanks to the extra power of Wolfe's mantle. *Fair fights are for suckers.*

"Alright, all three guards are down," Wolfe said. "Shel, care to bring me the computer, and we can head in?"

He leapt off the railing, enjoying his power as he landed on the ground outside the warehouse.

I wonder what they'll have for me?

CHAPTER 27

LOOT BOX

The door to the warehouse was locked with an old-fashioned padlock, which surprised Wolfe. Fortunately, the nearby dead guard—the one who had died without mess—was in possession of the key on a small keyring with a few others.

"Adam's salaries don't account for any more personnel here at night," Fern was saying through the headset, her awkward breathing also audible. "But please be cautious, Wolfe. I would be at least a bit surprised if there wasn't *something* as a backup to the guards. Also, until you hook up the laptop I gave you, I won't be able to advise or help you, except to tell you if someone is coming."

"Got it," Wolfe muttered as he placed the key in the lock and turned, half-expecting a trap right here after Fern's little speech.

But the padlock came open, and Wolfe pulled it from the door. There was a second lock, easily defeated by a different key, but nothing else happened. Wolfe entered the side of the warehouse. Next to him was a light switch, and he flicked it on.

A series of hanging flood lights lit up the warehouse. It was almost empty, most of the space unused. The center had a few crates and wooden pallets, however. Wolfe whistled low as he saw the contents—much of it was boxes of weapons. Wolfe's eyes widened, and he smiled. Perhaps it wasn't much to occupy a warehouse, and it was almost certainly nothing for a company of soldiers, but there were *a lot* of weapons from the standpoint of Wolfe and Shel and their team, such as it was.

Wolfe started to walk toward them, but Shel grabbed his arm and held the laptop up. "We should find any computer system they have and plug this in, so Fern can do... whatever she does."

With a quiet chuckle, Wolfe abandoned his beeline for the weapons and glanced around. There were stairs leading up to a small office overlooking the warehouse, as well as the door to the outside railing that ringed the building.

Wolfe pointed, still slightly in quiet mode from earlier, and the two of them walked the narrow stairs to the tiny landing outside the office.

Wolfe glanced in, finding a desk, chair, fan, and computer set-up in the otherwise empty room.

Wolfe pulled the keys out, but Shel put her hand on his arm. "I don't think the guards would have a key to the inner office."

"Will it hurt to check?" Wolfe asked.

Shel shrugged, and Wolfe went through the keys quickly, confirming Shel's suspicions. But he was wearing his new armored clothing, so he simply turned and smashed his elbow into the glass, hard. It broke, and large glass shards came raining down. He reached in and unlocked the door.

Shel, despite being in steel-toed boots, walked gingerly across the glass-strewn floor. She put the laptop on the table, turned it on, and then plugged it into the USB port.

"Got it?" she asked into her headset.

"I've got a connection, working on getting in. It has a very"—Fern stopped and let out a dark chuckle, the first time Wolfe could remember hearing mirth from her—"and we're in, the password was Gabriel, one of the preloaded ones I made for my system to try first, right after 'password.' Alright, I'm looking around, you guys go check out the goods."

Alright, everything seems to be going well. Please gods, don't fuck me now.

Wolfe headed downstairs, taking them normally rather than jumping off the edge like he had for the outside railing, as his mantle had faded. He reached the bottom and walked over to the pile of weapons.

He whistled again as he got close. He could see a bunch of military infantry weapons, including a bunch labeled XM7.

At that, Shel whistled. "Raphael reborn... that's the rifle that is supposed to replace the M4 in the U.S. military. Looks like Adam got his hands on some early versions, somehow. This guy is even more connected than we thought."

"Than *you* thought," Fern muttered darkly into the headset.

But Wolfe ignored had eyes for something else. "He has multiple *rocket launchers* here, and a solid amount of ammo."

"And a bunch of grenades," Shel said, pointing to another box.

"And heads-up displays, body armor, C-4, mines..." Wolfe said as he slowly pointed from box to box. "This is illegal as shit, and way more paramilitary than anything we had when I worked for Big Man Grimm. Overwhelming firepower isn't really a mob tactic ninety-five percent of the time."

Wolfe clenched his fist. "But *Damian* had it, right out the door. Second evening after Drop Night he hit us with a damned bazooka, remember."

"Like I was right there, because, spoiler alert, I was. I recall healing your eyes."

Wolfe shuddered. Of all the things that had happened to him, the time glass had exploded across both eyes was top five of 'injuries that he thought about late at night.'

"Right... I'm just curious, do you think Adam has been bankrolling the gangs all along?"

Shel shrugged. "I have no idea, but why does it matter?"

Fern's voice crackled into their ears. "Stop doing hypotheticals. I found the sequence that would have alerted Adam—or his team at least. If the light switch was flicked and a code wasn't entered within ten minutes, which I've done now."

This might actually work without issue? Wolfe thought with no small surprise.

"I also shut down and erased the cameras, which were conveniently digital. So I'll bring the truck around. I think we can safely take eight of the crates without being seen, what with the bed of the F-150. But the longer we stay, the more chance for something to go epically wrong. Which, with Adam, is always a real possibility. So, pick what you want quick and then we'll get out of here."

Wolfe nodded before realizing she couldn't see. "Alright, we'll do it."

Wolfe smiled again as he looked around. "This is better than an Overland Monster or Puzzle Room drop, effectively."

"What should we take?" Shel asked.

"A little bit of everything," Wolfe replied, and his smile went shark. "With a slightly higher focus on the explosives— rockets, C-4, and grenades all. Nathan blew a wall up next to me last time we met. I want to return the favor the next time we meet. But we should just move stuff around until we can consolidate eight boxes we can at least get out of the warehouse and into the truck."

Shel smiled, then bit her lip. Wolfe was worried she was getting sad or scared again, but she shook her head and stared up at him. "I'm going to summon the angels now that the light won't give us away. You get Malviere out and then put on your mantle. Let's do it."

Wolfe, Shel, and their companion cards spent the next fifteen minutes in a blur of activity. About five minutes in, Fern joined them, although she was almost useless at carrying things. But they managed to get eight crates of military gear loaded into Wolfe's backup truck.

Afterwards, Wolfe dragged the bodies inside the building, right to the center.

Then he broke open the remaining crates, and carefully opened up some of the ammo containers and spread them around. Wolfe then dumped nearly everything out that might be flammable, cut pieces of body armor off, broke the crates for kindling, and piled up a bunch of packing material.

Then he pulled some matches from his pocket and held them aloft.

He grinned at Shel. "Kinda romantic for us, right?"

She shook her head, grinning a tiny bit, but it faded quickly. Wolfe could see the worry in her eyes.

He shrugged. "Well, never mind. You guys should go get in the car, and I'll set this all off."

Shel nodded, and she and Fern fled.

Wolfe waited till he heard a second door close outside, then lit the match on the floor. He tossed it into the pile of material he had assembled.

He watched just long enough to see it catch, then ran from the building and leapt into the car. He shut the driver's side door and pulled out—quickly, but not enough to squeal the tires.

"Think we got away with it?" Wolfe asked as they drove away.

"For now, yes," Fern said, and he breathing was a touch steadier than before. "But I think it'll become apparent to Adam what happened at some point. I'm terrified, truthfully. But it changes nothing about how Adam will respond. This gives us a tiny bit better edge to fight back, is all."

Her voice went ragged again. "Because he was always going to come for us."

CHAPTER 28

ODDS AND ENDS

Wolfe walked into the kitchen in his workout shorts and a tank top, yawning so hard his eyes were closed for a moment. It had been that kind of couple days—his soul was tired.

He immediately noticed the smell of coffee and bacon, and opened his eyes to be greeted by a sight that felt like it should have been out of a harem novel, although a slightly weird one. Shel was cooking in the kitchen in just one of Wolfe's shirts, and her two lantern angels were working beside her. Each still couldn't put down the lantern in their off hand, so they weren't making as much progress as they could, but surprisingly to Wolfe, they seemed to know what they were doing.

He supposed Raphael was the Divine Lord of Kindness, and maybe cooking a nice meal was under that rubric. But it still wasn't something he would have guessed the lantern angels knew how to do.

He walked up behind Shel, who gave him a glowing smile over her shoulder before turning back to cooking. Wolfe wrapped one arm around her and then lightly goosed her. She pushed into him a bit and giggled.

No shorts, Wolfe thought, a slight stirring of his younger self coming through. Shel was gorgeous, and at the moment, she was downright sexy as well.

"You weren't at all interested last night, what changed?" Shel asked while snuggling back against him and continuing to cook.

"Eight hours of shut-eye," Wolfe said honestly.

Shel and even Sorenia laughed at that, which also surprised Wolfe—a sense of humor was up there with cooking skills in things he wouldn't normally assign the lantern angels.

"So what got you guys cooking?" Wolfe asked.

"Well, you *were* sleeping in, as you mentioned, so I thought I could make breakfast," Shel said. "It's hardly a thing, especially since you usually do it anyway. I got Sorenia and Liurenia helping me, and for a while Malviere was helping as well, but she, well…"

"Can't cook to save her—or anyone else's—life," Liurenia finished with a laugh. "I don't think that small, pleasant things are really the forte of the Infernal faction."

Then she held up her lantern. "Although this makes it a bit of a chore as well, I'll not deny."

Sorenia nodded hard at that.

"Well, I appreciate it, truly. Where's Cereboo?"

"We gave your mutt a double helping and sent him on his way," Liurenia said, very primly.

"Hey, you can't call him a mutt," Wolfe replied with a laugh. "I mean, his parentage is extremely prestigious."

"Who's his mother?" Liurenia asked with a smirk.

Wolfe stopped at that, briefly stunned by the question. "You know, I'm almost fifty percent sure you're just giving me snark over my Infernal companion, but that is honestly a question I'd like to know the answer to. Somehow, I've never thought about it."

All three of the women—one beautiful mortal and two cards—slowed at that, as if none of them had ever considered it either. After a moment, Liurenia shrugged and they picked the pace up again.

"Speaking of, do any of you know your parents?" Wolfe asked.

"We were born at the beginning of time as true angels," Liurenia said.

"Do you remember it?" Wolfe asked.

Liurenia and Sorenia had troubled expressions.

It was Sorenia that spoke, and her voice was hesitant. "No... I can't remember most of my life from before I came to this realm as a card. I remember a few things, and I can hear Raphael's voice instructing me, but I can't remember anything else about him. And only a few battles and moments other than that. I assume that there are things that I wasn't meant to be able to convey to mortals."

Wolfe could tell it bothered her, and he wasn't that interested in all the theological connotations anyway. "Well, how about we eat this food you've so kindly prepared for us, then call Rhett and Fern over."

"Rhett?" Shel asked nervously.

Wolfe tightened his arms around her. "Yeah... Fern has been talking to him. He's going to do what he's going to do, but he knows too much to just leave out now. At the very minimum, I need him to not be after me."

"Alright, I'll call them," Shel said, turning around in Wolfe's arms awkwardly before stepping back and holding a plate heaped high with breakfast food out in front of her.

Rhett sat at the table, slumped over for the first time that Wolfe could ever remember seeing him. His head was in his hands, and his elbows were on the table as he stared at Wolfe.

Everyone still on their extended team except Miriam and her remaining people were there as well—Shel, Fern, and the cards of all four of them. All stared at Rhett.

After a moment, Rhett spoke. "Fern tells me that you didn't choose any of this—that it was triggered because of things that they are doing to you, and to other good and innocent citizens. Is that true, Wolfe? Tell me straight."

Wolfe put his hand over his heart. "It is, I promise. I was planning on facing down he remaining Noimoire gangs, but I was planning to do it right this time—your way. I swear to you by my patron Cerberus."

"I've never heard you swear by a god before," Shel said.

"I'm trying to tell Rhett how much I mean it. Adam and his people brought this war to me, not the other way around. But he may have started it—I'm gonna finish it."

"And there's the cheesy one-liner," Shel said sotto voce.

Half the table had a chuckle, but Rhett remained dead serious.

"What are you going to do?" he asked, his finger tracing the outline of the demonic face on the table but his eyes boring into Wolfe's.

"We have four days, nine hours, and twenty-one minutes till Adam gets back," Fern cut in, her voice barely above a whisper. "Although he already sent Nathan, which I didn't expect. So my other predictions might be wrong as well."

"That doesn't answer my question," Rhett said, his eyes never leaving Wolfe's. "What. Are. You. Going. To do?"

"You know the answer, Rhett," Wolfe said, his voice heavy. "Do you want me to spell it out? Are we not doing the hypothetical thing anymore?"

"How many?" Rhett asked.

Wolfe knew he was asking about bodies.

"Three, if I get a perfect run. But reality, or the gods, have never been that nice to me. Good money is, the number will be far higher."

"Is it worth it?"

Wolfe hesitated for a moment, but then nodded. "I know it is, like the gods themselves told me, because one did."

"What?" Rhett barked out, leaning back.

"I saw a vision, Rhett," Wolfe said, his voice heavy as he remembered the night he got his cards. "A vision of Noimoire, a Noimore that was in chaos, pain, and suffering, with death everywhere, if I didn't take out the other family heads. Now, as a maybe separate thing, Adam wants to make the law tyrannical and use criminals, even people with baby crimes, for parts or, I don't know, sex toys or something."

Rhett stared at Wolfe as he talked. "How do I know you're telling me the truth?"

Wolfe shrugged. "C'mon, would I make some bullshit like this up?"

Shel laughed at that.

Rhett still didn't so much as crack a grin, but he nodded. "You've never been a big yarn spinner, that's true. You just clam up and lie by omission, most of the time. I suppose you're probably telling me the truth."

"Then I can count on you?" Wolfe asked.

Rhett hesitated, but then shook his head no. "I can't be a part of this. Maybe that makes me a coward, but turning away, for no profit for myself, after all the deep evidence of corruption that Fern showed me... maybe I can still hold my head high when I'm judged. But joining you on a rampage? It betrays everything I stand for. I'll watch after Fern when needed, and I won't stop you. But that's all I can do, Wolfe. I get it—when the law itself is unjust, revolution is justified. But this is still a borderline case. It's one individual is inside the system, poisoning it."

"So help me remove it," Wolfe said. "Then the system you love so much will work, right?"

Rhett didn't answer directly. "I hate myself for even going this far, Wolfe. For letting you go, knowing what you plan. It's as far as I fall…" His voice went softer. "For now, at least."

It didn't make sense to Wolfe, but he had never been a follower of the rules. He turned to Shel.

She nodded, which Wolfe took to mean that she understood Rhett and wanted him to drop it. Although Wolfe wasn't completely sure that was what Shel meant.

Wolfe turned back to Rhett. "Okay, well, I appreciate that."

Rhett nodded. "I'm going to head back home—I really don't want to be present for anything else. If you need a place of safety I'll provide it. Well, unless you go completely insane in your fight and innocents get hurt. I won't forgive that. But providing that protection is the most I can do."

He stood up. "I'll see myself out. I really hope you know what you're doing, Wolfe."

"We'll know soon enough," Wolfe replied.

Rhett gave one more tight nod of his head, and then turned and exited the room, his footfalls slow and heavy on the marble floor.

After a few moments, Shel let her breath out. "Whew. I was really worried about Rhett turning you in. What we're doing is… kinda crazy. Way off meta."

Sorenia chimed in. "I worry that we're corrupting him, although he could stand to be a bit more supportive of those trying to recover from having fallen."

Wolfe ignored that, instead turning to Fern. "So, next mission?"

"It's going to be a lot harder, but we need to take out the

Singh next. They've got multiple deckbearers, and, more importantly, way more gunmen. Of the two, they're the bigger threat than the Renfeldt. And, thanks to your humiliation of Gopal at the arena last year, they already dislike you. He's gunning for you himself."

Wolfe shrugged. "He's a chump among chumps."

Fern closed her eyes. "The chair I'm sitting on, the demonic carving under my fingers, my frustration held in check," Fern said, then opened them and stared at Wolfe. "You told me you were worried because Nathan almost took you out, because you didn't have the training, and ran in half-cocked. Don't make the mistake again, *please*. For my sake. Take the Singh seriously."

Wolfe rolled his eyes, but nodded. "I will, I promise. Sorry, they weren't ever the biggest threat back in my enforcer days."

"They've gotten stronger, both from picking up a lot of the pieces you left after your rampages, and now through Adam's patronage. They're stronger than the Grimm family was at its height, now."

Wolfe held his hands up. "I said I'd take them seriously. What do we need to do?"

Fern turned her laptop around and leaned over. "So, here's the plan..."

CHAPTER 29

TURNABOUT IS FAIR PLAY

Wolfe stared at the complicated drawings, guard rotations, and security systems all over the Singh mansion.

"So, all I have to do is defeat the initial security system, avoid a good forty guards, and then go defeat Gurjit Singh, who is an actual absolute badass?"

Fern nodded jerkily, her movements furtive and skittish. "It'll be hard, I know, but there isn't..."

Wolfe barked out a mirthless laugh. "It'll be near suicide, without something else. I've never actually charged an enemy stronghold before, you know. I'm not that dumb. A group on a mission, sure. But when we went after the Cobra's head, um—"

Wolfe snapped his fingers, trying to conjure the name.

"Klaus," Shel muttered.

"Right, that guy. When we went after him, Shel tricked him into coming out after me. The closest two I've done like that were going after Damian the final time, where I had inside help and nearly died, and going after Chester... where I *also* nearly died. I hate to admit this, but I'm not good enough to pull this off, not like this. Almost no one would be, not even champion deckbearers. We need a better plan. A *way* better plan."

"Well, I can turn off the security once you get the laptop to—"

"And the fact that there are almost *fifty* innocents, mostly women, inside the mansion? Any of which might scream or yell or tell what's going on?" Wolfe asked exasperatedly, sitting back in his chair and crossing his arms.

"If we don't stop them now, they'll surely come for us as soon as they learn where I'm at, assuming they don't already know," Fern said. "I already spent over two years in the clutches of those monsters. I don't want to spend more time there."

"Wait... wait wait wait," Wolfe said, holding his hand up palm out, his mind going a mile-a-minute. "They might come after us already? Once they know where you're at?"

"Maybe?" Fern said. "I mean, I stole a bunch from them, once. But if they learn where I'm at, Nathan will also likely learn that."

"And then he'll come for us as well," Wolfe said, musingly. "I'd rather face him later, when he doesn't have a ton of allies."

Or face him never, that would also be great. But I seriously doubt that's happening.

Wolfe was silent for a moment, contemplating his own thoughts. He knew the plan was here, but the specifics, and the details, eluded him for the moment.

Fern was staring at the etched table they all sat around, and Shel and her companions were all staring at Wolfe. But he ignored them, thinking it through.

"What we need, then, is something that would cause the Singh family to come out from behind their walls, right? Someone that would get Gurjit Singh to stop hiding and come out and fight... but wouldn't necessarily bring Adam or Nathan in."

Fern glanced up. "Yeah, that would be good, but how?"

Wolfe drummed his fingers on the table. "The families are still mostly independent, right? They don't just turn to Adam for everything?"

Fern was slowly nodding, her eyes as animated. "Yeah, they still handle almost everything themselves... why do you ask?"

"Well, I was having a thought... but it might mean we can't ever go back to the Rat Arena."

"I could handle that," Shel said.

"I don't think I'd ever go," Fern responded.

"Well, here is my plan then..."

It was broad daylight, and it made Wolfe nervous. He had conducted most of his life under the cover of darkness, and knowing he was about to engage in the kind of activity "the man" frowned on, in broad daylight, in a major city, was giving him near as much anxiety as Fern ran around with.

And, for reasons of her job, Shel wasn't here. Instead, Derek and two of Miriam's surviving enforcers were here to help him out. Derek had one of the new automatic rifles that they had picked up from Adam's warehouse, and his two companions each had a heavy caliber pistol.

He was staring at an empty parking lot, surrounded by a chain link fence, with one entrance in. A single man, a white guy that had so much acne scarring that Wolfe could make it out from across the street and down a bit, sat in a lawn chair, gently watching what was happening. He was so out of it he hadn't even picked up on Wolfe yet.

A voice crackled into his ear—Fern. "I see the limousine,

maybe a minute out. The van is still a couple minutes away. You should have a good window."

"Looks like we're doing this," Wolfe muttered.

"Hur-ray," Derek said, giving Wolfe a brilliant smile.

"Ha-ha."

A minute later, a limousine slowly drove up to the gate, turned in, and parked.

"Now?" Derek asked.

Wolfe nodded his head. "Yeah. But get your masks on first."

Derek nodded, and he and his two goons—who reminded Wolfe vaguely of Pete and Harry, from his old days, thick men with a stare that said the thickness ran upstairs as well—all pulled ski masks over their heads.

Derek clutched his rifle, and the two goons lifted their pistols off their laps, but kept them below window height.

"He'll just... get in the car?" Derek asked.

"He remembers me," Wolfe replied with a cold satisfaction in his voice. "He'll do what I say."

Derek nodded.

"No more talking. It's go time," Wolfe said, his voice conversational even though his stomach was tight with anticipation.

He drove into the parking lot, not screeching, but casually. The man in the chair at the entrance raised his hands, but Wolfe kept going, pulling his F-150 up to the side of the parking lot. The man in the chair got up and started lazily walking over to Wolfe, probably assuming that Wolfe was just a local worker bee trying to park for his job, or perhaps a guy here to sample one of the nearby eateries.

Wolfe dropped the window just as a hugely corpulent man, swarthy, with black hair and a thick black beard, heaved himself from the back of the limousine. He was dressed in a tailored suit that had to cost half as much as a car and still sat badly on his huge frame. He pulled a tiny, thin, mousey girl with auburn hair and a bruise on the side of her freckled face from the car behind him. Something about her walk and face told Wolfe she wasn't American born and raised—perhaps she was Eastern European.

Wolfe leaned out, his trusty Edge pointed at his target: Gopal Singh, cousin of the head of the Singh crime family, the god-gifted of Asmodeus named Gurjit Singh.

"Hello Gopal," Wolfe said conversationally, his tone so normal that no one had reacted yet despite the gun—no one except Gopal, who paled, his face going slack.

"W-Wolfe," the man stuttered, his demeanor entirely different than the blustering, cocksure fool that had challenged Wolfe in the arena a year ago. "W-what do you want?"

Derek pointed his automatic rifle out past Wolfe as other men stepped from the limousine.

"None of that, boys, or you all die. To answer your question, Gopal, I want a lot of things. But for the moment, I want for you to get in the car."

"You'll kill me..." Gopal whispered, his face somehow paling further. He had released the girl, who was pulling away from him, her own eyes flickering back and forth between the two different guns pointing from Wolfe's car.

One of the thugs poked his own hand cannon out the back window as the man that had been watching the entrance to the parking lot came up beside them.

"You might die, but I won't be the one that kills you, promise," Wolfe said, his voice deadpan almost to the point of disinterest. "Nor any of my people. At least not directly or intentionally. But if you don't move, I promise I'll shoot you dead here and now."

Gopal finally let go of the girl, who scrambled back into the limousine.

Then, after a moment, his eyes fell. "Okay. I'll come. Don't kill me."

"Tell your men to stand down as well."

"Guns down, guys."

No one had actually pulled a gun, but the men with him relaxed fractionally as Gopal walked toward Wolfe's F-150. One of Derek's enforcers got out of the vehicle, then had to help the corpulent Gopal to climb up into the back seat.

The other one kept his pistol pointed at the huge deckbearer—you could never be careful enough with a deckbearer, who only took about two-and-a-half seconds to summon their decks. Wolfe could remember Gopal's rat deck, although he wasn't sure the tub of lard was still using it.

Wolfe faced one of the guards. "Tell this guy's cousin, your boss, that if he wants his family member back, he needs to give me the Gate to the Infernal set card. He'll understand what I'm talking about. If he doesn't do it, I'm going to put a bullet in this waste of food. I'm giving him twenty-four hours. And if the cops show up, well, first Gopal here will still feed the fishes, and two, I'll release a ton of information I have on the Singh family operations to the same damn pigs that showed up."

Wolfe no longer thought of police in quite the same way he had before, and actually got along with a couple. But he was pretty sure that using the put-down on them would make him sound more serious to these men, which he needed.

Wolfe pulled his Edge back in and started the car, conscious of Derek covering the men with his rifle. No cars had stopped around them, and nothing seemed amiss about the day.

And the van with the Rat Arena workers still hadn't showed up.

"We clear?" Wolfe asked the air.

"You have time but don't dawdle," Fern replied in his ear.

Dawdle?

Wolfe pulled out, circled the parking lot, and carefully drove out into traffic, heading back to the Hellmouth Institute.

"Wait," Gopal suddenly said. "You promised you weren't going to kill me!"

Wolfe glanced into the rear-view mirror. Gopal was perspiring everywhere, and shaking slightly.

By the Divine, I did a number on this guy when I beat him to death in the Arena last year.

"I'm not going to," Wolfe replied.

"But, you just told my men that if Gurjit doesn't give you the—"

"I lied to them," Wolfe replied. "I know Gurjit won't give me the card. But I think he's going to try something else. But I'm not going to kill you, or not directly, at least. You have my word."

"You just admitted lying," Gopal said petulantly.

"Touché, douchebag," Wolfe said, irritated. "In the deck of crimes we're collectively responsible for, that ranks extremely highly, I'm sure."

Gopal didn't respond.

"What are you going to do if Gurjit *does* give you the card?" Derek suddenly asked.

Wolfe blinked. "I... I hadn't even considered that possibility. But if he does... well, then I'll hand ol' fatty there over and call it a day. Maybe I really could do things without a body count, like our mutual police friend wanted."

"Think it'll happen?" Derek asked.

"Not a snowball's chance in the Infernal Realms," Wolfe replied as he turned onto the ramp, headed for the freeway that would take him home.

CHAPTER 30

THE BEST OFFENSE IS A REALLY AGGRESSIVE DEFENSE

T he small, cramped space they were in smelled like the waiting room at a dingy criminal courthouse—a faint scent of desperation and fear-laced sweat, along with a fainter scent of aggression.

The harsh feminine breathing of Fern was new to Wolfe's experience, however. She was near to hyperventilating.

"You'll be fine," Wolfe growled, reaching across the short distance between them and placing his hand on her forearm.

Fern flinched away from him spastically, then looked at him guiltily and muttered, "Thanks."

Wolfe didn't respond as he withdrew his hand.

Wolfe, Shel, and Fern were all sitting in their polyester seats, with Wolfe having turned his around to face the back. Fern had set up three laptops on the back seat next to Shel, and was now facing the back seat as well.

One of the laptops had cameras watching the front of the Hellmouth Institute, and the other two had cameras along the interior, including the top, back room where Gopal was zip tied to a chair in just his gross tighty-whities. He was so covered in sweat that Wolfe could almost smell it as well.

A fourth laptop sat in Fern's lap, and she glanced down at it from time to time. It was running multiple programs, but the main ones she was paying attention to were the drone footage watching the four black S.U.V.'s headed along the freeway, presumably to the Hellmouth Institute... and a second drone that was circling, silent, far above a huge mansion, one that had two more SUVs next to it. Three streets over, a van with dealer tags was idling.

"I count sixteen, but they could have four more," Fern said. "I can't see the middle of the seats because I can't lower the drone enough without giving away its presence."

"We'll know soon enough," Wolfe responded.

The four vans took the exit at Juniper Street with near military precision, then turned East and headed right for the Hellmouth Institute. There wasn't much else out near Wolfe, and he had a fair degree of land around him, so it was almost positive they were trying to go get Gopal back.

Just like Wolfe wanted. Now that he had cleared everyone out, he much preferred the fight take place on his home turf. There wasn't anything there that he was worried about losing anymore, and the building itself was borderline indestructible.

"There they go," Shel muttered while tapping her leg, her cute face marred by a frown.

Sure enough, and exactly as predicted, the four SUV's pulled off Juniper and into the Hellmouth Institute parking lot, then drove to the front. Wolfe, Shel, and Fern all breathed quietly, as if they might be heard, as a full twenty men spilled from the four vehicles. They were all dressed in black and wearing ski masks, and...

"Of course," Wolfe muttered as he saw their armament.

While most of the men had the typical pistols one could find among gang enforcers—a collection of mostly half-rate ones that had been poorly maintained—four of the men were carrying automatic rifles.

And one had a rocket launcher, a twin to the ones Wolfe had stolen from Adam's warehouse the other day.

"I think we pissed them off," Wolfe said through a dark chuckle. "I haven't seen the gangs of Noimoire using a rocket launcher since Damian, that little shit, hit the convoy with Big Man Grimm two years ago."

"Why do you find that funny?" Fern asked.

Shel just smiled. "He finds a lot of screwed-up things funny. You get used to it."

One of the men that had spilled from the SUVs in the Hellmouth parking lot ran up the steps of the Hellmouth Institute and yanked on the huge doors that led into the front room.

Fern made the camera in the front room the primary, allowing Wolfe to more clearly see the people invading his home. The camera had been placed in the leaves of a large potted plant, facing the front, with a microphone attached, since you couldn't put anything into the walls of the Hellmouth Institute itself.

Wolfe and his two teammates leaned over a bit toward the monitor, eager to see and hear. The only sound in the vehicle was Fern's harsh breathing.

About half of the people invading his home had swarthy hands and black hair, and Wolfe was pretty sure that they were members of the Singh family—not just their enforcers.

"Should I start the defensive measures?" Fern asked.

Wolfe shook his head. "Let them get deeper."

"That's what she said?" Shel murmured, but no one laughed.

The men filed into the front room, one holding the door for his fellow enforcers. Before all of them had even gotten into the foyer, two teams of four had started heading down the halls, one team to each side.

Another four-person team moved into the room where

Mrs. Timo had once handled clients, leaping around corners with his gun pointed and then spinning to the other side like a bad b-flick.The camera in this room was on top of a large filing cabinet that had once held client files.

The last of the enforcers filed into the room, and the man holding the door let go. It fell shut with a click.

"Now," Wolfe whispered.

Fern brought up a program with numerous .exe entries, each of tiny file size, but hesitated just a second as the men moved a tiny bit deeper into the room, all of them in front of Mrs. Timo's desk.

Shel turned away from the screen.

One of the men glanced over at the file cabinet. "Is that a camera?" he asked, pointing.

Fern activated one of the files.

A fraction of a second later, the front of Mrs. Timo's desk exploded outward. The sound was loud even through the speakers, and Wolfe grimaced. The camera fell over, but Wolfe heard shouts.

But no screams—he assumed the four were gone in the directed blast he had built into the desk that morning with some of the explosives from Adam's warehouse.

Gopal, inside his chair almost directly above the explosion, pissed himself and squealed.

"Turn the sound on his camera off," Wolfe said irately. He didn't need the fat bully interrupting what they were doing with his reeking cowardice.

Wolfe turned his attention back to the lower-floor cameras. On the one in the foyer, he could see dust and smoke coming from the entrance to Mrs. Timo's room, as well as see a few splatters of... someone. Everyone was shouting and cussing, and one of the men touched his hand to his ear. "Report!"

Wolfe couldn't hear what was said, but the man rushed

into Mrs. Timo's room, and four more of his goons followed him.

The camera was pointed wrong, so Wolfe couldn't see what was happening, but he heard the same man say, "He was waiting for us—this is an ambush! He was prepared for what we would do if we didn't pay him."

There was a brief pause. "Yes sir. I'll make sure it happens."

Another pause, and then, "Everyone, search rapidly! Find and kill Wolfe and his bitch, then get Gopal. Go quickly!"

In the foyer, one of the three remaining men touched his chest, and pulled a deck of cards.

"Who's that?" Wolfe asked Fern.

Fern hesitated—everyone was wearing masks. But when the cards appeared, some glowed a deep crimson, and some glowed with a sickly yellow light. It was a giveaway.

"It's almost certainly Harjeet Singh, Gurjit's youngest son," Fern said. "He has an Infernal, Corruption, and Psychic deck that relies almost entirely on debuffs and creature stealing in Infernal and Psychic, and Corruption effects that make status effects dangerous to the enemy deckbearer."

Her eyes narrowed. "Like much of the family, paying for girls wasn't enough. He's had a few unwillingly."

Wolfe considered his options. While he would like to get Harjeet, both for moral and practical reasons, he needed to get as many as possible as soon as possible.

"Fire Two," Wolfe whispered. "They aren't doing what we need yet."

Shel was crying silently, but she didn't object.

Fern, dry eyed, nodded sharply once. Wolfe noticed that her breathing had become regular, and wondered if her being the hand that was smiting her once-oppressors was helping with her anxiety. He didn't know anything about trauma, but he knew it would help *him* with anxiety about abuse if he killed his abusers.

Fern touched another key, and the door to a closet inside Mrs. Timo's room pushed open.

Fern hit another button, and a drone, waiting inside the closet, took off. It wasn't a quiet one, and even before it exited the closet, the same man that had been talking before screamed, "Run!!"

The camera swiveled, and Wolfe got a brief view of the men trying to run back to the foyer as the drone flew at them fast. Fern hit another button, and the drone detonated.

Wolfe couldn't tell how many had been killed, and the explosive package on the drone was far smaller than the one that had been in the desk. But two men crawled from the room into view of the foyer camera, and each was bleeding profusely, although Wolfe was fairly sure non-fatally.

Fern stabbed a button again, and another explosion rang through the Hellmouth Institute.

Wolfe stared down, and she pointed to a now-black screen on one of the other laptops. "One of their teams reached the stair to the second floor. Only got one, I think, but they'll hesitate now."

Harjeet summoned forth what could only be a succubus —at Wolfe's eye level, he was staring at an incredibly shapely, red-skinned, bare rear end and back with bat wings—and then touched his own ear.

"We've lost eight, and two more are wounded too bad to continue. Wolfe's entire lair is one big trap, and we're basically down half—and you can bet him and his bitch are at the top, waiting for us. If you want this done, I need more men."

There was a pause, then Harjeet said, "I'll use my cards to clear the place, but they've got drones carrying explosives. I'm going to need more."

Another pause, then, "I'll do what I can while I wait."

"I think we did it," Wolfe muttered.

Fern shook her head. "Maybe. We have to wait and see."

The next five minutes were fairly boring, with the creature cards of the enemy slowly clearing trap rooms. Fern managed to wound two more with a flying drone attack, leaving eight healthy men.

Finally, on the last laptop, ten more men spilled from the mansion. They ran over to the remaining two SUV's and got in, six in one and four in the other. They drove out of the parking lot and headed out onto the road toward the freeway.

"Ten more headed to go and rescue Gopal," Shel said.

Wolfe laughed, but it was forced. His tension was rising. "I remember it like I was right there, because I was."

"Har har," Shel said to their common joke, but her own voice was tight.

"Let's go," Wolfe said. He reached behind him and grabbed a large backpack, then grabbed the door handle next to him.

On the same camera, off to the side, the doors to the dealer-plate van opened as Wolfe and Shel exited the vehicle.

CHAPTER 31

IMPROVED APPROACH

W olfe hurried out the side of the van while shrugging on the backpack. It was heavy with a familiar weight as he jogged toward the mansion ahead of him. The mansion that he was almost a hundred percent positive that Gurjit Singh currently occupied.

He was tense partially because Gurjit was nothing like his corpulent cousin. If you were what you ate, Gopal was cake and Gurjit was steak. The man was nearly as tall as Wolfe, more muscled, and even meaner. On the other hand, he was half a decade older and had considerably less street experience, especially recently. Wolfe would bet he could take Gurjit, on even terms, nine times out of ten. But in his own lair, with bodyguards? It was a dicey proposition at best, since Gurjit was a solid fighter on his own.

So Wolfe had hunted differently than he usually did—carefully. First, the allies. Then, the tools. Last, the distractions.

Now it was time to see if it would pay off.

Shel followed him out, carrying a small, awkward-looking rifle with a cylindrical canister under the barrel and a bracing stand—the second part of his plan to eliminate as many of Gurjit's people as quietly as he could.

Shel rushed after him even as Wolfe touched his chest, the two of them running down the sidewalk, past small, manicured trees on the street side, and the large mansions set back on the housed side.

Counting on his Bulgae Moon Chaser card to stop anyone from finding out about his deck, Wolfe pushed his hand out from his chest. Eight cards appeared in front of him—his base five and his effective three companions.

He immediately yanked Malviere out. Crimson light flowed to the ground, and Malviere appeared in a swirl of smoke that smelled faintly of dogs. She wore her usual black dress, to complement her black hair and nails.

"Where is big brother?" she asked as soon as she appeared.

Wolfe was briefly non-plussed as he ran, thinking about it. In truth, the last couple times that Wolfe had deployed Cereboo, he hadn't helped as much as Malviere had. But Wolfe tossed him next, and his pooch came out running on padded feet across the concrete of the carefully manicured streets in this ultra-rich neighborhood.

I wonder what he'll look like when I complete the set, assuming that I do, in fact, complete the set—and don't take the actual Hellgate.

Wolfe kept going, and pulled his 'companion' Obsessive Cultist as he did, but he didn't pull the second one, instead swiping his deck and looking for the next card he wanted. *Hope I get the Demonic Portal when the time comes.*

Shel hadn't pulled her deck, not wanting to alert people to what was coming. She was struggling a slight bit under the weight of her weapon—over the course of a thousand-foot run even a moderately heavy weapon was a chore to lug.

Wolfe saw that his second card was his Master of the Hunt mantle, and touched it. The light flowed across him and he *felt* the power. He took the odd rifle from Shel and carried it easily, one-handed, as they ran.

They reached the predetermined spot, a manicured bush a couple hundred yards from the front of the mansion. Wolfe set the odd-looking rifle down, popping the stand open and lying on the other side of the bushes, scooting through them until the barrel and scope poked through.

The red energy of his mantle played across him, his features slightly more bestial as he stared through the scope, rapidly searching the front of the estate, which was currently devoid of people and all but one car.

Shel, Malviere, and Cereboo all plopped down behind him, and Wolfe turned away from the scope momentarily to face them.

Shel shuddered dramatically enough to vibrate the bushes, then said, "I've been dealing with some pretty rough characters now that I'm in the police, but when you're in that mantle, your eyes all red... you put them all to shame."

Wolfe was unsure if her statement was positive or negative. *Probably positive since she's still with me.*

But his mind was on other matters, and he touched his hand to his ear. "Are they doing what we want still?"

Fern responded, her voice the tiniest bit tinny in his ear. "Yes, with their lowered numbers, they've moved to single-man patrols—just two guys on the outside patrol. Your trick with Gopal did what was needed, just like you said."

It's nice to be told you're right, Wolfe thought to himself with a feral grin. *Especially when it comes to something as serious as killing people.*

Fern kept talking over Wolfe's introspective moment. "First guy will come around the corner in just over a minute, most likely."

"Perfect," Wolfe whispered.

Shel pulled a ski mask from her pocket and put it over her

head, and Wolfe did the same. *Don't want any rando seeing us and being able to identify us to the police.*

Then he looked back through the scope of his FX Impact, taking his time now that he knew he had a few moments.

The Singh family mansion was large and ostentatious, even larger than the Grimm family mansion had been. Its front was shielded from view a bit better than most mansions with a lightly treed front lawn, but Wolfe still had a solid view of the majority of his target area–the large entrance area near the front of the house.

"One's coming around now," Fern said.

Wolfe watched quietly, barely breathing, as the man walked around the side of the mansion to Wolfe's far right, and started walking across the front. It was still a couple hundred feet to traverse the whole thing.

Even though Wolfe hadn't shot, Fern continued. "Remember, wait till he's far enough past that the next guy won't see him before you can get a shot."

Wolfe didn't say anything, just waiting as they had planned. When the man was about ninety percent of the way, and *probably* hidden by a pillar on the front of the house, he squeezed the trigger.

The FX Impact was an interesting rifle, powered by compressed air in the cannister under the barrel rather than gunpowder in the bullet. That, along with a subsonic bullet, meant that its stopping power was extremely low compared to similar rifles—it was best used for hunting small vermin, like coyotes.

But Wolfe had done some experiments earlier, and the interaction between his mantle, his perk, and Malviere meant that even though the rifle wasn't *normally* good at delivering good stopping shots, it was when powered by infernal magic.

The interesting—and most important—thing, however, was that it remained quiet. Its noise was barely that of a chirping bird, although quite unique, a metallic noise that had vague similarity to an insect buzzing past your ear.

The guard's head was perforated, a brief spray of blood through an extremely improbably large hole for what was barely different than a .22 bullet. He fell in the direction of the shot.

After about ten seconds in which Wolfe sat with coiled muscles, prepared to charge forward, Fern said, "No reaction that I can see."

Wolfe waited, and a few moments later, when the second guard came around the corner, he killed him too, dismissing the 'no experience,' notification.

"Go," Fern said, her voice urgent. "We don't know how long till they miss a check-in."

"There are only eight guards left," Wolfe said as he pulled back and then leapt over the hedge.

"Yes," Fern replied.

A savage glee, reminiscent of Wolfe's old days as a street enforcer, rose in him. "Will it even matter, then?"

"They still have *at least* two deckbearers, possible three, very improbably more if they hired them. And Gurjit is, as you reminded me, far tougher than his cousin. Be smart—you're the one that wanted to do this differently, and this was your plan."

Wolfe nodded, and reined in his savagery. Fern—or earlier Wolfe, really—was right. Even if he *could* kill them all the old way, in a blaze of talent-fueled glory, he needed to practice his new, more professional methods.

He ran to the gate, hoping that they didn't have some kind of sensor system—something Fern hadn't been able to figure out, but had figured against given the active guards and number of people constantly coming and going, and the lack of visible cameras.

Still, even as Wolfe accelerated, leapt, and flipped himself onto the top of the gate, his butthole clenched.

He relaxed when nothing happened, and held his hand down to Shel, who ran up, hit the gate and then jumped down inside with an assist from Wolfe, who followed her down onto the perfectly moved front lawn, lightly split up with carefully maintained trees.

Malviere ran up, Cereboo behind her, and Wolfe smacked himself. He unsummoned them, as well as the Obsessive Infernal Cultist, then flipped his deck as he hurried across the lawn. *I'll need to resummon them. I should have only brought out Malviere—she was the only one whose bonus I needed on that first part. Oh well, it's a tiny error, but something to remember for later.*

Shel glanced at him, opened her mouth, but then closed it and shook her head.

Yeah, it's mission time, we'll figure out whatever else is going on later.

"Don't forget there're a ton of innocent women in there," Shel said as they hurried across the lawn, from tree to tree.

Wolfe pulled his STI Edge as they got closer, but his mantle winked out.

"Innocent is hardly the term I'd use, but I understand what you mean," Wolfe replied to his fiancée.

As they reached the last line of trees, a sudden hissing, slightly mechanical, filled the air around them.

Wolfe whirled, expecting a monster, but he saw nothing. Shel glanced up, and Wolfe pointing his gun up, slightly panicked.

Then it hit him, just as the sprinklers popped up all around him.

But he hadn't seen anyone, so he grabbed Shel and ran forward from the lawn even as they went off. He was hit slightly, but hardly soaked as he rushed forward to the side of the house.

"Fucking cliché," Wolfe muttered, angrily, as they reached the edge.

She giggled, a tiny hint of the fun-loving girl Wolfe knew coming through Shel's tension, but she spoke seriously. "It'll still give us a tiny bit more cover, so let's count it as a win."

"Sure," Wolfe responded, gripping his gun tighter as he walked over to the front door.

He gripped the handle. "Let's go get card number five."

CHAPTER 32

ENEMIES GO BRRRR...

Wolfe opened the door quickly, slamming himself briefly against the outside wall on the off-chance someone had seen him and was prepared to shoot him coming in. When no one fired, he looked around the corner, and seeing no one in the entrance, moved inside.

The front room had all the tack that Wolfe would expect from someone in the service of Asmodeus, Infernal Lord of Lust. The four marble statues of naked women placed around the grand tiled foyer at least tried to be classy, although the level of detail was a bit too on point to really pull it off.

But the multiple paintings of women in various states of undress were not only garish, they clashed with the rest of the room.

And placing a grand chandelier in a room with a bunch of naked imagery just highlighted how *not classy* it really was. It took the eyes a moment to even see the two hallways leading off the front room, or the door in the back, what with all the insane and moderately clashing imagery around the front.

"What's with the crime families in Noimoire just openly

advertising that they serve the Infernal?" Shel asked with a grin.

Wolfe knew it was rhetorical, a joke to their time together and the Grimm family. He focused on the task at hand. "Alright, let's head to the study."

"Why the study?" Shel asked.

"Because, when I was head enforcer for the Grimm family, we always met in the study when we had serious business. Given that they think they're on a rescue mission to save Gopal, this is likely what they consider 'serious business,' and I'm willing to bet that they're congregated there, listening for updates and such."

"The very few times I was brought here by Adam we met there as well," Fern said into their earpieces.

Shel nodded, then hesitated.

Wolfe motioned to a hall leading to the side. "Down the hall, up the stairs, and then we'll head to the back. Or just follow me."

Wolfe ran into the hallway, toward the stairway visible at the end. He flipped his deck again as he did. He didn't have his mantle, instead summoning Malviere again from the cards that floated to the side. There was a decent chance that this whole situation wouldn't last five minutes.

A mostly nondescript, black-haired man stepped from a doorway into Wolfe's path. He carried a burrito-looking piece of food. His head was tilted as he took a bite with one hand under his food, not watching where he was going. Wolfe's whole plan went sideways, as did he, when he slammed into the man, propelling him back into the room he had come from and careening to the plush, carpeted hall floor himself.

The man hit the ground on his back, meat chunks from his wrap flying everywhere around his head. Wolfe rolled to the side, holding his Edge out. The man rose from the floor, staring at Wolfe's barrel with wide eyes—one green, the other brown.

Wolfe knew this man. Bart Fidel. Bart had been the lowest enforcer with a deck in the Singh family once, a 'nothing' man that had gotten a deck ten years before Wolfe and done jack-all with it.

He wasn't worth keeping alive, and might be dangerous somehow, given that he had a deck.

It must have shown in Wolfe's eyes, because Bart screamed something in a language Wolfe didn't know just as Wolfe pulled the trigger. 'Noggin salsa' joined the burrito pieces with a gunshot that reverberated throughout the house.

Wolfe shook his head, trying to dispel the ringing in his ear. *I wonder if Shel's healing fixes my slow accumulation of ear damage?*

Shel gagged at the sight, slightly green.

"What was that?!" Fern asked, terror in her voice.

Wolfe reached over and scooped up the ten cards that appeared on the man's chest, ignoring the disaster of the room. "Well, they had a third deckbearer, at least, but he's gone now."

Fern's breathing was harsh and choppy in his ear, but she didn't say anything else.

The backs of the cards were silver— a dragon deck. Wolfe knew it was more of a kobold deck than a true dragon one. Or it had been two years ago. Either way, it was money for later and not something he could use at the moment.

"Well, that was—" Shel began, hand already on her chest now that surprise had been lost. But someone leaped down the last flight of stairs at the end of the hall and fired a pistol at them rapidly. Shel grunted as blood sprayed from her back and she hit the hallway, coughing a spray of pink almost instantly.

Two bullets ripped into Wolfe's arm, but he ignored them in his *need* to finish the man shooting Shel. He dropped his

Edge, grabbing it with his other hand, but before he could shoot the bastard, Malviere—who had somehow not been hit —flung a death's-headed spirit dog from the aura around her into the man, who briefly screamed as he rotted before dropping dead.

"Never against the pack," Malviere whispered in her occult voice.

Wolfe knelt over Shel, who feebly pushed her hand out, calling her cards into existence.

"C'mon, Raphael, give her a healing card," Wolfe said, praying in his desperation to a faction that had clearly forsaken him.

Wolfe got not one, but *two* 'deckbearer draws a deck' notifications near him, but he ignored them in near panic.

Shel, arm shaking, touched a card in front of her and her Rookie EMT appeared.

The card knelt next to her, and color returned to the tiny part of her face that Wolfe could see. He almost wanted to rip her black hoodie off her to see how badly hurt she was, but knew that she would live now. His job was to fight.

"Into the room, and try and get set up," Wolfe said, standing and trying to help Shel to her feet with an offered hand.

She coughed, a wracking thing that sounded like an old man trying to cough his entire lung up. But instead, she coughed a bullet into her hand, wiped the blood from her mouth, and took Wolfe's assistance.

She backed into the room as Wolfe summoned Cereboo.

The three-headed dog appeared with a series of barks and then whined as all three heads trained on Shel. Cereboo jumped up and put his paws on her, all three heads alternating sandpaper licks and puppy whines, but Shel winced and Wolfe's pooch abandoned the efforts almost instantly.

Wolfe glanced around the room they were in. It was a huge kitchen, a massive stainless-steel workspace almost like a chef's cookery flanked by pantries carrying tons of food, and even vegetables hanging on racks next to a single massive kitchen. There was a large linoleum floor that included a ton of open space in front of the mess area, broken up only by a single small table. Besides the door in, the only way out appeared to be a double door with viewing holes to the side, looking into a massive dining hall.

"Divine crap, the Singhs did good once I knocked most of the gangs out," Wolfe muttered, not remembering anything this ostentatious from his few trips to the mansion. "How the hell did they even remodel this much?"

"Get ready, they have to be coming!" Fern said.

"Right," Wolfe muttered. "Shel, we need full set-up if you can draw it."

She nodded, and touched another card in her deck.

Stone Arch Fire
Unique Mythic equivalent Tier-1 equivalent Life [Civic]
Building
0 power

This creates the Stone Arch Fire. It adds +1 Fire power to the deckbearer, and doubles the effect of any other Civic Building in the deckbearer's deck.
This building card is not a null card. In addition to being placed as a building, it may be played as a persistent for 1 Life, 1 Fire, and 1 any power

Special: **All Healer [5]**: All allied deckbearers and cards heal 5 every single round
Special: **Civic Leader [1]:** All of the deckbearer's [Civic] subtype creature cards gain +1 to all non-health stats

Special: **Death Ward**: The deckbearer's creatures may not be killed by automatic removal effects while this card is in play
Special: **Fungible [Life, Fire]**: Life and Fire power may be spent as if they were the other

"Heat is life, cold is death. Never let anyone tell you fire is only for burning."

The linoleum space was covered in stone, with a fire burning in the middle. Immediately, the bullet tracks on Wolfe's arm healed.

"Behind the counter," Wolfe said, taking his own advice and crouching down so only his head, arms, and Edge were over the top of the counter.

"Don't we need to go kill them?" Shel asked as she joined him behind the steel workstation with a wince.

"Aren't you healed?" Wolfe asked.

She shook her head no. "The bridge only heals allied deckbearers, but it does other things for me. The EMT didn't fully repair me. I'll be full healing mode soon though."

Wolfe heard running feet, and refocused himself, preparing for what was coming.

Cereboo moved to beside the door, and Malviere walked behind the counter as well.

What came around the door, however, shocked Wolfe beyond belief. A beautiful demoness, flanked by a second one and a hellhound of a type Wolfe had never seen before.

The hellhound was rough, and the lesser demoness was also a chore for their decks.

Lesser Urban Corrupter
Uncommon Tier-1 Infernal [Succubus, Criminal]
1 Infernal, 1 Any Power

Health: 14
Attack: 4
Defense: 5
Magical Attack: 6[**Fire or Death**]
Magical Defense: 6

Special: **White Collar Criminal**: This card benefits from ALL Civic cards on the field as if it were Civic, but provides no benefits for being Civic.
Special: **Criminal Mentor:** All cards that benefit from criminal cards are treated as if there is one more criminal card on the field.

"Few of the Infernal benefit Mortal civilization, but many benefit from ensconcing themselves within it, weakening it from within."

Twice-damned Hellhound
Rare Tier-1 Undead/Infernal/Fire [Hellhound, Skeleton, Burning] Creature
1 Infernal, 1 Undead or Fire Power

Health: 13
Attack: 6
Defense: 6
Magical Attack: 7[**Fire**]
Magical Defense: 6

Special: **Agonizing Existence:** This creature cannot be controlled against the will of the deckbearer, and cannot be a target for any persistent cards.
Special: **Partially Incorporeal**: This creature takes half damage from all physical attacks.

Special: **Lock**: Any card that is slain by this card may not be replayed for the remainder of the fight.

"Even among the damned there are those that are pitied."

But Wolfe found himself staring in horror at the powerful card that faced him, hovering over the near-perfect form of the succubus that had led the way in.

Klireen, Daughter of Lust
Unique Legendary equivalent, Tier-2 equivalent, Infernal/Psychic [Succubus, Demigod] Creature
3 Infernal Power, 2 Psychic Power

Health: 20
Attack: 3
Defense: 5
Magical Attack: 15[**Fire or Psychic**]
Magical Defense: 15

Special: **Daughter of Lust:** When this card enters the field, it may take control of any creature card up to power 2, or any unique adult male creature card up to power 5. If anything would allow it to target any other entity for any reason, it can only affect those attracted to it.
Special: **Fade [1]**: The strongest attack against this creature each round is nullified.
Special: **Lost in the Dark**: If in the deck, the deckbearer does not trigger deck drawn warnings

"Deception and Desire, an extraordinarily powerful combination."—Klireen, Daughter of Asmodeus.

"I think we're still facing *three* deckbearers," Wolfe said, his voice tight as he stared at the powerful, unique card facing him even as he could still hear running feet.

CHAPTER 33

COMBAT OF THE ABSURD

A quick glance at the Stone Arch Fire card and back at the Lesser Urban Corrupter told Wolfe that it was going to be a huge problem if Shel got her deck going—it already gained plus one to all its stats from Shel's Mythic card.

But it was Infernal, and would take half damage from Wolfe unless he got his own mantle going. With a quick whispered invocation against his deck's usual luck, Wolfe swiped his cards sideways.

"Thank the gods," Wolfe muttered as, for a wonder, his mantle appeared in his next hand.

"Cereboo, Malviere, take out the Twice-Damned Hellhound," Wolfe said, touching his own mantle as two thugs came around the corner, firing guns.

He ducked back, but the enemy hellhound ran through the Stone Arch Fire and then leapt onto the wide, stainless-steel cooking counter, its claws scrabbling briefly on the top to find purchase.

The card held its head back, all burning dog skull with only a fringe of crisped skin on it, and howled insanely loudly in the closed space. But mid howl, Cereboo, with three barks that were half challenge, half playful, leapt into the hellhound and carried it back onto the other side, snapping and rolling.

I know he's just a card, but the fact he thinks fighting is fun makes the couple times he's been slain much easier to swallow, Wolfe thought.

As his mantle fell around him, Wolfe leaned back over. He took a bullet to the shoulder from an unusually accurate—or lucky—thug, but it felt more like a hard punch through his mantle and Infernal resistance than being shot. Wolfe ignored the now four thugs and plugged the Lesser Urban Corrupter in the chest, one-shotting it back into red energy that dissipated and flowed through the wall, giving Wolfe a rough estimate of where its deckbearer was.

A card briefly appeared in Wolfe's vision, a bleeding red crown, that sped and placed itself over the brow of Klireen.

Dark Regalia
Rare Tier-1 Infernal Persistent
2 Infernal Power

This equipment card may be equipped to a deckbearer, granting +2 to all stats and Infernal typing, or it may be equipped to any [Unique], [Demigod], or [Chosen] card that is already Infernal to allow it to benefit from status as if it were a deckbearer as well as gain the **Head-hunter** trait: allows creature to attack a deckbearer directly, regardless of the cards on the field

When the card this equipment is attached to is removed from the field, this equipment goes as well.

"In the realms of the Infernal, power and position can be conferred to particularly evil individuals, ones that stand out from the common ruck of demon."—Asmodeus, Infernal Lord of Lust

Before Wolfe could fully analyze how that changed the battle, Klireen, Daughter of Lust leapt across the field. She was merely human sized, but was a true demonic succubus in all her glory—red skin, massive bat wings, and tail—all wrapped in a shell of incredibly beautiful woman.

But it was her stats Wolfe feared the most. She landed on the stainless-steel counter and flung a broiling ball of fire into Wolfe, who screamed as his skin cooked. Her stats were insane, as befit a five-power Mythic, he supposed. She hit for a fifteen magical attack and he only defended with a nine; and his random roll dropped it to an eight. He took an actual twenty-eight damage, halved as it was Fire against Infernal. But even with his toughness and mantle, that cleaved roughly a third of Wolfe's life off.

Wolfe shot the demoness in the chest even as he burned, staring up at her.

Which gave him a great view of the ceiling as a miniature sun of rainbow-colored light rose, its luminance somehow mystical and comforting—a promise of a utopia to come in the warmth that washed across Wolfe's skin.

Quetzalcoatl's Blessing of Promise
Legendary tier-1 Divine/Life [Vitality, Civic] Persistent
2 Life or Divine Power, 2 Mortal Power

Target [Civic] Card you control with power cost 3 or less. This card becomes a token copy of it. While this card is on the field, [Civic] cards you own cost 1 less of any power to play and you may have 2 extra cards on field so long as they are [Civic]. Cards reduced below 1 power becomes cost 1 Any Power (available) and gain Speedy.

"Times are changing and a new age is arriving. I cannot
promise that it will be better and already there are omens that
it will be a dark age for your people, but I promise you, I will
care for you and watch over you, so that you may find comfort
and rest after your last days."—Quetzalcoatl

Wolfe grinned even as he fired at Klireen, who leapt from
the counter unharmed, thanks to the card's special ability to
resist the strongest attack each round. But Wolfe knew the
situation had just gotten way better for them. *Shel has both her
Legendary and her Mythic on the field. This ought to be
interesting.*

A duplicate of the Stone Arch Fire appeared, made
entirely of rainbow light. Each now duplicated the other's
strength, and the healing went to twenty per round for every
allied deckbearer and card on the field—basically, everything
on Wolfe's team except Shel herself.

Cereboo healed instantly, bites closing as if he had a
healing factor as he ripped the Hellhound apart. Wolfe's burns
faded to a light sunburn then disappeared.

As long as Shel doesn't fall, we're damn near invulnerable,
Wolfe thought, but then hesitated. *That card said it has a
fifteen magical attack with Psychic as an option, even if she used
Fire before like an idiot. One bad defensive roll and that could
end me, since she's got that damned crown. I gotta be careful.*

Although Wolfe felt a bit of greed for the card.

Wolfe raised up and fired multiple bullets at people.
Malviere whispered her ubiquitous "for the pack" and Wolfe
speeded up, even his gun somehow working faster. Two of the
four thugs died in seconds, holes the size of a fist blown clean
through their torsos. The other two leapt out of the room
before Wolfe could finish shooting them.

But a headless, naked woman floated into the room. Wolfe
briefly got a look at the card, which read "Object of Lust" and

had the same power as Klireen to control cards, but that worked upon first sight rather than being pulled from a deck.

Cereboo whined and turned to face Wolfe and his team, and Wolfe received a notification that Cereboo had changed sides.

Wolfe just laughed to himself. Clearly, no deckbearer had been brave enough to enter the room and see Wolfe's cards, or they wouldn't have used that tactic, as Malviere could always change all canine sub-type cards to Wolfe's side.

"*Always* for the pack," Malviere intoned, and Cereboo switched sides right back.

Wolfe didn't explode the Object of Lust, instead firing on Klireen again. It didn't do anything to her thanks to her power, but Cereboo jumped up and bit at her repetitively. While Klireen was insanely powerful on the attack and against magic, she was weak to physical attacks.

Cereboo, empowered by Malviere, ripped at the succubus demigod. The card screamed—something Wolfe hadn't expected as cards rarely reacted to situations with any emotion —as Cereboo lunged at it with three heads. Cereboo's base attack of five became six from Malviere—and then twelve against Infernal creatures.

Which was a hundred and forty-four damage, divided by the creature's five defense to become twenty-eight.

Per head.

Cereboo grabbed the succubus by one leg and both arms and *pulled*. Klireen was able to land a devastating hit, nearly killing Cereboo outright and setting him to burning with her Fire-based magical attack. But Cereboo detached both arms and bit the leg nearly in half before the brief screaming stopped and Cereboo hurled the armless torso and legs back through the door where the card dissolved into red light, the crown rolling across the floor for a moment before dissolving as well.

Then he, in turn, dissolved into red and brown light and returned to Wolfe's deck as the fire on him burned him to nothing.

Wolfe had seen numerous things in his life, but that one had to be near the top for 'most disturbing.' Although, slaying the demi-god child card of a major Infernal was pretty cool, and Wolfe knew Cereboo would count it as an absolute win despite being returned to the deck himself.

Plus Wolfe was hardly bereft of allies as Sorenia stepped up to his side, her lantern shining brightly.

"Do you need help?" Fern asked into a brief moment when neither gunshot, nor bark, nor scream marred the battlefield that was the Singh mansion kitchen.

"No, for a wonder," Wolfe replied, glancing around. The double Stone Arch Fire made Wolfe's situation nearly unassailable, despite the one-round kill of Cereboo. *I can't wait till I can make him more powerful. A two-power card for zero power will always be insanely useful, but at the level I'm currently playing at he gets taken out decently often. But if I get the six-card set...*

A voice came from outside, in the hallway. A voice that Wolfe recognized from his time as the head enforcer of the Grimm family. Gurjit Singh.

"That you, Wolfe?!" Gurjit yelled, his voice filled with rage. "If you've hurt Gopal, I'll have you raped to death by a horse!"

Wolfe chuckled quietly at his opponent's commentary—as if they hadn't tried to kill him seconds ago. He was pretty sure he'd survive this, although not nearly a hundred percent positive. But even if he didn't survive, he knew damn well they weren't taking him alive to torture regardless. They certainly weren't that much stronger than him. The idea was laughable.

At his quiet chuckle, Shel, sitting next to him, relaxed fractionally. She pulled out Liurenia to join Sorenia.

"Wolfe, you gods' damned dog, speak to me!"

Wolfe didn't deign to answer, instead taking his position behind the stainless-steel counter and waiting—nothing else in his hand called to him. Both of his guns were there, as was the Xolo Spirit-Warder, but he had a feeling this would turn into an 'overwhelm him with numbers' situation, and his attack power had proven brutally up to the task of individual targets.

A hushed conversation, filled with angry whispers, filled the hall.

"Ten bucks says they try and come in through the dining room door simultaneously and overwhelm us," Wolfe said, pointing.

Shel shifted to cover it, gun out.

"Get behind me, so you're protected in both directions," Wolfe ordered quietly.

"So I can watch you die?" Shel asked.

Wolfe rolled his eyes. "Because your setup heals me twenty points every thirty seconds, and doesn't benefit you. I'm a flesh wall that restores entirely, basically, every half minute. And I can handle the pain. Although if it's ever between you and me, I choose me to die. But in this case it's also just plain old-fashioned good sense."

"Right," Shel muttered, scooting around Wolfe so she was protected in all directions.

Shel pulled out another card, and a mantle settled around her, giving off heat and an almost spiritual warmth. At the same time, a poncho-like garment, colored in white, blue, and red but in very Amerind patterns, appeared around her shoulders. Her Stone Circle Fire Tender card.

Stone Circle Fire Tender
Rare Tier-1 Fire/Life [Civic] Mantle
1 Fire or 1 Life power

All other Civic Cards gain +2 to all non-health stats.

If the Stone Arch Fire is in the deck, all healing powers are doubled and may target any entity.

"Those that tended the Stone Arch Fire were the heart of the numerous Cowlitz tribes."

"Well, now I get healed too," Shel said, smiling.

Sudden feet thudding outside called Wolfe's attention. "Good, because I think we're about to start round two."

CHAPTER 34

COMBAT OF THE ABSURD, PART II

D espite the running feet, for a moment, nothing happened.

The doors to the dining room burst inward as an enraged ton of meat charged into the kitchen, quickly resolving itself into a massive, red-skinned warthog with pustules oozing yellow pus that Wolfe could almost smell. Its eyes were wide and pain-maddened, and one of its two tusks was broken, and infection on the end of it.

Pig-Greedy Soul
Uncommon Tier-1 Infernal/Beast [Punished Soul, Diseased]
1 Infernal or 1 Beast Power, 1 Any Power

Health: 20
Attack: 6
Defense: 4
Magical Attack: N/A
Magical Defense: 3

Special: **Infectious**: Anyone wounded by this card gains the

diseased status, suffering -1 to all non-health stats and 1 true damage per 30 seconds for 3 minutes. Anyone gaining a killing blow on this card gains the same debuff.
Special: **Squealing**: This card must be attacked by all non-infernal cards on the field first before attacking anything.

"The souls of those that sacrificed all their honor and goodness on the altar of Mammon, but accomplished nothing worthwhile and died poor anyway, spend their eternity as diseased pigs in his realm."

"What the fuck?" Wolfe asked, turning and shooting the pig. It died in a single hit, exploding, and Wolfe felt a sudden chill wash through him as boils grew on his arm and burst.

Even as Wolfe fired, two men came around the corner, firing Glock-17's at him. One missed entirely despite three rapid shots from maybe twenty feet, and the other caught him in the chest with all three. It hurt like heck, but the damage—almost half his life despite the Infernal mantle—healed rapidly.

Two more men came around the hallway side, flanking Wolfe. One was a powerful-looking, swarthy man in his mid-forties with black hair; a giant, black beard; and eyes so dark, they were also almost black. He wore a traditional red turban with a black gem—an actual onyx, not glass, in his case, to show his allegiance to Asmodeus, Infernal lord of lust. Gurjit Singh, head of the Singh crime family.

Next to him was his eldest son, Gurjit the younger, who was very nearly the spitting image of his father but a few inches taller and a touch leaner. Red and purple cards, six of them, floated in front of Gurjit the father; and four cards, two red, one a sickly yellow, and one a mix of both, floated in front of Gurjit the younger.

Gurjit the younger touched a card, a sickly yellow and red

mixed one, and Wolfe yelled as a gangrenous wound with a tiny creature or protuberance opened on his arm.

Festering Taint
Uncommon Tier-1 Infernal/Elder [Disease, Taint] Persistent
2 Infernal or 2 Elder Power

This Persistent may target any deckbearer, creature, or card with a Health stat. It does 1 true damage, and reduces all non-Health stats by one, each 30 seconds. If any stat reaches zero, the entity is slain.

"The taint of the lower realms can end someone."

At the same time, Gurjit the Elder threw a card out.

Infernal Taint
Common Tier-1 Infernal / Corruption Persistent [Decay, Taint]
1 Infernal or 1 Corruption Power

This card deals 1 true damage every 30 seconds to anyone on the field that has any Infernal or Corruption debuff or negative status effect, per incidence of each. Anyone wounded by an Infernal or Corruption creature suffers the same, but this does not stack with itself. This does not count as damage or an attack for purposes of removing card effects.

"Sometimes, you can't feel the taint of the Infernal until it has consumed you," Javier de Villalobo, Cardinal and Champion of Gabriel.

Between the pig and the two cards, Wolfe found himself down two stats in every category and taking three true damage every round—as well as losing a stat every round as well, with a mere seven rounds, or three-and-half-minutes, left to live.

"Do you have anything to heal me?" Wolfe asked as another bullet slapped into his arm near harmlessly, healed away instantly.

"No," Shel called, firing over Wolfe and ending one of the two remaining guards.

"Then I can't just live inside your healing aura forever, I'm on a countdown. Gonna fire in the hole this thing."

Wolfe felt Malviere's power entering him, but instead of firing, he took a minute to drop down, swiping his cards and whispering into his headset, "Initiate in twenty seconds six feet to your left of my position."

Fern's voice, sped up like she was being fast forwarded, came through the connection. "I thought you didn't want to do this?"

"I'm dead in three and a half minutes if I don't kill the deckbearers, Fern, thanks to an unusual attack form. Caution and careful expertise are no longer the path—if they even were when they found us here."

Fern, still speaking rapidly, said, "Okay, Wolfe. On it. Don't die."

"Working on it."

He checked his cards and saw that he had both his Obsessive Infernal Cultists, the Bulgae Moon Chaser, the Infernal Rift, and a Demonic Portal card.

With his increased power and speed, Wolfe kicked the backpack across the floor, hard, so that it entered the dining hall. Wolfe then popped over the edge of the steel counter again and used his Infernal Rift, targeting Gurjit's son—he would rather have gone for the father but given his last instructions to Fern he had made that a bad option. He also fired his gun vaguely in the direction of Gurjit senior, who promptly leapt back out of the kitchen, to Wolfe's left, and hid behind the wall.

The son disappeared, presumably to his ninety-second trip to a faux Infernal realm.

"Down! Everyone, person or card, down!!" Wolfe yelled, dropping behind the stainless-steel counter a third time and scrambling around the side, grabbing Shel whom he half-dragged behind as well.

He got a notification that his penalties had increased to three of every stat; two of them now down to six of nine.

Wolfe opened his mouth half-a-second before a massive explosion went off, blowing the dining room to pieces. A pressure hit him as fire washed over him and debris rained past him, speckling the wall of the kitchen with slashes to accentuate the new burn marks. For a fraction of a second Wolfe couldn't hear and his skin burned, but the healing kicked in almost instantly, fixing him.

Shel started to stand, but Wolfe grabbed her and pulled her back down. "Not yet!"

Wolfe got a notification of a deckbearer death and the disease effect from the boar disappeared, restoring a single stat in every category to him, as well as Malviere being slain – she hadn't made it behind the counter, Wolfe assumed. He also dismissed three deckbearer notifications past that.

A second later, a second explosion, smaller and more muted, sounded.

Wolfe rolled to his feet, still suffering from two of the debuffs and with a mere few minutes to live. He rushed from the room, over the still-active Stone Fire Arch and its rainbow doppelganger, and out into the hall.

The windows of the hall had been blown inward, the edges around damaged, and Gurjit was lying on the floor facedown. The rainbow lights playing from the kitchen made the crimson splash of his blood across the hall feel like a clash of genres, like sudden horror in a kid's movie. Two men were down and dead near Gurjit, and Gurjit himself was lying face down, his back raw meat.

"It worked," Wolfe muttered, aiming his Edge at Gurjit.

Gurjit rolled over onto his back, letting out a grunt of agony as he did, to face Wolfe. He tried to raise his pistol but seemed to lack the strength.

His face was a rictus of hatred. "Wolfe, I swear I'll—"

Wolfe didn't wait, raising his Edge and pointing it at Gurjit's face. The bang was loud, even with much of the wall missing, and Gurjit jerked once.

So easy, for a man that ran the crime family for as long as I worked for Big Man Grimm, Wolfe thought, surprised a bit by how little it meant to him.

A good twenty cards appeared on his chest, and Wolfe grabbed them quickly before turning around and walking back into the kitchen. Wolfe's fever was growing, and more and more pustules were forming and bursting. He could feel himself weakening rapidly, and his own breathing was becoming ragged. *That card is an absolute piece-of-shit card, and can end me past all my preparations,* Wolfe thought.

Shel came walking over the Stone Fire Arch as well, but Wolfe pointed her back toward the Dining room. "Go get the cards in there please, we have to leave as soon as possible. I may have been quiet with the Infernal airsoft plan, but needing to use the explosives means we'll have police on us in minutes."

Shel nodded and ran into the other room.

Wolfe raised his gun, waiting. Perhaps it was unsportsmanlike, but since he would be thirty seconds from dead by the time the guy appeared, it didn't feel unfair to him.

A moment later, Gurjit Jr. appeared, his head right where Wolfe's barrel was.

Wolfe pulled the trigger, and Gurjit Jr. blew backwards like a comic character, head first with gore exploding from it outward. Instantly, the feverish feeling left Wolfe, and he straightened, no longer in agony.

He grabbed the next set of cards, the ones that Gurjit had dropped on death, just as Shel came back into the room. She held up the cards from the deckbearer that had been exploded in the dining room.

Wolfe took an incendiary grenade from out of his jacket and tossed it into the room she had just vacated. Hopefully the fire would remove any DNA evidence, as Wolfe was nearly positive there wouldn't be anything else to track him to the scene.

Well, nothing else if those who knew him didn't get involved, at least.

"Let's go," Wolfe said, motioning to the newly aerated outer wall.

They ran out into the night, as fast as they could go, heading for the van and Fern, hoping that no police were following them.

CHAPTER 35

WAGES OF SIN

"No, no," Fern whispered, rocking a bit in the chair of the van as she drove down the moonlit road, keeping herself almost exactly three miles over the speed limit.

The police car driving toward them on the road—sirens on—slowed a bit as it passed them. Wolfe squinted as the passenger-side officer shined a flashlight across the window, the light briefly playing across Wolfe, Shel, and Fern.

"Just stay calm," Wolfe said.

Shel smiled and waved at the officers as the vehicle passed them.

The van was quiet for a moment as the police car kept going. Wolfe looked behind him, but the police car didn't break or turn, and after a moment everyone let out a collective sigh of breath.

"We're good?" Shel asked.

"Pretty sure," Wolfe said.

Then he glanced at the borderline arsenal lying all over the floor. "No police officer is gonna believe that we're the attackers with two cute twenty-something women in our car, so that flashlight probably did us a huge favor. If we'd been pulled over..."

"Yeah," Shel said as Fern's breathing briefly went ragged.

"So, what's the plan now?" Shel asked.

"Well... we have an absolute *ton* of cards... and I want to see the newest 'Gate to the Infernal' set card."

Shel passed her cards forward, then leaned up to stare at Wolfe. He was holding *sixty* cards in his hand, which was absurd. The majority were Infernal or Infernal and something else, although a few were different. Wolfe quickly skimmed through, looking for the set card first. After a bit, he found it.

The front of the card showed a powerful Infernal creature, arms akimbo, with wisps of light—a soul perhaps—flowing into it from behind while it stood on a night-time road in the rain.

Damned Soul's Road
Rare equivalent, Tier-4 equivalent Infernal Persistent [Gate]
1 Infernal Power

While in play, the first 4 unique Infernal creatures or minions in play require 1 less power of the deckbearer's choice. All Infernal, Undead, or Elder cards with the word Portal or Gate in their title or keywords cost 1 less power (minimum 1), even if brought to the field by another card rather than being played.

So long as this card is in the deck, all Infernal, Undead, and Elder creature and minion cards that are unique will have personalities as if they were companions.

Special: **Gate to the Infernal:** If all 6 are possessed in the same deck, the bearer will gain 7 Legendary Infernal or Beast card pulls. Additionally, the deckbearer may either gain the Mythic 'Gate to the Infernal' Building Card or evolve Cereboo. Each card was given to a member of the Noimoire underworld.

"When our lieutenants take the field in all but will, the time of ascension is nigh."—Gabriel, to Nurenda Whiteflame, 3103 BDN

Shel read over Wolfe's shoulder.

Then she whistled. "Wow... that's almost as complicated and bizarre as your Infernal Rift. It's like a baby enhancer card that's also a persistent that affects even side-decks or, theoretically, sacrifices that join you if they were unique."

"It's a doozy alright," Wolfe muttered as he stared at it, his mind racing.

"Do you have any unique creatures, by the way?" Shel asked. "You don't, right? Just companions?"

Wolfe nodded. "Yeah, although the Get of Xolotl will become one... and we know we just got Klireen."

Shel snorted. "Seriously? You want to have *Klireen* in your deck? A succubus daughter of an Infernal lord you opposed, the Infernal lord of lust I might add, and you want to give her a personality?"

Wolfe wasn't normally prone to embarrassment, but he felt his cheeks heating. "Klireen is a crazy powerful card, and even more so at four power."

"Uh huh," Shel said, her voice playfully doubtful.

Wolfe could see she was grinning. A touch hysterically, perhaps, now that they had gotten away, at least for the moment. But grinning.

Wolfe continued his musing as Fern drove down the streetlight-lit road. "Although I suppose playing this card first does almost nothing for me unless I get more unique creatures as well. Maybe I can put her in the side-deck and use her from there as a four-power equivalent."

"Did you get any other unique creatures?" Fern asked. "That might make it a bigger deal for your deck."

Wolfe rifled back through the cards again, glancing at types. After a moment, he shook his head no. "Nothing else here is unique. Maybe I should ask Mrs. Timo for Tuvagi back."

"That's a companion, not a unique creature," Shel said.

"Right, sorry." Wolfe shuffled through the cards more slowly. "I do have some really interesting cards in this set, though. There's a Death and Life combo enhancer card, no power cost, called Deck Slayer that gives two percent life increase for every deckbearer you've killed and a flat plus one each to defense and magical defense."

"Wow, you could live forever," Shel said with half a laugh, her eyes wide. "That's straight-up Thousand Card Killer stuff."

"The serial murderer?" Fern asked.

Shel nodded.

"I have killed quite a few," Wolfe said, counting absently. "I wonder if it counts the two I got before becoming a deckbearer myself?"

"Doesn't say it doesn't," Shel said.

Wolfe nodded again. He would age quite slowly with just that one card—perhaps, if everything went as he hoped, he could live with Shel for the majority of her extended lifespan, given that she had the Cowlitz mountain 'set' of cards.

"It's a good future," Shel said as if she could read his mind, then put her hand on his arm. "But keep your mind on the here and now—we have to live through the next couple days first."

Wolfe chuckled darkly. "There is that."

He searched the rest of the cards quickly. "There's a lot of stuff here, and a ton of it is good. But most doesn't fit my deck. Control and damage over time cards are the majority of the stuff I've got here—none of it fits."

"So you said," Shel muttered, and Wolfe blinked.

Then it hit him—he'd repeated himself. He ignored her teasing.

"I was hoping to get more than just two cards I can use out of the *sixty* that I had."

"We can always trade them to Gavin's in return for other, better cards," Shel said.

"It almost always takes more than four days, and I wanted them before we went after the Renfeldt. I think that at this point Nathan and whatever other toadies Adam has are gonna figure out what I'm up to—and I am... concerned about meeting up with Nathan again. I'd rather be as strong as possible."

"Speaking of, how many levels did you get?" Shel asked.

"Two, the vast majority of it from Gurjit himself. You?"

"About two-and-a-half," Shel replied.

Wolfe returned to the previous conversation. "Levels aside... I need a way to turn cards into other cards, fast."

There was a moment of silence as Fern turned off the highway onto their street, broken only by the noises of the car and the faint tap-tap of Shel clicking her fingernail against her teeth as she thought.

"Well... we could use the underground card markets. Those guys have way less variety than the main market, but they seem to be able to get the cards fast, or at least they were able to last time."

Wolfe laughed. "I kidnapped Gopal right from the parking lot that the Rat Arena uses—I doubt they're gonna let me just walk on in with no consequence."

"Well... what if we gave Gopal back?"

In the excitement, Wolfe had somehow forgotten all about

Gopal. "Ah, shit. Did he even live?" Wolfe asked Fern. "And did they already get him and take him out?"

"He did live... but he didn't escape. No one else either lived or escaped. My traps got them all."

"...We're returning to a house that's a complete bloodbath, aren't we?" Shel asked, her voice tired.

Wolfe glanced back and saw that her eyes were glistening, but she shook her head when Wolfe opened his mouth.

Either ignorant of the exchange or unwilling to acknowledge it, Fern responded to Shel's question. "Well, I got the remaining two vans worth of them on the highway with the drones while you guys were out, but still... yeah. Twenty people are dead in that place. More cards, though—Harjeet didn't make it either."

Wolfe whistled, running his hands through his hair. "Wow."

"How do we get this... handled?" Shel asked. "Clean and body free?"

"We can call Miriam and have some of her people handle it..." Wolfe said. "The Dungeon of Loowitlatkla's Fall is still there, even if we beat it... if they take the bodies there, they can dispose of them. Bodies dissolve in dungeons, right?"

"Yeah, but we're gonna have an absolute ton of work to do, regardless," Fern said. "And more people from Miriam seeing it means more problems. I killed ten people on a highway, twenty more disappeared at your place, and you murdered ten and set everything on fire. Even by deckbearer standards this is gonna be a huge deal. We might need to vacate the state soon. Maybe the country."

Wolfe nodded. *Yeah, forty bodies in the thorough, borderline military way we handled it, even if they only figure out half of them is gonna cause some issues. Forget buying cards from the underground market—I'll need to sell cards to them as well, just to keep off the radar.*

Speaking of the radar... "So we release Gopal?" Wolfe asked. "That's the plan? Don't you think he'll squeal?"

Fern shook her head as she turned into the parking lot of the Hellmouth Institute. "He won't. He's here on a temporary visa, and thinks very differently about this stuff— he'll assume the police will take your side, or are bribed. I know him from my time with Adam. He'll flee quietly, trust me."

It's a risk, but I have to take one somewhere... "Alright, I'll head upstairs and get him, set him free. Shel, call Miriam and get her working. Fern, track everything you can and make sure we're not about to be raided."

Fern nodded but said, "I don't have that much access to active police communications, but I'll try."

She came to a halt past the four black SUV's, right at the front door to the Institute.

Wolfe opened the door. "It's gonna be an all-nighter after a raid, peeps. Get started as fast as you can—I, for one, am already tired."

CHAPTER 36

WHEELING, DEALING, AND WARNINGS

"**I**'m surprised you let that fat fuck go," Miriam said over the table they all sat in the Ekron Eternal. Wolfe noted that even though it had only been a few days, the bullet holes and blood from his assault here were gone— and despite being in the early afternoon, Miriam was keeping the place dim and foggy, its ambiance restored from when Wolfe had last seen it.

Although she isn't playing the club music, thank the gods.

Derek and a new guy named Anthony were talking. Anthony was Miriam's replacement deckbearer with the Egyptian/undead deck, with the same chiseled Egyptian features as the dead and barely lamented Ahmed, although he was a couple inches taller even than Wolfe's six-foot-two, which was impressive.

Shel and Fern and even Malviere were talking as well, and Cereboo lounged at Wolfe's feet, panting happily.

Wolfe yawned, his hand over his mouth as he involuntarily did an impression of a snake eating an egg. It had been a *long* night, even with Miriam's crew, cleaning up everything... to the extent it had been cleaned up.

Miriam gently rapped a silver-and-black stiletto onto the table, leaving the tiniest groove, which she frowned at. "I *said*, I'm surprised you let the fat fuck go."

Wolfe focused on Miriam again, blinking slightly. She was dressed with her usual 'panache,' a white, semi-diaphanous gown over a black slip that left her barely decent, with a silver and onyx necklace that drew the eye, even in the dim light of the club.

"Yeah, well, it's my only chance to get cards before I have to face the Renfeldt family, and with the rate things are moving, probably Adam's stooge Nathan as well," Wolfe said with a grimace, taking a sip from his whiskey before continuing. "Fern doesn't think he'll tattle on us—she thinks he's gonna run. Given how bad my one beating of him last year broke his spirit, I suspect she's right."

"That's an awful risk to take," Miriam replied, leaning back and snuggling between Derek and Anthony before crossing her thin arms over her chest.

Fern glanced up from her conversation. "We're already fine on that front at least."

"What?" Miriam asked, startled enough to immediately lean forward again. "How do you know?"

Fern placed her laptop on the giant table and turned it around, facing the group. "A credit card registered to Gopal bought a plane ticket to Pakistan half an hour ago. He'll be gone in less than an hour."

The screen showed a bank transaction list, and second from the top, below a hefty 'lobby concession' purchase, was a ticket on Elemental Lines.

"He could still call the police from outside the country," Miriam said.

But Wolfe was more concerned with Fern's other choice of words—she didn't tend to use language in a manner other than precise. "What did you mean when you said 'fine on *that* front *at least*?'"

Fern didn't answer directly, instead turning the laptop around and tapping on it for a few seconds. After, she turned it back around. Everyone leaned in.

It was a memo from Chief Huang, head of the entire Noimoire police department, to the heads of every single precinct.

Wolfe read through quickly, his frown deepening with each line. "So, basically, they're going to be putting everything into finding out who killed the Singh family, and bringing them to justice?"

Fern turned the computer back around, nodding. "Yeah. Given that it was a borderline paramilitary-style hit and left two flaming wrecks on the freeway and one giant flaming mansion in a posh neighborhood..."

"Yeah," Wolfe said, grimacing again. "Even for deckbearer fights that was a bit past the norm."

"It was a very blatant hit, even if you hid *who* did it semi-well."

"So, we're on a clock before I'm an out-and-out bad guy again?" Wolfe asked. "Only we don't know how long till they figure out it was me?"

Before anyone else could respond, Wolfe's phone buzzed in his pocket. He glanced down at the phone, seeing 'Lieutenant Righteous Prick' on his phone.

Wolfe held a hand up for silence. "Guys, hold up. Rhett's calling."

He answered the phone. "Didn't think I'd be hearing from you, at least till um... everything blows over, let us say."

Rhett's voice was tight. "I wanted to give you a heads up, just in case you're involved with the Singh family situation. Chief Huang of the Noimoire police has made it his absolute top priority to find and arrest the ones responsible."

"We know," Wolfe replied.

"Did you also know that he sent out calls to all the other police departments around, including my Joliet one, and that the FBI has been called in?" Rhett asked.

Shit. Wolfe glanced at Shel, whose eyes were very large. Then he glanced at Fern, who shook her head.

After a moment, Wolfe responded. "No... didn't know that. Thanks for the heads up."

"If you were involved, *William*, you might want to find a way to get out of town... fast. They'll track it all to you soon, one way or another."

"I read you loud and clear," Wolfe said.

"Alright, I've got criminals to catch, I'll talk to you some other day." With those clipped words, Rhett hung up.

"Shit," Wolfe said, lying back against the booth and putting the arm with the phone across his face. "Shit, shit, shit."

"I... I think I'm going to have to quit being a police officer," Shel said, quietly, her eyes staring out into the statue-and-fog-filled dance floor, but obviously seeing nothing.

"At least here, yeah," Wolfe responded to her, then hit his fist on the table. "*Shit.*"

"You have a ton of money, and you said Cerberus himself gave you a quest," Fern said quietly. "This is just a setback... you'll likely have decades longer than usual to be together, and to build a life somewhere. But this is another time-table... and a variable one that we don't know the end point for yet. We can still win and we can all get to safety."

Shel pulled her head back around. "Yeah, that's true. And the first step..."

"Is to see about trading cards," Wolfe replied.

It was Miriam's turn to hold up her phone, which she did before rapping her fingernail on the table. "Well, in good news... they've agreed to meet you. But we all bring guys."

"Guys?" Wolfe asked.

"Guys with guns," Miriam said, "So that, and I quote, 'nothing untoward happens.'"

"Lovely."

The meeting place was a fancy restaurant that wasn't officially open yet, called 'Louie's,' something that felt to Wolfe more Quebecois than Noimorian, but whatever floated their boat, he supposed. They met in the back, in one of the fancy secluded dining rooms for special occasions.

It was an uncomfortable fit, regardless. Miriam and Derek and her new guy were all here, as was Wolfe and Shel. On the other side of the table sat Hans and Lisa Berwick; the two they had traded cards with at the Rat Arena over a year ago.

Hans was still tall and overweight, but not grossly so. Wolfe remembered his eyes as kinda sad, but now, they darted from side to side and he was visibly sweating and rubbing at the huge wart on the inside of his arm. Next to him sat Lisa, a cute, blonde-haired girl who was obviously trying to hide her looks. She was dressed like a pile of laundry—she had on baggy, black sweatpants and an oversized black hoodie; it was so similar to the one before Wolfe had a brief doubt she had changed clothes, even. But this time she sat hunched and had the hood up.

Wolfe wasn't sure why they were so nervous—they had four guards with guns with them. Any attempt to do anything here, in a closed room, would result in dead people on both sides, and no one wanted that, least of all Wolfe. He would never forgive himself if he got Shel killed, and even losing Miriam would hurt him quite a bit, he admitted to himself quietly.

"So, what have you got for us?" Hans asked.

Wolfe took the cards he'd gained from the fight—every single one except Klireen, the Infernal Gate set, The Infernal Regalia, and the Deck Slayer card—and passed them over. At the sight of the huge pile, Hans's eyes widened.

But Lisa was the one that picked them up. "Give me a few minutes... or near an hour, really. I need to see what this is all going for, and what we'll trade you for it."

Wolfe didn't actually know who Hans and Lisa worked for, which concerned him. He had always assumed that the six 'families' were the real crime powers in Noimoire, but the Rat Arena and Han's guys had been a surprise. Wolfe wondered if he was missing anything else.

He glanced around the tiny room as Lisa began slowly shuffling through cards and banging away on the keyboard.

"Parcheesi, anyone?"

Twenty minutes into the waiting, it had occurred to Wolfe that this might be a trap even though it hadn't triggered yet— something to get him to wait around. But when he queried Fern, she texted that she hadn't seen anything, and that it made total sense they had to check the cards.

Forty minutes later, despite the reassurances from Fern, Wolfe was on edge enough that he was giving at least slight thought to leaving, Lisa finally looked up.

She pushed her glasses up on her forehead and rubbed at her eyes before staring at Wolfe. "My organization will give you thirty-seven million in trade for all seventy-seven cards."

"What?!" Shel asked heatedly, leaning forward. "How is that fair? Gavin would give us forty-five million in cash—there was some rare stuff in there, even a legendary! Plus, I know the cards you sell us will be marked up as well! We're gonna get barely more than half value of the cards, if we're lucky!"

Lisa shrugged, her face elaborately unconcerned. "You'll get it in untraceable cards, and you'll get it within twenty-four hours, even if our selection is far more limited and a touch more expensive than Gavin's. Take it or leave it—this isn't a charity or a debate society."

Shel sat back and crossed her arms over her chest, but Wolfe got it. Close to sixty percent on 'stolen' goods—even if they were cards, about the most value-to-weight thing in the entire world—was actually damn good.

"We'll take it," Wolfe said, ending the debate. "What have you got?"

"I need you to be more specific than that."

"Unique Infernal creatures," Wolfe replied. "Rare or Legendary Civic, Mortal, or Divine cards. Anything that benefits orphans in Mortal, Divine, Beast, or Infernal. Plus any cheap Xolo Spirit Warders, Twice-damned Hellhounds, or Angry Hellhounds you have."

Lisa reached down and tapped the computer for a few moments, then turned it around in a motion reminiscent of Fern, showing them a list of cards.

Wolfe, Shel, and Miriam all leaned in to stare at the list.

CHAPTER 37

WHAT CRIME PAID

W olfe decided to look at the Unique Infernal creature cards first. He was going to look for canine ones first, but as he scrolled down the list, he realized, with growing frustration, that it wouldn't even come to that. There were literally only two unique creatures mentioned, and neither were canine subtype.

The first unique creature card was imp subtyped. The card front showed a thin, sneering imp with a hand on the end of its tail—a hand with improbably long and slender fingers.

Bartrill, the Fifteen Fingers
Unique Uncommon Equivalent, Tier-7 equivalent Infernal
(Imp) Creature
1 Infernal Power

Health: 9
Attack: 4
Defense: 4
Magical Attack: 4(**Fire**)
Magical Defense: 4

Special: **Filch**: When this card comes into play it steals any one equipment card that any opposing deckbearer or creature card has equipped and equips it regardless of other requirements, gaining any numerical bonuses as if it qualified with all keywords.

Special: **Speedy**: The first card with the speedy keyword played per 30 seconds doesn't count against cards played.

"Envy manifests in many ways, and forms the basis of multiple Infernal lords' profiles. Bartrill has worked for more than one of them, taking a cut on this theft or that."

Wolfe glanced at the price. *Six million. Holy shit.*

"That's... expensive," Wolfe said.

Lisa answered for the duo as usual. "No other card like it in existence. Plus, you'd need seven hundred and twenty-nine uncommon cards to make a tier-7 uncommon card. Even if they were a mere hundred k for each, that's over seventy million I'd remind you. This is, dare I say it, a *steal* at this price."

"Ha ha," Wolfe said, dryly. "Why the cheap price, then?"

"A lot of reasons," Lisa said, her face bored again. "Probably because the card is so situational, one. Also, you could make seventy-two deckbearers with those uncommon cards. Lastly, most people don't drive to the truly absurd levels, usually settling for tier two or three, really. Tier seven is for emperors and world-bestriding business owners."

Hans finally stepped in. "Except for the orphan cards. Those seem to go up in tier fairly easily."

Lisa brushed her blond hair from her shoulder but didn't respond.

"I wonder what the personality of fifteen fingers here would be like," Shel muttered.

Wolfe snorted. "Unpleasant six days of the week, and utterly intolerable the seventh."

He raised an eyebrow as Fern actually giggled from next to him at the tiny table. *Didn't expect that weak joke to land with anyone, much less her.*

Wolfe checked out the second card. The card showed a giant, legless demon, vaguely humanoid, with clouds of green gas wrapped around it and spewing from it.

Sligrethak, The Choking Land
Unique Rare-equivalent, Tier-4 equivalent Infernal Creature
4 Infernal, 4 Any Power

Health: 50
Attack: N/A
Defense: 17
Magical Attack: 17(**Corruption**)
Magical Defense: 17

Special: **Incorporeal**: This creature does not take damage from physical attacks
Special: **Choke the World:** This ability does 5 true damage every round to everything, except this card, Corruption creatures, and the deckbearer, that is on the battlefield as Corruption damage, modified only by resistances and weaknesses, every round. All Nature, Plant, Beast, [Land], [Point of Interest], and [Civic], buildings and persistent have no effect in the aura. All Corruption creatures have their stats doubled.
Special: **Corrupt the Game [20]**: Every deckbearer that is slain has a 20% chance to have every card (checked per card, not as a whole) matching the types above change to either an equivalent Corruption card.

"Sligrethak is a top minion of the Infernal Lord Belial, lord of impurity. He pulls on the worst of industry to choke the life from the land and cities both."

"Gross," Shel muttered as she stared at the card.

"Yeah, I'm sure *its* personality is absolutely delightful," Miriam muttered with a laugh.

Wolfe wasn't very impressed by the card either—it was hugely powerful, but it cost his entire power load to cast, couldn't be used with his Demonic Portal cards, and hurt his allies as well.

He glanced at the other side of the screen. *The price is an insane fifty million as well. I couldn't afford it without dipping into reserves.*

"They don't have any really useful unique cards... what about other things?"

Wolfe glanced at the list again. They had a *bunch* of cheap Angry Hellhounds, but nothing really notable from any of the other categories Wolfe had asked for.

"What can we get in cash?" Fern suddenly asked, leaning forward.

"What?" Wolfe interjected before anyone else could say anything. "Why would we take cash?"

Lisa started typing furiously into her computer.

Fern hesitated, her fingers tapping out a rhythm on the table before she answered. "Well... we couldn't sell the cards through Gavin's because we need the cash fast, and Gavin's auctions take time. But we can go to their local store, as well as the rest of the Noimoire card exchange, and *buy* the stuff they already have there. If we have cash, or money in a bank account, really, that can't be traced. You can get access to a huge variety of cards, maybe even some professional help."

"Professional help?" Wolfe asked, briefly intrigued.

"Yeah, they have deck specialists, who make their living

studying cards and combos and sell the expertise, not to mention keeping tabs on what's available at the stores."

Lisa suddenly spoke. "My principal will give you twenty-eight million in cash for the cards."

For the second time, that's both highway robbery and better than I expected, Wolfe thought.

He turned and stared at the women with him. "Do you think this is a good idea? I'm hardly in a good position with the police right now, given..."—Wolfe glanced at Lisa and Hans before finishing—*"everything*. Shouldn't I keep a low profile? I mean, it'll be pretty obvious where I am."

Fern shook her head, a slight smile playing over her usually pensive features. "It may raise questions, since you'll be spending a lot of money with no obvious source—if anyone pays enough attention. But Gavin's doesn't report to any agencies in the government, thanks to longstanding deck secrecy laws, so they'd have to have someone there watching, and why would the police just happen to have someone there."

"Hmm," Wolfe said, scratching his chin.

"Plus, you'll be acting the opposite of suspicious—you'll be appearing in public, openly going about your business. It's the perfect disguise!"

Wolfe hesitated, casting his eyes over at Shel. She smiled and nodded.

Wolfe turned to Lisa and Hans. "I saw you have another eleven Angry Hellhounds for some reason, for the price of twenty thousand each. Can I get those, and then, I guess, the rest in cash?" Wolfe asked.

"Of course," Lisa replied.

"We should make a day of it," Shel said from the front passenger seat.

"What?" Wolfe asked, startled from his musings on his upcoming battles. "A day of what?"

"I want to be a part of the day!" Miriam said from the back of the Ford 150.

"*What* day?" Wolfe asked again, his hands gripping the steering wheel tight as he pulled around a silver sports car that wasn't using even an ounce of its get up and go.

Shel answered. "We should make a day out of going to the card exchange. We haven't been to the Three Fires Arena, which is right next to it. We can get cards, have a nice dinner, and catch a couple matches along with doing what we need."

"I have days at best to figure out finishing off the Renfeldt family," Wolfe said as he pulled back into his lane, headed for the Card Exchange.

Fern started to say something, but Wolfe held up his hand. "I know, I know, you have the time down to the minute."

In the rearview mirror, Wolfe saw Fern flush, and Miriam fake punched her arm, grinning.

Shel leaned over. "C'mon, it'll be fun! It'll also add to your cover, because it *is* incongruous behavior for someone that just committed a massive hit on a crime family. But mostly, you're not likely to go after your enemies in broad daylight, and you're unlikely to need the whole day to get cards for your deck. Besides those cards, you're as ready as you're ever going to be."

"It seems pointless," Wolfe muttered as he pulled around another car. "Why go have fun like nothing's happening when we're in the middle of a war?"

"By the end of this, I think there's a good chance we're going to have to flee the country," Shel said quietly. "I think that enjoying the city of our birth and casing some of its highlights might be the best thing we can do."

Then Shel laughed. "Besides, shouldn't we celebrate getting engaged?"

Wolfe chuckled a bit himself. "I thought we did that the other night."

Shel fake slapped his arm with a laugh. "You."

Then she sobered. "Seriously, though, let's make the trip something to remember."

Wolfe sighed, then signaled his turn. A moment later, he slowed and pulled onto a side street. "Alright, alright, I've never been good at saying no to you. We'll do the whole thing, one last slice of normalcy, so to speak."

Shel clapped her hands.

"Why'd you turn down this street?" Miriam asked as they passed some high-end shops. "The card exchange is the other way."

"You don't know?" Wolfe asked. "This is where we can get some high-end clothing. If we're gonna go to the card exchange and the Three Fires Arena, I think we should dress the part."

CHAPTER 38

PRIVILEGE OF WEALTH

The entrance to the Card Exchange reminded Wolfe of his recent trip to Michelle's to get a ring for his beautiful new fiancée. The building was a three-story, Art Deco-style building with huge windows and white-and-gold accents, directly across the street from the Three Fires Arena.

It didn't, strictly speaking, look like Michelle's. But the ostentatious display of wealth, in such stark contrast to the majority of Noimoire, made it *feel* the same. No litter or trash, no homeless druggies anywhere, and everything appeared to have been recently power-washed.

But the biggest similarity was the pair of armed guards out front.

Once again, however, looking like you belonged was the biggest way to avoid trouble. Wolfe was dressed in a smart three-piece suit, tailored a bit loose, with his Edge in a holster underneath his suit jacket. Derek was dressed about the same.

Shel, next to Wolfe as they walked up from the closed parking lot, was in a sexy green dress that might have been spray-painted on, and Miriam had chosen a slinky black dress that also left little to the imagination.

Only Fern appeared sedate in a gray pantsuit with a large gray jacket over it.

Wolfe wasn't used to doing these things—or anything, really—as a group of five. Despite the last two years of his life having a ton of people in it, the previous twenty years before that had been nearly devoid of anyone, and old habits, or thought patterns, stuck.

But, against his better judgement, he was enjoying having people around him.

He stepped up to the door, and the guards, after a brief and perfunctory once-over, waved him in, their attention already on the hundreds of others entering.

He pushed through the crowds and into the Card Exchange. The inside was even more impressive than the outside, although the carnival feel of too many people in too small a location took away a bit—in that regard, Michelle's it wasn't.

But the Card Exchange, and its patrons, reveled in the Great Game, their passion clear. Huge posters of famous deckbearers and equally or even more famous legendary and mythic cards adorned the walls, were placed on poles near intersections, or, in a few cases, hung from the ceilings as near tapestries—and a fourth of the people here were dressed as some card, the floor crawling with costumed people.

Stores having everything to do with cards were crammed into all available nooks and crannies. Some were obviously suffering hard times; mostly the old archive footage watching locations, which had been failing since the internet archives became prevalent. But most stores were clearly packed, with a wide variety on display. Stores selling fake cards or custom card cakes competed with outposts of Gavin's and numerous similar but smaller purveyors of cards for attention, and every place got something.

Wolfe stepped away from the entrance a few feet and then turned to Miriam. "Where's your guy?"

"My guy?" Miriam asked, her musical laugh nearly drowned out by the cacophony around them. "You mean the card specialist?"

Wolfe nodded.

She made a lazy air quote. "'My guy' is the undead one, which won't help you much. Just look for the Infernal card specialist, or maybe a Beast deck specialist."

Wolfe furrowed his brow. "So, where am I looking?"

Miriam stepped close to Wolfe and pointed back and up. "Most are on the second floor, nearly behind us, off to the side there. All clustered for your convenience. I'd bet the Infernal card specialist is next to the Undead one, so it should make it easy."

"Let's go then, Fern's clock is counting down."

In the scale of Wolfe's life, getting there was indeed easy, but it was annoying regardless. He had to traipse up the escalator on the far side, walk away from his target, cross a bridge, and then walk back. All the time jostling through people. But a few minutes later, he was where he wanted to be —a door with a couple feet on each side, looking into a 'store' barely bigger than an office building. The sign read "Pedro's Card Advice."

But it appeared to be free of people, which was a plus in Wolfe's book. Well, except for one guy in the back at a desk, whose face was hidden behind a computer.

"This is it? Just... Pedro?" Wolfe asked. "How do I know he even specializes in what I want?"

Miriam pointed to the top frame of the door, where the tiny, stylized devil face symbol of the Infernal faction was inlaid.

"This is barely more than a hole in the wall," Wolfe groused as he looked at it. "Is this guy any good?"

"Just go in and find out," Shel said with laughter in her voice. "You'll be able to tell if he's useful quickly, I'm sure."

"True." Wolfe pushed the door open, stepping into the deep but narrow store. A chime in the back rang.

"One moment!" the man in the back called.

Wolfe glanced around as the rest of his team crowded around him.

The walls of the store had a couple giant card posters hanging, all infernal, as well as multiple deck examples, from ten cards to a hundred-card monstrosity, all with names on them, many famous—Elizabeth Bathory, Kim Nguyen-Young, and Al Capone just a few examples.

The man came out from behind the desk. He was an astonishing six and a half feet tall, but he looked like a scarecrow—an albino one with thick glasses. His skin was sallow, and he walked hunched over, as if embarrassed by his height. But his eyes, despite the glasses, shone with a burning passion.

"I'm Barry, Barry Vivendi. How may I help you?" he asked.

"My friend here," Wolfe said, jerking a finger back at Miriam, "said I should seek professional help finding some good cards for my deck, and said the best in the region hang out at the card exchange... so I guess that's you."

Barry nodded absently. "You need help with an Infernal Deck?"

"That's why I'm here, like I said."

Barry smiled, excitement in his eyes. "I can't wait to see what you've brought me." Then he glanced at the people around Wolfe. "Normally, I do this confidentially..."

"I trust these guys," Wolfe responded.

"I appreciate it, hun," Shel said, kissing his cheek. "But

there're no seats, and I'm very familiar with your deck. If you don't mind, I'll just look around."

"Same," Miriam said, and Fern nodded as well.

"That makes it easy," Barry said as everyone filed out. He walked after them and closed the door, putting up a 'consultation in session' sign.

Then he sat down behind the desk and pushed a computer screen around so Wolfe could see it, while keeping one facing himself. "So, tell me about your deck."

Wolfe pulled his deck up in his mind, then started listing his cards.

"I've got Cereboo—"

"List of capabilities, please," Barry said.

Wolfe gave them to him as Barry typed madly into his computer.

"Also, Malviere,"

"List of capabilities, please."

Wolfe volunteered that information as well.

"And, as my last pseudo-companion, an Obsessive Infernal Cultist."

"Tier?"

"You don't need me to list the stats?" Wolfe asked, surprised.

"I just need the tier, so long as it's one we've seen before. I know the card."

Wolfe whistled. "That's... impressive. How do you know that?"

Barry looked up and smiled. "My entire livelihood is to know Infernal cards and cards that stack well with them. That's it. I'd be a bad advisor if I couldn't keep even relatively obscure ones in my mind."

Wolfe nodded, and kept going with his card list. It surprised him, somehow, to note that a good half his cards were unique or modified to be temporarily unique.

After Barry had written down everything, the thin man sat back in his chair, rubbing his chin thoughtfully but awkwardly.

I wonder if he does that normally, or if he's trying to look smart?

"So, you're running an entire advanced deck at three power or less, focused almost entirely on portal cards as a way to get creatures onto the field?" Barry asked.

"Obviously," Wolfe responded.

"Hmm..." Barry said. "Plus a heavy canine synergy... and you need interesting unique cards as well?"

Wolfe nodded again.

Barry went into a fury of typing, and after a moment, two cards popped up on Wolfe's screen.

The first was a monstrous creature, a demon with a dog's head but intelligent eyes, and a mane, which was carrying a weird torch-whip. Fire covered it and spilled from its mouth, and seemed to somehow radiate beneath its fur.

Bahkark, Gehennan Kennel Half-Breed

Unique Tier-4 equivalent, Legendary equivalent Infernal [Canine] Creature

2 Infernal Power, 3 Fire or Beast Power in any combination

Health: 31
Attack: 8
Defense: 5
Magic Attack: 8[**Fire**]
Magic Defense: 6

Special: **Motivation**: When this creature enters the field or attacks, any creature with a matching sub-type may make an additional attack.

Special: **Gehennan Leadership:** +1 to Attack and Magical

Attack to any Creature [Canine] for each of the types it matches among Fire, Beast, and Infernal.

Special: **Called to Canine:** This card costs 1 less power for each [Canine] already on the field.

"Who did what to whom to make Bahkark has always been a subject of much speculation"—Anonymous Gehennan Kennel Master

The second card showed a pack of wolves, each with different magical attributes—ice, fire, demon's horns, and the like—worrying at the legs of a massive being, inflicting gross amounts of damage.

Strength of the Pack
Uncommon Tier-1 Beast Persistent
2 Beast Power

So long as this card is in play, each card gains an additional attack for the square of total matching allied sub-types, to a maximum of an additional 100% capacity.

"Together, we can fell the mightiest Titan."

The third showed another demon, but this one was a pale girl that stood about eight feet tall, obviously demonic, holding a glowing red chain while standing in front of an old, fat man in a corporate office.

Vatya, Claimer of the Corrupt
Unique Tier-5 equivalent, Rare-equivalent Infernal [Civic, Criminal] Creature
3 Infernal Power

Health: 20
Attack: 3
Defense: 5
Magical Attack: 3
Defense: 5

Special: **Claim the Corrupt**: If any creature, minion, or persistent costs 4 or more base power and has any debuff on it, this card may slay it instantly.

Special: **Wages of Sin**: Each time an enemy creature, minion, or persistent with a debuff dies or changes sides, this card create a 'Wages of Sin' persistent token that adds 1 Infernal power and 1 card on field to Vatya's deckbearer and has a standard time in play.

"When the Infernal collects a soul, they might use any number of minions, but Vatya is one of their favorite."

"This one seems more like a corruption deck card than one for mine, why this?" Wolfe asked, hesitantly.

Barry smiled. "Well, before we talk that, we need to talk price. You can have this information for free, but if you want to purchase these cards through me, and get the next one I'll show you, my fee is five percent."

Wolfe frowned. *I feel like everyone is taking a cut...*

"*If* I take your suggestion," Wolfe ground out.

"Of course, only if. It assumes you like the next card..." Barry said, pulling some forms out and passing them over. "Let's just take care of this, and I'll show you a card that'll let you defeat an entire category of decks... It's one of my favorites, Corrupt the Pillars of Civilization."

CHAPTER 39

INTERLUDE INTERRUPTUS

"The Nagiri is amazing," Shel said as she laid her chopsticks down, across the small table from Wolfe. "You should really try some."

Wolfe rolled his eyes and forked a piece of meat into his mouth.

He grimaced. "I'll stick with the teriyaki beef. Sugar sauce is about as exotic as I like to get. I'm more of a beer and breakfast food kind of guy."

"Pretty sure that combination is considered at least *slightly* exotic."

"Not in my line of work—or my old line, I mean. Eggs and beer at 2 pm is how most of the enforcers liked to start the day. Maybe some Tylenol thrown in for variety."

Shel chuckled briefly and picked another piece of sushi—what exactly Wolfe didn't know—and fed it into her mouth, chewing briefly and then swallowing. She sat back and let out a contented sigh.

A waiter dressed in a tuxedo stepped up next to them, his hands behind his back. "May I get you anything else? Dessert perhaps? We have a variety of Mochi."

Mochi? Wolfe almost laughed—the place they were in, the *Imperial Garden*, was an extremely high-class restaurant, with spotless white walls, older-style Japanese artwork, and crystal chandeliers.

Mochi felt like an offering every two-bit Japanese hole-in-the-wall joint offered, however.

"No thank you," Shel said. "I'm content with what we've had."

Wolfe nodded, although he wouldn't have minded some dessert—just not Mochi.

"Of course, madam. Shall I leave the tab then?"

Wolfe pulled his wallet out and passed two hundred-dollar bills over. "Keep the change."

Inside, Wolfe cringed a bit. Objectively, he knew this was cheap by honeymoon standards, and that he had the money. But the roughly hundred-and-sixty-pre-tip lunch bill still made him feel like he was being taken for a ride, somehow.

"You don't want to see the bill?" the waiter asked.

"I added it up when we ordered it, and I don't want to be reminded of the foolishness of paying this amount for a bit of rice and fish."

The waiter nodded, the tiniest hint of a smile tugging at the corner of his mouth. "Very well, sir, and thank you. Feel free to stay as long as you'd like."

He retreated with the cash.

"Thanks for taking me out," Shel said. She put her chin in her hands and smiled at Wolfe from across the table.

"Of course," Wolfe said, a smile tugging at his own features in a mirror of the waiter at her cute display. "Did you want to go look at cards for you now?"

Shel shook her head no. "I've got a *ton* of powerful cards at the moment... and you spent most of the money, right?"

Wolfe grimaced. "Yeah. We could be set for years with the

amount I have left, but as far as buying new cards, we're about out. At least if we want decent ones."

She stood up from the table. "So let's just enjoy the rest of our day out. Tomorrow, you can go about your business."

"Killing people."

Shel looked around nervously, but no one was paying attention at all. Which Wolfe had known.

She gave him the stink eye. "Ha ha."

Wolfe stood up as well, stretching. Between sitting at the table with Barry and working on cards, and now sitting at this table for lunch, he was feeling stiff.

"Where should we go, then?" he asked as he brought his hands down.

Shel glanced around again, then leaned in slightly. "Actually, I wanted dessert... but nothing here was calling to me. They had a fancy pastry shop a few stores back, though. On the other side. Care to go check that out?"

Wolfe shrugged. It didn't make a real difference to him. If they weren't going to do anything important, he figured Shel might as well enjoy herself—without her, he'd just be home brooding anyway.

"Lead on," Wolfe said.

The two of them walked out of the overpriced sushi shop. The only way to get across to the other side of the second floor was to either go down and across, or to take one of a couple glass bridges. Wolfe didn't really like them—he wasn't normally a fearful person, and had recently been thrown from a three-story building, but something about it made him uneasy. But he tolerated it for Shel's sake as she led him across the thing.

"I thought you said it was back a few stores?" Wolfe muttered as he glanced down through the glass, his mind on how fragile the thing looked.

"Well, it is, but I said it's also across—" Shel began.

Wolfe grabbed her arm and pointed. "That's Benjamin!"

Shel jumped slightly, her eyes wide, and stopped talking. A moment later, after a quick dirty look at Wolfe, she stared along his finger at the man he was pointing out. The man, Benjamin, was about six feet tall and muscular without being particularly large. Benjamin was in his late thirties, brown haired with just a hint of white. He was walking across the floor of the Card Exchange with four large men around him.

A couple pushed past Wolfe and Shel, eyeing them irritably as they half-blocked the path across the glass bridge.

"Who's Benjamin?" Shel asked once the couple had moved on.

"Benjamin *Renfeldt* the 3rd, our next target." Wolfe whispered after a quick glance to make sure no one was nearby. "He's the grandson of the head of the Renfeldt family —also Benjamin, but everyone calls the older one Ben, kinda a reversal—"

"The next head of the Renfeldt family is just walking down there? Just like that?" Shel asked, then continued, "And he's your next target?"

"Yeah," Wolfe said. "Fern said he's the one with the card we need, not his old man. If I—"

It was Shel's turn to interrupt, putting her finger across Wolfe's mouth as another couple came walking across the glass bridge. Wolfe sat silent as the couple passed, instead following Benjamin with his eyes as the man went into a large card store called '*Collector's Park*.'

"We could get the sixth card right now!" Wolfe hissed after they'd left.

Shel pursed her lips, then reached up and twisted her hair in her fingers. "Please, Wolfe—this place is crazy crowded. Either you'll be seen, or you'll hurt innocents. Probably both. You said you didn't want to go off half-cocked anymore. We don't have the specialized gear, we don't have Fern as a guy in the chair. It's not worth it."

Wolfe ran a hand through his hair, remembering his near-fiasco on the ship when he had gone after the Weeds, the supposedly weakest of the gangs, compared to his success against the Singh family.

He also remembered how much trouble Nathan was with all his training.

Shel was right.

He sighed deeply. "Fine. That's fair. Let's just go get dessert. I'll go after them when I'm prepped and ready."

Shel smiled at him, her hand dropping down. "Thank you, love."

Wolfe rolled his eyes. "Yeah, yeah. C'mon. Time to go salve my ego with strudel or cupcakes or whatever the Infernal you buy at a pastry shop."

Shel forced a chuckle, kissed Wolfe quickly, and then linked her arm with his, leading him away. But despite his agreement with Shel, Wolfe couldn't help but keep his eye in the direction of Benjamin. A moment later, the number two of the Renfeldt crime family walked out of *Collector's Park*, then headed to the next store over.

"He just went into *Nature's Bounty*," Wolfe muttered.

"Benjamin?" Shel asked. "So what?"

"Remember Fern's presentation? I don't think any member of his crew runs a Nature deck."

"Maybe he's getting a gift for a mistress or something," Shel said, shrugging and then rubbing Wolfe's arm. "Why does it matter?"

"It just feels off," Wolfe muttered, but he couldn't place it either. A moment later, they walked past the point that Wolfe would be able to see them when they emerged. He felt himself relaxing, although he hadn't realized he was so worked up.

He sighed and turned his head back to where Shel was guiding them.

She took them to the pastry store called the *Sweet Victory*. It had a picture of some made-up card—of course—with a ridiculously over-powered candy monster on the front as its entry sign.

"Does *everything* here need some kind of tie-in to cards?" Wolfe asked, irritable for no reason—except perhaps that Benjamin was here, going completely un-attacked.

Shel just rubbed his arm again as they entered.

"Two?" a thin waitress in a bubblegum-pink outfit asked, and Shel nodded.

A moment later, the two of them were seated at a table, looking at a menu that was almost as garish as the sign outside and the waitress's outfit—but Wolfe did see a *huge* variety of desserts, and he was still in the mood to eat. More than just pastries, a lot more.

"What're you thinking?" Shel asked as Wolfe perused the list.

"Lotta options here, not sure," Wolfe said as he scanned everything from ice cream to pavlova.

Shel leaned in and spoke quietly. "Decision paralysis from a guy that can fight three cars full of twelve dudes and never hesitate on who to shoot first?"

"Har har," Wolfe said as he placed the menu down and then glanced up at her grinning face. "I'll get the lemon tort."

"Kinda a fruity dessert for a tough guy," Shel said, smiling at him and twisting her finger in her hair very obviously while glancing at the ceiling.

Wolfe enjoyed the gentle teasing and flirting. "And what the hell dessert is for tough guys, smarty pants?"

"Ooh, I think that one was from your kindergarten years," Shel said with a smile, briefly sticking her tongue out.

Wolfe snorted again, but before he could continue the

playful back-and-forth, a meaty hand fell on his shoulder, interrupting him. At the same time, a chair was pushed across the floor right next to him.

Wolfe turned his head as a man sat in the chair—six feet, brown hair turning white, a countenance that Wolfe recognized—Benjamin Renfeldt.

What the fuck?! Wolfe's right hand shot into his jacket, headed for the holster, as he clapped his left hand over his heart, fingers splayed.

CHAPTER 40

A PLEASANT SIT-DOWN

"Whoa whoa whoa!" Benjamin said, eyes wide. He held his hands up, palms facing Wolfe. "Whoa! I'm not here to fight, I swear—I just want to talk."

Wolfe felt the power of his deck, waiting to be called. He didn't remove his hand from his chest, but he did release his grip on his Edge, pulling his hands out from his jacket.

He nodded his head sideways at the hand on his shoulder. "What about the goons then?"

"Sorry, I think that's just old habit for them. Charlie, Nick, you can wait outside."

"You sure, boss?" the guy holding Wolfe said, but he was releasing his grip even as he asked.

"Yeah," Benjamin said, then waved his hands around at the thirty or so people packed into the sweet shop. "We'll be safe here—no one is starting something here."

Wolfe glanced around, mirroring the guards. *Yeah, Shel and Benjamin are both right. This is a safer place to talk than even the heavily armed bunker we were in with the card sellers— Hans or whatever. At least safer for enemies, although we're gonna need to be quiet to not be overheard.*

Wolfe removed his hand from his chest. The power dissipated. Shel let out a sigh, and the two guards backed away to stand just outside the pastry store on the second-story balcony.

"Where are your other two guards?" Wolfe asked.

Benjamin chuckled. "You saw us, huh? Well, it was our ten other guards, actually, one of whom let me know you were here. I've been looking for you."

"You could have just called."

Benjamin shook his head. "No... we were ordered to look for you by Nathan, and I'm pretty sure that whatever system Fern set up for Adam still monitors us. He would have asked questions if we contacted you. But once Kendra called and said she saw you in the parking lot here, well, we're just looking for you anyway."

Wolfe shrugged. "That's all fascinating, but get to the point, or let's go our separate ways. I've got some tort to eat."

"I feel like there's a joke there, but I'm not sure what," Benjamin mused.

Shel snorted laughter, even though Wolfe could see her own hands were still clutched.

Benjamin smiled at her, quite charming. "Look... can I ask you to indulge me for just a tiny bit? I have a couple questions."

Wolfe rolled his eyes but nodded.

"Excellent!" Benjamin said, tapping his fingers together.

He leaned in, giving Wolfe a knowing smile, one of a co-conspirator.

Wolfe found himself half-liking Benjamin, but reminded himself they were enemies. *This guy is trying hard to get me on his side, it has to be for some reason.*

"For my first question," Benjamin said, still smiling. "Is the war over cards, or is it against us? You obliterated a couple gangs, but in other cases, like the Weeds, you killed one or two people and took their cards, and that's it."

Wolfe glanced around again, conscious that they were in a high-end but still somewhat closely packed pastry shop, and not the seedy bars and VIP nightclub tables he was used to. This kind of talk could get them arrested.

But although a few people were glancing at them, none were super close, or had cameras out or anything that Wolfe could see.

He was also tempted to lie, on the theory that giving an enemy information wasn't the brightest idea, but he couldn't think of any advantage to him in lying.

So, he leaned in even closer, his face only a couple inches from Benjamin's grinning mugshot. "It was personal with Damian and the Cobras. In every other case I wanted the Gate to Hell set cards."

A slight darkness flashed across Benjamin's face, although he kept his smile in place. "You were willing to kill what has to be close to a hundred people at this point, just to get some cards?"

Wolfe grimaced, an expression that came easily to him these days. "It wasn't like that. I had reasons."

Benjamin spread his hands slightly, still grinning. "Do tell."

Wolfe hesitated again, looking over at Shel. She shrugged.

I've got five of the six cards, and I'm aiming for the sixth regardless... what the hell possible harm can it do to tell him.

Except the gods never talk to mortals. He'll think I'm crazy.

"Look... I already know you won't believe me if I tell you, and either way I'm coming for you, so it doesn't really matter. Sorry, legit. Your family is like the Grimm family, before Damian. So I'm sorry. But it is what it is."

Benjamin, still smiling, spread his hands again. "Try me."

Wolfe rolled his eyes. "Fine. Cerberus, who is apparently

my patron god, told me that unless I acquired all six cards, Noimoire would go up in flames."

"He told you that?" Benjamin asked, his eyes wide.

But Wolfe didn't see disbelief, for some reason.

His own thoughts drifted back to that message, that was burned into his soul. "Well, not technically. Technically, I got a vision of the city, and the holders of the cards. And darkness and pain spreading from them, engulfing the city. And then... two sentences. I guess I don't know who said them, but I am almost positive it was Cerberus."

Wolfe paused again, more from the emotion of that remembered moment. Then he spoke in a voice as close to the one he remembered, hungry and vengeful... "I was told... 'This is the fate if you do not hunt them down, and claim the cards for yourself. It will be as your failure from before, but far, far worse.'"

Benjamin shivered. "Well, I can see why you're on the warpath. Do you think the 'hunt them down' portion is important, or can you just claim the cards?"

"Wait... you believe me?" Wolfe asked. "I was pretty sure no one would ever believe me, since no one has ever been known to talk to the gods before."

Benjamin leaned back a bit, talking a tiny bit louder. "Well, a ton of people have *claimed* the gods talked to them... but of course, no one knows. But, well... a *lot* of people made that claim after this latest round. A lot. And there are two new card types... and there are documented cases of overland monsters with sentience, now."

Wolfe whistled, the fact that he was supposed to kill this man moving to the back of his mind, ignored if not forgotten. "Seriously?"

"Yeah, we had an incident just after you killed the Cobras, when you were out of the loop, some Shadow monster that could talk. But since then it's come up across the world.

Personally, I think some critical mass is being reached in the world. It doesn't surprise me at all that the gods might speak to you. And from the little I interacted with you before, and the things I've heard since, you don't strike me as the type that would make up bullshit to justify burning someone down."

Everyone shut up as the waiter came over. Wolfe ordered his tort, Shel a chocolate lava cake, and Benjamin an éclair. It gave Wolfe a moment to think about everything as well.

Once the guy had left, Wolfe pointed the little dessert spoon that had been left at Benjamin. "Alright, you believe me. What difference does it make? Why do I care, and why, after all this, are you here?"

"That's a lot of questions," Benjamin said with a smile.

"It's three," Wolfe said.

"Well... I was serious about the question about whether you needed to hunt me, or if you can just take the card by other means. I'd really rather not have a fight with you, given the mortality rates of my dearly departed colleagues."

This guy talks like a used car salesman and a university professor had a baby.

But Wolfe had to admit, he would prefer to get the card some way other than violence, if he could. *I must be getting old.*

"So.., you'll just give it to me, then? To leave you alone?" Wolfe asked.

Benjamin smiled. "Ah ah, not give. Sell."

Wolfe frowned. "I'm not sure I can afford a legendary, unique, set card, to be frank."

Shel interjected with, "That would be... insanely expensive, if our recent forays into card purchasing are anything like accurate."

"I won't charge full price, but I should get something. I mean, I'm pretty sure I could just sell it to Gavin's or something and you'd stop hunting us."

"Then why come to me," Wolfe said with a growl. "You also make a lot of assumptions that I won't kill you just for being a criminal—don't press me."

Benjamin laughed. "I do remember you and Big Man Grimm were tight—and he had honor. Me and my faction are hardly a big deal, or the kind of criminals you need to worry about. We run illegal gambling dens, mostly for rich people that can afford to lose it. As you well know. Hardly worth a death sentence. The Singh family was evil, as were the Cobras. I do notice you let Miriam continue her money laundering operation."

Fuck... I really should have operated a bit more quietly, back in the day.

"I admit nothing... but let's pretend I won't kill you out of hand and you're not going to sell it to Gavin's. What do you want?"

"Thirty million," Benjamin said, spreading his hands again.

"Fuck me," Wolfe said, mostly for effect. Inside, he was a bit less upset. *I can sell some cards back pretty easily. We've had more than that on hand twice, and I can get it back. Although I wish he'd asked a mere twenty-four hours ago.*

"That is *very* reasonable," Benjamin said. "I'm doing you a favor."

"Well, I don't have thirty million at the moment," Wolfe said before taking a bite of his tart, preparing for some serious negotiation.

"We might be able to work out payment in forms other than cash," Benjamin began.

Suddenly, Shel burst out laughing. "By the Divine, I get it. I know why you're here and what you want. You're not doing us a favor, *we're* doing you a favor."

For the first time, a shadow of doubt crossed Benjamin's

face. "What? That's a great price. I'm willing to negotiate as well."

Shel leaned in. "You're not worried about *Wolfe*, you're worried about *Adam*. He's been running your entire family, as well as everyone else except Miriam. You just want Wolfe to pass you by and go kill Adam! I mean, you're probably worried about Wolfe as well, but still, you're afraid of Adam! This is all a negotiation for that! You're a sheep that wants the wolf and the bear to kill each other."

Benjamin frowned, and his eyes glittered dangerously. "Really? You're calling me a sheep?"

Shel blushed. "No no, sorry, that was wrong of me. I just meant you want your enemies to go kill each other, and leave you in charge of the city."

Benjamin relaxed again, but he also looked around. While Shel had explained his supposed plan quietly, she had made her first proclamation loudly. As Wolfe followed Benjamin's gaze, he could see that numerous people were now looking at them.

Benjamin leaned forward again and whispered. "Alright, I *do* want Wolfe to go kill Adam. But I'm pretty sure that'll happen one way or another. What I really want is for a certain file to disappear. Fern found a *ton* of information on us, and Adam has our nuts in a vice. But I still want some cash, for after. So, I guess we can skip to the chase. Are you going after Adam?"

Wolfe nodded. "Yeah."

Benjamin nodded. "So have Fern access and erase the file, your word on it. Pay me fifteen million. Don't attack us. Give me all that, and you can have the card."

Wolfe glanced over at Shel, but she shrugged.

"Ten million."

"Twelve."

"Deal," Wolfe said, then held his hand out. "Card please."

But Benjamin shook his head. "Not so fast. I'd like to at least get the twelve million before I give you the card, since there's still a good chance you die going after Adam and I see nothing from it. That'll at least be something."

Before Wolfe could respond, he heard faint gunshots, and screams came from the area outside the pastry shop. Wolfe looked up just in time to see a shower of glass fall, some of it hitting people on the walkway who were scythed down in a welter of blood.

A fraction of a second later, Nathan, in full dragon mode, fell down and spread his wings, arresting his fall and slinging him in a circle. He used the momentum to throw a grenade into the pastry shop, right at Wolfe.

No one would be foolish enough to fight here in broad daylight... "Down!" Wolfe screamed, grabbing Shel and pulling her down, placing his body over her before kicking the plastic table into a shield.

Benjamin dived to the side, half a second behind Wolfe, just as the world exploded in light and sound.

CHAPTER 41

ROUND TWO

The table was blown against and then over Wolfe from the force of the explosion. He felt something sharp bite his ass. The adrenaline dump muted the pain, but Wolfe cussed regardless from sheer irritation.

I would have bet real money that no one would have been stupid enough to attack us here. I'm paying for my lack of imagination.

He shook his head to clear it and dismissed the 'three damage' notification. He grabbed Shel with one arm, placing his hand on his chest even as he rolled her back to another table. She yelped, but didn't fight him as he desperately tried to get her to safety before another grenade landed, or bullets ripped through them.

Feet thudded all around him—and a few clipped him—as people fled the pastry shop, screaming. A few were lying on the floor and screaming as well, or even more ominously, lying silent.

Gunshots rang out, but nothing ripped through Wolfe—he didn't even hear the telltale ping of ricochets. He risked glancing up, keeping Shel down briefly. Nathan was flapping in place, but he had turned, and was firing at one of Benjamin's guards.

Now or never, Wolfe though. His cards appeared in front of his chest, and he threw Cereboo out without thinking about it. It probably wasn't the best play for a set-up, he knew, but he needed space and time and Cereboo would buy him both.

He grabbed Shel by her shirt and lifted, nearly exposing her before she got to her feet.

Wolfe pulled her as he ran. "Let's go! I can't fight him in full dragon mode without some sort of advantage. I already tried that and failed."

"Advantage?" Shel asked as they pushed through the crowd, heading to the back of the pastry shop.

She dropped Sorenia off, who promptly took to the air herself to get a better vantage point and fired a beam of light at Nathan.

"Card setup, an ambush, *something*," Wolfe muttered as he glanced around, trying to find their erstwhile dinner guest.

He pushed a few people aside and gazed at the ground. Benjamin was there, his legs both shredded, blood soaking his suit and starting to pool on the floor.

Shit.

Wolfe grabbed Benjamin by his suit coat and hauled him up, ignoring the scream of pain from the Renfeldt mob family number-two. He threw the man over his shoulder and tried to barrel through the crowd, pushing to the back.

There was more gunfire, and a woman next to Wolfe, maybe late forties, collapsed like a puppet with her strings cut. At the same time, Benjamin screamed.

"Healing!" Wolfe yelled.

Shel tossed one of her Rookie EMT cards onto the counter of the pastry shop as the three of them made their way around behind it, taking temporary refuge in the safety of the counter. A couple bullets hit the counter, and Wolfe hissed as one sliced along his arm.

Two of the ladies that had been working the counter, and were now crouched behind it, briefly screamed as Wolfe and his crew stopped behind it.

A brief glow surrounded Benjamin, and Wolfe figured the thug leader was healed enough to walk. Wolfe dropped behind the counter, followed by Shel, and dropped Benjamin into a crouch that the man easily fell into, apparently unharmed again.

Wolfe tossed Malviere onto the field, and she poked her head up and threw one of her death-energy wolf attacks.

Then she briefly screamed and dropped back into the deck as a wave of fire washed across the entire shop, passing over the heads of the three deckbearers.

Wolfe got a notification that Cereboo had dropped as well.

"Fuckface has something huge on the field," Wolfe guessed. "I need a moment to get set up, he's overpowering my attempts to drop stuff with what he already has on the field."

Shel glanced at the door behind the counter. "Think that goes anywhere?"

Wolfe eyed it. It didn't look promising, but the fire, screams, and running on the other side of the counter looked even less promising.

"One way to find out," Wolfe said. "Follow me."

"Wait!" one of the girls crouching behind the counter said. "It doesn't have an exit, except the freight elevator!"

Wolfe paused, although his shoulder-blades crawled with the thought that Nathan was headed for them at the very moment. "Can't we just take that? It seems fine."

"Umm... yeah, you could!" the girl said, her eyes lighting up. "Take me with you!"

"I think he's gonna go where we go," Shel said, gently.

"You'd be better off hiding at the end and letting him go after us."

The girl hesitated, but then nodded, far more composed than her hyper-ventilating coworker. "The code is cupcake. For the lift."

Wolfe nodded, and then launched himself scuttling across the floor. As he went, he switched cards and tossed his Bulgae Moon Chaser out, more to keep whatever creatures Nathan had off his own body than out of any real hope that it would do anything.

And once again, no mantle.

Benjamin and Shel followed his scuttle, with Benjamin fumbling to get a phone out as he did. The three of them made it into a kitchen area, and Wolfe stood, rushing around the side—and some cowering cooks—to head for the door in the back, the other two following.

His Bulgae died just before he made it to the door, and a step after that a blast of submachinegun fire covered the area. Wolfe cussed as pain spread through his back, dropping to the floor, but Shel's cry of agony chilled him even more than the hole in his chest.

Benjamin hit the ground as well, still clutching his phone.

Wolfe rolled over and yanked his Edge and fired rapidly back the way he came and was rewarded with the brief sight of Nathan ducking out of the way. A huge dragon came flying over the counter, knocking a cook to the side as it did and landing on another, who screamed and died. Wolfe threw a Demonic Portal down despite its bad rate of return and brought forth the Smoke Demon. Even as the demon appeared, Wolfe immediately used its Sacrifice Obscured ability so that no creatures could attack them for ninety seconds.

Smoke exploded across the battlefield, and Wolfe could hear Nathan briefly choking and coughing. Wolfe rolled over to check on Shel. He had to get close to see her through the smoke infesting the whole area, but he saw her leaning against a metal cabinet on the floor, her blood leaking down behind her. But her cards were out, and she touched one.

Immediately the Stone Arch Fire appeared across the center of the room, a burning beacon mostly obscured by the thick fog. A couple bullets flew through the fire portion, and Wolfe assumed it was Nathan attacking.

Wolfe started to heal from the arch.

Benjamin was dialing on his phone, and Wolfe could hear it ringing, as he crawled over to Shel.

"Heal *yourself*," Wolfe whispered in Shel's ear, putting his Edge on the ground and grabbing her.

She coughed quietly but shook her head. "I need one of my Rookie EMTs. All my other heals only target allies. Good thing we did the dungeon though, I'm already past the point to kill me as a normal mortal."

Wolfe grimaced. It hurt like hell when you reached that point, he knew.

"I can switch cards in about fifteen more seconds," Shel muttered as she leaned back against the metal storage cabinet, eyes half closed and her blood leaking on the ground.

Benjamin was speaking into his phone. "Send everyone. Nathan is here, and his guys probably aren't far behind. Send everyone. They're trying to kill me."

Something clicked in Wolfe's mind, and he rushed over to Benjamin, grabbing him and staring him in the eyes. He mouthed, as clearly as he could. "Just like he killed the Singh family the way he promised he would."

Benjamin's eyes widened, and he coughed. "Sorry, the smoke is getting to me. Nathan's here to kill me, just like he promised he would, the same as he promised he would kill the Singh family right before he did. You've got to send everyone *now*."

Wolfe started to smile, but something set his danger sense off—vibrations in the floor, the movement of the smoke, he wasn't sure. But he turned and lunged up from the ground just as dragon-Nathan came looming through the smoke. He pushed the gun up even as Nathan fired, and the rounds hit the ceiling and ricocheted off. But before he could do anything else, Nathan kneed him in the side so hard Wolfe heard cracks.

Wolfe doubled over, barely able to think through the agony, but he held the gun which was ripped from Nathan's hands. He turned the gun and fired at Nathan only for it to click on empty.

Nathan thrust his knee up a second time, slamming into Wolfe's sternum. Despite it being nearly the most protected location on the human body, Wolfe heard another crack and was tossed back onto the ground in front of Shel, stunned and barely able to breathe.

But Shel's Stone Arch Fire card was still working, and Wolfe recovered enough to grab his Edge from the floor and fire it into Nathan repeatedly. Nathan was still protected by his mantle, and the shots weren't close to fatal, but they obviously hurt and Nathan ran back into the smoke.

Wolfe switched his own cards and finally saw his mantle. He threw it on, and immediately felt better. More health, more attack. Power for his other cards.

At the same time, another Rookie EMT appeared and healed Shel, and a demon with a roulette wheel for a head appeared as Benjamin, completely unharmed, walked from the smoke.

"Thanks for the healing," he said, then glanced at the huge dragon just hanging out on the side of the room. "What's that thing doing?"

"It can't attack for another fifteen seconds or so," Wolfe responded, raising his gun. "We should finish it before Nathan comes back."

Shel and Benjamin pulled guns as well, aiming them at the dragon, and pulled the triggers. Shel and Benjamin did tiny amounts of damage, but Wolfe blew chunks out of the card.

Nathan exploded out of the smoke and slashed his claws across Benjamin's throat, and they came out the other side followed by trails of red blood from the Renfeldt's jugular. The demon with the roulette wheel disappeared as Benjamin fell to the ground, briefly grasping at his throat before he fell prone on the carpet.

CHAPTER 42

DESPERATE PLAYS

A pile of cards appeared on Benjamin's back, and Nathan reached down for them, but Wolfe shot him with the Edge again. The first shot caught him in the shoulder and blew a small hole in him, knocking him back, but the second pull of the trigger clicked on empty.

Wolfe cussed, pulling a magazine from his pocket and inserting it into the chamber of his Edge, but Nathan kicked Benjamin's corpse so hard that the body slewed sideways and the cards went flying. Then the dragon-mantled asshole jumped back around the side of the kitchen work area that split the room in two.

Wolfe cussed, following him around the corner, prepared to shoot or dodge if Nathan turned around again, since the bastard had proven extremely willing to engage in combat when most people wouldn't—probably a trait from his training, to keep people off balance.

It wasn't Nathan that appeared, however. A smaller dragon materialized in front of Wolfe and he skidded to a stop. It instantly breathed fire on him, doing almost no damage, and he got a brief look at the card as he raised his Edge and emptied mantle-empowered bullets into it.

Ravenous Hatchling
Rare Tier-one Dragon [Drake]
1 Dragon Power (available)

Health: 9
Attack: 4
Defense: 4
Magical Attack: 4
Magical Defense: 4

Special: **Mystic Ambush [0]:** This creature makes a single magical attack as soon as it enters at +0 Magical Attack.

"Drakes are hungry out of the egg, but this one takes it to a whole new level."

Nathan leapt forward and kicked Wolfe's gun, hard, just as he finished the hatchling off—he had found the perfect moment to strike Wolfe again, somehow. Wolfe's gun went flying into the smoke that still filled the kitchen, and before Wolfe could recover, Nathan dropped his first leg to the ground, pivoted on that foot, and kicked Wolfe hard with a straight kick to his stomach. Despite Wolfe's mantle, he was thrown back—Nathan's mantle had more power than Wolfe's defense, it seemed.

"I've had about enough of you," Nathan growled as he stomped forward. "You've messed with Adam's plans one too many times. I'm his right-hand man, and I've never failed him. You won't be the one to stop me."

"Cool story, bro," Wolfe muttered as he played another Demonic Portal, bringing out his ubiquitous two Angry

Hellhounds and one Lost Hellhound Puppy. Without his Obsessive Cultist setup the portal card drained him to zero power. But having his mantle and the three cards would make him far more dangerous.

Master of the Infernal Hunt
Unique Tier-5 equivalent Infernal Persistent [Mantle]
2 Infernal Power

+10 Health, +3 to all remaining stats.

Special: **Cerberus's Champion:** All other [Canine] Cards gain +5 Health and +1 to all other stats, and all [Canine] cards gain advantage against Infernal cards.
Special: **Versatile [Infernal]:** This card alters to fit its wearer so long as they have at least 2 Infernal Power
Special: **Grand Pack [Canine]:** [Canine] cards do not count against cards on the field
Special: **Favorable Façade [Canine]:** Count as a Beast [Canine] card for all purposes except type match penalties.
Special: One of the 'Gate to the Underworld' cards. If all 6 are possessed in the same deck, the bearer will gain 7 Legendary Infernal or Beast card pulls. Additionally, the deckbearer may either gain the Mythic 'Gate to the Underworld' Building Card or evolve Cereboo. One card is held by each of the crime families of Noimoire, and the sixth is held within the city by another.

"Sometimes, the demons call a hunt on other demons, and a hunt master is always chosen to lead the chase."

Nathan kicked one of the Angry Hellhounds in the head so hard it instantly dissipated, but the other one attacked, doing slight damage, followed by a tiny bite from the Puppy.

More importantly that the damage, however, the creatures finally gave Wolfe a chance to breathe and take back the momentum of the fight.

He healed from the Stone Arch Fire as he scrambled across the floor toward his pistol, but Nathan launched himself in the same direction. Wolfe grabbed his Edge but Nathan wasn't going for it—he landed on the ground about ten feet from Wolfe and grabbed a handful of cards off the floor.

Wolfe shot Adam's minion, and a light beam hit him as well. But Nathan smiled through the fight and dived behind a small mobile card filled with metal tubs. The dragon-encased man called out, "If you want your card, come and get it. I'll send you the address, and we can have it out when I'm not outnumbered. You've only survived because of your friends, asshole. Next time we meet I'm going to have a bunch of *my* friends."

"Why are we talking about friends? The police are just gonna arrest you," Wolfe said as he fired into the metal tubs, hoping to penetrate them.

A grenade sailed over the side, and Wolfe dived back over the workspace splitting the kitchen as well, praying that Shel—whom he couldn't see—was either already out of the blast or would follow him.

There was a bang, and Wolfe heard no screams. But his remaining creatures were killed off the field. *By the Divine, this guy is too fucking good at this! He never lets me get set up and has already seized the initiative back!*

Wolfe did get the five power he had spent back, however, since the last creature the portal had summoned was dead.

And the healing he got from Shel suddenly boosted as well.

Nathan called back with a voice filled with haughty derision. "Of course they will, in a day or two. When they do, Adam will just have me pardoned. But you'll never see the card again. Your only chance is to come get me before they get here."

A large dragon dropped into the center of the room, on Nathan's side of the counter. At the same time, Wolfe brought forth another Demonic Gate, calling forth three more doggos on the right of the dragon. A beam of light hit the dragon as well, and Wolfe ran out from behind the counter, curving left around the dragon as it fought his hellhounds.

Bullets whizzed past Wolfe and one clipped him, doing decent damage that the massive healing from Shel almost instantly fixed. The shot did knock Wolfe off balance, however, and send him skidding to the ground.

Where did he get the gun? Wolfe wondered briefly as he scrambled for the questionable cover of the other side of the tiny mobile tub station Nathan was hiding behind. *I thought I tossed his gun.*

Nathan exploded out over the station, a single leap carrying him into the air as he flew past Wolfe.

"Come and get me if you dare," Nathan taunted. A single bullet from Shel hit the dragon-mantled warrior as Nathan sailed out, but without the backing of a powerful mantle, Shel's shot did almost nothing.

There was a brief couple seconds worth of growls, roars, and a Glock-17 firing as Shel, Sorenia, and Wolfe's minions finished off the dragon. Wolfe kept his Edge out but didn't fire, eyeing for Nathan's return or another grenade. But this time, finally, nothing happened. It seemed his nemesis had fled the field.

Wolfe holstered his pistol back in the shoulder holster. The smoke from the expended Smoke Demon card was finally clearing, and Wolfe walked over to Benjamin's body. He was dead, but Wolfe saw that his phone was on his body, open, and his last call was to 'Lil' Brother.'

And the phone was undamaged.

Wolfe crossed his fingers. *Here's hoping.*

Shel came and put her arms around him from behind. "I'm sorry for your loss."

Wolfe shrugged. "I barely knew him—a few meetings from my time before in the family, and this. I guess I'm a touch sad we aren't getting the card without violence, and I would *really* have preferred to have it before we fight Nathan again... but I've seen an absolute ton of people die, and killed quite a few myself. I'm more sad we probably have to go after him than I am about Benjamin."

"It's your empathy that I love about you most," Shel said.

Wolfe snorted before continuing. "Well, I'll not deny he seemed like a decent guy. Still, we've seen much better people die."

He kissed her hands before gently unwinding her arms from him, then bent over and gathered up the cards, checking each one to see if it was the last card of the Gate to Hell set. He didn't have much hope, but it was possible that Nathan had screwed up, grabbing the wrong cards in the smoke.

After a few moments, Wolfe sighed. *No such luck, of course.*

A moment later, a voice floated in from the outside of the pastry shop they were in. "Dismiss your decks and come out with your hands up! This is the Noimoire Police, Card division!"

"Ah, shit," Shel said. "I'm gonna get arrested by people I know."

"Maybe it'll help that you're one of them," Wolfe replied. Then he leaned in. "Don't admit we were involved with the Singh thing if asked."

Shel raised one eyebrow in an "*oh, really?*" gesture but didn't otherwise react to his comment. Instead, she dismissed her cards, then held her hands up with the badge in one.

"I'm Lieutenant Lyons! I'm coming out with my hands up and my badge out. My fiancée, private detective William

Madison, is with me. We have two dead at least, as well as possibly two more wounded or dead."

Wolfe heard brief muttering, then, "Okay Lieutenant Lyons, we'll be waiting!"

Shel slowly walked out, and Wolfe followed, keeping his hands up and open. They cleared the back room and walked past the sales counter. Blood slicked the floor of the pastry shop, and people were moaning and crying nearly everywhere. There were already police treating the numerous victims of Nathan's rampage, but in many cases it was, or would shortly be, too late.

Amid the carnage it took a moment to notice the seven police officers that awaited them, all with guns drawn. Two had multiple cards out, one running a Divine deck from the cards, the other a Psychic/Golem one—the only other time Wolfe had seen that combination was Fern's deck.

The officer with the Angel cards was a six-foot-one tall, recruiting poster type that looked like a younger image of Rhett—a touch leaner and less harassed-looking, but with the same chiseled jaw line, muscles, and striking blue eyes.

"You okay, Shel?" he asked as he came up, his pistol trained on Wolfe.

"Hey Tom. I barely made it, and only did thanks to William. As a healing specialist, however, the only wounds are in my mind," Shel said.

Tom glanced at her shirt, which had two bullet holes and was almost entirely soaked in red. His eyes widened, and he nodded, but he didn't holster his pistol. "I can see that."

He turned to Wolfe. "Thanks for saving her, Detective Madison."

Wolfe nodded. "Well, she is my fiancée. I didn't do it for you."

The man nodded, but still kept his pistol trained on Wolfe. At the same time, the other man walked up with a pair of cuffs. He towered at least two inches over Wolfe's six-foot-two and his ebony skin was corded with muscles.

Wolfe glanced at the newer officer, then back at Tom. "By the Divine, when did the police get so damn buff? You guys weren't nearly this good when I was living in the bad parts of town—I swear those guys were paid to eat donuts and harass hookers."

The new guy laughed. "Well, they don't send the desk jockeys when they have a serious card fight and numerous dead people. They send people that can mess a guy up. I'm a bit of overkill to chase hookers off street corners, am I right or am I super right?"

Wolfe laughed, perhaps a touch hysterically. "Fair."

There was an awkward moment, but Shel finally pointed to the gun. "It's a nice tool you've got there, Tom, but why're you still pointing it at William?"

"Uh... well." Tom looked embarrassed. "I have an arrest warrant for William, and so, even if he saved you here, I need to take him in."

"Lovely," Wolfe muttered, but he held his hands out and together.

Tom smiled in relief and finally holstered his pistol. The second cop reached out with the handcuffs, giving Wolfe a half-apologetic smile. "I'll keep them loose."

CHAPTER 43

AND THE EVIDENCE SAYS...

"Thanks for bailing me out," Wolfe said as he pulled himself into the passenger side of their spare armored F-150.

"Of course," Shel replied, leaning over for a quick kiss to his cheek. "Given the situation, waiting was completely out of the question."

"Yeah," Wolfe half-grunted.

"What's the plan?" Shel asked when he didn't continue.

Wolfe had been thinking of the plan he wanted to pursue the entire time he had been in jail—overnight, the morning, the holding cell before the judge pronounced his bail, and the time it had taken Shel to handle things after that.

It all relied on one thing he had heard Nathan say, and one rumor he had heard about the leader of the Renfeldt gang back in the day.

Well, that and a card.

"Do you have the cards from the shop by any chance?" Wolfe asked. "I need them to win this."

Shel nodded, reached back into the cab, and passed a small, locked chest forward. "Code is one-two-nine-eight."

Wolfe nodded, put the code in, and briefly stared at the three cards inside. Bahkark, Gehennan Kennel Half-Breed, Corrupt the Pillars of Civilization, and Vatya, Claimer of the Corrupt.

"I need to make some alterations to my deck really quick," Wolfe said. "Then we'll be ready to go."

"You'll tell me the plan?" Shel asked.

"No plan," Wolfe said. But when Shel turned to him, he mouthed 'Tell you later' as obviously as he could.

She didn't respond, which Wolfe took as acceptance. So, he turned his attention back to the cards and pulled out his deck.

Getting the two unique cards into his deck was easy—he had room in the combined portal side deck, and he just slotted them in. However, getting the Corrupt the Pillars card in was a bit of a challenge—his main deck was rather stuffed at the moment.

He had three leveling pips left, enough for another five cards in hand, but Wolfe really wanted to save for another building slot. So, instead, he took a long look at his cards.

He needed them all in his build, badly, except, perhaps, for three cards. Two were from the Infernal Guns set, which were nice but not critical—except they gave him another power. The last was his Get of Xolotl, which Wolfe was pretty sure would turn into an amazing companion—but not soon.

And he had only had it in his deck for a few days.

With a heavy sigh, Wolfe removed the card from his deck and replaced it with the 'Corrupt the Pillars of Civilization' card.

As a last change, he pulled one of his Tier-3 Angry Hellhounds and used his recently acquired copies of the card to finally raise another one to Tier-4. Then he pulled up his expanded character sheet.

Ethan Madison Wolfe Status:
Level 39 Mortal [3 pips remaining]

Deckbearer Perks:
Lost and Lonely God-gifted Start: +1 Companion card

Deckbearer Perk 1: In the Thick of it: +50% to all numerical benefits gained from mantles

Deckbearer Perk 2: Man's Best Friend's Best Friend: Gain 1 Beast Power. May have one extra card in play so long as it's a Beast (Canine or Hybrid Canine).

Level 25 perk: Master of the Lost and the Lonely: Orphans gain +1 Tier when they evolve, and any card packs or non-orphan cards gained from orphan advancement are gained twice. Any one [evolved orphan] card of no more than 2 power may be treated as if it were a free-slot companion card with a 0-power cost.

Deckbearer Flaw: Fallen: May not gain Divine Power, nor use Divine cards unless they are also Infernal or Corrupted.

Deckbearer Stats:
Cards in Deck: 20 (3 pips)
Cards in Hand: 5 (3 pips)
Cards in Play: 4 (1 pips)
Length of Play: 5 minutes

Specialty Cards:

Companion: 3 (three free from perks and cards, 1 must be an evolved orphan acting as a companion)
Building: 2 (5 pips, one free from cards)
Minion: 3 (3 pips, 1 free from cards)
Enhancer: 3 (6 pips)

Total Power: (upgraded 5 times): 8 -1 (Infernal Rift) +1 (Infernal Gun set) = 8. (Total pips 15)
Type 1 and Power: 5 Infernal (5 -1(Infernal Rift) +1 (Infernal Guns))
Type 2 and Power: 2 Beast
Energy 1 and Power: 1 Fire

Personal Perks:
Inborn Perk 1: Vicious Killer: +25% to all Attack and Defense, check twice for Attack modifier and take the best

Inborn Perk 2: Tough as Nails: +10 Health

Acquired Perk 1: Crafty Street Fighter: +3 Attack and Defense

Personal Stats:
Health: 30/30
Attack: 10
Magical Attack [None]: 0
Defense: 10
Magical Defense [None]: 5

Deck: (20 cards, 3 companions, 2 Buildings, 3 Minions, 2 Enhancers)
Specialty:

Companion:
1x Cereboo (Gate to the Infernal set card 1)
1x Malviere
*1x Obsessive Infernal Cultist

Building:
1x Hellmouth Institute
1x Infernal Library (Library Wing of the Hellmouth Institute) (locks Obsessive Infernal Cultist to the first pull)

Minion:

Enhancer:
1x Caretaker of the Lost
1x Conduit of the Infernal Six (Enhancer, Gate to the Infernal set card 4)
1x Deck Slayer

Standard:
Mantle:
1x Master of the Infernal Hunt (Mantle, Gate to the Infernal set card 3)

Persistent:
4x Demonic Portal (each adds a side deck of 5 Infernal creatures, 20 creature total side deck)
1x Cerberus' Home for Wayward Hellhounds
1x Damned Soul's Road (Gate to the Infernal set card 5)
1x Corrupt the Pillars of Civilization

Immediate:

1x Infernal Rift (Gate to the Infernal set card 2, adds 1 minion and 1 building card)

Creature
1x Obsessive Infernal Cultist
1x Bulgae Moon Chaser

Equipment
1x Hellfire (Infernal Gun set card 1)
1x Brimstone (Infernal Gun set card 2)

Side Deck: (20 Infernal Creatures)
1x Gehenna Kennel Master
3x Tier-4 Angry Hellhound
1x Tier-3 Angry Hellhound
2x Tier-2 Lost Hellhound Puppy
1x Fireborn Hellhound
1x Smoke Demon
1x Chain Demon
2x Xolo Spirit-Warder (modified to Infernal by Conduit of the Dark Six)
1x Bahkark, Gehennan Kennel Half-Breed
1x Vatya, Claimer of the Corrupt.
1x Klireen, Daughter of Lust

After he had made the adjustments, he rattled off his stats and cards to Shel.

"You think you can beat Nathan with that set-up?" Shel asked, her voice carefully calm and neutral.

"As much as I hate to admit it, probably not," Wolfe said with a shake of his head and a grimace. He had never encountered someone as good at fighting as him before, and it frustrated him no end that in their two match-ups, all Wolfe had been able to do had been to frustrate his enemy's purposes in one and survive in the other.

"But you're going to try anyway?" Shel asked, laying her hand on his arm. "The last card isn't worth your life, Wolfe. You can't die."

Wolfe stared at her for a moment, running the conversation back in his head.

Then he laughed. "Don't worry, that's not what I meant. I meant that the deck as is, by itself, isn't enough. At least not given what I think Nathan has done. I need to talk to the Renfeldt family, quietly and without using a phone. I have the glimmering of a plan that might get me through this thing alive and unincarcerated."

Shel smiled at him. "I don't think that's a word, hon. I think the word is just 'free.'"

"Well, you know what I meant," Wolfe grumbled.

She bowed her head at him, and glanced at him from under lashes before returning her gaze to the road. Her smile turned into a full-on grin for a second. "Of course I do, hon. Everyone knows what you're talking about."

Then her grin slipped and she rubbed her belly with her free hand. "But tell me about the plan that'll keep you alive."

"First I need to call Rhett," Wolfe said. "Do you have my phone?"

She fished it from her pocket and passed it over. Wolfe dialed, but after a minute, it went to voice mail.

Wolfe frowned, then quickly googled the Joliet police department and dialed the main number.

"Joliet Police Department. If this is an emergency, hang up and dial 911. Please listen to the following as our options have changed. For hours of operation and…"

Wolfe pushed the button and leaned back with a sigh. "He's not answering."

Shel pulled her own phone out and dialed someone one-handed while driving.

Wolfe heard a faint male voice from the headpiece but couldn't make out the words, then "Hey Tom, it's Shel—yeah, Shel with the Noimoire Card Police," Shel said. "I was wondering if you knew where Rhett was. I need to get ahold of him."

A brief pause. "Yeah, Rhett Walker."

Another brief pause. "I see... thank you, Tom. I appreciate it."

Shel hung up and turned to Wolfe. "Rhett... Rhett turned in his badge, Wolfe. He retired two days ago."

"What!" Wolfe asked, shocked silly. "Rhett quit? Really?"

"I just found out too, but it seems like it, yeah."

"Huh."

Wolfe stared ahead for a moment, staring at the traffic they were driving through without really seeing it, as he collected his thoughts.

After a moment he shook his head. "Shouldn't matter too much... Let's head to see the Renfeldt family. I think we can still make this work, even without Rhett."

"Do you think we're doing the right thing?" Shel asked. "I mean, Rhett was a good guy. If he quit over this..."

Wolfe gave it some thought. "I've never really understood Rhett, but I think if he thought we were wrong, he'd have turned us in. The fact he didn't is significant in my opinion."

"Why'd he quit then?" Shel asked.

Wolfe shrugged. "You know him as well as me."

"Just give me your best guess," Shel replied softly and rubbed her free hand over her belly again.

"You know why," Wolfe said, clenching his fist. "It's not about goals. On that, he and I agree. It's about methods. But I know the vision I received, and I know what I need to do. You have to believe me, Shel. I wanted to do this Rhett's way. But you know what Fern showed us. Adam has way too much influence in too many organizations for us to take him down the right way, and he's gunning for me personally thanks to his stupid shit of a son getting killed backing Damian."

Shel nodded slowly to his words, her face firming. "You're right. Give me the address to the Renfeldt house. We have to end this."

"Damn right."

CHAPTER 44

A BETRAYAL MOST EXPECTED

The Renfeldt mansion looked about the same as every other mob family base Wolfe had gone to, even the Grimm family mansion before he had exploded it.

The details were different—style of architecture, colors, the plants, etc. But the basics were the same, because the needs of the families were the same. *Function begets Form,* Wolfe thought, a hazy recollection from his childhood spent in an unusually educated if utterly dysfunctional family.

The mansions were all set back from the road quite a distance. Always fenced to the limits allowed by the local zoning codes. Plants everywhere to block public view. Usually at the ends of a road.

It made it hard for the police to sneak up or observe you unawares, but it also made it easier for Wolfe and his ilk to raid the places without getting caught—if he could get past the guards, of course.

But there would be no Infernal airsoft tricks this time. He didn't *want* to get past any guards. He had traded seats with Shel, so he would seem even less threatening, he hoped. He drove right up to the gate, his hands clearly on the wheel of his car.

There were two gate guards, both bored-looking, but both obviously packing heat. One stayed leaning against a metal fence while the other held a hand up and then slowly walked out to Wolfe's truck, which he obediently slowed down.

The guy was a bit older for an enforcer, closer to thirty from his looks, with brown hair and brown eyes that wouldn't have looked out of place on a cud-chewing cow in the fields. But when he got close and saw Wolfe, his eyes widened in alarm, and he pulled his gun from its holster.

"Whoa, whoa!" Wolfe said, his back crawling as he carefully did not move his hands or make any sudden movements. "I'm not here to cause problems, I promise. I just want to talk to Ben Renfeldt. Peacefully. I promise."

For once, I wish I wasn't recognizable to every enforcer with more than three years experience.

The man stared at him for a moment. "I'll check."

He started to pull his phone while keeping his gun pointed into the truck, but Wolfe interrupted. "I know that your phone system is compromised. Does your intercom still work?"

The man stared at Wolfe suspiciously, his phone halfway to his ear. Wolfe sat, tensely, as the man cogitated.

But after a moment, he put it back and called over to his fellow enforcer, "Jamie, call the boss on the intercom. Tell him *Wolfe* is here and wants to talk to him. See if he wants to talk to him or if we should send him packing."

The phrasing left Wolfe a touch concerned, but not too concerned. He was pretty sure, based on Benjamin's last cellphone call, that he would be welcomed in.

A moment later he was proven right, as Jamie walked back over. "The boss said to take your guns, but to be polite and let you in—he's been expecting you, apparently. He wants to meet you right now."

"So..." Wolfe said, not sure exactly how to proceed.

"Park your car on the side of the road, we'll frisk you, and then Hector will walk you up," Jamie said. "Both of you, if you want."

"Alright, give me a moment."

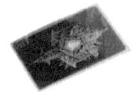

About fifteen minutes later, Wolfe found himself in a kitchen. An old man, nearly seventy from the looks of him, was making sandwiches while multiple enforcers hung around. An even older man, almost a hundred from the looks of him, with spotty skin and wispy white hair, sat at a small wooden table in the center. His eyes were red and puffy.

Wolfe knew him—Benjamin Renfeldt the first, head of the Renfeldt crime family, called Ben by everyone.

Jamie gently pushed Wolfe forward into the room and announced him. "Wolfe and Shel are here, Benjamin, sir."

Ben turned, trembling slightly, to face Wolfe. Without preamble, he asked, "You were there when my grandson was killed?"

The man making sandwiches slammed his knife down extra hard on the counter and stared at Wolfe, saying nothing. Wolfe was pretty sure that was Benjamin the second, but he honestly didn't know—none of Ben's kids had been very involved in his business, or at least not in ways Wolfe had ever encountered them through.

"I was, yes," Wolfe said. "I failed to protect him, I'm truly sorry."

He was sorry. He didn't much like the Renfeldt family,

but he bore them no ill will, and Benjamin had come to give him the card. He felt a bit responsible.

He would solve his grief like he always did, however. By killing the one responsible. Or die trying, anyways, if this meeting went badly.

"And Nathan was the one to do it?" Ben asked. "Adam's dog?"

Wolfe nodded again.

"Did my boy die well?" the man at the counter—now almost certainly Benjamin the second—asked.

Wolfe sighed—it wasn't worth talking about. "He died quickly."

"Did he kill his enemies?" the man asked, leaning forward.

"That's enough, son," Ben said softly. "We're here for other business. You want us to help kill Nathan, yes? You assume we want revenge for Benjamin?"

Wolfe nodded.

"Before we address that, I have to know—how did Nathan know to find my grandson?" Ben asked, his voice an angry, wavering rasp.

"Fern Wachowski didn't actually remove the tracking program that she placed on you guys all those years ago—she just changed it for Adam's benefit, after he tortured her enough. The program also sent your texts. I never cared because I was planning on killing all of you, and I didn't think about it in the ten minutes or so I was talking with your grandson before Nathan showed up."

"I'll give you ten million to turn her over to us," Benjamin the second said.

"Hush, son," Ben interrupted. "If Wolfe was the kind of person to betray his allies, the entire history of this city's underworld over the last twenty years would be different. Don't be any more foolish than the gods made you."

Benjamin the second grabbed his knife again and began chopping vegetables rapidly.

"So, you'll help me then?" Wolfe asked.

"Not so fast," Renfeldt said, holding one trembling hand up. "Just because my son is a fool who asks for something you won't give, doesn't mean we aren't negotiating. I want Nathan dead, and given what've you told me, I need him dead soon. But I have other options—countries I can flee my family to, for example. But, I know you want that card. Badly."

You don't know *that, or your grandson would have known*, Wolfe thought, but did his best to keep his face clear.

Ben didn't seem to notice as he continued. "So, you need my help more than I need yours. I have a proposal—everything in the house is mine, especially the cards, except that you get the last Gate to Hell set card and whatever Nathan had—but everything else is mine. In return, every deckbearer we have, and the vast majority of our enforcers, will help you attack the compound."

Wolfe winced—he knew, from Fern, that there were *a lot* of really good rares, as well as some legendary cards and even a few mythic ones, in Adam's house. But, since Renfeldt would be sending multiple deckbearers—most of them, in fact—Wolfe wouldn't argue too much.

But he needed to argue just a bit, for formality's sake. He hunkered down to begin the argument.

A few hours later, Wolfe sat next to Shel in the Ford-150. Behind them, Fern was tapping away at multiple computers. Her drones were up in the sky.

Ahead of them was Adam's massive compound. It wasn't, at the most fundamental, any different than the compounds of the Noimoire crime families—he had the same needs, after all. But any sense of Déjà vu was lost by the sheer *size* of the thing —it utterly dwarfed the mansions of the Grim, Singh, or Renfeldt families.

"Does he know we're coming?" Wolfe asked.

"He does—or, at least, he is prepared in case," Fern replied breathlessly from the back. "Guards are everywhere. No one is slacking. They're in large groups to prevent the kind of quick kill operations you did before, and give them warning. No way you could have done this on your own."

"Deep breaths," Shel said, reaching back. "We won't be on our own, not even close to it."

"Why didn't you ask Miriam to help?" Fern asked. "I told you to get her help."

"I can't bring her into this," Wolfe replied, irritated slightly. "It will cause problems."

Wolfe understood why Fern was scared, but he didn't have *time* for this. "Just let me know when Renfeldt starts to move. Then, use your card, give us an illusion, and Shel and I will handle this."

"You have to finish him," Fern said. "And you can't die, or the Renfeldt family will kill me."

"Wolfe won't die," Shel said, smiling. She rubbed her belly again. "He can't die. We're going to be parents."

CHAPTER 45

FULL CIRCLE LONE WOLFE

"What?!" Wolfe said, staring at Shel with wide eyes, feeling as if he had been hit by a Lightning elemental.

Shel took his hand and placed it over her belly, although all Wolfe felt was the armored jacket. "I'm pregnant. So you have to live, and we have to set the date soon."

"I thought you were on..." Wolfe trailed off.

"I was... but it didn't work, apparently. That other day, when I got nauseous—it got me thinking. So I took a test."

"You didn't tell me till now?" Wolfe asked. "You got shot! Twice!"

"The baby is okay—nothing happened to it. I didn't tell you till now because I didn't think it was necessary, but now... I want to make sure you live."

"During the fight, if you'd been hit in the—"

Shel held a hand up, interrupting him. "I wasn't. I didn't expect a fight then, either. And I don't want our child growing up without his father."

Wolfe stared at her for a moment. "You can't—"

429

Fern squeaked from the back, her voice nearly panicked. "They're going right now!"

Shel started to reach for the door, but Wolfe grabbed her. "I'm doing it alone! I know you want to save me, Shel. But this is my job... and if I don't make it, take care of our baby. No matter what. Don't try and avenge me, just... just have this one thing of me left in the world. A piece of me that can get it right."

Shel stared at him. "I didn't want—"

Wolfe interrupted again. "I know. I get it. But I've got this!" He turned to Fern. "Hit me!"

His appearance shifted—brown hair, a blander face, brown eyes, a touch taller but proportionally leaner. Features that were similar to the features of the Renfeldt family.

He grabbed his Edge, stuck it in his holster, and ran out the car, heading around to the back of the compound, through the woods that guarded the rear.

"Turn right a bit," came Fern's voice in his ear.

"Did Shel stay?" Wolfe asked as he adjusted slightly, running through the dark woods.

"I did," Shel's voice came through the headphones, tight but controlled. "Fern had a second pair of headphones in case of emergency. Surprise. Stay focused, and don't think about me."

Wolfe kept running. He could hear gunfire breaking out in front of him—and a few howls, roars, or screeches from various inhuman creatures. He smiled—the single most important thing was that whatever deckbearers Nathan had brought were engaged with the ones that the Renfeldts had brought.

I really hope I've read Nathan correctly—as well as read how he sees me, Wolfe thought as he dodged through the trees.

"You're almost there," Fern said, "and it's clear of enemies. The guards have been pulled from the back fence."

Wolfe grabbed wire-cutters from his pants pocket and went rapidly to work, cutting a tiny hole for himself. He missed all the gear he had taken from Adam's warehouse, but he couldn't use it here—he had to rely on the Renfeldt family to balance the capabilities of his enemies, as well as Fern's knowledge of the compound.

He scooted through the hole he had made at ground level, dragging the chain links along his body as he did, but he got through and the fence snapped back with a loud rattle. He leapt up and ran forward.

"Code is nine, eight, seven, etc., back to one to open the door with the override I left," Fern said.

Wolfe ran to the back door of the house. It wasn't a fortress, and he could probably easily have broken in, but the code was faster—and quieter. He had only a small amount of time before the illusion faded.

He busted the door open and ran inside.

"Have you found Nathan yet?" Wolfe asked into his ear piece.

"Not yet. The drone cameras haven't seen him and the Renfeldts at least haven't reported him."

"Wait, if you have the codes to the door, how come you can't just see Nathan through the cameras?"

"The inside ones have been removed—which will likely work both for and against us. I think he might guess that I still have access. The outside ones are still in place, however, so I can see what's happening there."

Son of an Infernal. "How's the rest of the strategy going?"

"The Renfeldt family have reported multiple, overlapping persistent cards in play, although they're not really responding to all of my requests for information the way they should be."

Shel broke in. "Understandable, given that they're officially running this show and the history you have with the Renfeldt family."

"It's inefficient, and this is too important to screw up," Fern said, and then her voice went ugly. "And they had it coming, given what they did to my brother."

Shel answered that, but Wolfe was mostly ignoring their cross chatter as he ran through the building. It was an extremely impressive dwelling-slash-fortress. He passed underneath crystal chandeliers, and ran across marble tiled floors covered in expensive-looking Persian carpets. What he noticed most as he ran through the empty portions of the house, however, were bronze and marble statues of Gabriel. The Divine Lord of death and punishment was shown in many poses, always accomplishing great things—but violent ones, like vanquishing Infernal creatures and smiting the unworthy, frequently sinners cowering from him in fear. It gave Wolfe more of an insight into who Adam was than all of Fern's pronouncements and charts—this was the art he had chosen for himself, and somehow, Wolfe knew it was how Adam viewed himself.

"Fucker thinks he's the good guy," Wolfe muttered. "A good guy with the courage to do what *must be done*."

Wolfe disliked the evil of the people who thought that way. But even more than hating their evil, he hated their *pretension*. They acted like they were the one child of destiny whose vision was so right, and that their shit stank so little, that the Divine themselves had somehow given them the right to kill everyone for the greater good.

At a certain level, he preferred a straightforward villain like Big Man Grimm, who killed people when they screwed with his business without pretending his desires were some great moral accomplishments.

Wolfe was brought back to the moment as Fern muttered, "They've reported four persistent cards in play that match the requirements."

Wolfe touched his chest and pulled his deck, immediately

tossing the Obsessive Infernal Cultist out. It cost him nothing, leaving him his full eight power, and made any Demonic Portal cards he drew cost four power.

The sounds of gunfire were heavy, and all coming from the front of the building. But Wolfe slowed down—he was almost positive that Nathan would expect him, and he didn't want to run into an ambush.

He was also pretty sure that he had more companions and wanted to get them out fast, now that he was close enough the time in play likely wouldn't run out.

The ostentatious room Wolfe was in had multiple exits, both open hallways and doors. The sounds of gunfire and yelling was clearly loudest from one of the hallway entrances. Wolfe took it. He moved slowly and cautiously, constantly on the lookout for Nathan and any members of Adam's team that might be around a corner.

He needed to find the nexus of the fighting—or at least a place he could be close to as many of his enemies at the same time as possible.

But he didn't need to die doing it.

He brought Malviere out to join the Obsessive Infernal Cultist as he walked, holding his finger up to his mouth as he did. Malviere grinned at him, her eyes alight. It was a feral expression, but she nodded silently to his gesture.

A man came around the corner, and Wolfe raised his Edge. But the man was facing away from Wolfe—he had backed around the corner. He was holding his arm, which leaked blood. As soon as he was around the corner, the man dropped to the ground and began ripping at his shirt.

A moment later, the man stopped bandaging his wound, reached his hand out, and touched something in front of him. Sickly yellow light left his hands and turned into a gibbet holding a barely alive woman covered in pustules and blisters and surrounded by flies. The gibbet barely fit inside the hall, despite its massive size and tall ceilings.

Wolfe immediately felt feverish, and a sweat sprung out. Fear entered him, making it harder to clench his gun, and whispering to him he should run.

He stared at the gibbet, and the card popped up.

Carrion Maker
Rare Tier-1 Persistent [Corrupt]
3 Corruption Power, 1 Any Power

All enemies on the field, deckbearer and card, suffer a point of true damage per turn. All enemy deckbearers and cards suffer -2 to all non-health stats as well, modified as if it were damage by typing modifiers.

"Hanging Bloody Mary and leaving her as a warning is about the worst mistake you could make."

Slowly, pustules started to form on Wolfe. He had a brief, dark déjà vu moment to his previous fight with the Singhs, and was tempted to end the deckbearer from behind.

But instead, he half-smiled through the building pain. The deckbearer's card, and his choice to play it rather than creatures, confirmed what Wolfe had suspected—and he further suspected that his enemies had massive overlapping buffs as well.

He almost gave in to the temptation to shoot the deckbearer in the back of the head just to see what overlapping defensive buffs showed up in the attack and damage calculation, but didn't give in to his desire.

All Wolfe needed was to find Nathan before Wolfe died, and then survive the fight long enough to get his deck right. Easy.

Right.

He stepped sideways into a massive bedroom to the side, just as opulent as everything else in Adam's mansion. He swiped his deck. For a wonder, his mantle came up. He put it on, more to extend his lifespan since he was being actively affected by the ticking true damage.

Malviere stepped in after him, staring dubiously at the growing blisters and pustules. "Shouldn't we kill the corrupt deckbearer, alpha? The Infernal realms await his tainted soul hungrily."

"Not yet—I need Nathan."

"Cause an uproar?" she asked, her voice reverberating with something otherworldly.

Wolfe gave it honest thought, but he didn't want to summon a bunch of the other combatants first. "Let's just try and find him some other way—I don't want us getting mobbed."

He tapped his ear. "Have you seen Nathan yet?"

"No," Fern answered. "But the situation is getting out of hand. We have multiple dead enforcers on the Renfeldt side, a couple for-sure dead members of Adam's people, and the police just got a call about it. I suspect fifteen minutes till they show up maximum, even in your secluded location. You have to move."

"Best place to find him?"

Fern hesitated. "Again, he removed the internal cameras. Plus, he hasn't shown his face on the external cameras or where my drones can see him. So, I still don't know. Sorry."

Wolfe tossed Cereboo onto the floor of the room. Cereboo looked at him, his three pairs of eyes intense on Wolfe's, his expression somehow more serious than his usual 'good-boy' vibe.

Wolfe stared at him. "We'll have back-up for the whole

thing, but we're starting this shit the same way we did it back in the day—with you on point."

All three of Cereboo's heads nodded, and somehow, Wolfe could sense his excitement.

"Flame out the window when you find him," Wolfe said, then motioned to Malviere. "Go into twenty more seconds."

A moment later, she surged with power, and Cereboo exploded from the room.

CHAPTER 46

PENULTIMATE FINALE

Wolfe instantly flipped his deck. *Third pull.* Still not the card he wanted.

As Cereboo tore from the room, Wolfe ran around the corner. The wounded man had pulled his Glock and fired rapidly at Cereboo, hitting him once from the notification Wolfe got. But it wasn't enough, and the yells and thuds from the hallway told Wolfe that either Cereboo or the fusillade of missed shots had caused everyone to take cover.

Wolfe ran toward the man from behind. He started to reach for his ear, similar to how Wolfe had done, but Wolfe grabbed his hand and yanked the pistol from it. Then he slammed his fist into the man's nose, specifically trying to not seriously disable him, but put him out of the fight for a few seconds.

Blood squirted from the man's nose and he half-yelled, slumping against the wall holding his face, tears blinding him. Wolfe simply tore around the other side into the front hall. At the same time, he hit a card, playing it to the field.

Damned Soul's Road

Rare equivalent, Tier-4 equivalent Infernal Persistent [Gate]
1 Infernal Power

While in play, the first 4 unique Infernal creatures or minions in play require 1 less power of the deckbearer's choice. All Infernal, Undead, or Elder cards with the word Portal or Gate in their title or keywords cost 1 less power (minimum 1), even if brought to the field by another card rather than being played.

So long as this card is in the deck, all Infernal, Undead, and Elder creature and minion cards that are unique will have personalities as if they were companions.

Special: **Gate to the Infernal:** If all 6 are possessed in the same deck, the bearer will gain 7 Legendary Infernal or Beast card pulls. Additionally, the deckbearer may either gain the Mythic 'Gate to the Infernal' Building Card or evolve Cereboo. Each card was given to a member of the Noimoire underworld.

"When our lieutenants take the field in all but will, the time of ascension is nigh."—Gabriel, to Nurenda Whiteflame,
3103 BDN

Five power left, Wolfe thought as he ran. The card he needed most would be in the next pull, but he had to make one more play before then. Unfortunately, a single power would be all it could be—he needed four left.

A roar reverberated through the halls, coming from a door on the front side of the hall. It was immediately followed by three cut-off yelps of pain.

"Nathan's in the—"

"I know," Wolfe replied, leaping around the door, his Edge

held out. He had a brief impression of a massive and opulent study, filled with a massive desk at one end and multiple couches near where Wolfe was. Paintings of Gabriel adorned the walls. But Wolfe took that all in as half an impression as red-and-brown particles flowed back into him, briefly casting a crimson glow over the three figures in the room.

Two men and a half-dragon, Wolfe thought.

Wolfe fired a quick series of shots into one man's chest before he could react and dived behind the couch as the other two fired back. Three bullets *blasted* through the couch, two clipping Wolfe and doing five and seven damage despite the protection and Wolfe's mantle.

"Wolfe!" Nathan boomed out, his voice filled with contempt. "You can imagine my surprise that you idiotically took the bait! A thug is all you are, and a thug you'll die. Every time you've faced me you've had allies—but this time you're outnumbered."

"Shut the fuck up," Wolfe muttered quietly. He heard yelling outside and knew he had mere moments before he was attacked from behind as well. He spun and ran from the couch on the opposite side from the one he was facing, firing at the other man as he did. That guy took an Infernal-mantle-empowered shot to the head—which exploded in a fine mist. He dropped to the ground as Wolfe dived behind the other couch and touched a card at the same time.

The second Obsessive Infernal Cultist popped out, and Wolfe whispered, "Stay down!"

A series of bullets ripped through the couch again, miraculously missing the cultist somehow, but one clipped him again. Between his increasing sickness and the three bullets, he was down to a mere five health, and had added another one-point wound penalty to the disease impairment of his stats.

A voice crackled to life in his ear. "Wolfe, the enemy

deckbearers are taking a terrible toll on the Renfeldt outside—we're going to lose soon."

"Tell them to hold for twenty-five more seconds," Wolfe whispered to Fern.

He grabbed a spare magazine, ejected his and slapped the new one in. Then he chucked the old one over the couch in a parabolic arc toward Nathan, standing as he did, a half-formed prayer to Cerberus on his lips. Thankfully the half-dragon was diving behind the couch as Wolfe came up, probably thinking Wolfe was throwing one of the grenades he had stolen from the warehouse.

Instead, Wolfe came to his feet, firing. He caught Nathan with a single shot as he dropped, and saw the numbers pop up in his combat log—Nathan had *ten* points of defensive buffs on him from various persistents all his allies had played, besides his mantle and training. Nearly a twenty-five in his defensive stat.

Perfect.

Nathan was behind the couch, and a single thug—or maybe mercenary—was coming in through the door. Wolfe turned and pulled the trigger on his Edge, firing at the thug, who actually managed to dodge and leap behind the door. Wolfe slowly fired a bullet every second, alternating his shots into the couch Nathan was behind and the doorframe, till he had emptied his magazine of his eighteen bullets.

Wolfe was, essentially, bluffing. He was bleeding everywhere, he was sick and losing health from the card, and Nathan could have easily taken the hits from a weakened Wolfe.

But Nathan didn't fear Wolfe's intelligence, only his strength. A terrible error.

Wolfe's pistol clicked on empty. Red wings flared above the couch, and Wolfe knew that Nathan was coming. He swiped his deck as Nathan flew over the couch, claws out and hatred on his face.

One trembling hand touched the card Wolfe had been waiting for, right there in Adam's study, surrounded by all the different deckbearers fighting the Renfeldt members outside.

A cloud of black particulate matter that smelled faintly of decay exploded into existence.

Corrupt the Pillars of Civilization
Rare Tier-1 Infernal/Corruption Persistent
4 Infernal or 4 Corruption Power

All persistent and equipment cards on the field, except this one, that have a power cost of three or greater, have their bonuses and maluses reversed. They may not leave the field, and their power does not return to their deckbearers, even if their time in play runs out, until this card has left the field.

"When a higher institution of a civilization is corrupted, it does not merely remove itself from play, it actively works against its own."—Kithrilkik, Spreader of Discord

Nathan's claw slammed into Wolfe's cheek, and Wolfe's head moved maybe an inch. He barely felt it.

Nathan stared in horror at Wolfe, then turned his head to stare sideways—at the card.

"Your play was obvious, too, Nathan," Wolfe said, unable to hide the feral glee in his voice. "You've always been a follower, a team player—and you dismissed me so much you *told* me you planned on bringing in allies this time—the thing you blamed your inability to finish me off on."

Wolfe pushed his gun into Nathan's chest as his own health ticked up from the 'disease' he was experiencing. "Your next move was *obvious*."

He pulled the trigger. Nathan, now reduced to an effective one defense, exploded entirely into a fine red mist, having taken almost four hundred actual damage from the combination of Wolfe, his perks, his mantle, and the benefits from the gibbet card that was now enhancing him.

"The deckbearers are weakened," Wolfe said after touching his ear. "The Renfeldt can move up."

Wolfe bent down to grab the cards that appeared in the puddle of blood whose name had once been Nathan. The move saved his life as a bullet whipped through the air above him.

Wolfe dived to the side, cursing, and scrambled in front of a couch, putting it between him and his attackers.

"Right, you just accused Nathan of hubris and nearly got killed by a random mook because you forgot the penalties don't affect non-deckbearers ninety percent of the time," Wolfe muttered. Although he wondered, given how high his stats were, if he'd actually have died anyway.

Despite the danger, however, he dismissed his mantle. It returned two power to him, and Wolfe tossed down a Demonic Portal card. It had reached a new low, costing him only a single power to use. He brought forth his usual two Angry Hellhounds and single Lost Hellhound Puppy.

He needed guardians more than the mantle at the moment.

As his doggos ran into the fray, amid barking and screaming, Wolfe took the thirty seconds while he searched through Nathan's cards, quickly coming upon the only Infernal one. It appeared as a pitted iron bar with demonic symbols carved in it.

Bar of the Gate
Unique Rare-equivalent, Tier-7 equivalent Infernal
Equipment

1 Power

When this equipment is carried, all other Infernal cards on the field cost 1 more power, and no portal cards may be played on the field except the wielder's. The wielder's named Infernal cards with five or more total power cost have their power cost reduced by one, even if summoned by portals.

Special: **Gate to the Infernal:** If all 6 are possessed in the same deck, the bearer will gain 7 Legendary Infernal or Beast card pulls. Additionally, the deckbearer may either gain the Mythic 'Gate to the Infernal' Building Card or evolve Cereboo. Each card was given to a member of the Noimoire underworld.

"You should not have removed that."

There was gunfighting outside, and screams from inside. No one was in the study with him, and Wolfe slumped back. Not everything was over, since Adam lived and would almost certainly come looking for revenge.

But almost three years ago, Cerberus had given him a mission. Wolfe held the Bar of the Gate card aloft, his hands slightly trembling. He couldn't believe that he had actually gotten all six of the cards.

Wolfe risked a glance around. Despite yells, gunshots, and screaming all around him—and two bodies and a puddle of blood in his room—Wolfe was in a small oasis of safety, at least for the moment. He switched his deck and brought Cereboo forth. Then, with trembling hands, he touched another card in his hand, the Bulgae Chaser.

He willed it to switch with the card in his hand.

Trumpets sounded briefly, nearly scaring Wolfe silly despite the cacophony already around him. A spectral gate of pitted black iron rose from the floor, and creaked open, its hinges the screams of the damned.

Briefly, Wolfe caught a glance of a massive being, looming beyond the gate. Three pairs of red eyes stared out at Wolfe.

Cereboo barked joyfully, and two of the heads dipped slightly, one to Wolfe, and the other to Cereboo.

The gate slammed shut and disappeared.

Two cards appeared in the air, hovering about two feet from Wolfe, a foot farther than his own deck cards, but closer to eye level than chest. Each was swathed in crimson flames.

Wolfe stared at them.

Cereboo Evolved

Unique Mythic equivalent, Tier-10 equivalent Beast/Infernal [Demi-God, Canine] Companion

0 Power

Health: 25
Attack: 8x3
Defense: 10
Magical Attack: 11[**Fire**]
Magical Defense: 8

Special: **Fungible [Beast, Infernal]:** While in play, Beast and Infernal power may be spent as if they were the other.

Special: **True Companion**: This companion does not count against the total companions someone may have.

Special: **Preferred Typing [Beast, Infernal]:** Gains all the better type matchups of both Infernal and Beast.

Special: **Hunter of the Fallen:** +100% damage against Infernal, Elder, Undead, and Corrupt

Special: **Gatecrasher:** Anytime a Portal or Gate card is played by this card's deckbearer, Cereboo may return to the field, no matter where he is in the deckbearer's deck.

"A pup of Cerberus, who was born into a particularly frisky litter. Cereboo was the runt—not quite as strong, nor as tough, as his litter mates. Few thought he would amount to much. But, through the companionship of Ethan Madison Wolfe, he became one of the most powerful of the get of Cerberus, travelling from the Infernal halls of the damned to Wolfe's side at will, bringing ruin and punishment to those who would do harm to the good."

I'm mentioned in the cards? Wolfe thought, stunned and a tiny bit alarmed.

He stared at the other card.

Gate to the Infernal
Unique Mythic equivalent, Tier-10 equivalent Infernal
[Portal] Persistent
3 Infernal, 3 Any Power

So long as this card is in the deck, all Infernal Creatures cost 1 less power, even when summoned by portal. This does not stack with other things that reduce power cost. If a card's cost would drop below 1, it remains at 1.

Create a ten-card Infernal creature side deck. This may combine with any other Infernal portal card side decks. When this card comes out, bring ten power worth of creature cards to the field in any combination. If this card leaves the field, all creatures brought to the field with it leave as well. All cards together count as only one card on field.

"And the bar was cast from the gate, and the armies of the Infernal Lords poured from their realm to obliterate the worlds of the mortals and take their souls as playthings."

Explosions sounded and gunfire rang, but Wolfe stared, hands reached out. *The power of either of them is insane...*

He stared at Cereboo, who seemed to shrug.

Wolfe reached for the cards.

The End of Book 3

THANK YOU SO MUCH FOR READING!

Please consider leaving a review—any and all feedback is much appreciated!

Also, check out these super helpful Facebook groups!
https://www.facebook.com/groups/LitRPG.books
https://www.facebook.com/groups/Dungeonstories
https://www.facebook.com/groups/LitRPGsociety
https://www.facebook.com/groups/litrpgforum
https://www.facebook.com/groups/LitRPGReleases

"To learn more about LitRPG, talk to authors such as myself, and just have an awesome time, please join the LitRPG Group."

About the Author

John Stovall loves Shami, gaming, reading, math, his friends, his family, and his dog, and probably a whole lot of other things he can't think of right now. He obtained his BA in political science, and then later his JD from Humphrey's School of Law, but his real passion lies in writing. When he isn't thinking up number systems for his own homebrew Dungeons & Dragons game, he's thinking up cool plotlines for his books.

MORE STUFF!

If you're interested in more work from me, please check out my author page for other series, or sign up for the newsletter! I have a lot of other books, all LitRPG, but with a great deal of variance therein.

If you'd like to contact me directly, the easiest way is my Discord. You can also find me on Facebook (be prepared for questionable photography skills), or can email me at John.W.Stovall@gmail.com. You can also support me and read advance chapters on my Patreon.

www.ingramcontent.com/pod-product-compliance
Lightning Source LLC
Chambersburg PA
CBHW030756260626
47169CB00001B/76